CONQUER THE THAW

BOOK 10, THE THAW CHRONICLES

TAMAR SLOAN

HEIDI CATHERINE

SEQUEL HOUSE

GRACE

*J*oy pumps through Grace's veins with the same force as the grief that had gripped her only moments ago. Raze is alive. Barely. But still, he spoke to her, which means there's hope.

"Raze," she says, as his eyelids slide closed once more. "Stay with me."

She'd thought she was going to have to lead the Outlands alone. She'd thought Rusty—*Corbin*—was the only friend she had left in the world. But a thousand Corbins don't equal a single Raze.

She trails her fingertips down his face, trying to wake him. This strong handsome man who refused to harm her, knowing the decision would likely cost his life. She owes him everything. If only fate will allow her to pay her debt.

"Come on. I need you, Raze," she pleads. "Don't you dare leave me."

He doesn't wake, but she can feel the warmth of his breath just as she can see the gentle rise of his chest. He's still here. And her first job as Commander is to make sure he stays here.

Fatigue washes over her at the thought of everything that's

led to this moment, and everything she must still do. But how can she complain? At least she's here to feel the tiredness in her bones.

She glances to the sky, wondering if Gray is watching over her with Lexis by his side. She has to stay strong. All of what they went through in the Tournaments can't have been for nothing. She has to make Gray proud.

Tearing a piece of cloth from the bottom of her shirt, she rolls Raze onto his side and packs it into the wound on his back where Evrest stabbed him, stemming the worst of the bleeding. The injury is bad. But Raze is tough. She's seen him survive impossible situations before. He can do it again.

"You're going to be okay," she tells him. "Just hang in there until we can get you somewhere safe."

"Commander Grace," comes a deep voice from behind her.

She turns to find Corbin waiting for her.

"He's alive," she says, remaining crouched beside Raze. "He just spoke to me."

Corbin tilts his head, not looking as happy as Grace feels. "He doesn't speak. Like...ever."

"He did," she insists. "He spoke to me in the final Tournament. And again, just now. He's alive."

"We can't stay here." Corbin crosses his arms. "And he's too weak to come with us. So, we have ourselves a bit of a problem."

She stands to level eyes with him. "You're saying that Raze being alive is a problem?"

"Not to me." He indicates over his shoulder to the restless crowd who just appointed her their leader. "But it will be to them."

"Don't be an idiot," Grace says, brushing away Corbin's advice. "We're not leaving him behind. We'll carry him"

"Oh, fish shackles, Winter!" He sighs loudly. "That's Evrest's son you're talking about. He's not exactly flavor of the month out here. Don't you understand? We need to leave him behind."

2

"Firstly, I've already told you my name's Grace." She glares at him as she straightens her spine. "Secondly, have you forgotten I'm the Commander? I decide who we take and who we leave behind. And thirdly, what in the world are fish shackles?"

Corbin suppresses a smile as he sweeps out his hand toward the people, not answering any of her questions.

She steps forward, determined to prove him wrong. These people will agree to carry Raze if it's what she asks them to. It was only moments ago they were cheering her name and declaring her their new Commander.

"People of the Outlands," she says, trying to get their attention. "We need to leave this Ring of death and find a new home."

There's a murmur of agreement but not everyone is listening. These people are exhausted. They want to get moving, not stand here talking.

"If we can just decide on where we—" she begins.

"Easy decision," growls Brik, his tattoos rippling across his large forearms. "Fairbanks is a damn sight better than it is out here. Shelter from this stinkin' sun and the occasional rat to feast on."

"Along with thousands of bugs," a skinny Cragg woman with bright red hair complains. "We should go to the mountains."

"Perhaps if we—" Grace tries again.

"Why do we even need a base?" a Never man asks. "Better to roam the land and find what we need."

Grace holds back her frustration. She can't even get a sentence out without someone cutting her off. Although, at least the people cutting her off are actually listening to what she has to say, unlike the many others who are wandering around the Ring. They may have appointed her their Commander, but it seems it's going to take a whole lot more to gain their respect.

"We need a base because we need to make a plan," says Grace, calmly. "We need to gather weapons and bide our time if we're going to invade Askala."

"Then we should go to Rust," says the same Never man who just spoke about not needing a base. "We can't get to Askala from the mountains, but we can sure get there by boat."

"What's your name?" Grace asks, smiling.

He looks around as if checking she's talking to him. "Feather."

Brik sniggers. "Sounds like a girl's name."

"Says a man named after something as thick as his head," the skinny Cragg woman pipes up again.

Brik sneers and Grace wonders if this woman knows what kind of a cruel man she's insulting. Although, if she grew up in Cragg, cruelty wouldn't exactly be an unknown beast.

"I like your thinking, Feather," says Grace, trying her best to show Corbin what a good leader she can be by getting things back on track. "You'll be useful when it comes to strategy."

Feather seems to grow a foot taller with her praise.

"And what's your name?" Grace asks, turning to the Cragg woman.

Her eyes widen. "Scoria."

"Excellent," says Grace. "We now have ourselves a representative from each of the *former* factions to help us move forward as one. Scoria, Feather, and Corbin...if I could have a word, please?"

"Oi!" Brik turns a purple shade beneath his tattoos. "What about Fairbanks?"

Grace opens her mouth to say that she represents Fairbanks, then decides as the leader perhaps it's better she remain neutral. "And Brik," she adds. If he really is as thick as his name, he shouldn't be too hard to outsmart.

Leading them over to Raze, Grace squats down to make sure he's okay. The dressing is soaked but the bleeding seems to be slowing. Satisfied he's still breathing she squeezes his hand, then stands to face the small group.

"Raze will represent Cy," she tells them.

"But he's dead," says Scoria.

"Not dead," groans Raze at their feet.

"He can talk?" Scoria's jaw drops. "Thought he was a mute."

"He just didn't have anything worth saying before." Grace tugs at her too-short shirt. If she can't find another piece of cloth to help Raze, she's about to get awfully sunburned. "Raze is an important part of moving forward. Without him, we don't have all the factions represented."

"*Former* factions," Corbin corrects.

"That's right." Grace nods, not having time for him to be so pedantic.

"We don't need no Cy scum," says Brik. "Cy are just as much our enemy as Askala."

Grace shakes her head. "He's not the enemy. But he understands the enemy better than anyone else here. Isn't that worth something?"

"We should take him with us," says Feather.

"Boar's ass!" spits out Scoria, making Grace wish she chose another representative for Cragg. Although, looking at the remains of her faction wearing their animal hide clothing and snarls on their faces, she isn't sure anyone else would've been a better choice.

"Let's take a vote," says Grace, unsure if this is about to be her worst decision yet. Because she's taking Raze with them, no matter the outcome. "All in favor of having someone who understands our enemy on our side, please raise your hand."

Feather puts his hand high in the air and nods. Corbin's hands remain firmly at his side, as do Scoria's. Brik is too busy glaring at Scoria to vote.

"Brik, so good to see that you are aligned with Scoria," says Grace. "I thought after she called you stupid…"

Brik's hand shoots into the air, and he gives Scoria a smug look.

"Corbin?" asks Grace, wondering why he's being so resistant

to the idea of helping her with this when all through the Tournaments he'd been her annoying guardian angel.

Corbin shakes his head. "Sorry, Win—Grace—Commander Grace—but I vote no."

"Two votes yes, and two votes no," says Grace. "Now I'll cast my deciding vote…"

"You don't get a vote!" snaps Scoria. "That's like Fairbanks having two. It's not fair."

Grace balls her hands into fists as she drags in a deep breath. This Cragg woman is a piece of work!

"Yes," says Raze, very quietly but very clearly. "I vote yes."

All eyes drop to him, and Scoria opens her mouth to complain again.

"Excellent," says Grace, moving on quickly. "Now we need to decide where we're going. All who vote in favor of seeking refuge in Rust, raise your—"

An almighty roar cracks through the air and Grace's head snaps up to see the Ring lined with Cy warriors brandishing spears.

Evrest stands with them, and Grace realizes his earlier retreat was only giving him a chance to regroup. To gather his army and show them all who's really in charge around here. Grace may have the numbers with her motley army, but they're nowhere near as coordinated at the Cy. And Evrest knows it.

"There were seven Tournaments," Evrest says to the stunned crowd. "And now, I give you to the count of seven. Anyone who remains in this Ring after that time will be treated as a competitor. And they will die."

Grace turns to the others in desperation as her mind whirls over her next best move.

"Run!" cries Corbin, leaving Grace standing beside Raze. Scoria is right behind him.

Evrest claps his hands just like he did in the Tournaments as his warriors bang their spears on the ground. "One!"

People shriek and scramble as they climb out of the Ring.

"Help me, Brik!" Grace pleads, crouching down beside Raze. "I can't carry him alone."

"Two!" Evrest claps again, the sound echoed by the dull thump of spears.

"There's no time." Brik turns away, heading back to his loyal follower Mason who'd traveled with him to the Tournaments.

"I'll help," says Feather, trying to lift Raze. Except his frame is wiry, and Grace decides he has even less chance of moving him than she does. They don't even have much hope if they try together.

"Three!"

Grace dashes after Brik to the sound of thumping spears and grabs him by the arm. "I'll make you my second in charge."

He looks at her and blinks twice, his tattoos straining underneath his bulk. He could practically carry Raze with one finger.

"Four!"

Brik grunts something to Mason, then moves quickly, scooping Raze from the ground. If he hurts him, Grace has no idea. Pain doesn't seem important right now. This is all about survival. Which means getting Raze out of this Ring.

"Five!"

"Hurry!" Grace shouts, as Brik stumbles toward the edge. Almost everyone is out now, running in all directions in their panic, not one of them believing Evrest will be satisfied when he reaches the count of seven.

"Six!"

Grace climbs out with Feather beside her. The sixth thud of the spears, accompanied by Evrest's clapping is like thunder in her ears. Aware their time is almost up, Grace and Feather reach down, helping Brik with Raze as he hauls himself out.

Raze's eyes are open now and he's clearly suffering.

"Hold on," Grace tells him. "You have to hold on."

"Seven!" Evrest claps a seventh time as he surveys the empty Ring.

If Grace learned anything about Evrest during the Tournaments, it's that he doesn't like to lose.

"Keep moving," she says through gritted teeth. "We need to get off Cy land."

"Come on," says Feather. "I know the way to Rust."

The Cy warriors turn to put their backs to the Ring.

"We start again!" calls Evrest. "One!"

Each warrior bangs their spear and takes a step away from the Ring. The warrior closest to them sneers as he angles his spear at them, taking aim.

"Second in charge?" Brik asks Grace, eyeing her suspiciously.

"Yes!" she squeaks. "Let's just move it. And be careful."

He picks up Raze, holding him against his colorful broad chest.

"Two!" calls Evrest.

This time his men bang their spears and take two large steps away from the Ring as they fan out into their surrounds. The warrior with his spear pointed at them moves in their direction.

"Three!"

"Come on!" Feather motions for them to follow him.

Grace nods, hoping she hasn't messed things up so soon in her command. She runs beside Brik through the village that Raze called home his whole life. She's not sure what her promise to Brik is going to mean just yet, and she really doesn't care.

Because they're on their way out of here. And without Brik, she'd never have been able to save Raze.

When she left Fairbanks, she hadn't ever thought she'd find a new home. But she knows without doubt that now she has.

Raze is her home. Now all she has to do is find a way to keep him safe.

RAZE

*R*aze's life has been defined by pain. Physical beatings. Deprivation. Mental anguish. All underscored by the absence of hope.

But as agony jolts through him with each one of Brik's steps, shredding his nerves and fragmenting his thoughts, Raze realizes a part of that formula is now missing. He no longer feels the helplessness. The despair. The belief that his life had only one reason for existence—to die.

Suddenly, the pain is bearable, no matter how much the stab wound feels like a crater in his back. In fact, his father's attempt to kill him freed him in so many ways. It was a catalyst, a cleansing. The scar he'll always carry will mark the beginning of his future.

Raze swallows even though his mouth is as dry as their surrounds. He can speak. In fact, he's said more words today than he has in the past decade. He was never sure if the capacity was forever gone, the ability forgotten by the muscles and nerves of his throat.

And not just his future has changed, but that of the

Outlands. All the factions have promised to unite, bar one. Raze registers Brik's panting breaths and low grunts. The man—Feather—speaks occasionally, giving them directions to the ocean. And the coward Corbin will be back soon, Raze is sure of it, like the bad smell he is. No doubt, he'll have that Scoria woman with him, who seemed keen to see how unity could benefit the Cragg.

All this...hope is possible because of a beautiful young woman.

"Careful, you're jostling him," she says to Brik, who just grunts a response. Raze doubts he cares whether he's causing pain. In fact, each time Raze has opened his eyes, the man seems to step in a divot or hoists him with a loud grunt. Considering he's straddling the hazy line between consciousness and oblivion, Raze hasn't bothered to look around again.

As long as he knows Winter's nearby, he's willing to ride the painful wave of healing.

Not Winter, he corrects himself. Grace.

Raze mulls over her new name. Winter is a season. One that no longer exists. Probably like the naïve girl who arrived at Tournaments. Instead, a strong leader has been born. Despite the odds. Because of the odds. In fact, because she was so different to every one of the contestants.

He almost smiles. Grace is not only who but what needs to lead the Outlands.

Pretending Brik's trudging steps have the power to lull him to sleep, Raze frees his hold on painful consciousness. He floats, barely aware, but not totally free of reality. His lifetime of training won't allow him that luxury, not when he's being carried by a man he'll never trust. He wills the miles between them and the ocean to melt away.

"I need a break," mutters Brik.

A bolt of pain that feels a thousand times bigger than his

body slices through Raze as he's jostled. His legs drop heavily, and he registers warm sand beneath him. The dressing on his back pushes into the wound, protecting it, but also plugging it with pain. Then Brik's arms are gone, and Raze almost wonders if the agony tearing him from the inside out is worth the relief of being away from the man.

"Careful," Grace hisses. "You could reopen the wound."

Brik grunts. "I'd probably be doing us all a favor."

Soft hands flutter over Raze's face and chest. He cracks his eyes open, bright sunshine punching straight through his brain. A shadow falls over his face as Grace shuffles close. "Are you doing okay?"

Raze nods, the pain having robbed him of breath.

"According to Feather, we're almost there," she says.

Raze lifts a hand and brushes it over her soft cheek. Grace traps it and holds it there, closing her eyes.

"I wish I could carry you myself," she adds.

His lips twitch up at the image. "You'd...look like a piece of...flatbread."

Her eyes fly open, surprise and humor lighting the dark depths. "But I'd be a happy piece of flatbread," she murmurs.

Sand scrunches nearby as someone steps closer. "How long are we going to spend here?" Feather asks tensely.

"Not long," responds Grace. "Just enough time for us all to rest."

"Good, because we're very exposed."

"That's because we're not in Fairbanks," snaps Brik. "Plenty of shelter there."

"Along with even more malaria and dengue," says Feather. "I'd rather fight an enemy I have some chance of defeating."

"Winter, I mean, Grace. As your second in command—"

"Someone's coming."

Feather's urgent voice has Raze's eyes flying open. Grace

11

immediately places her hands on his shoulders. "Stay still. We can take care of this."

Raze remains where he is, even though he has no intention of staying flat on his back if they're attacked, wound or no wound. There's nothing he won't do to protect Grace.

His every sense is on high alert as he lies on the ground, waiting to see if they're being approached by enemy or friend. A Commander may have been chosen, but it's going to take time for unity across the factions to be accepted by all.

The Cragg woman's strident voice punctures his haze of pain and Raze unwinds a little.

"It's Scoria," says Grace as she pushes to her feet. "And Corbin."

Raze's muscles coil again, and he levels his breathing out as his body objects. He knew Corbin would come slinking back.

"Winter," Corbin calls out in greeting. "We backtracked so we could look for you."

Of course he did. He needs to make amends for running like the coward he is.

Brik steps up beside Grace. "The Commander's name is Grace."

Corbin narrows his eyes. "Who are you to remind me?"

"I'm the Commander's second in charge." Brik puffs out his tattooed chest.

"You're what?" Corbin gasps. "Wint—Grace, what's going on? I've done nothing but help you, and you appoint *him*?"

Scoria sidles up next to him. "Corbin deserves the role. He's a far better man."

Brik takes an ominous step forward. "That puny Rust?" he scoffs. "I could kill him right now if I wanted."

For a second, Raze considers remaining where he is. Brik taking care of Corbin means he doesn't have to refrain from killing the waste of space himself. Except Grace takes a step forward, slipping between the two men.

"Enough. I made the decision I had to." She levels a gaze at Corbin. "With those who were by my side."

Corbin frowns and flushes simultaneously. Raze waits, gathering the shreds of strength he doesn't have, ready to leap to his feet. Grace's first decision has already divided the factions. And she did it to save him.

"This isn't over," Corbin promises. His eyes flash as he steps back and turns away.

Scoria remains close to his side, making Raze wonder if these two have already formed a relationship of some sort. "The people who count know who you really are."

Raze frowns. What's that supposed to mean?

"We will all have a role to play in defeating Askala," says Grace. "We leave in a few minutes."

She kneels beside Raze again as the others shuffle a few feet away. Feather keeps his gaze on the horizon, seeming to have ignored the strutting of Corbin and Brik. Raze makes a mental note that the Never seem determined to remain neutral. That could be an asset, but it also makes him unpredictable.

Grace brushes a lock of hair from his forehead. "I have no idea what I'm doing, Raze," she whispers. "Is uniting the factions even possible?"

"With you it is."

And if it's not, then Lexis and Gray died for nothing.

Her face softens. "With us."

"Always." He never intends on leaving her side.

"Let's get you somewhere with shelter so you can rest." She stands again, turning to the others. "Brik, thank you for carrying Raze. We don't have far to go."

Except Brik doesn't move. "People die of smaller wounds than he has. It's not worth dragging him back to the Rust village."

"We had an agreement," she grinds out.

"I'm not wasting my precious energy on a dead man."

13

"He's got a point," Corbin mutters. "The only good Cy is a dead one."

The desire to thump Corbin flushes through Raze, but he keeps his eyes half-closed, pretending he's not aware of the conversation. This is Grace's second test as a Commander.

Sand softly crunches as Grace's feet press further into the ground. "If this were you, would you want your leader leaving you behind for dead?" She glares at Corbin. "Or you?" Then Scoria and Feather. "Or either of you?"

Four sets of eyes slide away.

"The people of the Outlands must work together, or we'll never win against Askala. That's why you're going to carry Raze, Brik."

Brik grumbles under his breath but stoops and picks up Raze. This time, he throws him over his shoulder. "Let's hurry up and get to the Rust village."

Raze feels like a bomb has detonated in his back, shattering his spine and annihilating his muscles, but he grits his teeth with everything he has. He's not giving Brik the pleasure of hearing him groan. Nor is he going to cause Grace more worry by showing his pain. If this is how Brik's going to carry him, then so be it.

They set out, the sun high and harsh above. Raze tries to hold onto consciousness, but the agony pulsing through his body overwhelms him. Brik periodically hoists him as he slips down, only compounding the pain.

It becomes painful to breathe. To feel the blood throbbing at his temples.

It hurts to be alive.

But for the first time in his life, Raze is glad he is. Which is ironic, because this is possibly the closest he's ever come to dying.

The trip becomes a blur of Brik's inked back, bleached sand,

and brief glances of Grace's worried expression. Time becomes as hazy as his senses. He has no idea how far they've come or how long it takes.

All he can do is use every second to cling to life.

To a future with Grace.

Hours or days could've passed when she leans in close. "We're here, Raze. We're at the Rust village."

He glances up, blinking as he tries to bring her cherished features into focus, realizing they're on a sand dune of some sort. The prospect of being able to lie still, to be off the hard shoulder digging into his pelvis, has sweet relief flowing through the pain.

Grace moves away and Raze tries to look around. Even semi-conscious he attempts to stay alert for danger. He sees flashes of moving red sky and he frowns, then realizes he's upside down. That's the ocean. He twists his head, hissing through his teeth as white-hot pain slices down his spine and finishes somewhere beyond his toes.

He's about to put his head down when he sees something in the distance, a flicker of an image distorted by heat.

Two figures. One male, one female, both running. The sun glints off the yellow tresses of the woman.

"Lexis," he mouths silently.

Raze blinks and the mirage is gone. Lexis is dead, just as Gray is. It's just Raze and Grace now, trying to forge a future that their twins died for. The thought punches grief through him, quickly followed by hard determination.

He and Grace have a responsibility to do whatever it takes to win against Askala. But it's more than that. They have to prove that the fight for survival can't be done alone.

Shade engulfs him as Raze is lowered, not expecting or being afforded the luxury of having it done gently. The last blast of pain steals his consciousness, no matter how hard he fights it.

They've arrived at Rust, which means their journey has just begun.

And Grace has shown she'll lead with compassion, unlike any of the other contestants who entered the Tournaments would have.

It will either be her strength...or her undoing.

GRAY

"*L*exis!" Gray comes to a halt, panting heavily as his bruised ribs scream at him. "I need a second."

Lexis stops and breaks into a grin.

"Yes, you're fitter than I am." He shrugs, rolling his eyes for dramatic effect. "And a better fighter. And better looking. You're also far better at coming back from the dead than I am."

She tilts her head, seeming troubled.

"And I'm fine with all of that!" he reassures. "In fact, it's just the way I like it."

He hopes she believes him. Because he's not intimidated by her. He's in awe of her. He's always been hopelessly in love with her, but since he learned of Winter's death, Lexis has become his sun, his moon, and all his stars. He could happily orbit around her for the rest of his days.

"Why are you looking at me like that?" she asks.

"Because I love you." He drags in a deep breath trying to halt his panting and stands up straight to look into the blue of her eyes. "And there's nobody else I'd rather be running away with."

Lexis shuffles her feet, not yet used to this kind of open display of affection. It's just fortunate he doesn't need her to tell him she feels the same. He knows it. There's no way she'd have agreed to leave the village of Rust with him otherwise. Especially given that they're heading in the opposite direction of Cy. Far away from everyone she's ever known.

"It's probably safe to drop our pace now, anyway." She slips her hand into his and he squeezes the warmth of her. The girl who used to walk clutching her spear now holds his hand instead.

Lexis looks over her shoulder as if double checking it really is safe. Thankfully, Rusty's mom had alerted them to the Cy warriors approaching in time for them to get away from the village. They'll be expecting them to head back to Fairbanks. Which is precisely why they're walking the other way.

He adjusts the heavy bag on his shoulder that Rusty's mom had handed them as she'd practically pushed them onto the path leading away from Rust. She was a strange woman. A nervous sort. She definitely has some kind of story to tell. It's just a shame they couldn't hang around long enough to hear it.

"What do you think's in the bag?" Lexis asks. "Looks heavy."

"Should we check?" He pats the oddly shaped items protruding from the hessian.

Lexis scans their surrounds, spotting a scraggly bush several yards away. "Over there. It's safer. Less chance of us being seen."

He nods, once again in awe of the way she's always thinking one step ahead, just like a true warrior.

They deviate off the worn path and take shelter in the patchy shade of the bush. How it survives out here is a complete mystery. No doubt, soon, it will be as dead as the miles of barren land that surrounds them. Mother Nature letting one more thing slide out of her grasp in this war against a burning planet.

Gray groans as he sits down, his feet throbbing inside his worn shoes. Lexis squats beside him in her ever-alert warrior's pose.

"Sit down," he tells her. "Rest."

She shakes her head. "I'm fine."

"They're not following us." He pats the hard ground beside him. "We'd have seen them by now."

"You're too trusting." She remains in position. "It'll get you killed one day."

"Winter used to say that about my optimism," he says. "And look where that got me. Or, rather, look who it got me."

He'd always known if he waited long enough, life had something wonderful in store for him. Turns out it was Lexis. Which is even more wonderful than even he'd expected.

"Just give me the bag already." She puts out her hand, but the pink tint to her cheeks tells him she's pleased with his words.

He slips the bag from his shoulder and hands it to her. She quickly undoes the string and pulls out a large flask. His mouth instantly aches for some of the cool liquid inside. They both take a sip. It takes all his self-control not to down the entire thing.

"Have some more," he tells her, holding it out.

"Only if you do." She raises a brow to show him she means it. "Sip for sip."

He considers faking his sip, but she's too smart for that. Besides, there's no way he wants to lie to her. Not even if it's for her own good. "It's okay. We should save it."

"You know who taught me that?" she asks. "The sip for sip thing, I mean."

He shakes his head, waiting for her to tell him.

"Your sister." She laughs gently. "It's how she got Raze to eat."

This makes him smile. "That sounds like Winter."

Lexis reaches back in and takes out a jar in the shape of an animal.

"Is that a polar grizzly?" She hands it to him.

"I think so," he says, trying to open the lid. It's stuck tight. He can't even begin to guess how many years ago it was sealed.

"Here, let me." She takes the jar back and with a solid twist, the lid undoes.

"Stronger than me, too," he says, adding to his earlier list.

"What is it?" She holds the open jar to him so he can see.

His eyes widen at the golden syrup inside. "I think it's honey. I've heard about this stuff. Here, let me try it."

"It could be poison." She holds it away.

He raises a brow. "It's not poison, Lexis."

Reluctantly, she hands it over and he dips a finger into the warm thick goo. Bringing it to his mouth he closes his eyes and lets out a deep moan as the intense sweetness floods his senses. It's so good, it's almost too much to handle.

"Oh, Lexis," he says, passing her the jar. "It doesn't matter if it's poison. You have to try this."

She looks at him cautiously.

"Look." He waves his hands at her. "I'm not dead. In fact, I feel great! It's safe."

"What is honey?" She sniffs at the jar.

"It comes from bees," he says.

This doesn't seem to make it any clearer to her.

"Little flying insect things that sting you," he says. "They're pretty much extinct, but I saw one in Fairbanks once."

"So, why's the jar in the shape of a polar grizzly if the bees make it?" she asks.

"Good question." He shrugs as his mouth waters at the thought of more honey. "Just have some already!"

Lexis dips her finger and brings it to her lips. Her tongue darts out and her eyes widen as she immediately jams her entire finger in her mouth and sucks on it. Crumbling to the ground, she goes back for more. "Oh, Gray."

"Told you it was good!" He smiles, enjoying watching her being so happy.

She passes him the jar and he goes back for seconds.

"We shouldn't eat too much," she warns. "It might make us

sick. We're not used to it. Never in my life have I tasted anything so sweet."

He licks his finger and a wave of bliss rolls through his tired body. "Maybe just one more each."

"One more." She nods as she takes her third helping. "Actually, maybe just two more."

Gray readily agrees. Before he knows it, half the jar is gone, and Lexis snaps on the lid.

"We really have to stop," she tells him. "Honestly, we're going to be sick."

"It would be worth it." He lies down on his back and puts his hands on his stomach as the honey gets to work feeding his depleted body. "I think I'm in heaven."

Lexis stretches out beside him. "What's heaven?"

"Mom said it's the place we go after we die. Up in the sky." He blinks at the sole cloud floating above. "It's where I thought you went the whole time I carried you to Rust."

"Do you think Raze and Winter are there?" she asks.

He nods. "Definitely. They're eating honey on that cloud right there, laughing at us because they know we ate way too much and we're both going to be sick."

"I do feel a bit sick," she says. "But you're right. It was totally worth it."

He laughs. "It really was."

"We should look what else we have in that bag," she says, propping herself up and reaching into it.

She lays out their spoils. Some dried fish wrapped in hessian. A sharp stone that could be used as a knife. And a folded piece of netting.

"Why would she give us all this stuff?" Lexis asks.

"The same mysterious reason her son helped me and Winter right through the Tournaments, I suppose. Who knows!" He waves a hand. "But right now, I don't think we're in the position to knock back any offers of help."

"And you really think we're going to find somewhere nice to live?" she asks.

"I really do." He sits up and touches her gently on the cheek. "If Askala exists then there have to be other places like it. We can find them."

"Why not just go to Askala?" She takes his hand and holds it. "It might be simpler."

"We've been through all this," he says. "Because your father is going to invade it. We want to live in peace, not war. There'll be somewhere else like it. Have some faith. And maybe in this new place the people won't be as selfish as they are in Askala. Maybe they'll be willing to share what they have with us."

His sweet Lexis nods as she takes this in. "If you say so, Gray."

"I do say so." He leans forward to kiss her gently, the taste of honey still fresh on her lips. "And if we can't find another Askala, then we'll make our own."

She either likes these words or she's had enough of hearing them, because she presses her mouth against his, kissing him with the kind of passion he's come to associate with this fierce girl.

His stomach clenches in a whole new way that has nothing to do with his recent overdose of honey. The things this girl does to him...

Lexis climbs onto his lap, straddling him to press her torso firmly against his. He tilts up his face, not wanting their kiss to break as she wraps her arms around him.

He already knew he'd do anything for this girl, but the reality of this settles in his heart as he slides his hands up the smooth skin of her arms.

She reaches for the string on her bodice, and he braces himself, knowing what's to come and hoping he can contain the excitement building inside him.

But just as she's about to pull down on the string, her entire body stiffens as her head snaps up.

"I heard something," she hisses, listening intently.

"That's just my heart beating." He tries to urge her lips back to his, not ready for this moment to end.

"I mean it, Gray." She shoots him a stern look as she climbs off his lap, scanning the horizon in all directions.

"It's probably just the polar grizzly wanting his honey back." Gray mumbles as he pulls himself to his feet.

She lifts a steady hand and points. "There."

Gray squints, trying to see what she is. But it seems the flatbread she grew up on must be good for eyesight, because he can't see a thing.

"Get ready." Lexis slides her spear from her leather belt. "We're under attack."

LEXIS

*F*ive figures appear on the horizon. Lexis's body winds with the familiar tension of preparing for battle and she shifts in front of Gray.

"They might not be dangerous," he points out.

She slowly unsheathes her spear from the scabbard that runs parallel to her spine. After being unable to use her favored weapon in the Tournaments, it feels good to be reunited with her best friend. "Everyone is dangerous in the Outlands."

Gray shades his hand over his eyes. "They've seen us."

The men are pointing at them, and the faint sound of a shout reaches them.

"They could be excited to see us," he adds, even though he no longer sounds so convinced.

Lexis narrows her eyes. "They're Rusts." The bleached hair is unmistakable in the harsh sunlight.

"Why would they be coming after us? We just left them."

"Because of the food," Lexis mutters.

And they have plenty of it, and water, too. Both the highest commodities anyone could possess out here. Far more than anyone in their right mind would've sent with two people they barely know.

"But Rusty's mom gave it to us. She insisted."

Lexis doesn't say anything as she bounces on her toes, warming up the muscles of her calves. If she knew what was in that bag, she would've asked a few more questions. But there wasn't time. People were approaching the village.

And whomever has won the title of Commander, isn't someone Lexis wants to be ruled by. She wouldn't be surprised if Evrest himself claimed the title despite everything they'd all been through.

Even after Raze and Winter were killed.

The men approaching them begin to gain form. They're thicker than she expected, more heavily built. It seems the Rusts have been eating better than they thought. It also makes them more formidable foes—just the way Lexis likes it.

"There's two of us and five of them," she tells Gray. "That's good odds."

He shifts his weight. "Ah, more like one and a half of us. I'm not much of a fighter."

"Yes, I already allowed for that in my calculations."

He chuckles, something that should be impossible at a time like this. "True, you definitely make up where I'm lacking."

"Grab the stone shaped as a knife. You're going to need it."

Gray quickly does as he's told and pulls out the rough looking dagger. He then takes the bag and tucks it under the bush.

"Good thinking," says Lexis.

He grins like she just gave him the sun rather than a compliment. "Thanks."

Lexis turns back to watch the approaching men. Gray's soul is beautiful in a way that shouldn't be possible, especially in the world they live in. The fact that it does, shows how precious it is.

It only reinforces that Lexis will do everything she can to protect him and the beautiful, gracious gift that he is in her life.

She glances around and picks up a rock small enough to fit in the palm of her hand. With her other hand, she grips her spear. "Stay behind me."

Gray instantly moves back a little, and she loves him all the more for it. He's not some macho Cy warrior who wouldn't be okay with taking orders from a woman, let alone allow her to be the one to face these men.

The moment the Rust men are a few yards away, they break into a run. They raise their arms, a medley of knives and weapons in their hands, and they roar a battle cry.

"Nope. They're not here to have a chat," says Gray.

They're here to kill.

Normally, Lexis would run at them, too. Back when Raze was her shadow and shield. But she can't afford to leave Gray unprotected, nor can she assume he knows to follow closely behind. She'll be facing these enemies right here.

Which is fine. She likes a challenge.

The closer they come, the faster the men run. Their faces come into focus—twisted with hate and snarling their need for blood. Lexis pushes her feet into the soil and strengthens her stance. She's the impenetrable wall they'll never get past. She'll die protecting Gray.

One man streaks ahead of the others and she drops her chin, focusing on him. Moving away from the group is his first mistake.

He raises the long stone knife he's holding.

That's his second mistake.

With a wild roar, he barrels at Lexis.

His third mistake.

She winds back her arm and executes a powerful throw, sending the rock she was holding hurtling toward him. With his arms up and his body open, his head is an easy target, one very similar to the smaller and smaller bullseyes she used to train with. The stone hits the man between his eyebrows, a sickening crack punching through the air. A trickle of blood runs down the middle of his face.

The man's mouth falls slack and he drops. Dead.

But there's no time to mourn or celebrate, or whatever emotion it is that she's supposed to feel, because the remaining Rusts scream their outrage.

Lexis grabs her spear with both hands, noting that the men divide, two moving a little to the right.

They're going after Gray.

Which means she'll deal with them first.

With a battle cry, she launches at them. One has a thick spear like hers, the other clutches a stone axe. She goes for the guy with the axe first, seeing as he poses the most danger. He doesn't raise it high like his comrade did, no doubt learning from his mistakes. Instead he slashes it wide and low, aiming for her torso.

Lexis leaps back as it slices through air, only inches from her stomach. As the momentum pulls the man's arm around, she swings her spear like a bat, swiping at his legs. There's a *crack* as it sweeps through his knees. The man tumbles like a pile of rocks, his back arching with pain although he doesn't cry out. She leaps, slamming her spear across his throat.

There's a gurgle, then silence.

There's no time to check, because the Rust with his own spear leaps and strikes. Lexis blocks, the movement instinctive and programmed into her muscles when she was just a child. She jumps over the fallen, probably dead, Rust, wanting to create more space between them and Gray.

She jabs and parries, strikes and blocks. Her opponent does the same. The clash of wood on wood echoes through the barren air, each one making Lexis angrier and angrier. She wants this man out of the picture. To no longer be a threat.

"Lexis!"

A quick glance over her shoulder shows the two other men closing in on Gray. He waves the knife from side to side, trying to keep them at bay. Except one has an axe of his own, the other a stone knife, too, but much larger than Gray's.

The wood of the spear connects with her temple as the Rust she's fighting makes the most of her split-second glance. Pain shoots through her skull as her head snaps to the side. She ducks, knowing a second strike will try to follow the first, the knowledge that Gray is about to experience pain, too, hitting her just as hard. Not unless she stops them.

From her crouch, Lexis vaults forward, shooting toward the Rust like a bullet. His eyes widen, having never expected her to try for close combat. She grips the spear in her left hand, then punches him in one eye socket, then the next in quick succession. His head has just snapped back when she clasps her spear once more and powers the tip into his solar plexus. A pained wheeze belches out as he doubles over. Lexis drops the spear on the back of his head and he collapses.

She spins around, already running toward Gray. The remaining two Rusts have widened the distance between themselves, meaning Gray's eyes are frantically leaping between each of them, his head twisting farther and farther each time. The Rusts are making sure he can't keep an eye on both of them at the same time.

Lexis injects every ounce of energy the honey gifted her in covering the short distance between them. She digs her spear into the ground, leaping into the air and tucking her body into a somersault. She sails over one of the Rusts and lands beside Gray.

"Wow," he whispers.

But Lexis is already facing their remaining enemy. "Leave or you die, too."

The Rust with the axe curls his lip in his hardened face. "Or we stay and you die."

"We just left your village," Gray points out. "Why would you try to kill us now?"

"Corbin said you stole our food," says the man with the too-big knife as he takes another step to the side.

Lexis doesn't know who this Corbin is, but she already doesn't like him.

Gray shakes his head. "We were given it."

"Sure you were," snarls the first Rust. "We would never give anyone our honey."

The Rusts glance at each other, and Lexis knows that was their agreement to attack. She has a split-second to decide who she'll meet. Who she thinks she can end before the other reaches Gray.

Just like before, the man with the axe poses the greater danger. She has to finish him. And quick.

She blinks away the sweat, ignoring the flash of tiredness streaking through her muscles. The energy injected from the honey no longer exists, but she's fought all her life without it. She doesn't need it to do what needs to be done.

She lifts her spear, ready to attack as the Rust's gaze flares at the prospect of bloodshed. She swings, but the man side steps, swiping his axe down, even though a couple of feet still separate them. It crashes into the spear and knocks it out of her hand.

Lexis instantly changes her trajectory as her weapon rolls over the dirt. She roars her frustration at now being so defenseless, but she doesn't let it stop her. She spins, using her momentum to launch herself back. It's dangerous, considering she's unarmed, but it's not something her opponent will be expecting.

And she fully intends on fighting until her last breath.

The Rust raises the axe, victory pulling his mouth into a

grin. She'll have to evade the deadly weapon and try to get a strike in. If she doesn't...

Something slices past her head, slashing the air before embedding in the chest of the Rust.

The pale-haired warrior jerks back, the axe dropping as he registers the hilt jutting from his breastbone. He looks at Lexis in surprise, then beyond her. His eyes glass over and he drops.

Lexis spins around, realizing Gray threw his knife to save her life. Which has just left him unprotected.

The Rust across from him whips his own knife through the air and Gray leaps back. The man keeps approaching, swinging, stabbing, slicing. Gray's sharp reflexes have him moving out of the way each time, his body twisting and jumping. But he won't be able to do that forever. He'll tire just like Lexis. The Rust will get in a lucky shot.

Gray will end up the second person with a knife impaled in his body.

Picking her spear up, Lexis is running once again. She lets out a scream, trying to distract the final Rust. Except the man keeps his gaze pinned on Gray. He swipes the knife again and Gray takes another leap back, but this time the Rust keeps moving forward, bringing his hand back in a large arc. The hilt hits Gray in the temple, instantly dropping him.

"No!" Lexis screams.

She throws her weapon, using it in the way a spear was designed. It sails through the air, an arrow aimed for the Rust. But the man sees it coming and nimbly side steps. The spear lodges into the ground, skewering the soil instead of its intended victim.

Once again without a weapon, Lexis keeps running. She has every intention of being between Gray and the Rust. Her panicked gaze keeps flicking to him. With relief, she sees his eyes flicker as his chest pulls in shallow, panting breaths. He's down and he's in pain, but he's alive.

The Rust turns to face her, once again swinging his large stone blade. Lexis curves her body so the weapon misses, but she stops short. She's on the defensive in this battle.

"No Cy is ever getting anything from us," mutters the man.

Lexis blinks at the hatred in the man's voice. It's practically burning from his eyes. Was uniting the factions even possible?

The man powers forward, bloodlust blending with the hostility. Lexis meets him, her hands grabbing his as he tries to bring the knife down. She locks her arms just like she was trained, stopping the weapon from moving any further. The Rust man snarls, his tendons straining as he raises his other hand to push down.

They struggle for long seconds, both straining. Lexis tries to push, desperate to get the upper hand. She just needs something to give her an advantage. Except she doesn't have Raze with her, protecting her back, making her two warriors in one. Her temple throbs from the hit. Her energy reserves are gone. Gray is hurt.

The Rust's leg sweeps out and knocks Lexis over, and she finds herself on her back, dust peppering her eyes. Her gasp is cut off as the Rust lands on her chest, quickly pinning her arms with his legs. She struggles, determined to buck him off, when something presses against her throat.

The knife.

"You should never have stolen from us," the man hisses, his face only inches from hers. "That's our food."

There's a flash of shadow. "You mean this food?" Gray asks, as the bag slams into the man's head.

The Rust's eyes roll back, the whites flashing a second before they flutter closed. Lexis pushes him off before his body slumps forward, unconscious or dead, she's not sure.

Nor can she bring herself to care.

She leaps to her feet, finding herself in Gray's arms. The only place she's ever belonged.

They hold each other for long seconds, both breathing heavily. Lexis runs her hands over Gray's head, neck, shoulders, back. She needs to know he's okay.

He cups her cheeks and pulls her face to his, pressing a tender kiss to her lips. "I'm fine. I had less of a knock than you."

Which he made himself vulnerable to because he threw his knife at the Rust attacking her.

"Thank you," she whispers.

He grins softly, his handsome face still achingly close to hers. "Hey, I had to take out more than one, or I'd be totally living in your warrior shadow."

"We make a good team." She presses another quick kiss against his lips, sealing the words.

Gray's sigh brushes over her. "The best."

There's a soft groan, reminding Lexis that not all the Rusts are dead. She pulls back. "We need to get out of here."

They need to disappear, now, more than ever. The Cy people could be looking for them. The Rust now have a blood debt. And a food debt, it seems. Lexis isn't sure which has a higher price in the Outlands.

Gray nods, taking her hand. "We have each other, which is all we need."

Lexis nods, her gaze sliding to the bag. The one that he used to knock out the Rust. Gray may be her world, filling her heart in a way she didn't know was possible, but there will come a time when her stomach won't agree with what he just said.

But if they have food and water, as well as each other, then anything is possible. Even the crazy future he painted.

Lexis's eyes widen. "Oh no..."

The bag dangles from Gray's hand, and he looks down, too. "What?"

A large, sticky stain is spreading over the hessian.

Their honey is gone.

GRACE

*G*race isn't sure what she expected from the Rust village, but it certainly wasn't what she's looking at now.

As they'd approached the ocean, the smell of its acidic depths had intensified, along with the rise and fall of the undulating land. They'd ended up on a clifftop above an expanse of flat ground. The landscape is barren, but not as harsh as the desert conditions they'd walked through. Out here there's an occasional clump of grass hanging on by shallow roots or a scraggly bush trying to suck moisture from the air, the struggle to survive extending far beyond the desperate humans who remain.

But it's the backdrop on the horizon that's holding Grace's attention, not the earth itself. She wishes Raze would wake up so he can see this. Because there's only one word for it...

Spectacular.

Beyond the soft grains of sand, in the distance, lies an ocean of translucent red. Not quite the color of blood, with its shades of deep crimson and vermillion. She can see why the people who live here are called Rust. The water reminds her of the

33

oxidized iron beams that crisscross the rubble in Fairbanks. Her older sister had come here once with her warrior, and a young Winter had hidden behind a wall as she'd listened with wide eyes as her sister told her friends stories of making love to him on the sand.

"Oh, Corbin," gushes Scoria. "This is even prettier than the mountains."

"You haven't seen nothing yet," says Corbin, clearly pleased with the compliment. It's rare for a faction to say anything nice about where their enemy chooses to live. Perhaps that's a sign that the task of uniting the people has already begun.

"Where do you live?" asks Brik, jostling Raze roughly on his shoulder. "I can't see no huts."

Corbin laughs. "We don't live in *huts.*"

"Wait until you see it," says Feather. "Even I was impressed the first time."

"When did you see our village?" Corbin's brows shoot up.

"The Never have seen everywhere in the Outlands," says Feather, shrugging. "We just haven't found anywhere we liked enough to make us want to stay."

Corbin grunts at this, clearly preferring Scoria's reaction to his homeland.

He leads them down a narrow path and Grace takes a few quick steps to catch up to Feather.

"Have you been to Askala?" she asks, needing to know as much as she can about this mysterious land she's been tasked with invading.

He shakes his head. "I said everywhere in the Outlands. Too dangerous to go to Askala."

"I thought they were peaceful people?" She glances around to make sure Brik is following with Raze.

"They are peaceful," he says. "But the acid in the ocean will eat you alive trying to get there. And if it doesn't, then the leatherskins will."

Grace nods, thoughtfully. They certainly sound like formidable obstacles. But not insurmountable ones.

The path winds down the side of the cliff and as they round a bend at the very bottom, Corbin comes to an abrupt halt. He plants his hands on his hips and nods proudly.

Grace blinks a few times, trying to take in what she's seeing. There's a large set of steel double doors in the cliff face, just above the level of the sand.

"What is that?" she whispers to Feather.

"A container," Corbin replies, turning to her before Feather can answer. "They wash up on the shore from time to time when we have a big storm."

"What do they contain?" Grace frowns, not feeling any clearer.

"Sometimes nothing," says Corbin. "But sometimes they have food, or furniture, or clothing, or plastic toys. Anything, really."

Grace scratches her head. "But how did they get in the ocean?"

Corbin shrugs. "They're shipping containers. Who knows how they end up here. Maybe they sat on docks before they went under. Maybe they sat on ships before they sank. The ocean swallows everything eventually. Occasionally, it likes to spit something back out."

"And you live in one of them?" Scoria asks, still right by Corbin's side.

"More than one." He nods proudly. "We've positioned them so they interconnect with tunnels. We have dozens of them. What you see here is only the tip of the iceberg."

Grace just hopes these containers fare better in the future than the icebergs themselves. That cliff has a heck of a lot of sand for a metal box to have to hold up.

"Is it dark inside?" asks Feather, beads of sweat forming on his brow.

"We use solar power," says Corbin. "We're not savages."

Grace bristles at the way he looks at Raze as he says this word.

"Can we get on with it?" grumbles Brik. "I'd like to put this lump of flesh down at some point."

"Raze is not a lump of flesh," Grace bites out. "Nor is he a savage. He's a trained warrior and our representative of Cy. We need him on our side if we're going to defeat Evrest and invade Askala."

"He's more of a ghost than a warrior right now." Brik repositions him on his shoulder.

Raze groans, but his eyes remain closed.

"Let's move," Grace says to Corbin. "Raze needs proper rest."

"Don't worry about the poor bastard carrying him," mutters Brik.

"Come on, Corbin!" Scoria pulls on his arm. He looks a little startled at first, then puffs out his chest, shoots Grace a smug look, and allows this mountain girl to drag him down the path. "I'm so excited to see where you live."

They approach the set of steel doors, and Corbin lets go of Scoria to stand directly in front of them.

There are bits of metal hanging off the front, which Grace assumes used to be the locking mechanism.

Corbin raises his fist and knocks three times slowly, pauses for two beats, then knocks twice in quick succession. He steps back and smiles, clearly enjoying showing them how this system works. Actually, now that Grace thinks of it, why is he showing them all of this? Although, if it's a trap they're well and truly ensnared now.

There's a loud clunk and the door on the right swings out, revealing a woman with bleached hair hanging down to her waist. She smiles at Corbin, reaching out to cup his face in her claw-like hands.

Scoria is visibly upset by her new competition but she's not seeing what Grace is. The line of this woman's nose, the exact blue of her eyes, the rounded shape of her face tells her she's Corbin's mother.

"My son," the woman says. "You're back. I did as you asked me to. I sent them aw—"

"Mom." Corbin pulls her to his chest, muffling her words. "Let's not bore our guests with things that don't concern them."

Grace tilts her head. She wouldn't have minded hearing what his mother had to say. Who exactly had she sent away? Had Evrest's men come looking for them already?

"You brought me visitors!" Corbin's mom pulls back and claps her hands. "I just love visitors. Come in! Come in!"

Grace plants her feet. Something isn't right. Nobody in the Outlands loves visitors. She looks over at Brik whose eyes are darting around. He knows it, too.

"You'll have to excuse my mother," says Corbin. "She's..."

"I'm *what* Corbin?" she asks without any hint of resentment. "Mad? Crazy? Nothing in my head except a bunch of fish shackles?"

Corbin swallows. "I didn't say—"

His mother looks directly at Grace. "My name is Kallini. Please excuse my son's rudeness for not introducing us. If you'd like to come in, I have food and water for you. I might even be able to find you some honey."

Grace's mouth instantly waters. Surely, they don't actually have any honey here?

Corbin frowns. "Mom, if you don't keep out of the food supplies, Barnacle's going to kill us both."

She waves her hands. "We have plenty. Another container will wash up soon enough. Now, who do we have here?"

Grace nods, realizing it isn't that something's not right in this situation. It's Kallini who's not quite right. It's in the way her eyes are darting around as she talks, never quite making eye contact with anyone and not at all comfortable with any silence in the air. Still, Grace can't help but like Kallini a whole lot better than she likes her son.

"I'm Grace." She pulls back her shoulders, being clear with her words. "Commander of the Outlands."

"That's nice," says Kallini in such an empty way that Grace wonders if she even heard because she certainly didn't seem to understand.

"This is Feather, Scoria, and Brik," Grace presses on. "Our friend, Raze, is injured. Can you help us?"

Kallini nods, only to quickly recoil. "He's Cy?"

Grace stiffens, wondering how many times she'll have to say this. "Raze is nothing like his father, Evrest. He saved my life."

Blinking, Kallini doesn't move. Her hand flutters to her throat. "Evrest's son?" she whispers.

"The next time I see him," Raze groans quietly. "I'll kill him."

Kallini beams. "Well, if that's the case." She steps back. "Come in, come in."

Corbin and Scoria step into the dim light, closely followed by Brik who's glancing around cautiously. Grace nods at Feather to follow.

"I'll wait out here," he says.

"You think it's a trap?" Grace asks. Perhaps he's wise to be cautious given it was a Never who killed a Rust in the first Tournament.

Feather shakes his head, and she sees that he's trembling. "I'm just more comfortable where I can see the sky."

This reminds Grace of her mother's fear of open spaces. A same kind of phobia as Feather's, brought on by the exact opposite cause.

"Are all the Never like that?" she asks, wondering if this is part of the reason they haven't made themselves a permanent home.

"Most." He points into the container. "Go on, Commander. I'll be right here keeping watch."

"Do you think it's a trap?" she asks again.

"Unlikely," he says. "They didn't know we were coming. Besides, you don't have much choice now that Raze is inside."

He's right, and hearing this has her taking quick steps into the dim light behind Brik.

Blinking as her eyes adjust to the cavernous space, she looks around, her nose wrinkling in the stuffy air. Maybe Feather was right to wait outside. She can't see any of the food supplies or furniture Corbin had mentioned. The space is empty apart from half a dozen chairs and some empty tin cans scattered on the floor. If it weren't for the fact Corbin was in here with them, she'd be very nervous right now.

"If you try anything funny, I'm going to break your skinny neck," Brik growls at him. "What is this?"

Corbin goes to the very back of the container and presses both hands to the rear wall. With some grunting he slides a panel across, revealing a hidden door leading even deeper into the cliff. Grace doesn't even want to think about how many tons of sand are above their heads.

One of the chairs has wheels on the feet, and Kallini rolls it over to Brik.

"We can push your friend on this," she says. "Give your arms a rest."

"He's no friend of mine." Brik lowers Raze onto the chair and Grace rushes to support his weight so he's sitting upright.

Brik stretches his arms, clearly glad to be free of his load.

"Thanks," says Grace, meaning it. "I couldn't have gotten him here without you."

"Second in command," he says, drilling his eyes into hers. "We made a deal."

She nods, shifting her attention back to Raze as she bends forward. His skin is pale and clammy, his hair slick with sweat. He needs water. And some proper rest.

"You did so good," she tells him, pressing her fingertips to his cheek. "We're here in Rust. We're getting you help. Everything's going to be okay. Please, just hold on."

His eyes flutter to show he heard her, and she squeezes his hand.

"We'll take him to the infirmary," says Kallini, wheeling the chair toward the opening at the back of the container.

Grace follows closely, determined not to let Raze out of her sight.

"Did you like our trick?" asks Kallini over her shoulder, giggling like a child. "We make the entrance look abandoned. If anyone attacks, we can hide further in and keep quiet. Nobody has to even know we're there."

Grace wonders if Kallini tells everyone she meets these secrets. It's no wonder Corbin is keen to keep her quiet. Although, discretion hasn't exactly been his strong suit either.

They step through the secret entrance and Grace draws in a gasp, blinking in surprise. This container is far bigger than the empty one they just walked through and it's bursting with possessions. Crystal chandeliers hang from the ceiling with flickering globes casting shadows across the plush burgundy carpeted floor. There's a long timber table in the center of the room with ornate chairs. It's been set for a feast with brass candlesticks, fine china and sparkling silver cutlery. The paneled walls have been decorated with the heads of hundreds of fish, preserved and stuck to the boards, their eyeballs watching Grace in an eternal stare. This is equally the most fascinating and terrifying room she's ever been in.

The enormous jaws of what could only be a leatherskin sit at the far end of the room and people are stepping through them from what can only be another container buried even further in the cliff. The people stand around the edges of the room, staring at their visitors like they've arrived from outer space.

It seems Corbin hadn't lied about the series of tunnels his

people had created. There is a whole labyrinth lying quietly underneath the earth like a sleeping giant.

"This is amazing," gushes Scoria from behind Grace.

"It's our meeting room." Corbin puffs out his chest. "This is where we make all our decisions."

A tall man with a long beard steps through the jaws, ducking his head so he doesn't snag himself on any of the sharp teeth.

"What the hell is going on, Corbin?" he growls. "I've had about enough of you."

Corbin seems to shrink by about a foot as his shoulders hunch over. So, it seems he doesn't have as much power in this faction as he's made out. Even more reason why he's trying to align himself with Grace.

"I've b-brought you the n-new Commander of the Outlands," stammers Corbin. "The Tournaments are over."

The man immediately fixes his eyes on Brik, taking in the size of him.

"No, Barnacle," says Corbin. "Not that one. The girl. She won. She's our new Commander."

Barnacle looks to Scoria, aghast. "A Cragg won?"

"He's talking about me," says Grace, stepping forward. "I'm Commander Grace from the faction formerly known as Fairbanks. I'm here to unite the people so we can take our share of what the Earth has left to offer."

Somehow, as she says these words, they feel a little emptier than they would have before she'd seen the riches this faction is in possession of.

"Is this some kind of joke?" Barnacle asks Corbin, not even acknowledging anything Grace just said. "You expect me to believe this skinny girl won the Tournaments? The very same Tournaments that killed Trout in the first round?"

"It's true." Corbin nods, taking a step back. But he's not fast enough and Barnacle's large hand strikes him across the face, sending him sprawling.

41

"You mock me, boy!" Barnacle stands over Corbin with his fist clenched.

"She did win," says Scoria, squatting beside Corbin and holding out her hands for the violence to stop. "None of us expected it. Or even liked it. But it's true. She was the only one left at the end, along with him." She points at Raze. "Although, he's practically dead anyway, so he doesn't count."

Barnacle leaves Corbin to stalk over to Raze, still ignoring Grace.

"Cy scum." He spits at Raze, a large glob of saliva landing on his chest. "I should just put him out of his misery and end it for him now."

"No!" Grace pushes herself in between Barnacle and Raze. "He's a good man and we came to you for help. He knows things about the Cy people. We need him."

"So, he's a traitor as well as scum?" Barnacle scowls.

Grace pulls back her shoulders and draws in a deep breath, shifting her gaze around to take in the wide eyes of the silent people of the Rust watching on. "We've come here with a representative from each of the factions. We—"

"I don't see anybody from Never," Barnacle interrupts.

"He's waiting outside." Grace clenches her own fists. "The Never don't like the dark."

"And I don't like the Never." Barnacle grins and his people snigger in return.

"We've united the factions," says Grace. "We have the Never, Fairbanks, Cragg and Rust. With Raze's help, we'll soon have the Cy as well."

"Well, doesn't that sound cozy." Barnacle runs his fingers down his beard as he sits at the head of the long table. "We can all have a tea party!"

"We're going to invade Askala." Grace remains steadfast by Raze's side, ignoring Barnacle's jest. "We can achieve so much more together than any of us can alone."

Barnacle reaches for a goblet and drains it of liquid. "I think we're doing pretty well already. Although, I wouldn't mind a pretty wife like you."

"Aren't two wives enough for you?" Kallini asks, boldly.

The room falls into a hush as they wait for Barnacle to react.

He roars laughing. "Never enough. Although, I'm not desperate enough to take you just yet, Kallini."

A sick feeling winds its way through Grace's gut. It seems women are no more respected in this faction as they are in any of the others she's come across. Which is going to make her job as their leader twice as difficult.

"We need to unite all the factions," says Grace, trying to get the room to listen, even if Barnacle seems like a lost cause. "Which means I need your help to heal my friend so we can defeat Evrest and convince the rest of the Cy people to join us. We'll be stronger than ever. We can do this!"

She looks to the people, expecting to see a few nods or a sign of support. But instead, she sees amusement on their pale faces.

Barnacle leans over the table. "I've got a better idea, little lady."

Four of his men step up to stand beside him.

"What do you propose?" Grace asks, already feeling apprehensive.

He gives her a sly smile. "How about we put your friend out of his misery, then invade Cy and finish the rest of them off?"

Grace glances to the door, noticing it's been closed. They're trapped. She's failed Raze in the worst possible way. She brought him here to save him, yet now it seems the Rust will do what the Tournaments had failed at.

They're going to kill them both.

RAZE

*R*aze lifts his head, burying the pain that's writhing through the muscles and sinew of his back. His and Grace's lives depend on the next few minutes.

He glares at Barnacle. "And you don't think Evrest and his men are planning on doing the same to you?"

Barnacle's head whips around, surprised but quickly recovering. He narrows his eyes. "Are you threatening me, Cy boy?"

"No more than you just threatened me."

Barnacle's eyes become slivers as they turn shrewd. "How do you know what Evrest plans?"

"I'm his son." His only surviving heir.

Raze says the words simply, ignoring the acid that burns his tongue as they slip past his lips as a gasp or two punctures the room. There's nothing he can do about his parentage, except use it to his advantage.

Barnacle's lip curls and he spits on to the carpet beside Raze's feet. "It's decided. We'll kill you now."

Grace shifts closer to Raze. "Or you could listen to what he has to say. Raze knows better than anyone what Evrest is likely to be planning now that he's lost the Tournaments."

Which is exactly how his father would see it. Evrest intended on Cy winning those fights to the death.

Grace being the Commander isn't an outcome he'd be willing to accept.

Barnacle puffs out his chest. "We'll end Evrest and whatever army he has the moment they step on Rust soil."

Raze snorts. "He'll slit your throat before you know he's here."

A couple of people standing near Barnacle recoil as the woman, Kallini, whimpers. All a testament that Evrest's carefully crafted reputation has done what it's supposed to do. They know he's cold. Brutal. And a master in the art of death.

Barnacle crosses his arms. "What are you saying?"

"I'm suggesting you prepare for war, and not against Askala." Raze glances at the others in this dank, gloomy room. "The people of Cy won't stop until they rule the Outlands."

He slides a glance at Grace, hating the words even though they're the truth. *Because* they're the truth. The Tournaments were little more than a guise, a means to an end. Evrest always planned on being the ruling faction.

She stiffens, but it's the only sign his words have an impact. Grace keeps her shoulders back and her chin high, a pillar of strength beside him. He consciously matches his breathing to hers, uniting them in more ways than one. She's his strength just as much as he is hers.

"He's lying," someone shouts from his left. "He wants us to fight their battles for them."

Raze holds Barnacle's gaze. "And if I'm not?"

The man's arms tighten across his chest, almost as if the words were an attack themselves. Good. He understands the consequences if he doesn't take Raze's warning seriously.

Grace rests a hand on his shoulder, her touch giving him something to focus on apart from the thick tension in the room.

"Or we could unite. Become a strength formidable enough to defeat any threat."

And right now, Raze isn't sure which enemy feels more daunting—his own people, or Askala.

Barnacle's nostrils flare as he draws in a sharp breath. "We don't need no Cy scum or Fairbanks ghosts."

Raze's jaw tightens. It seems working together, rather than continuing as warring factions, is the first hurdle.

"But we'll keep you alive, for now," Barnacle continues. "See if you have any useful information to share."

The band around Raze's chest unwinds a little. They have what they need—time.

Kallini claps her hands with childlike excitement. "Wonderful! Let's get them settled in, shall we?"

Without waiting for a response, she moves back behind Raze and pushes his chair to the other end of the container. The Rusts divide as Grace stays close by their side. The air already feels thick and stale. She glances at him and Raze nods. He doesn't like moving further into the bowels of this cliff any more than she does, but they don't have much choice.

And he hates being pushed like some invalid, but he knows he's too weak to move very far on his own. Right now, he needs to do everything he can to get strong, and that includes being escorted around on a chair with wheels like a child.

Corbin rushes up and helps get the chair through the giant leatherskin jaws, flashing a glance at Grace that sets Raze's teeth on edge. Having that Rust slime anywhere near her almost annihilates his good intentions and has him pushing to his feet. His hands wrap around the arms of the chair and Grace's hand is instantly on his shoulder again. "Where are you taking us?" she asks Kallini.

"To the infirmary," the woman says cheerfully, as if they just left a celebration rather than the fight that would've inevitably led to their deaths. There's no way Raze could've fought in his current state. "I'll have this young man better in no time."

The chair clatters over the lip of the container and they find themselves in a passageway lined with nothing but rock. The light from the meeting room they left steadily fades, and although there's a light ahead which must be another container, there's a patch of black in between. The band around Raze's chest constricts again as he takes Grace's hand. "How many exits are there out of this place?" he growls.

Corbin rolls his eyes. "Like I'm going to tell you that."

There's the sound of running feet and Raze spins around, pain slicing down his spine. But it's just Scoria rushing to catch up with them.

"I'm coming with you," she tells Corbin.

His jaw twitches. "Fine."

Scoria beams, either ignoring or failing to notice Corbin's cool response. She pushes past Raze and Grace to get to him, her shoulder brushing the wall. The sound of tumbling gravel grates over Raze's ears.

"Careful!" Corbin snaps. "Don't touch the walls."

Raze feels Grace's hand tense. She probably just realized what he did—this place is as sturdy as it appears. Which is not very.

Scoria huffs. "Well, if you waited for me, I'd already be there with you."

They reach the black stretch of passageway and Raze straightens even though it hurts. If the Rusts were going to attack, now would be the time. But it's Grace's hand that brushes his cheek, making him startle. She's making the most of the privacy the darkness affords them. Her hand strokes down his jaw, trailing over his neck. It has shivers of delight dancing over his skin. He catches her hand and brings it to his lips, kissing her fingers. Her hand curls tightly around his, conveying her own promise.

No matter what waits for them beyond this unknown, they'll face it together.

"This way," Kallini says, suddenly turning the chair even though Raze never noticed any intersecting passageways. But they don't crash into a wall, instead trundling over more gravel and rock.

Ahead, fingers of light pierce the darkness and Raze once again braces himself for what they'll find. The door to this container is open and as they maneuver over the lip, he prepares to defend Grace with every last shred of strength he has.

But the room they enter is just as much a marvel as the last one. This one has what looks like three low lying tables down one wall with blankets on them. Shelves line the opposite wall, jars and tools sitting on them. The room is well lit, spacious, and clean in a way Raze hadn't known was possible.

"This is the infirmary," Corbin says proudly.

Scoria moves to the first table with blankets. "Ooh, is this...a bed?"

"Yep. May as well be comfortable while you're sick."

She runs her hand over the nearest one and Raze watches in fascination as it seems to sink. She glances at Corbin. "I'm sure this would've been more comfortable for other things, too," she murmurs coyly.

Surprise spears through Raze, quickly followed by a jolt of nausea. Corbin and Scoria have been far closer than he realized, and although it's useful information to know, it's an image he can do without.

Kallini pushes Raze to the closest bed. "Yes, they're wonderful to sleep on, too. I stay here most nights, in case someone needs help." She smiles. "I like to help."

She brings her hands together, wringing and twisting them as she waits, her smile hovering uncertainly. Sympathy pierces Raze's chest. There's a fragility about this woman that he understands on a level he almost wishes he didn't. She's scared. She's broken. And she's doing the best she can.

Which is essentially the story of Raze's childhood.

He stands, keeping the movement steady and slow. Agony still twists through his gut as the muscles of his back contract and flex, the flesh of the cut feeling ragged and raw. "Are you familiar with knife wounds?"

Kallini's eyes light up. "They're one of my favorites."

"You said that about burns and broken bones," Corbin mutters.

His mother ignores him, smoothing over the blankets of the bed they're standing beside. "Here, lie down and I'll get some supplies."

Grace moves in closer as Raze gently lowers himself. His eyes widen as his backside hits the surface and continues to sink. It's one of the softest things he's ever felt. Soft has never been good in his world. Then again, neither was love or tenderness, and he's realized how essential they are to survival.

Kallini turns to Corbin. "Why don't you go give this girl a bit of a tour?" she asks, indicating to Scoria. "She'd probably like some food and water."

Scoria's already at the door. "Are there any more beds?" she asks, the coyness back.

Corbin hesitates, appearing torn. It's clear he's determined to stay close to Grace. And yet, Scoria is offering him something Raze doubts has been dangled in front of him too often. Just like Raze knew he would, Corbin grabs her hand and pulls her out of the infirmary. "I'll show her around."

Once they're gone, Raze pats the bed beside him. Grace sits down in a blink, shuffling close to him. "How's your back?"

Kallini returns before he can come up with a convincing lie that it's fine. "Shirt off and lie down," she says, sounding almost eager. "Then I can help."

Raze goes to draw his shirt over his head only to hiss with

49

pain. Grace tuts, grabbing the edge of the material and carefully pulling it up and over. He bites back the groan of pain as he has to lift his arms.

"Lie down," Grace says quietly but firmly, her own face strained. "You don't need to be strong right now."

"On your side, with your head here." Kallini pats a folded blanket at the top of the bed.

Raze does as he's told, exhaustion suddenly dragging at every cell in his body. He braces himself as he lies down, but the softness of the bed seems to absorb most of his pain. He places his head on the folded blankets, grateful for the support.

Grace shuffles further up, clasping his hand in both of hers. Behind him, he feels Kallini's cool hands on his back. The sensation is so gentle and delicate it almost feels pleasant. But then she presses at the edges of his wound and Raze has to stop himself from turning around and shoving her away. Actually, punching her away. All his training taught him to hurt anyone who hurts you.

But he remains where he is. Grace shifts down so her face is level with his. "You're stronger than you realize," she says with a small smile. "And kinder."

Raze blinks, never having associated that word with himself. He's Cy, and Cy aren't kind. They're the opposite of kind.

Except, the factions need to dissolve. Those lines they define themselves by no longer exist. By asking others to unite, he's thrown the shackles of his father and his faction.

The thought is freeing and terrifying all at the same time.

"It's a clean cut," Kallini observes, possibly sounding a little disappointed. "I'll sterilize it then stitch it up. You're a strapping young man, you'll be back up and about in no time."

"Thank you, Kallini," he murmurs.

The other Rusts have extended nothing but hostility and the promise of death. And yet this woman is fussing over him, offering to heal.

"I like to help," she repeats, her voice soft with pleasure.

What follows doesn't feel like help. Kallini flushes cool liquid over his wound, and it's like she doused it in fire. She murmurs encouragement the whole time. Raze has to force his eyes to stay open, fighting the wave of black trying to steal him away. He focuses everything he has on Grace's beautiful face, clinging to the faith shining from her eyes.

Except he realizes he's holding her hand far too tightly. He goes to loosen his grip, but she tightens hers as she shakes her head. "Let me help how I can."

When Kallini begins stitching his tattered flesh back together, he bites his tongue so hard it bleeds. He's struck by the irony that he's spent most his life not talking, and yet now he has to work hard to stop any sound from escaping.

Grace brushes a hand over his forehead. "It's okay to let it out, you know."

He pants, sweat beading over his skin. "But—"

"Rest, Raze," she whispers. "I'll be here."

He lets his eyes drift shut, craving the promise of oblivion even as he wishes he didn't need to sleep. With a sigh, he allows it to steal his consciousness. Grace is right. He needs to rest.

He needs to heal.

Because there's no doubt in his mind war is coming far sooner than they anticipated.

GRAY

*G*ray and Lexis trudge over the hot, barren land until he forgets what it feels like to stand still. They can't stop. Firstly, there's nowhere *to* stop. No more lone shrubs or scraggly trees. Just dirt. More dirt. And then a whole lot more dirt.

Their water is long gone, the sticky remains of the broken honey jar licked clean. All they have is the dried fish but neither of them is game to put those morsels in their parched mouths in case it sucks away what little moisture they have left.

"There's nothing out here, Gray," says Lexis, not breaking her stride.

"That's the whole point," he tells her. "We're finding our own place to call home, not someone else's. We'll find something soon. Let's keep going."

"We have no choice. We've come too far." She looks back over her shoulder. "If we turn back, we'll die for sure."

"The sun will set soon, and it will get easier." He wipes some precious sweat from his forehead, aware that they can't survive much longer without finding something to drink. Surely, there has to be a cactus around somewhere that they can slice open to drink the juice? If they just go a little further they have to come across something.

She nods. "Will you be okay to walk until dark?"

He puts a gentle hand on her back. "Will you? You worked far harder than I did in the attack. I'm still impressed that you won against five men."

"You took care of two of them," she reminds him. "So, really it was only three."

He goes to protest, but the effort needed to form the words is too much. It's taking all his energy just to keep putting one foot in front of the other.

They walk on until eventually the sun dips below the horizon, providing sweet relief from the burning rays. But despite this, the air remains stifling. He feels like he's breathing in fire. He told Lexis he could walk until dark, but now he's really not sure. Every cell in his body is screaming at him for rest.

"What if we dig?" Gray fights the dizziness swarming in his head. "There might be a water table under here."

Lexis pauses to turn to him. "This ground is like your concrete walls in Fairbanks. And what would we dig with, anyway?"

He reaches into his pocket and produces the sharp stone Corbin's mom gave them.

"This." He grins at her through cracked lips.

"Go on then." She nods at the ground.

He crouches down and slams the stone into the earth. Pain slices up his arm at the hard impact. The rock slips from his hand and his head spins like it's filled with a thousand mosquitoes buzzing to get out.

"Fish shackles!" he shouts.

Lexis raises a brow. "Fish shackles?"

He shrugs. "It's catchy, okay."

Lexis stoops to pick up the stone and hands it to him. "Are you going to try again?"

He lets out a long sigh and sits down before he falls. "Not a chance. You were right. Again."

She crumples beside him. "You want to know something else I'll be right about?"

He loops an arm around her, the weight of it feeling like lead. "What?"

"That once you sit down, it's much harder to continue on." She rests her head on his shoulder. "We should've kept walking. Sitting here is a mistake."

"Just five minutes," he says. "My legs are cramping."

"That's dehydration." She puts a hand on his thigh and rubs. "I'm going to guess you have a monster headache as well?"

He nods. Now that he thinks of it, there's no part of his body that doesn't hurt.

"What about you?" he asks, realizing that Lexis must surely be feeling the same effects. "Are you okay?"

She nods. "I'm used to it. Don't forget I delivered all those invitations to the Tournaments."

He's not sure he believes her. It doesn't matter how used to it you are, your body still needs water. Especially when you've just spent the day walking in the hot sun.

"Let's just lie down for a moment," he says, stretching out and groaning.

Lexis remains sitting. "Gray, that's not a good id—"

He pulls her down so she's resting in the crook of his arm. "Sorry, were you saying something?"

"Never mind." She puts a hand on his chest. "Your heart is racing. Maybe you should rest for a bit. I'll keep watch."

"There's nothing out here to watch," he tells her.

"Then I'll watch you." Her blue eyes blink at him and he feels a wave of comfort wash through his aching body.

"You should rest, too," he murmurs, fighting the urge to sleep. "Then we can find our forever home."

"That's what I'm worried about." Lexis's eyes turn to the sky. "I'm not ready to join Raze just yet."

His brow crinkles, not understanding what she means.

"We'll die out here, Gray." She lets out a sigh. "Our forever home is looking more and more likely to be up on one of those clouds."

Shaking his head in protest, he gives in and allows sleep to claim him. He's instantly sucked into a vortex of confusion and torment.

He's back in the Tournaments with Winter by his side. He looks across at her, his heart aching with love and regret. He feels the familiar warmth of her hand as she slides it into his. He's missed her so much. Why did Evrest have to kill her? She had so many more years left to live. So much good she could have brought to the world.

But something isn't right. He looks down and Winter's fingers have morphed into a tangle of baby vipers. He lets go with a yelp, swatting at the snakes, trying to get them away from his twin.

"Gray," Winter hisses, a forked tongue darting from her lips. "Gray! Gray! Gray!"

He takes a step away, and Trakk is behind him.

"Trakk!" He grabs hold of his friend, his eyes burning with tears. "You're here."

But Trakk isn't smiling. He grips Gray by the shirt. "You didn't save me. You let him kill me. Why didn't you save me?"

Gray shakes his head. "I wanted to. I wish I could have—"

His words are cut off by the sound of Trakk's loud whistle, telling him it's time to run.

"Gray!" Winter continues to cry. "Gray! Gray! Gray!"

His heart rate picks up and he turns to run, but Trakk is still gripping his shirt and his feet are planted on the hard earth.

Trakk whistles again, and this time a horde of rats come scurrying toward them. They run straight for Gray, climbing up his legs and into his clothes, nipping at his neck and face. He tries to bat them away, but his hands don't move, so instead he thrashes his head from side to side, trying to dislodge them.

"Gray!" Winter shouts. "Gray! Don't you dare leave me! Gray!"

"Winter!" he screams, as his eyes fly open.

But it's Lexis in the shadows before him, not his sister. Her eyes have a sunken look and she's breathing faster than he's seen before.

"Gray!" she gasps, slapping him repeatedly on the face. "Wake up, Gray!"

He blinks. "Lexis, rats, snakes, Winter. Quickly, Lexis. We have to move."

He tries to get up, but his body is stuck to the ground, his muscles refusing to work.

"You were dreaming," she tells him, her palm now resting gently on his cheek. "I couldn't wake you."

"Trakk's here," he says, looking around. "He has rats. Winter's here, too, but her hands are snakes."

"Stop it, Gray." She bends forward to rest her forehead on his chest. "Just stop it. Please."

He frowns, feeling even more confused. Surely, she should be interested in knowing Winter's here. Raze might be, too. Doesn't Lexis miss Raze?

"Be careful," he tells Lexis, trying to keep her safe. "Don't let them get you."

"You're not making any sense, Gray," she sobs. "You need water. We both do."

"We're finding a new home," he says. "Just you and me. It's going to be so beautiful. Like you, Lexis. You're beautiful."

These words seem to upset her, although he doesn't know why. Doesn't she want to find a new home with him? Maybe it's the rats? She's worried their home will be infested with them.

He opens his mouth to tell her he'll keep the rats away, but the dark shadows that surround them turn to black, dragging him into silence. Is it night-time or have his eyes closed again?

He tries to call Lexis's name. He tries to lift his hand to her face. He tries to still the rapid beating of his heart. But the only thing he can manage to do is give in to the force that's pulling him under and tell himself that everything's going to be okay.

It always is. Isn't...

LEXIS

*L*exis is scared.

It's a feeling she hasn't felt often in her life. She had to stamp out the precursor to panic from a young age.

Fear clouds your judgment. It rules by emotion. It robs the ability to make necessary decisions.

But with Gray lying on the hard ground, his cheeks sunken and his lips cracked, the coils writhing and tightening around her chest are most definitely fear. He breaks his deathly stillness, his head thrashing from side to side as he mutters incoherently.

They're dying, their bodies progressively and painfully being drained of moisture. Her own end she made peace with long ago.

Gray's death is one that shreds her with pain she didn't know existed.

She brushes his hair over his forehead, trying to uselessly create some shade over his face. The sun is almost gone, taking its harsh rays with it, but leaving behind its legacy of heat. It draws into her lungs with each breath, desiccating her from the inside out.

Lexis looks around, refusing to sit here and do nothing. She has to do what she can to save Gray. She always planned to go down fighting.

But the twilight landscape is flat and barren, an endless stretch of hopelessness. There's no way to tell which direction they should walk, even if Gray was capable. Lexis would carry him, drag him, if she knew that a few more miles would mean shelter. But a few more miles are far more likely to mean wasting what little energy she has left.

Right now, it feels like they're in the middle of a never-ending wasteland. There are no signs of life, no curls of smoke breaking the harsh horizon.

Lexis startles. Smoke! If they can't find signs of habituation, maybe they can create some for others. She pauses. The reason they're in such dire straits is because they're trying to get away from humanity. The other factions are dangerous. Deadly. The Rust may still be after them, wanting their debt repaid.

But the Rust will have water she can bargain for. Or kill them and take.

Gray moans again and she folds down, stroking his cheek. "I know you wanted to find our haven." Their place of peace and happiness. "But we didn't."

Gray would tell her they haven't found it *yet*. Lexis smiles despite their fragile situation. She never really believed such a place existed, but she still followed him and his foolish hopes. As she feels her lip crack, she has no regrets. She'd rather be here with Gray than anywhere else.

But that doesn't mean she can't fight for their lives, and if that means trying to attract people to them, then that's what she's going to do.

Her spark of hope flickers when she realizes she needs something to burn if she's going to create smoke. She glances at her clothes. Burning them will mean no protection when the sun rises again, but if it means there's a chance Gray could be saved...

Lexis shifts, a part of her looking forward to peeling the sweat stained material from her skin, when she feels the scabbard on her back. Her spear!

She quickly removes it, admiring the smooth length. Two depressions sit close to the center, handholds worn from her years of training with it. This spear was her first toy, the protection she depended on as surely as she did Raze. The thought of it becoming firewood hurts.

But that doesn't stop Lexis from jabbing it into the hard ground, holding the top, and slamming her foot through the center. There's a sickening crack as the wood splinters but it doesn't snap.

"Now isn't the time to be tough," she mutters to her faithful friend.

The second kick has her foot slicing clean through. A jagged half is now held in her hand, the other still quivering as it juts up from the dirt.

"I'm so sorry," she says quietly, hanging her head. Beside her, Gray moans, as if he can feel her pain. Lexis grits her teeth. "But we need to save him."

Lexis sits cross legged, holding one half between the soles of her feet. She takes the other and pushes the tip into the center of the rounded wood. Flexing her shoulders, she wipes her brow as if that will rid her of the exhaustion creeping through her mind and starts to twist the upright half between her palms. She's started fires like this before, but it takes time. And patience.

And energy.

"Lexis," Gray moans fitfully. "We're going to be so happy."

"We will," she croons, not taking her focus off the rapid twirling of the wood. They need to be alive first.

Slowly, a divot wears below the point of the spear, the wood paler than the aged outer skin. The cramps start sooner than Lexis would've liked, constricting between her shoulders and clamping around her joints, but she breathes through it. Friction will create heat. Heat will create fire.

Darkness is closing in around her, oppressive and eager, when the first tendril of smoke creeps up. Lexis gasps, hope climbing alongside the fragile coil.

She rubs her hands faster, grimacing as her muscles beg for her to stop. Her body is parched and exhausted, and it no longer cares about fire or finding a way forward. Or the belief that there's hope they can survive.

But her heart must've been touched by Gray's optimism, because she keeps going. The curl of smoke grows and gains substance, now a silvery smudge in the dusky air. Lexis keeps her gaze glued to the point where the friction is

She blows gently, eyes stinging with dry tears when a flame is born. She nurses it like the fragile tendril of hope that it is, and it slowly grows, creeping across the top of the half-spear, greedily devouring the wood.

When a solid flame has established, Lexis sits back, breathing as if she just fought an army to bring the fire to life. Like a giant candle, she spears it into the ground, jamming the second half next to it so it can burn, too. Smoke coils up, smudging the dark air. The flame is small, the smoke a negligible mark of their existence, but it's something.

It's all they have.

Her shoulders sag as exhaustion makes her light-headed. Lexis curls up beside Gray and even in his barely conscious state, his arm wraps around her. She rests her head on his chest, watching the flames eat away at her spear. They probably have an hour or so before the small fire reaches ground zero and is extinguished.

She runs her dry tongue over her peeling lips. Although she told Gray she's used to this, she can't remember feeling so incredibly dry, as if each of her cells is slowly calcifying. She idly wonders how long before she turns into just another parched rock in this vast wasteland that is the Outlands.

Her eyes drift shut; her eyelids now too heavy to be held open. Lexis tells herself it's exhaustion, but deep down, she knows it's death creeping up on her. She tucks herself closer to Gray, trying to shield him from it. She can hear his heartbeat fluttering too fast, feel his panting breaths.

"Gray," she whispers. "Thank you."

He showed her love.

He gave her hope.

He touched her soul, when she thought it was dead.

Lexis slips in and out of consciousness. Each time she opens her eyes, the world is blacker and the spear has burned further down. Time is slowly eating away at their final moments. She takes Gray's hand and threads their fingers together. As her own pulse starts to hurt, her heart struggles to pump her thickening blood, she smiles. "I love you."

When she hears a voice, she smiles even wider, thinking Gray heard her. But then the sound comes again, and she realizes it's the wrong tenor and it's not soft, but far away.

Someone's coming!

Lexis leaps to her feet, only to stagger back and fall over. Gravel grazes her palms as she hits the ground, but she's already trying to push herself up. The Rust are here, and she needs to defend Gray and herself long enough to try to bargain. And if that doesn't work, she'll need to kill them and steal their supplies.

Her legs give out again, this time the rocky soil digging into her knees. She moans, the sound grazing her parched throat. She has to protect Gray.

Before she can push up again, there's the crunch of gravel and something prods her chin. Lexis raises her head, and the spear slides down her throat to rest at the base.

"Don't move," warns a voice.

She blinks in the dark, the dying coals of her own broken spear shedding enough light to show that it's not a Rust standing before her.

A Never man is holding the weapon to her throat, his flowing, ragged clothes hanging from his lean frame. Her thick thoughts try to process what that means. The Never are even more of an unknown than the Rust.

Except it doesn't matter. She needs the same thing, no matter who it is.

"We need water," Lexis wheezes through dry lips. Her gaze flickers to Gray, keeping the rest of her body still. "He's dying."

"We all are," scoffs the Never. "I can finish him quickly if you like."

"No!" Gray would never choose that, no matter how hopeless things looked. "He just needs water. And some food."

Another Never appears beside the first. "And what makes you think we're going to give him either of those?"

Lexis blinks as the robed bodies multiply, wondering if she's hallucinating. She doesn't have the strength to stand, let alone fight. But if there's several of them, then she'll be dead before she gets a strike in.

"We would like...to...bargain," she pants.

Someone snorts. "You're half dead. You have nothing."

Lexis's blurred mind can't think of anything they'd have to offer. Her head droops. Right now, she looks nothing like the proud warrior she believed she is. And Gray's light is dimmed, no longer shining. They look like little more than a burden.

The man nudges the spear and she drags her gaze back up to him. "We will save you," he says. "But there will be a price."

Lexis nods. There always is.

"I agree," she mutters hoarsely, closing her eyes as the last of her strength fades away.

They have no choice. It's owe the Never or die.

GRACE

Grace blinks in the darkness of the infirmary wondering if it's morning. It's impossible to tell the time down here. Kallini had turned off the lights as she left Raze to rest, kindly allowing Grace to curl up beside him.

Scoria and Brik are nowhere to be seen, although Grace has no doubt Scoria will be glued to Corbin's side. Most likely in his bed. Maybe Brik has gone back outside to find Feather. Grace smiles at this thought, realizing it's ridiculous. Those two men are as opposite as the origins of their names.

Besides, the only person who matters right now is Raze. Kallini had worked some magic on him, and for the first time since Evrest stabbed him, Grace feels a sense of confidence he's going to be okay. She can hear him snoring gently. It's possibly the most beautiful sound she's ever heard.

Deciding that sleep is overrated when it comes to her own needs, she kisses Raze gently on the cheek. He stirs and she slowly withdraws, not wanting to disturb him. He needs his rest.

She gets out of bed and stretches, unable to shake the feeling she's just slept in a lion's den. These people of Rust may have helped them, but they're not her friends.

Not yet.

If she's going to bring them on side then she needs to get to work. Corbin clearly holds no power here. It's that awful Barnacle she has to befriend. Although, the comments he made about her in the meeting room have set her on edge. It was bad enough having to swat annoying Corbin away with his unwanted advances. Barnacle is a whole new level of danger.

But she didn't win the Tournaments by being a pushover. She's smart. She's resilient. She's strong. She can totally do this.

There are three doors leading into the container that forms the infirmary and she pauses at one of them, questioning if it was the one Kallini had ushered them through. She'd been so focused on Raze, she hadn't paid enough attention. Which is a mistake that could be deadly. If she's going to be a good Commander, she needs to be better than that.

Deciding to give it a try, she slips through the door and blinks, feeling her way along a damp wall made from stone. These tunnels connecting the containers have been dug out of the cliff. Surely, that can't be stable? The thought of how vulnerable they are right now causes beads of sweat to break out on her forehead.

She reaches what feels like an opening and walks through it, keeping one hand on the wall and the other in front of her. It's quiet in the tunnels with a musty smell that can't be healthy to breathe in all day. Maybe Feather was the smartest one of them all, choosing to sleep outside.

After a few more turns, Grace soon realizes she's made a mistake wandering the halls in the darkness. If she'd gone the right way, she'd have reached the giant leatherskin jaws by now and would be back in the meeting room. Instead, she's... Actually, she has no idea where she is.

Coming across what feels like a few closed doors, she leaves them as they are, afraid of waking an angry Rust. Besides, the last thing she wants to do is accidentally stumble into Barnacle's bedroom. He'd surely take that as an invitation, no matter how many wives he has sleeping next to him.

She turns around, deciding she'd be better to head back to the infirmary before she gets too far away from Raze. But it doesn't take long to discover this is just as impossible as finding her way to the meeting room.

Determined not to let this get in her way, she quickens her pace, turning left, then right, then right again, then pushing on in a straight line. She survived men twice her size trying to kill her in the Tournaments. She can beat this maze. How hard can it be?

After several more minutes, she realizes how hard it can be.

Too hard. She's completely lost.

"Oh, fish shackles," she grumbles.

A low sound behind her has her spinning on her heel.

"Who's there?" She holds herself still, waiting for whoever it is to reveal themselves.

The sound comes again, and she realizes it's someone stifling their laughter.

"Corbin?" she asks, hoping for a return of her annoying guardian angel. Not because she wants to see him, but because all other options are far worse.

"I preferred it when you called me Rusty," says a familiar voice. "Nobody's ever given me a nickname before. Well, not one that wasn't offensive."

"I'm lost," she says, getting to the point.

"I know." He laughs again. "I've been following you. Most entertaining thing I've seen in a while."

"How can you see me?" She holds both hands out in front of her, hoping Corbin doesn't try to come any closer.

"Hold on." She hears some retreating footsteps, then a click.

Soft light fills the tunnel, and she sees Corbin standing beside a switch high on the wall. He has some goggles pushed up on his forehead.

"All you had to do was turn on the light." He grins as he points to the goggles. "Or wear a pair of these."

"I thought goggles were for water," she says, not feeling at all comfortable at having been observed without her knowledge.

"These are for night vision," he explains. "Although, if any more water seeps through these walls, I might need them for swimming."

"How comforting." She wipes more sweat from her brow. "How can you live down here? It's not natural."

He shrugs. "What is natural in today's world?"

"That's very deep, Rusty." She smiles. "Now, do you think you could lead me back to the infirmary please? Or to the meeting room? I wouldn't mind a chat with Barnacle."

"Be careful of him," Corbin warns. "He can be harsher than he acts."

Grace wasn't sure he'd acted any differently to her definition of harsh, but she nods to show she understands.

"He'll kill Raze the first chance he gets." Corbin takes a few steps closer to her. "If I were you, I'd get him away from here. Find an excuse to hide him in Fairbanks so you can do what you need to do here."

A cold shiver runs down Grace's spine. As helpful as Corbin's been, she can't help but think he'd like any excuse to get Raze out of his way so he can get to her.

"I'm the Commander," she reminds him. "I don't need to find excuses. I can do whatever I like."

"Right now, you're the Commander in name only." He steps a little closer. "I can help you earn that title."

Her back stiffens. "I'm sorry, but last night it didn't look like you had much power to do anything."

"I work behind the scenes." He taps his forehead. "I pull all the strings around here."

Grace draws in a breath, wondering how much truth there is to that. It doesn't seem like much, but then again, no one expected her to become the Commander. Looks can be deceiving.

"I've got some information you might find helpful." He lowers his voice to a whisper. "Barnacle wants to build a fleet of boats to attack Askala."

Grace nods, unsure how this information is helpful. Building boats isn't exactly her specialty.

"I can tell you more useful things if you like." Corbin sidles closer. "If you make me second in command."

"I've already given that position to Brik," she says, almost relieved for the excuse not to grant this wish.

Corbin grimaces. "I still don't understand why you made that choice."

"I had to promise him something," she says. "I didn't exactly see you offering to help me carry Raze."

"Why do you like Raze so much?" The light is dim, but it looks like Corbin has tears stinging his eyes. "What does he have that I don't? I really like you, Winter. I always have."

"You know what he has?" She raises a brow. "Respect for me. And do you know how I know that?"

"How?" he squeaks.

"He respects my wishes and calls me Grace." She glares at him. "He understands how important that is to me. Winter is dead. She died in those Tournaments alongside her twin."

Corbin nods, pulling himself together. "I'll take you to Barnacle, Commander Grace. He's in the meeting room."

Grace follows him through the winding corridors, certain she'd walked these very steps in the darkness. They turn a sharp corner and Corbin presses on the light. The giant leatherskin jaws illuminate at the end of the tunnel.

Relief washes over her in a wave.

"Thank you," she says, trying to let him know she wants to do this alone. "You go back to Scoria."

"She means nothing to me." Corbin holds up his hands. "I swear it."

"Which is just another reason why I'm in love with Raze," she tells him. Raze would never toy with a woman purely to satisfy his primal needs. He hasn't done any more than kiss Grace despite having slept by her side on more than one occasion. But she doesn't say any of this. If Corbin had the emotional intelligence to understand that, then perhaps he wouldn't have been so far out of the running for her heart in the first place.

She continues down the corridor alone, steeling herself for what is sure to be a difficult conversation with Barnacle.

As she steps through the jaws, she's surprised to be greeted by the sound of raucous laughter. Brik and Barnacle are sitting on opposite sides of the table taking large gulps from goblets she's certain do not contain water.

"Commander Grace!" slurs Barnacle when he sees her. "Come and join us. I've just been getting acquainted with this fine man who tells me he was the ruler of Fairbanks."

"That's right," says Grace, keeping a safe distance. "It was a shame that he didn't rate his chances enough to enter the Tournaments so he could prove just how *fine* he is."

This is about as close as she's prepared to get to calling Brik a coward. Although, judging by the look on his face, it was a little too close for his comfort.

Barnacle ignores this comment and pours a dark red liquid into Brik's goblet, then his own.

"Would you care to join us?" he asks, reaching for a third glass and filling it to the top. "That is, if you're old enough to drink."

Grace glares at him as she takes her seat and picks up the

goblet. She forces down a large gulp, trying desperately not to show on her face the effect it has on her. The alcohol burns at her throat and a dozen balloons seem to float into her skull and burst one by one.

"Enough talk of the factions and who leads them," she says, delaying taking a second sip. "We are united now."

Barnacle seems to find this amusing. He looks across at Brik who lets out a deep chuckle. Grace hadn't even realized he knew how to smile.

"How long will your boats take to build?" she asks, trying to steer the conversation toward something remotely like business.

Her question wipes the smile from Barnacle's face. "How do you know about my boats? I haven't even started building them yet. Who told you?"

She forces down another sip of liquid, despite needing to keep her head clear.

"Was it that rat, Corbin?" Barnacle leans toward her, and she can smell his stinking breath. Or is it the rot that's growing in his beard?

She ignores him, not wanting to implicate anyone.

"I bet it was the mad woman," Barnacle says. "I don't know why we keep Kallini around sometimes."

"Does she have hidden talents?" asks Brik with a leer.

"It wasn't Kallini," Grace says quickly, not wanting to get the woman who worked so carefully to heal Raze into trouble.

"The boats will take years." Barnacle sits back in his chair. "We're going to build a fleet."

"Years?" When she'd been tasked with invading Askala, she'd imagined a period of months, not years. "That's too long."

"Just as well I'm not building them for you then, isn't it?" Barnacle grins at her and Brik breaks into more laughter.

Grace can see she's not going to get anywhere right now. These men are far too intoxicated for a sensible conversation.

And she really doesn't like the way that drink has gone to her own head either.

"If you'll excuse me." She takes another sip of her drink, being careful not to actually consume any more of the liquid. "I need to check on Raze."

"Don't tell me that Cy scum made it through the night." All humor has leached from Barnacle's voice. "I knew I was way too soft on him."

"We need him." Grace stands, suddenly feeling anxious. "You'll see. He's a very valuable piece of the puzzle."

Barnacle scowls. "And what if it's a puzzle I have no interest in completing? We were fine here before you came along. We don't need to play your games."

"Then why did Rust enter the Tournaments?" she asks, sweeping from the room before he has a chance to think up a smart reply.

She steps through the leatherskin jaws and looks around. With the corridors now lit, the path to the infirmary is obvious. Shallow grooves have been hollowed out in the dirt floor from when Kallini had pushed Raze in the chair with wheels. All she has to do is follow them.

Increasing her pace to a jog, she rounds the final corner and sees the infirmary door ahead. Why had she thought it was a good idea to leave Raze?

She pushes open the door to find a commotion in the dark. There's clattering and gasping and a few choice curse words.

Scrambling for the light switch on the wall, she finds it and flicks it on, just in time to see a figure escaping through one of the doors on the far wall.

Raze is on the floor on all fours, panting.

Practically pouncing on him, she ignores the racing of her heart as she throws her arms around him.

"I need to go after him," says Raze, attempting to get up. "He tried to kill me."

She looks at the door and shakes her head. "It's too danger-ous," she says, trying to figure out how she's going to tell him what she now knows is true.

Corbin is right. Raze can't stay here.

She has to hide him in Fairbanks.

It's the only way he'll stay alive.

RAZE

*G*race sits on the bed, her gaze heavy. "You can't stay here, Raze."

The pain in his back instantly fades into the background. "What are you talking about? We just got here."

She shakes her head, her dark hair brushing her face. "If you stay, the Rust are going to kill you. We need to go to Fairbanks."

Raze straightens, welcoming the flash of agony down his back. His wound is a testament of what he stands for. "I'll die before I leave you."

Grace won't be able to stay in Fairbanks. She needs to unite the factions.

"I'll leave before you die," she shoots back, her eyes full of steel and sadness.

A new pain, a fresh pain, slices through Raze's chest. He moves to sit beside Grace, taking her hands. "What are you saying?" he whispers.

"I'm saying you dying for me is never what I'd want. That would break my heart." She caresses his face. "I love you, Raze."

His breath disintegrates. He pauses, realizing this is why he hasn't spoken for so long. Words are hard. They hurt as much as they heal. "It's because I love you that I don't want a life without you."

He kisses her, pressing his lips to show her the depth of these feelings. The breadth of them. The way they sear his very heart.

But as he pours himself into their sweet connection, Raze finds Grace giving as much as she's receiving. And her love is just as deep as his.

He groans, clasping her closer. Her soft curves mold to his hard lines, heat scorching everywhere they touch. Her hands streak into his hair, tugging as if she wants more. As if, just like him, she can't get enough.

A subtle but undeniable *creak* has them pulling apart. The door to the infirmary opens and Kallini steps through, smiling as she carries a hessian bag. "Oh, you're up," she says breezily. "That's wonderful."

Panting a little, Raze and Grace glance at each other. They smile surreptitiously, but then Grace bites her lip. They still have a lot that needs to be discussed.

Kallini sits the hessian bag on Raze's lap. "You eat and drink while I check your wound."

Grace frowns. "Someone attacked Raze this morning. They tried to kill him."

Kallini looks stricken for long seconds, her hand fluttering to her throat, but then she visibly unwinds. She even smiles as she walks toward the shelves. "Well, how lucky that they were unsuccessful!" She pulls down a jar and some cloth. "People can be so silly sometimes."

Raze arches a brow. Grace shrugs then shakes her head. She takes the bag and opens it, finding a canteen of water, some flatbread, and what looks like dried fish. There's even a small jar in the shape of a bear.

"Thank you, Kallini," Grace says, looking impressed.

Kallini waves away the gratitude. "I like to help, remember?"

Raze and Grace make quick work of sharing the water and bread. He's not sure either have ever tasted so good. His mind flashes to all the times Grace insisted on him eating if she was going to. No wonder he fell so hard and fast for her.

Kallini moves to his back, carefully peeling the bandage. "The stitches are fine," she observes quietly. "Apart from a new dressing, there's little here for me to do."

The heavy note in her voice has Raze turning around. "You've extended me kindness, Kallini. That takes courage few have."

She flushes. "Oh." Then frowns. "From what I can tell, a lot of people just think I'm crazy."

Raze shakes his head. "We're all broken in some way," he says quietly.

Grace grasps his hand and squeezes it. "Which is what makes us stronger."

Kallini claps in childlike happiness. "I like you two," she announces. "I like you two a lot."

She goes back to redressing Raze's wound, humming to herself.

Raze places his other hand over Grace's. "What did Barnacle say?" he asks quietly.

She frowns. "That he doesn't want a Cy in his midst."

Raze shakes his head. That's not what he was asking, and she knows it.

"That's because Cy are evil," Kallini whispers and Raze feels the way her hand trembles.

She steps away, shuffling back to the shelves with her shoulders hunched.

"I'm Cy," Raze points out gently. Maybe she missed that when he arrived.

But Kallini shakes her head. "No, you're not," she responds, glancing over her shoulder. "Cy have no heart."

Her eyelids flicker and she quickly turns back to put away her supplies.

Grace watches the fragile woman for long moments before turning back to Raze. "You think the Cy are coming, don't you?" she whispers so Kallini can't hear.

Raze nods. "He wants to rule," he says simply, knowing Grace will understand he's talking about his father.

And Kallini's right. Evrest is heartless. He'll stop at nothing to become Commander.

Suddenly, a loud clanging echoes from beyond the infirmary, as if someone is banging something on metal. Then another round of noise picks up from a different direction. Then another.

Kallini freezes. "The alarms," she whispers, clearly horrified.

Raze shoots to his feet, Grace beside him. "The alarms for what?"

Kallini's eyes open until the white seems to dominate her face. She tries to move her lips only to fail. Grace rushes over, gripping the woman's shoulders. "What's the alarm for, Kallini?"

A single tear spills over her pale cheek. "Attack."

Adrenaline drenches through Raze's muscles. "They're here." His father and his warriors have come far sooner than anyone expected.

The words make Kallini flinch. "They'll kill us all." She shudders. "After they've finished with us."

More clanging echoes from further away, as if the sound is being passed through the labyrinth of tunnels and containers. Kallini starts trembling, the sound of fluid trickling onto the ground telling them that she just lost control of her bladder.

Raze takes her hand and pulls her to the door as Grace opens it. "We need to get out of these damned tunnels."

Kallini pulls back desperately. "No! Leave me here! I'll hide."

"The Cy love finding little gifts, as they call them," Raze tells her. "We're not leaving you."

Grace glances out the door, pulling back as several people rush past, everyone silent but panicked looking.

"They're running further in," Grace gasps.

"Fools," Raze mutters. They're running to their death.

Grace leads the way, Raze tugging a silent Kallini as they work their way through the tide of Rust heading into the bowels of the cliffs. "We need to talk to Barnacle," she shouts.

Raze nods. They need to know what the plan is.

Kallini trips as they step through the bleached leatherskin jaws, and Raze quickly catches her, pulling her up to his side. "Leave me," she moans.

"No," he responds. "I won't leave you behind."

They enter the container, finding Barnacle and Brik there with several Rust warriors. Barnacle's frown only intensifies at seeing them. "Keep it down," he hisses.

The men are standing stock still, heads cocked.

They're listening. For the Cy.

There's a *thump* from beyond the other end. They're in the entrance container.

Grace steps forward. "And you think we don't need to unite?" she whispers fiercely as she points in the direction of the sound. "We have an enemy on our doorstep, let alone the one over the ocean."

"They don't know we're here." Barnacle scowls, keeping his voice low. "Plus, once I build my boats, I can attack Askala all on my own."

"Not if the Cy have killed you," says Raze.

And the moment they get through that door, that's exactly what will happen. The Rust are trapped in their own decaying tunnels.

"And not if your warriors are exhausted when they arrive in Askala," Grace adds. Something jolts through her—the ripple is subtle but Raze notices it. "Do your boats have sails?"

"Material that size isn't easy to come by," Barnacle snaps,

then quietens his voice. "You don't think I would have sails if I could?"

"What if I got some for you?"

Brik straightens a little, suggesting he has an idea what she's thinking.

Barnacle's eyes narrow. "I'd be willing to talk."

There's a bang and everyone freezes. Kallini whimpers, pulling away from Raze to tuck herself in the corner of the container.

Raze scans the ceiling, then glances over his shoulder into the dark passageway. "Is there an exit out of this death trap?"

"Of course there is," says Barnacle.

Brik's gaze sharpens. "The hole you have to crawl out that you were bragging about?"

"It's an exit," Barnacle responds defensively.

That will only let one person out at a time, leaving everyone else to be slaughtered.

"You need to let them in," Raze states flatly.

"What?" Barnacle gasps.

"They're coming in," Grace says in a low voice. "Today or tomorrow or the day after that, whether you like it or not."

"The Cy won't stop," moans Kallini. "No matter what."

Raze wishes he could go to her. Comfort her. Ask her how she seems to know so much about the Cy. But a thud on the other side of the container reminds him they have little time.

"We know you're hiding in there, Rust!" a deep voice growls. "You're a bunch of cowards. If you don't let us in, we'll break the door down and make you pay for your lack of hospitality."

"Send someone out through the exit to get a message to Feather," Raze says. "Tell him to collapse the entrance once the Cy are through."

There's an uncomfortable murmur from the Rust warriors.

Barnacle removes a knife tucked into a sheath on his belt. "You're suggesting we fight them?"

Raze stills, unsure who the knife is for. "I'm suggesting we trap them before they trap us."

"That's exactly what we need to do," says Grace. "Show the Cy we're fighters, not moles hiding and scurrying away."

Corbin appears in the jaws of the leatherskin. "I came as soon as I could," he pants, and Raze doubts that's even a shadow of the truth. He wouldn't put it past Corbin to have been hiding in the shadows, listening to decide whether he was going to take part. "What can I do?"

Barnacle's gaze snaps around the room before coming back to rest on Corbin. "Take Brik to the exit. He has a message for Feather."

Corbin nods sharply. "Of course," he says confidently.

"And take your mother with you," adds Raze. "She needs to be away from all of this."

Corbin's gaze flicks to Grace, then to his mother cowering in the corner. "I was just going to do that."

He takes her hand and Kallini curls into his side. "Corbin, they're coming," she whimpers.

"I'll keep you safe," he murmurs, his gaze flickering once again around the room as if to make sure everyone heard him.

Brik quickly slips past the others to join him. He pauses beside Grace. "This had better work."

She glares at him. "That depends on everyone working together."

Pride infuses Raze. He never could've predicted this woman whose spirit was born in the rubble of Fairbanks would be exactly what the Outlands needs, but she's just that.

"Rusts!" comes the deep voice again from the other side of the door. "Your time is up! We're coming in."

The warriors in the room shuffle and glance at each other. Barnacle's hand tightens reflexively around the hilt of his knife. "We fight, warriors of Rust. Our allegiance will not be taken by force."

There's a round of nods and Raze feels a cold calmness settle over him. The battle has been decided.

"Here." One of the Rusts passes Grace a stone knife and she smiles in thanks. Raze isn't offered a weapon, probably because they hope he'll die during this fight, but that's fine. He doesn't need one.

He was trained to be deadly from the moment he could walk.

He looks toward one of the men near the door, the ones the Cy are on the other side of. "Open it when I give you the signal."

The Rusts all tense, their bodies wired to fight. A quick glance around the room reveals each one is holding a knife or a club, their faces blank in the way warriors are before battle. They're either making peace with their possible demise, or doing everything they can to not consider the possibility.

Raze smashes the chair on the table.

"Hey!" calls a voice on the other side of the door. "I just heard—!"

Before the Cy have finished, Raze gives the signal.

The Rust warrior shoves the door open, revealing a dozen Cy soldiers on the other side. More than Raze expected. All armed. All with bloodlust painted on their familiar faces.

He lifts the leg of the smashed chair and throws it. The makeshift dagger slams into a Cy's throat and lodges there, blood gushing down his chest. The man collapses with a gurgle.

One down.

The Cy let out a roar, one that is quickly matched by the Rust and the room fills with the quest for blood. The Cy pour in, weapons swinging and thrusting, swarming around the table in the center of the room. Three jump on it, smashing dinner plates and kicking over vases.

The Rust rush forward, grunts and thuds quickly filling the room. There's a cry as a Rust is quickly impaled with a spear.

Grace goes to step around Raze, but he stops her. "We can't let them past this room," she says urgently.

"We won't," he says, the scent of blood already staining the air. "You need to be ready to evacuate with everyone else."

He doesn't have a chance to see whether she understood, because a Cy runs across the table, straight at them. Raze leaps up, ignoring the slice of pain through his back and picking up a couple of silver knives on the way through. He throws one just like the chair leg, but the Cy warrior is ready, blocking the projectile with his mace.

The Cy swings the studded club back, and Raze curves his body as it narrowly misses him. The warrior is about to swing again, leaving him little time to recover, when the man arches his spine and lets out a scream. He looks down, and Raze sees Grace quickly step back toward the jaws of the leatherskin, leaving a fork impaled in the Cy's leg. Knowing she just created an opening for him, Raze leaps forward, slamming his fist into the man's jaw. The Cy spins and crumples, his head landing on the table with a thud and a bounce.

Raze leaps down again, just as a grizzled-looking Rust falls to his left, a hideous scream bouncing off the metal walls. A dagger protrudes from this chest. The Cy he was fighting leaps on him, withdrawing the weapon and stabbing it several more times just for good measure.

Raze takes quick stock. Several Rust are already dead, along with a handful of Cy. They're outnumbered and out-skilled, but he knew the latter would be true. Cy are walking assassins. The Rust could never win in a battle, which is exactly why they need this plan to work.

Raze glances toward the door the Cy came through, desperately hoping to see a flicker of movement. But the dark opening reveals an upturned chair and little else.

Barnacle takes several steps back as he throws a candlestick and it clangs off a Cy's head. He glances at Raze, then Grace. "If you've been working with the Cy all along..." he growls threat-eningly.

Another Rust screams in agony, his blood spraying across the unblinking eyes of the fish decorating the wall.

Raze's gut clenches as the red haze only fuels the Cy. They're running out of time.

A flash of movement beyond the container catches his eye, and relief courses through him.

"Retreat," he shouts.

The Rust respond instantly, some turning and running toward the leatherskin jaws. Several of the Cy's faces flash with premature victory, and they straighten a little, giving them-selves a moment to regroup before they begin their slaughter.

But they fail to see Feather and Brik behind them, slamming the doors closed. The *thuds* that follow tell Raze they're doing exactly as they're supposed to.

They're trying to collapse the ceiling of the entrance.

A Cy comes from the back and Raze instantly recognizes him. Arc. The cold-blooded bastard who killed just to come on the journey to announce the Tournaments. He grins at Raze. "We're here to kill the traitor, anyway." He thrusts his spear into the air. "No mercy!"

Raze shoves Grace behind him. "Get everyone out!"

Scuffling sounds reach him as the last Rust rush past him, but Raze doesn't turn to look. He keeps his eyes on the enemy as they break into a run, realization dawning on their faces. In a few seconds, they'll be the only ones in the container.

There's a *boom* and Raze freezes at the unexpected sound. Several of the Cy stumble, glancing around, trying to locate where the explosive noise came from. Raze looks over his shoulder, seeing Barnacle and Grace behind him, the remaining Rust behind them.

The *crack* and *crunch* that come next are just as loud, but somehow far more ominous.

Raze slowly turns back, horror echoing through him as he realizes what's happened. He planned to trap the Cy, but not this... Feather and Brik collapsed the roof of the entrance container, but they've triggered an avalanche.

With a deafening wrenching of metal, the back end of the container caves.

"Run!" screams Arc, using the man beside him to shove off in a desperate attempt to get more speed.

"Raze!" Grace shouts.

Like a wave, the length of the container implodes, metal snapping and twisting as the tons of earth above it crush it flat. The sight is awe-inspiring and terrifying. Raze leaps back through the leatherskin jaws, compressed air seeming to push him through.

He takes hold of Grace and keeps running, the sounds of destruction seeming to tumble over each other behind him. Ahead, Barnacle is directing his men down one of the intersections.

"Raze!" comes a scream through the deafening rumbling. "You bastard mute!"

He turns around to see Arc still running for the exit, a moving wall of metal and dirt right behind him. Raze remembers the second silver knife he's holding. He doesn't blink as he raises it and flings it.

It impales right through Arc's eye socket, and the Cy scum reels backward, hitting the wall of death still powering forward.

The leatherskin's jaws slam shut as the last of the container crumbles, instantly cutting off the noise.

And stopping the wave of destruction.

Raze finds himself in the passageway, Grace beside him. They're both breathing heavily. He stares at the jaws of Mother Nature that just swallowed Arc. The man whose final words were to call him a bastard mute.

"I just never had anything to say to you," Raze mutters.

Grace takes his hand as Barnacle approaches them, his men behind him. Several sets of eyes are still wide, the whites bright in the gloom.

"You're lucky you didn't collapse the whole place," Barnacle growls.

Grace straightens her shoulders. "You're welcome," she says. "Your people are safe."

Several of the Rust men mutter as they shift their weight.

Barnacle drops his shoulders and lifts his chin. "What do we owe you?"

Raze realizes that's what this is about. Barnacle doesn't like knowing he's in debt.

"There is nothing to pay. That's what happens when factions work together." Grace raises herself another inch. "Take us to the exit."

"Where are you going?" he asks, still looking suspicious despite everything that's just happened.

"Go look after your people, Barnacle," she says, her hand tightening around Raze's. "We'll get you your sails."

GRAY

*G*ray stirs, gradually becoming aware of Lexis drizzling water through his cracked lips. Everything hurts. His head. His feet. His stomach.

He reaches for Lexis's hand and squeezes it.

"I'll always love you," he tells her, wanting her to know just how much she means to him.

Forcing his eyes to open, he blinks. The first thing he notices is that he's inside a tent. The second thing is that it's not Lexis's hand he's holding.

There's a bemused old man crouched on the ground next to him with a damp sponge in his hand.

"Hey, I know you're thirsty but declaring your undying love for me might be taking things a bit too far." He lets go of Gray's hand and places the sponge in his palm so he can administer the water himself now that he's awake.

Normally Gray would laugh. Except Lexis's absence fills him with fear.

"Where is she?" He tries to sit up, but the effort is too great. "Where's Lexis?"

"Your woman's in the female camp." The man puts a

steadying hand on his chest. "She's alive. In better shape than you from what I'm told."

Gray relaxes just a bit, hoping he can trust him.

"Who are you?" he asks, studying the deep creases on the man's weather-beaten face. "Where am I?"

"My name's Chicago." He removes his hand slowly when he sees Gray makes no further attempt to move. "And you're in the Neverlands."

"The what?" Gray tries to sit up again.

"The Neverlands," he repeats, forcing Gray back down. "It's what we call the parts of the Outlands no faction has claimed. It's where we live."

"You're from the Never?" Gray asks, unsure if this is some weird hallucination.

"Sure am." Chicago lifts Gray's hand to force the sponge to his lips. "Drink."

Gray sucks on the sponge, suddenly aware of just how dehydrated he is. "Do you have a flask? I think I need more than this."

"The sponge will do you for now." Chicago nods. "Water's in short supply out here."

"What happened?" Gray asks, rubbing his forehead with his free hand. His temples are pounding as vague snatches of memories try to piece themselves together. And his feet are killing him. Just how far had they walked?

"We saved your lives," Chicago says. "You were almost dead. But lucky for you, your woman could still talk."

Gray nods, not surprised. His warrior girl is tough. Much tougher than he is.

"She agreed to the price." Chicago stands. "Hardly anyone agrees to the price."

"What price?" Gray sits up this time without Chicago close enough to stop him.

The bemused look returns to Chicago's face. "The price to save your lives."

Gray isn't sure what exactly Lexis agreed to, but he's happy she did. Because it means she's still alive. And he's still alive to see her.

Chicago turns to leave the tent.

"Wait," calls Gray. "You didn't tell me what the price was."

He grins. "Oh, you'll figure it out soon enough. Rest now. While you can..."

But Gray doesn't want to rest. He wants Lexis. He hauls himself to his feet, realizing all the pain is coming from a burning feeling in his left foot.

He steps forward and overbalances, toppling and landing hard on his butt.

Cursing, he gets up again, his head thumping, his vision blurring, his left foot screaming at him in protest.

This time, he takes one step toward the exit of the tent before he crashes back to the ground. Was there some kind of alcohol in that sponge? He just can't seem to get his balance.

He pulls his foot up to inspect what the problem is. It's been bandaged in rags and he unwinds them, needing to know what's underneath. Wincing as he gets down to the final layer, his eyes open wide.

"What the—" Vomit races up the back of his throat and he only just manages to stop himself from bringing up the precious water he'd consumed.

The big toe on his left foot is missing. In its place is a jagged wound like it was hacked off with a blunt saw.

The price of saving his life was his toe? What the hell is wrong with these people?

Cradling his head in his hands, he thinks of Lexis, hoping that somehow the price applied only to Gray. She's so precious. So perfect. The thought of her being mutilated in that way is too much for him to bear.

"Chicago!" he calls out. "Come back here! Chicago!"

The old man pokes his head back in the tent. "That was fast. Takes most people longer than that to figure it out."

"What's going on?" Gray tries to stand, but the knowledge of what's wrong with this foot has him even more unsteady than before. "I want to see Lexis."

Chicago rolls his eyes and steps back into the tent. "How many times do I have to tell you to rest?" He forces Gray back to the mat he'd been sleeping on.

"You cut off my toe!" Gray glares at him, daring him to deny it.

"Well, technically, *I* didn't." Chicago stands over him.

Gray groans. He's getting nowhere. No closer to Lexis. No closer to understanding why these barbarians have both maimed him and saved him.

"Please," Gray begs, looking up. "Tell me what's going on. I need to see Lexis."

The older man sighs. "Resources are limited out here, as you and your woman discovered when you ventured into the Neverlands."

"Her name is Lexis," Gray bites out.

"You needed water," he continues. "Your woman promised you to us for five years in exchange."

"Me?" He puts a hand on his chest, not understanding.

"Both of you," says Chicago. "You and your woman belong to us for five years."

"B-belong?" Gray tilts his head. "What does that mean exactly? Because if any of your men lay a finger on Lexis I'm going to—"

"We're not savages," Chicago snaps. "We're the Never, not the Cy."

"You cut off my toe," Gray yelps. "That seems pretty savage to me."

"We need to know you're not going to run away," he says.

88

"Sadly, our first few volunteers scampered the first chance they got. You'd be amazed at how the loss of your toe slows you down and upsets your balance."

"Volunteers?" Gray glances down at his foot, not feeling all that much like a voluntary participant in all this.

"Your woman volunteered you." Chicago runs a hand through his silver hair. "You weren't in a position to speak for yourself."

"Lexis agreed to *this.*" Gray points to the wound on his foot.

Chicago shrugs. "There wasn't a chance to explain it in fine detail when we found you both."

"Please tell me you didn't do this to her as well?" Gray feels the anger bubbling up in his gut.

"That's up to the women," he says. "We keep our camps separate."

"Can I ask why that's necessary?" Gray wraps his foot back up, deciding keeping it clean might be the only way to stop it getting infected.

"Is this a world you want to bring a baby into?" Chicago asks. "I already told you that resources are scarce. Interaction between the sexes is strictly supervised. We don't want children in the Never. All we want is to live out our remaining days in peace."

No children? Gray's never heard of a society like this before. And while he can see some sense in it, he's not even nearly convinced. Removing digits doesn't sound like anything a peaceful society would partake in. And they entered the brutal Tournaments...

Chicago plants his hands on his hips. "Any more questions?"

"You haven't told me what belonging means?" says Gray. "What have we been volunteered for?"

"Whatever we say," says Chicago. "Digging wells. Fetching supplies. Tending the sick. Hunting for food. Defending the Never from attack. Borrowing from the other factions."

"You mean stealing?" Gray clarifies.

He shrugs. "Same, same."

"So, I'm a slave then?" Gray thinks he may just have encountered his very first situation where he's struggling to put a positive spin on it. At least in the Tournaments he had Winter by his side. From what Chicago just told him, he's not going to see Lexis for five whole years.

"We prefer the word *volunteer.*" Chicago smiles.

"I'm sure you do," Gray grumbles. "But I like to call things what they are."

Chicago chuckles. "All the volunteers are like this to begin with. You'll soon settle in."

"How do I see Lexis?" Gray gets to his knees and clutches at the rags Chicago calls clothes. "You have to help me. Please. I need to see her."

"Today is your rest day." Chicago brushes him off. "If I were you, I'd make the most of it. Because tomorrow you'll begin volunteering. Forget your woman. She's history to you now."

Gray slumps back on the mat. Lexis will never be history to him. He can wait five years for her. He can wait five lifetimes if necessary.

"If you try to leave this tent, you'll be killed." Chicago goes to the exit and lifts the flap of animal hide. "Rest. I'll bring you a refreshed sponge a little later."

A warm rush of air hits Gray in the face as the tent closes behind his captor.

He tries desperately to think of all the positives in this situation.

He's alive.

Lexis is alive.

He's...he's...he's...dammit! He can't think of one other thing.

Then he's hit with Winter's words when she was trying to convince him to enter the Tournaments. *I know we don't stand much chance, Gray, but it's still a chance.*

He can hear his twin just like she's standing beside him in this suffocating tent.

Who would have thought her words of hope would be the thing he'd cling to to get out of this hopeless situation?

There's still a chance.

He and Lexis can still get themselves out of this mess. The life he imagined for them can still happen.

A loud scream pierces the air, vibrating through the thick humidity.

Lexis. That was definitely Lexis.

He leaps to his feet, stumbles, then rights himself. It's only a toe. He can walk without it, no matter how much it might hurt.

Limping to the exit, he opens the flap of the tent.

The scream comes again and this time he's even more certain it was Lexis.

"Lexis!" he cries out, scanning the makeshift camp surrounding him. "Lexis! I'm coming!"

A shifting shadow catches his attention and he turns to see a flash of gray hair and a club rushing at him.

Pain shatters his senses as he's knocked to the ground.

Still trying to call Lexis's name, blackness swallows him once more.

LEXIS

*L*exis roars her frustration once again. "You monsters!"
She takes the small, bloody package that was just given to her and throws it with all her might.

The Never woman standing in the opening of the tent, Nocona, doesn't flinch as it hits her chest and drops to the floor. "It's customary to do this with all volunteers."

"You cut off his toe!" Lexis screeches, revulsion like a thrashing serpent in her gut. Poor Gray. This was never the price she imagined he'd be forced to pay.

She's seen amputated limbs before, those much deadlier than a toe, but Lexis can't bring herself to look at the red-stained bundle now sitting in the dirt. Gray's soft soul should never have been subjected to something so barbaric.

"You wanted proof he's still here, now you have it." Nocona flicks a matted dreadlock over her shoulder. "What's more, it will ensure you cannot run."

The Never have tried three times to come at Lexis with a knife. The first time, the two women sent to do the job while she was barely conscious were surprised to find a spitting, snarling Lexis on their hands. The second time, the three women all sported bruises as they walked away. The third time, the knife they'd brought had ended up impaling the soil between one of the woman's feet.

Lexis didn't know what the Never women were trying to hold her down for, but she certainly does now.

"You will not be doing the same to me," she growls.

"It seems we don't need to. You've been here two days and you haven't tried to leave." Nocona angles her head. "You won't leave without him."

Lexis's hands clench convulsively, hating that the words are true. She could've left here the moment the Never rationed her some water and food. She could've snuck out under the cover of darkness, killing anyone who tried to stop her.

But Gray is here. There's no way she'd take a step outside this village without him by her side.

Her gut clenches. With one less toe, which means once again he'll be too injured to travel.

Not that they have anywhere to go…

"You heartless bastards," Lexis spits.

"You're alive, aren't you?" says Nocona. "It's more than the Cy would've allowed."

That's also the truth. That slim hope is why she agreed to the price even before she knew what it was. Her last seconds of consciousness were used to pin their lives on the knowledge anyone is more merciful than the Cy.

"I want to see him," Lexis demands, keeping her voice hard. Her captors don't need to know this need is a desperate one.

Nocona sighs. "I'll not explain it again. Men and women remain separate. Any contact is strictly supervised."

"Then supervise it," snaps Lexis.

"For us to help you, you must help us."

She grinds her teeth. According to the five years of slavery she's apparently agreed to, she has no choice but help them. "What do I need to do?"

If she has to do some work in order to see Gray, then she'll play the Never's game. For now.

Nocona's dirt-streaked face lights up in a smile. "I'm so glad you asked."

She turns and leaves, and Lexis realizes she's expected to follow. She exits the tent cautiously, scanning her surroundings. She hasn't left the suffocating space she woke up in, meaning she has no idea what's about to greet her.

A handful of other tents have been pitched in a half-circle, all made of the same rags the Never clothe themselves in. Several yards away, a second half-circle of tents can be seen, most likely the men's quarters. The center is open and naked, nothing but bleached dirt and blinding sunshine.

Sneaking out to look for Gray will be difficult. But not impossible. Lexis is determined to find a way.

"This way," Nocona says, turning right and moving beyond the tents.

Lexis follows, for a moment considering breaking into a run in the direction of the men's quarters, but she quickly discounts it. The Never's hospitality—as they call it—won't extend to a prisoner who injures or kills one of them. And Gray needs time to heal. For now, she'll pretend she can stomach being a slave.

Nocona continues to walk away from the encampment, not bothering to check whether Lexis is following. Not even caring that she has her back turned to her. Lexis grinds her teeth. No one would've considered turning their back to her a few days ago.

She's not only a slave, she's a harmless one.

Lexis sees a small shape blurred by the heat ahead, and she tightens her muscles. Her fingers reflexively twitch, missing her spear. There's always the chance the Never will still try to kill her.

But the shape quickly reveals itself to be a small child, hunched over the dirt. As they come closer, Lexis sees it's a girl, crouched in the middle of a large depression. Her hair matted and the color of dust, she's stabbing the hard ground with a thick stick in her hand, over and over. She doesn't glance up as they arrive, just monotonously chips away at the rock as if she's uselessly trying to dig a hole for herself to disappear into.

Lexis's stomach tightens. Just like Gray, she's missing a toe.

Nocona stops a few feet away from the child. "We have a well that needs to be dug."

Lexis notes the lines scraped into the depression and wonders how long it took to etch them out. "That will take months." Possibly years.

"Yes, and it's back breaking work. That's why we have volunteers do it."

"You're using a child?" Lexis asks incredulously.

Nocona shrugs. "Children have the least value to the Never. And this one is a Cragg." She sneers. "And she doesn't even talk."

Just like Raze.

Nocona nudges the girl with her foot. "We borrowed Shale from the Cragg. The way they treat their children they didn't even notice her go missing. May as well put her to use here."

Lexis frowns, but quickly hardens her heart. It doesn't have room for the suffering of others. She needs to focus on freeing Gray and herself.

Nocona picks up another stumpy, thick piece of wood sitting at the edge of the depression and holds it out to Lexis. "We'll bring your water and food rations at noon." Lexis goes to take it, but the woman yanks it back. "You use this as a weapon and you'll find something similar in the chest of your man."

Lexis snatches the tool, furious at the image Nocona just painted. The impulse to end this impassive, almost congenial, woman here and now flashes through her. Lexis would already be running toward the men's quarters before Nocona's lifeless body hit the ground. She'd tear apart every tattered tent until she found Gray. She'd cover any Never who tried to stop her in blood.

A movement in the corner of her eye has Lexis glancing at the girl. Shale tucks her head down, her shoulders hunching up to protect it. Her bony body contracts within itself.

Lexis blinks. The girl may appear mindlessly absorbed in her task, but she sensed that Lexis had violence on her mind. She's deeply attuned to any sign of danger.

Just like Raze.

Lexis grips the stick and turns away from Nocona. "Don't hurt Gray and I won't have a reason to use it as more than a useless digging tool," she mutters darkly.

"If you don't show some gratitude, then your midday rations will be given to someone who does," snarls Nocona before turning on her heel and striding away.

Lexis is left standing in the sun with Shale stab, stab, stabbing away at the hard ground. The need to scream is overwhelming as frustration bubbles up. She spins and throws the stick, gaining a small sense of satisfaction as it impales the ground.

Shale's intake of breath is subtle, but Lexis has spent years honing her senses. She hears the gasp the little girl tries to subdue. The sign of fear the girl doesn't want to show.

"Sorry," Lexis mutters. "They just make me so angry."

Shale doesn't look up, simply resumes her rhythmic chipping. Lexis watches for long moments, almost mesmerized by the repetitive actions. As the sun dries any sweat before it even forms, she realizes Shale will do this for hours. In fact, Lexis could stand here all day, reserving her energy, gaining her strength back with each ration the Never give her.

She squats down, looking more closely at the little girl. Her skin is caked with dust, her clothes even more ragged than the Never's. She doesn't look up, doesn't acknowledge Lexis's presence or stare. She just stab, stab, stabs away at the hard ground.

Lexis wonders how long it's taken her to etch out the depression she's in now. And whether Shale realizes that this will likely be her future during her time with the Never.

Probably.

"You don't get angry, do you?" Lexis asks quietly.

Not even Shale's eyelids flutter in acknowledgement of the question.

"My brother stopped getting angry, too." He coped by accepting.

Stab. Stab. Stab.

"You know, he didn't talk either," Lexis muses, wondering why she's making conversation at all.

Maybe it's because she's used to a silent companion.

Maybe it's because she knows Shale is hearing far more than she's letting on. Just like Raze did.

Stab. Stab. Stab.

"But a lot of the time he didn't need to," Lexis continues, her heart aching for her twin. "People say so much without ever saying a word."

Stab.

Lexis stills when she notes that Shale just paused.

Stab. Stab.

Lexis narrows her eyes as she keeps her gaze on the hazy horizon. "It also meant people forgot he existed. I think he wanted it that way." She frowns. "And I never questioned that."

There's silence and Lexis realizes Shale has completely stopped. Lexis turns back to see two wide eyes looking at her. The girl stays stock still as she watches Lexis, barely breathing, barely blinking.

She's waiting to see what Lexis will do next.

Lexis almost frowns, unsure how this moment came to be. She should turn away and end this one-sided conversation. She should tell Shale to get back to work.

But Raze's face rises in her mind. His eyes used to watch

others just as intently. He'd wait to see what people would do next.

The whole time he was wanting to disappear. As he wanted to be seen.

Lexis shuffles forward, flapping her hand. "Move out of the way," she says gently but firmly. Shale simply stares at her. "Go on, I'll do some digging. And sit behind me, may as well make the most of the shade."

Shale blinks but does as she's told.

As the small girl settles behind her, close but not quite touching, Lexis knows Raze would be proud of her. Actually, so would Gray. For a bittersweet moment, she feels their presence as keenly as she feels their absence.

Frowning, she stabs the thick stick into the dirt, grimacing when the force rebounds straight back up her arm. The water table could be a mile below them, and the ground will only get harder.

Which just makes her angry.

Lexis lifts her arm higher and hits harder. All the furious helplessness at the situation she's found herself in is channeled into the dirt. She chips away at the layers of rock, telling herself every tiny shard is a victory.

She'll dig her way to Gray if she has to.

GRACE

*T*here's a breeze in the air as Grace leaves Rust. Only time will tell if Mother Nature will vent her anger at the remaining humans on her sorry planet with one of her storms.

Grace has already experienced enough anger to last a lifetime. Although, something tells her it's only just beginning.

"Storm's coming," says Raze, confirming her fears. "We'll need to walk faster if we're going to reach Fairbanks before it hits."

"How are you feeling?" she asks. "Are you sure you can manage?"

"I'm much better." He looks to his other side. "Thanks to Kallini."

The older woman smiles at Raze like he's the sun and the moon. "It was nothing. All I did was patch you up and get you fed and watered."

"And that's all I needed." Raze puts a gentle hand on Kallini's back and Grace feels tears prick at her eyes. These two are developing a special bond. It's a beautiful thing to watch.

Kallini suffered greatly in the Cy attack. Firstly, with the fear of what might happen to her, and then later with the blatant rejection by her own son.

Corbin had made a show of looking after his mother when the Cy first ran into the tunnels of Rust. But it wasn't long after that Grace and Raze had found her huddled in a corner, shaking and alone. Corbin had other priorities that didn't involve caring for what he seemed to consider his *mad mother*. Such as that awful Scoria...

It was Raze's suggestion that she come with them to Fairbanks, seeming to instinctively know they needed to make her feel useful. She'd come to life in the infirmary when caring for Raze. That spark could be ignited again. If they left her at Rust, no doubt that corner she'd hidden in would become her new home. Corbin had made it clear she wasn't welcome in the infirmary anymore after *the mess* she'd left there when the alarms had sounded.

"Tell me again about curtains," says Raze, returning his attention to Grace.

She laughs softly. Raze has been fascinated with the concept of curtains ever since he heard her mention them to Barnacle as a possible solution to the lack of sails for his boats. Fairbanks has loads of fabric hidden amongst its rubble. Some of it torn, but some still intact. If they get lucky, each one of Barnacle's boats could be fitted with sails.

"They're large lengths of fabric," she says. "Like the stuff my clothes are made from. And they used to hang from the windows in the buildings to block out the light. You'd pull them closed at night, then open them up in the daytime."

Raze shakes his head in amazement. Resources in the Outlands are far too scarce to consider using precious fabric for something as unimportant as blocking out light.

"And what color are they?" he asks.

"Lots of different colors," she says. "It depends on what color the person wanted to decorate their house."

"People really cared about that?" He lets out a slow breath as he walks. "Like they actually minded if the things in their home were blue or yellow?"

"I know." She shakes her head. "It's crazy, but it's true. They really did care. But that was before they had real things to care about."

"It must've been so strange to live in those times," he says. "I wonder what they did all day."

Grace shrugs. She might know a whole lot more than Raze about how people in cities used to live, but most of her knowledge has been pieced together from snippets of stories she's heard, or the rare book she'd found in the rubble. She has no idea what it might have felt like to live in those carefree days.

"Why did they have to come?" Kallini interrupts, pointing ahead to the trudging forms of Brik and Mason. Some of the others from the Tournaments, including Mason, had eventually found their way to the Rust, arriving just in time to see the tunnels begin to collapse.

"We need someone to carry the sails," Grace explains. Although, the real reason she'd agreed to them coming was in case they needed to carry something else. Something tall and blond and incredibly handsome. Something with a deep wound in his back that Grace is just as deeply concerned about.

"We could carry the sails," says Kallini. "The three of us are strong."

Grace walks on, pretending she didn't hear. Raze won't be carrying anything to Rust. Because he's not going back. She's going to make sure of it. She just hasn't gotten around to telling him that. Or figuring out where that leaves her.

"I'm looking forward to you showing me your home," says Raze.

Her brows knit together. "You saw it when you delivered the invitation to the Tournaments."

"But you didn't show it to me," he says, quietly. "It's different this time."

"Oh." She smiles, thinking back to the time she first laid eyes on Raze. Never in a million years could she have imagined what he'd end up meaning to her. "Well, let's see what's left of it first."

A bug lands on Grace's nose and she swats it away. "The welcoming committee has found us."

Raze freezes, looking from left to right. "Where?"

"I mean the bugs," she laughs. "You're going to want that netting Kallini found."

Kallini proudly pats the roll of netting she has strapped to her back. "How many bugs will there be? Hundreds?"

"Millions," Grace laughs. "Although, the storm will keep them away for a little bit."

She tips her head to the sky, noticing thick clouds gathering. Brik and Mason have picked up a pace that's impossible to keep up with. Not that it matters. She'd rather not walk with them now that she knows Raze is fit enough for the journey. She can find them in the rubble of Polaris later.

"We need to go faster," Raze says, as if reading her thoughts.

"I like walking," says Kallini, moving a little faster. "It makes me feel free."

"You are free," Grace points out. "We're just lucky to have you with us to help out."

Kallini smiles a healing smile and Grace is certain she's going to be okay.

Raze urges them to walk even faster as the clouds close in, robbing them of the harsh sunlight.

Kallini points ahead with a squeal of excitement. "Is that it, Grace? Is that your home?"

Grace squints at the jagged shapes on the horizon as she turns that word over in her mind. *Home.* Somehow, it both applies perfectly to Fairbanks but at the same time it no longer applies at all. "Yep. That's it."

Kallini claps her hands, and the three of them break into a jog as large raindrops land on their heads.

At first, the rain is soothing. It cools their sunburnt skin and washes the sweat from their bodies. But the closer they get to Fairbanks, the cooler the temperature becomes and the more the wind picks up.

Soon, the raindrops are stinging Grace's skin and she finds herself wincing and squinting as they run and the shapes on the horizon grow.

By the time they reach the ruined city and find a slab of concrete to shelter under, the storm is in full force. Claps of thunder have Kallini jumping in fright as the lightning cracks open the sky in regular intervals.

They huddle together, shivering. Raze sits in the middle, a protective arm around each of them while they wait to dry off.

"It sounds louder out here," says Kallini.

It takes Grace a moment to realize what she means. Storms must be a bit of a non-event from the safety of the Rust's underground village. Although, she doesn't like the idea of all this rainwater running into the tunnels. Hopefully they're better at drainage than they are at ventilation.

"How do we know the lightning isn't going to hit us?" Kallini asks.

"It won't," says Raze confidently, even though that's not something he can promise. But Grace doesn't blame him. They need to keep Kallini calm. "We're safe here."

Grace reaches in her bag of supplies, passing around their flask of water. With this amount of rain, now isn't the time to ration their supplies.

Feeling secure under their sturdy shelter and Raze's flimsy promise, Kallini fusses about checking Raze's wound while Grace takes the empty flask to the edge of the concrete slab and sets it down to collect the steady stream of rainwater.

A noise a few yards away catches her attention and she tilts her head to listen. Is there someone else out here? Surely, Brik or Mason have no need to sneak up on them. They'll be back at Polaris picking through the rubble and ruing the day their castle fell.

Wandering back out into the rain, she picks her way over the slab. Maybe she'll get lucky and stumble across a rats' nest. Or maybe the noise was just a shifting of the rubble under the weight of rain. But all the years spent out here tell her it's neither of these things. Someone's watching here.

"Grace!" Raze calls out. "Grace! Where are you?"

She holds up a hand silently, without turning around. Now isn't the time for her to reveal her position to a potential enemy. Nor does she want to raise Kallini's stress levels again when she's only just settled down.

"Grace!" Raze calls again, clearly not being able to see her. "Grace!"

She lets out a long sigh. "Just taking a private moment!"

This seems to satisfy him.

She continues down the slab and hoists herself over a steel beam, slipping a little on the wet surface.

Turning a corner, she gasps as a man steps out from behind a crumbling brick wall. While he's dressed in the kind of clothes a Fairbanks person would find in the ruins, his features tell her unmistakably that he's not from here. He has the dark hair, square jaw and prominent nose favored by the men of Cy. Well, most men, given Raze's genetics seem to have had a mind of their own.

With rain dripping from his long hair to his broad shoulders, he holds out his palms to show her he means no harm. But, still, Grace's heart beats wildly.

"He called you Grace," the man says. His voice is rough, like it hasn't been used for a time. "Why did he call you Grace?"

"Who are you?" she asks, ignoring his question. "What are you doing here?"

"He called you Grace." There's so much emotion in his voice that she decides it's impossible he means to harm her.

She takes a few steps to her left until she's under the shelter of a thick glass window lying on its side. With her head, she indicates for the stranger to follow her.

"You're Winter." He runs a hand through his tangled hair to shake off the rain as he steps under the glass. "I know you. Why did he call you Grace?"

She narrows her eyes. "I don't know you. And he called me Grace because that's my name."

"You're her sister," he says. "You look like her. You're Winter."

She studies him more closely, and as she does, the years fall away from his weathered face and she sees a young warrior hiding in the rubble waiting for her sister to sneak away from Polaris for one of their secret trysts.

"It's you," she says, certain she's placed him right. "I thought you were dead."

"I thought you were dead." He points in the direction of Polaris.

"What are you doing here?" she asks.

He shrugs. "I...I couldn't leave her. And I couldn't le—"

Grace's eyes widen. "But she's dead. You know that. You carried her home yourself."

"Her spirit's still here," he says. "I see her everywhere I look. I see her in you. Even more up close."

"You've been watching me?" she asks.

"From time to time." He looks away. "Just to make sure you were safe. But not for years now. Not since your friend caught me. I stayed away from Polaris after that."

"Trakk," she says, a deep longing for her friend winding its way around her heart.

He pulls something out of his pocket and Grace braces herself, ready to fight.

But it's a wooden object he's holding. It looks almost identical to the figurine Raze carved of Trakk—the one that fell out of her pocket when she was trying to get Raze to safety. Except, this figurine isn't Trakk.

It's her older sister, and she finds herself staring into a face that she hasn't looked at for far too many years. She'd thought she'd forgotten what Grace looked like, but as she stares at her sister's features, all her memories come rushing back.

"I use her name now," she explains. "To honor her. I'm trying to keep her memory alive. To make her proud..."

"Grace, are you—"

She spins to see Raze approaching. His eyes widen when he sees she's talking to someone, and he immediately folds into his warrior's stance.

"It's okay," she tells him, holding out her hands. "I'm okay."

Raze shifts from Grace and slowly his stance unwinds. "Hatch? Is that you?"

The Cy warrior's jaw falls open. "Raze? You've grown. And... you talk."

Raze joins them under the shelter, standing protectively close to Grace. "*This* is where you went when you disappeared? I thought my father killed you."

"He wanted to," says Hatch. "I was spending more and more time here over the years. He found out and called me a traitor. I got away before he could get to me."

"Why here?" Raze asks, rubbing his temples.

Grace holds up the figurine. "My sister. He loved her."

Raze blinks like this is too much for him to take in, then his head snaps up as he seems to remember something. "You told me the woman you were seeing was having a baby. Was that—"

"You heard me say that?" Hatch looks surprised. "I never thought you heard anything I told you. Not once did you answer me back."

"The baby died," says Grace, not having the patience to

explain that just because someone doesn't talk doesn't mean they don't listen. "My sister died giving birth. Hatch was the one who brought her home to us."

"I have to tell you something." Hatch swallows as he fixes his gaze on Grace. "The baby didn't die. We left him in Fairbanks. We had no other choice."

Grace's knees buckle and she presses herself to Raze for support.

Her family isn't all dead like she believed them to be. Her sister's baby is alive.

RAZE

The first rays of dawn touching Fairbanks bring many things. The low hum of insects. The glare of bleached concrete.

And shadows. So many shadows. Some angled and jagged, some curved and worn, some little more than a speck. Others reach for body lengths, never ending as they blend into the next.

As Raze stands beside a rusting hulk of metal, he realizes he likes shadows. The Cy village, sizzling in the Outlands' vast openness had afforded little opportunity for shades of gray to linger. It's like even shadows knew there was nowhere to hide.

But here, in Fairbanks, he can cloak himself in darkness whenever he wants. Despite his initial opinion of this crumbling city, Raze has never felt so...safe.

Grace slips into his arms, pressing her hand to his chest. "What do you think of my home?"

He tightens his hold around her, losing himself in the same safe darkness of her eyes. "I found my home when I met you."

Which was right here in Fairbanks.

She smiles softly. "Yes, home will always be with you."

She presses her hand more firmly over his heart as she

pushes up to press her lips against his. Raze sighs, losing himself in the sense of rightness while he has it. When every moment of their future is so uncertain, he's going to revel in the glory of the present.

"You two," admonishes Kallini as she appears from behind a slab of concrete.

They pull apart, eyes glinting before they separate. Last night, under the cover of darkness, they'd done far more than kiss. Hands had roamed and explored, mouths had tasted and sighed.

Hatch leaps down from the top of the cement. "Your sister had a passionate heart, too."

Raze nods, acknowledging the loss laced through his old friend's voice, but also the love. When Hatch first started disappearing for longer and longer stretches of time, Raze had resented it. Hatch was the only adult who didn't get creeped out by his silence. Not only that, he gave Raze a way to communicate—carving.

But now, he understands. Hatch had found his own home.

Grace nods. "She really did. And she loved you very much, too, Hatch."

Hatch nods sharply, quickly looking away. He clears his throat. "So, why are we going to Polaris? That rubble is still shifting."

Grace angles her head. "We need material, and Polaris had a lot of curtains."

"Apparently they're what people used to cover their windows," Kallini says, sounding dubious.

Hatch chuckles. "People used to do a lot of strange things." He turns to Grace. "But yes, Polaris would probably be one of the few places to still have fabric seeing as it managed to stay standing for so long."

Raze frowns. It was the Cy coming to announce the Tournaments that sparked the collapse of the old building. He was one of the people responsible for its destruction. He looks to Grace. "I'm sorry. For what we did."

She shakes her head. "It was slowly decaying, just like everything else here. And if it hadn't fallen, I probably never would've left."

And the Outlands wouldn't have the Commander no one expected. The Commander they need.

Hatch pulls the netting wrapped around his head over his face. "Let's get going before it's too hot."

Raze does the same, as does Grace.

Kallini arranges her own. "There's no need to rush, is there? We could talk as we go." She flushes. "I like to learn almost as much as I like to help."

Hatch raises an eyebrow. "Sure," he says, uncertainly. "I can tell you what I know."

"Oh, thank you," Kallini pipes up, clapping her hands.

Raze suppresses a chuckle. Kallini won't be giving Hatch an adjustment period now that the man has company after so long alone. He'll be remembering how much he loved to share knowledge in no time.

Hatch and Kallini fall into step, finding a trodden path among the rubble. Raze takes Grace's hand, ready to follow but she stays where she is.

She grins from within her protective layer of her own netting. "I say we meet them there."

Raze shrugs. "I'm happy to run." The wound in his back is little more than an annoying throb now.

Her smile impossibly grows. "We won't be running," she says, her eyes alive with excitement. "We'll be flying."

Before he can ask what she means, Grace is gone. She leaps, landing on the concrete slab Hatch appeared on.

"Hey!" Raze calls, but there's no response.

His own grin surging across his face, he does the same, surprised to find it higher than he expected. Grace made it look as if it was a much smaller jump. Once he's landed, he sees she's already a few yards away.

She glances over her shoulder, a smile flashing within the depths of her netting. "Try to keep up."

Her laughter carries on the early morning light as she leaps again, landing on a metal beam. She balances across it, never once losing speed.

Which means Raze had better get moving.

He breaks into a run, following the path she's creating. Except when he jumps on the beam, it wobbles. He slows, throwing his arms out for balance. The sound of more laughter has him grinning. It seems Grace has a playful, somewhat competitive side.

He reaches the end and jumps onto the next rubble pile, wincing as his wound reminds him it's still there. Up ahead, Grace is gaining more ground. She vaults, grabbing an exposed pipe above her and swings. She lands gracefully, barely contracting before pushing on again.

Raze watches her as she navigates her city. Lithe and quick, she moves with familiarity and confidence. He closes in on her as he follows her lead, but he suspects she lets him. She and her brother got away from Raze and the other Cy the last time they were here.

But unlike that day, he doesn't want to catch her. Watching her freedom has joy singing through his veins.

Grace reaches a flat length of concrete and executes a cartwheel and Raze laughs. Happiness makes him lighter, has him jumping higher. But it's still not enough to keep up with Grace. Just like she said, she's flying. Her feet barely seem to touch the ground. She spends more time in the air, the wind her foundation, the sky her backdrop.

She reaches a large pile of rubble and begins descending, hopping from one chunk of debris to the next, never landing long enough to disturb anything. Raze realizes that although one pile looks much the same as the last, they've arrived at their destination.

He joins her, navigating the shifting pile with far less poise before coming to stand beside her. "I never stood a chance."

Grace is panting a little, making the netting flutter. "Maybe one day you'll be able to catch me," she teases.

Raze shakes his head, pulling up his netting so he can see her better. "No, I meant falling in love with you."

Grace is beautiful. Strong. Inspiring.

She flushes. "Oh."

He tugs her under the protective shade of an overhang, lifting her own netting enough to expose her lips. Tenderly, he presses his mouth to hers. "And when you leave Fairbanks," he says softly, "I'm coming with you."

She huffs, curling into him and pressing her cheek against his chest. "You can't come back to the Rust."

"We need to talk to the Cragg and the Never, yet."

Grace sighs. "I know. Let's see where we're going next, then figure it out."

"There's nothing to figure out. I'm coming."

She huffs again. "This is why you didn't talk for so long— you're as stubborn as a stone."

The sound of footsteps has them pulling apart. Raze presses a quick kiss to her forehead before pulling his netting down. "Thank you for the compliment," he says lightly.

That elicits another huff as Raze steps past her, watching as Hatch and Kallini approach them. Hatch is pointing as he talks, Kallini nodding with enthusiasm.

"Polaris was the last to go," Hatch says. "I can't believe it stayed upright as long as it did."

Raze turns around and sees what Hatch is describing. An expanse of rubble is splayed several yards away, and it's hard to imagine this used to be the building that Grace and Gray locked themselves in when Raze and the others were last here.

Now, it's little more than a sea of mangled and mutilated materials.

"The fabric is in there?" Raze asks dubiously.

"Yes," says Grace, subdued. "Hopefully not too far down."

They approach the destruction like it's a slumbering beast. A gust of wind whips over the rise and fall of devastation, stirring up eddies of dust.

"Where are Brik and Mason?" murmurs Grace as she looks around.

"Probably asleep," mutters Raze. He doesn't trust either of those men.

"Well, there's no point waiting," she says. "I suggest we take a section each and search. But be careful. Don't go anywhere that looks unstable."

Hatch indicates with his head to Kallini, who's wringing her hands. "Let's start over here." He leads her to the left, where the rubble hasn't mounded as high.

Raze catches his gaze and nods. Kallini is too fragile to be climbing over shifting debris. Keeping her to the edges is a good idea.

He and Grace go right, picking their way over shattered concrete and twisted metal.

"Look!" Grace says. Not far ahead, a corner of material sticks up.

Raze takes one step and notices another small shred exposed between some cement. "Here's another. I'll get this one."

Grace nods and skips over the rubble in that light-footed way of hers. Raze squats, shoving away chunks of concrete, being careful of the shards of glass littered everywhere.

"I've almost got it," Grace calls.

"Me, too."

"But mine will be out first," she responds, a smile in her voice.

Raze finds himself chuckling, but he sets to work at uncovering his piece of material even quicker. He's just freed a piece about an arm's length wide and long, when Grace appears beside him.

"It's out." She's holding up a shred that's about as big as his chest.

"Mine's larger," he points out.

Her beautiful face scrunches in mock consternation. "Then who won?"

He grins, pulling Grace to him.

"It seems we both did," he says a moment before he pulls her into the shadows of the half-standing wall and presses his mouth to hers.

Grace's arms slip around his neck and she molds her body to his. "Raze," she murmurs, and the way she says his name sends shivers over his skin.

He pulls her closer, wishing the shadows were night.

Grace pulls back. "One piece of material, one kiss," she says breathlessly.

"You're on."

They spend the next hour digging with enthusiasm. When one finds a shred of cloth, no matter how small, they run to the other to claim their prize. Raze quickly realizes he's experiencing something he never has before—the feeling of having fun.

It doesn't take long for a small pile of material to accumulate.

But when they finally stop, Grace surveys the dusty, crumpled collection. "I thought there would be more pieces that were large enough."

Raze frowns. Of varying colors, some could cover a window as they were first designed to, but most would fail to make a shirt for a child. They were so caught up in their game, that they hadn't noticed that much of the material wasn't what they needed it to be.

It's going to take a fleet of boats to invade Askala. And each one of them will need a sail.

"I could sew them together," says Kallini as she and Hatch approach.

Grace's face lightens. "Yes! We could make as many as we want, then."

Raze jerks his thumb toward his back. "Well, my wound has certainly held together."

"I like to help." Kallini smiles, her cheeks flushing with pleasure.

Hatch hoists his hands on his hips. "What do you need this much material for?"

"To make sails," says Raze, wondering how this hadn't already come up.

Hatch glances at the pile a little incredulously. "For how many boats?"

Grace straightens. "For a fleet. The Rust are going to build them."

"They can't build that many," Hatch responds, shaking his head. "There's not that much timber in all of the Outlands."

Grace and Raze glance at each other. Barnacle failed to tell them that.

"And why so many boats?"

Grace lifts her chin. "To attack Askala. It's time they shared what they're so greedily keeping for themselves."

Raze nods, pride filling his chest. Hatch will want to be part of this fight.

But Hatch frowns. "Attack Askala? But they are a peaceful people."

"They are as selfish and uncaring as the Cy," snaps Kallini, sounding angry and bitter in a way Raze didn't think was possible. "They leave us here to die while they live like kings."

Raze feels the familiar burn of anger at the injustice of it all.

If things were different, the Tournaments would never have been necessary. Lexis and Gray would still be alive.

Hatch shuffles back a little, as if he needs space. "I don't think that's true."

"What are you talking about?" Raze demands, conscious Grace has gone very still beside him. "They're the ones who could change all this."

But Hatch is shaking his head, slowly but resolutely. "I've seen them."

"You have?" Grace asks.

"They came here, to Fairbanks. They took my son back with them."

Grace's eyes widen, no doubt knowing that's her nephew Hatch is talking about.

Hatch pulls his shoulders back. "I was going to stop them, but then I saw how they treated him. Those two souls carried more love than I've seen in all of the Outlands."

Silence creeps between them. Raze tries to process what he just heard, but it's like trying to fit a chunk of rubble through a keyhole. If anyone else had told him this, he wouldn't have believed them. But Hatch is one of the few people he trusts...

"I've even built a raft, ready to go there," Hatch continues. "To go and see my boy." His sharp gaze locks with Grace's. "In peace."

Raze turns to her, unsure whether this has changed anything. "Commander?"

Grace holds his gaze, her dark eyes simultaneously calm and turbulent.

"We need to go to Askala."

GRAY

*G*ray wakes and for one precious moment he forgets what's happened and where he is. Then it crashes back to him with such force he sits up and gasps. He's had some terrible nightmares in his life. But this is the first time where his reality is far worse than his dreams.

Lexis.

He heard her scream just before he'd been knocked out. Please don't let her be hurt. Or worse.

Blinking, he tries to work out if it's day or night. He crawls forward and peeks out of the tent to find it's daytime—possibly late morning—but the sky is blanketed in storm clouds making it impossible to tell for sure.

"Rain's coming!" cries Chicago, running toward his tent. "Get out here and help!"

The older man's face is alight with excitement. Gray almost returns his smile out of habit, then remembers this is the same man who knocked him unconscious for trying to get to Lexis.

Deciding he has a far greater chance of finding Lexis out there than inside his tent, Gray limps forward. He yelps, wondering if it's possible his foot hurts more today than it had yesterday. He overbalances but stops himself from falling by taking hold of the tent, almost toppling it in the process.

How can one toe impact so much on his ability to move around? A toe that he'd never really given a lot of thought to. Does that serve him right for having it taken away? He sweeps a flash of gratitude through his body to all the other parts of himself he's never thought much about but clearly still desperately needs.

"Hurry!" Chicago shouts. "Follow me. Now!"

Gray takes a few steps, cursing as he almost falls over again. Men are emerging from their tents and heading in the same direction as Chicago. He sees some women in the distance and his heart leaps.

"Lexis! I'm here!"

But raindrops are falling now, and they drag his words down into the deep cracks in the arid soil.

A warm body slides in beside him, urging him forward. For one blissful second, he thinks it's Lexis. But this body is too short. Too thin. Too silent.

It's a child. A girl with a dirty face and tangled hair.

"I thought the Never didn't have children," says Gray, trying not to burden the skinny girl with too much of his weight.

The girl doesn't answer. She tucks herself under his arm on the side of his injured foot and pushes forward, meaning for him to use her as a crutch.

"Do you know where Lexis is?" he asks, stumbling as the rain runs down his cheeks. "She's new here. Have you seen anyone new?"

Again, she says nothing.

He tries to support himself with his next step and falters. As he looks to the ground, he notices the girl's bare feet.

The girl has nine toes.

"You're a volunteer." He grips her around the shoulder, now not just using her for support but offering her his own support.

This poor child. How could the Never mutilate her like that? Surely, they don't force her to work? But why else would they need to stop her from running away? This is barbaric!

The girl grunts as she tries to hurry him along. The confident way she's holding her balance gives him some hope for the future. Maybe when this storm has passed, he can ask her to teach him how to walk properly.

"Where are we going?" he asks.

She points and he sees the dirt caked under her cracked nails. Forcing them to a stop, he takes her hand and studies it. Her palms are covered in scratches and blisters. These aren't the kind of hands any little girl should have. Her hands should be soft and pink from playing with her friends. Not worker's hands.

"What do they make you do?" he asks, unsure now if the rain is still running down his cheeks or if it's tears. "Do they hurt you?"

She pulls her hand away and grunts, urging him forward.

"I don't blame you for not talking," he says, taking another step. "Lexis's brother never spoke, either. Sometimes it's just not worth saying anything."

They pick up a slow rhythm and the sounds of the Never shouting to each other become louder over the steady falling of rain.

"Mind you, I don't think I'll ever stop talking no matter how bad things get," says Gray. "Winter—that's my sister—she says I'll keep talking even after I'm dead. Except, she's the one who's dead now. But that's another sto—"

His eyes widen as he sees what's happening beyond the camp of tents.

The Never have an enormous sheet made from soft plastic and the men are standing around its edges. The sheet is pulled taught, angled so it collects the rain. It funnels down to the women who are scurrying about with buckets collecting the precious liquid.

The girl slips out from his side, either afraid of being seen helping him, or frustrated at how slow he is.

With an uneven gait, she runs to a woman at the edge of the plastic sheet, and with surprising strength takes the full bucket of water. She carries it toward another group of women who are busy lining up flasks and shouting orders at each other. It rarely rains in this hot world they live in, but when it does, it seems the Never make the most of it.

Gray limps closer, still trying to get a glimpse of Lexis. There are people everywhere but not one of them is *his person*.

The young girl glances quickly around with a serious expression, then spits in the bucket. Looking at Gray to make sure he saw what she did, she turns to a woman and hands it to her. She immediately begins pouring it into a flask, oblivious to the additional ingredient courtesy of a child who clearly has so many more layers than anyone out here realizes.

Gray can't help but laugh, aware his heart just grew in size to cradle this quietly rebellious girl neatly inside. She may not speak but she just told him she doesn't like what these people have done to her, either. He'd be willing to bet she has a whole jumble of words inside her just waiting to get out.

He doesn't know if he and Lexis are ever going to be able to escape this hellhole they call the Neverlands, but he's certain if they can, they'll be bringing this child with them. He'd rather die than leave her behind.

"Get over here." Chicago appears by his side and drags him over to the other men, forcing him to stay upright with a tight grip on his arm. He places him beside a Never man with a long beard. "Take over from Shui."

The bearded man steps away with a grunt and Gray grabs hold of the plastic sheet, using it to steady himself.

"Careful," the man beside him growls. "Not like we have another one of these. Don't pull it."

Gray bites his tongue to stop his sharp reply. Maybe if they hadn't cut off his toe, he wouldn't be having so much trouble standing up on his own.

The rain is cold now and Gray shivers as it soaks through his clothes. The men around him angle the sheet to take advantage of as many drops of water as possible. They have this down to a fine art. One that Gray is clearly yet to learn.

"Too high," the man beside him says. "Lower it."

Gray does as he's told, allowing his eyes to stray to the women collecting the water. The young girl is still helping but there's no sign of Lexis.

Where? he mouths to the girl. She knows what his eyes are searching for. And he's pretty sure she also knows the answer.

The girl sets down her empty bucket, pretending to scratch at her leg. As she stands, she points directly to one of the tents. Then, like it never happened, she gets back to work.

Gray turns back to the plastic sheet and notices he's let his hands rise again. Not wanting another admonishment, he lets them drop. The water on the sheet rushes at him, looking for a way to escape, and the sudden shift in weight sends him crashing to the ground, a shower of cold liquid cascading over his head.

"Get away!" The man beside him kicks him hard in the ribs. "You wasted it. Don't ask for a ration later. You've had yours."

Gray flinches, crawling out of reach as the man's foot rises once more.

The man called Shui returns to take his place once again and Gray crawls in the direction of the tent the girl had pointed at.

This could be his only chance. He has to move while these people are distracted. This rain could stop as suddenly as it arrived, taking the opportunity to see Lexis with it.

The rain intensifies, acting as a shield and Gray moves

forward, reaching the tent and rising to his knees to pull back the flap.

And there she is.

Lexis.

His Lexis.

The reason he's still fighting in this world that's told him more than once he doesn't stand a chance.

"Gray!" she gasps.

He stumbles forward, seeing that her ankles and wrists have been tied together.

"Did they hurt you?" he asks, tugging at the twine.

"They tried." She leans forward and catches his lips with her own.

His fingers pause as he kisses her desperately, the rainwater running from his hair down his face and onto her parched skin. He didn't think he was going to see her again, let alone have the chance to do this.

"I know they hurt you," she says, pulling back and casting her eyes down.

"I'm fine," he lies. "I can still run. We have to leave. Like, now."

"You crawled in here." Her voice is full of sadness. "We can't run. They'll catch us. We need to be smart about this. Choose our moment. When you're healed."

"But..." His protest dies on his lips. She's right. Out here, there's nowhere to hide. When they do make a break for it, they need to make sure they can move faster than the Never. Right now, he couldn't outrun a toddler. "Then you need to go alone. Get out of here, Lexis. You can make it without me."

She shakes her head, and he gets back to work on the twine binding her wrists, wondering how he can convince her. There's no point both of them dying here.

"Don't untie it completely," she instructs. "Just loosen it so I can get my hands out when I need to."

Smart. *Always smart.* If they find her unbound, they'll only tie her twice as tight next time.

He does as she asked, and she slips one hand out of the twine.

"Perfect." Her palm goes instantly to his cheek, and she presses it there.

"There's a child," he says urgently. "A girl."

"Her name's Shale," says Lexis. "She was taken from the Cragg."

"They cut off her toe." He swallows. "They make her work."

Lexis nods sadly, bringing her free hand to his other cheek to cup his face. "It's not right."

"You need to get her out," he says, hoping this might be the thing that convinces her. "Leave me here. Take her and run. She can move fast."

"I'm not leaving you," she says firmly. "So, stop asking. We'll leave together. And we'll move faster without a child to slow us down."

He sighs. "Well, that's a shame. Because I'm not leaving without her."

Lexis's brows shoot up at his threat. "We don't know how to look after a child."

"True." He nods. "But I'm certain we can do a better job of it than the Never. I can't leave her, Lexis. And I know you can't, either."

Lexis's eyes dart around his face as she thinks about this.

"Okay. We'll take her home to the Cragg." She kisses him again, satisfied she seems to have found some kind of compromise. "Only because you insist, not because I'm being kind."

He smiles. She's being kind and they both know it. Her heart of ice has been melting since the moment he met her.

"Next rain," he says against her lips. "We play nice, and we wait. Next rain, we run."

She kisses him harder with the kind of passion he's come to

associate with his warrior girl. His world spins, then centers as he pulls her closer.

"I love you, Gray," she murmurs. "And I'm not leaving here without you. Please, don't ask me that again."

There's a noise at the opening of the tent and they break away from each other to turn.

It's the girl. Shale, as Lexis had called her. He wonders how much of their conversation she just heard.

Shale blinks at them, her expression inscrutable.

"Next rain," she says. "Next rain, we run."

LEXIS

There's a shout beyond the tent walls and they all still. Frustration throbs through Lexis that her time with Gray is already over. She only just reunited with him. He can't have to leave already.

But he gets up, the rain slicking down his face running through lines of regret. "I have to go." He turns to Shale. "And yes, next rain, we run."

Shale nods solemnly, her mouth once again tightly closed, as if her soft words were never uttered.

Gray presses a short, fierce kiss to Lexis's lips, then turns, promptly stumbling to the left. Lexis tries to stand, but is hampered by her tied hands and feet. It turns out she doesn't need to. Shale is already tucked underneath Gray's arm. She helps him hobble to the tent opening.

"I'm going to have no pride left by the time I leave this place," he mutters under his breath.

Lexis smiles, her chest filling with warmth. Gray has the least ego of anyone she's ever met—he's too busy looking for rainbows and the good in people.

It's one of the countless reasons she fell in love with him so totally and completely.

With a last glance in her direction, Gray slips out. Shale hovers by the tent side.

"Go help him," Lexis says softly. "He needs to get back quickly."

Shale nods, and scampers after him. Beyond the tent, the sound of the rain eases, and Lexis realizes he left just in time. A few minutes more and his absence would definitely have been noticed.

Alone again in the tent, Lexis adjusts her bindings so they look like they were never tampered with. Her body aches from chipping away all day at ground that resembles concrete. She wasn't given her midday rations either—punishment for not being more grateful.

Lexis would spit that last word out if she had any spare saliva.

Instead, she runs her tongue over her lips, catching the moisture Gray left behind. And it tastes even sweeter because she can taste him.

Although it's dark in the tent, she can sense that evening is coming. Lexis doubts she'll be seeing any food or water today, so she curls up on the sleeping mat. If she and Gray plan on running the next time it rains, she needs to be in as good condition as she can. That means being well rested, and being... grateful.

The thought grates over her nerves. Being subservient to these cruel people is going to be her toughest challenge, especially when she wants to show them exactly who would win in a battle. No matter how many Never come at her.

But she draws in a breath and lets it slowly out. Gray's life depends on her playing nice, as he called it.

And she'd do anything for Gray.

There's a faint shuffle for the door and Lexis sits up,

instantly alert. It's either Nocona bringing food and water, or another Never bringing trouble.

Except it's neither. The flap to the tent closes behind Shale as she stands with her hands behind her back, unmoving. Lexis watches her, curious about this girl who refused to talk, but could talk all along. Was Raze the same? Would he have spoken if he'd found a reason to?

One of Shale's hands comes to the front, and Lexis sees that she's holding a small canteen, no doubt full after all this rain.

But she shakes her head. "It's yours."

She's not taking a child's rations, no matter how thirsty she is.

Shale grins, her other hand coming out to show a second canteen.

Lexis grins back. "Now you're talking."

The girl darts in, sitting cross-legged a bit closer than Lexis would've liked. She passes the second canteen and Lexis takes it, deciding that a little proximity is fine. Shale's a child after all, not a bloodthirsty warrior.

And apparently she's coming with them.

Lexis drinks the water more quickly than she means to, reveling in how good it feels with each mouthful. When she brings the canteen back down she finds Shale watching her.

"Next rain, we run," the little girl says in a small, hoarse voice.

Lexis hesitates. "Yes, that's right."

Shale's gaze falls away as she thinks this over, chewing her lip. She scratches her matted hair, frowning, before looking back up. "Where?"

Lexis's brows shoot up. This girl is cleverer than she gave her credit for.

"Somewhere else that's not here."

Shale shakes her head. "That's stupid."

And blunt, it seems.

Lexis opens her mouth only to find no answer has formed. She snaps it closed again, her own frown powering down her eyebrows. Where will they run to? They can't go back to the Rust. The Cragg will be equally as dangerous. And they've already discovered how vast and deadly the Neverlands are.

They have nowhere to go.

Except Gray would say that leaves them everywhere to go.

"We'll be away from here, so that's a start," she snaps. She lies down, curling up on her side, tucking her tied wrists and ankles in as comfortably as she can. It's time to end this conversation. "Thank you for the water. It's time to get some rest."

She even closes her eyes to make her point.

Lexis waits for the sounds of Shale leaving, only to be met with silence. She frowns internally, making sure to keep her face neutral. If Shale wants to sit here and stare, she won't stop her.

Several minutes pass and finally Lexis hears the little girl move. She unwinds a touch, admitting it was unnerving lying here with her eyes shut with another person in the tent.

Except Shale doesn't move toward the exit of the tent.

Lexis's eyes fly open as she feels something brush her legs. She stills in silent shock as Shale slips in between her arms and tucks herself beside her. Shale curls up, her back to Lexis's front, then goes still herself.

Lexis barely breathes, unsure of what to do. Her first instinct is to shuffle back. To push the bold little girl away.

But then she notes the way Shale hasn't moved. Hasn't twitched. Lexis isn't even sure she's breathing.

She's reminded of Raze, waiting and watching to see how people were going to respond to him. Preparing himself for the rejection.

And Lexis knows she won't be moving or pushing Shale away. She'll just have to pretend she's not here as she tries to get some sleep.

As the minutes draw out, Shale slowly unwinds, her skinny body fitting into Lexis's more snugly. Her breathing begins slow and careful, but quickly evens out as she relaxes. She even lets out a little sigh.

Lexis's eyes widen. Protectiveness floods her, warm like a gust of wind, but powerful and full of force like a storm. She's never held anything so fragile in her life. A silent vow to shield this precious child from harm sears her mind before she's even realized the words have formed.

She instinctively tugs Shale in a little closer, despite her bound wrists. The child completely relaxes, becoming a rag doll that Lexis could manipulate any way she wants.

But Lexis just lies there, breathing in the scent of earthy soil and fresh rainwater. As time passes, she feels herself becoming drowsy. She assumes Shale's already asleep, only to be snapped back to wakefulness by the girl's soft whisper.

"I know where we could go."

"The Cragg will accept you," says Lexis. "But Gray and I cannot stay there."

Shale shakes her head, her hair gently rubbing the inside of Lexis's arm. "I don't want to go back there. They told me they killed my mom. Everything and everyone else is so...hard. I'm talking about going somewhere else."

Lexis waits, wondering where Shale's talking about.

"We should go to Treasure Island."

Shale must've found some old books that have survived the ages. "Places in pages no longer exist," she says, trying to make her voice gentle but not quite succeeding.

Shale shakes her head, this time more vehemently. "No, the Never talk about it, at night. Especially when it hasn't rained for a very long time."

When the world is even more bleak than usual.

"They say they're not from the Outlands," Shale continues. "That there are others out there."

Shale must be talking about Askala. Lexis is about to point out that no one from that selfish place would ever come here. They're too busy hoarding their wealth and keeping it to themselves.

"They call them the Origins," says Shale, her voice becoming hushed. "People who live on a large floating island. Treasure Island. They hide from everyone else, not wanting to be found."

Lexis is left speechless, blinking in the dark.

"But some people didn't want to stay on Treasure Island. I think they got tired of being in just one place. They wanted to see what opportunities were in the Outlands."

"They were fools."

"They're the Never," Shale says, as if that explains everything. She rolls over to face Lexis. "Treasure Island. That's where we should go."

Lexis stares at the young hopeful face that she's somehow holding in her arms. She suspects most people wouldn't want to see that expression fall. That they would feel the need to keep it alive.

But that would be cruel. The Outlands are full enough of disappointments without adding to it.

"We can't go there, Shale," she says firmly. "There's no place called Treasure Island. These stories are what people tell themselves so they don't lose all hope. They want to believe there's something better out there, waiting for them."

The hope on Shale's face dissolves quickly, almost as if it never had any substance. She chews her lip in thought. "Is there?"

Lexis is about to say no, but Gray's sweet face rises in her mind. There was something better out there for Lexis, but it wasn't a place. It was a person.

"People's hearts are where hope is," she says softly, marveling at how much Gray has changed her. She never would've thought such words would come out of her mouth. "It's home."

Shale's face remains serious as she processes the words. "So people let you in? To their hearts?"

Gray certainly did that with Lexis. "Ah, yeah, sure." She shifts a little, now getting uncomfortable with how this conversation is evolving. She wanted to give Shale a dose of reality, not some mushy words that she doesn't really understand yet.

"Like when you did my digging for me?" Shale asks. "And let me use your shade?"

Lexis is left speechless again. How did she find herself in this position?

"Enough talking," she says gruffly. She nudges the girl's shoulder. "Roll over. We need our rest."

There will be more digging tomorrow. And the day after that. And for as many days as it takes for the rain to return.

Shale does as she's told, this time snuggling her body in until it's tucked right into Lexis's. She lets out another sigh.

Lexis finds her lips softening, almost tipping up. But then a thought strikes her. Her very own dose of reality and her face hardens.

She nudges Shale. "Don't tell Gray about Treasure Island."

The little girl twitches in surprise.

"Promise me, Shale. He can't know about it."

She nods, and Lexis hopes she understands this is important.

Shale doesn't know Gray and his perennially optimistic soul. If he learns about the mythical Treasure Island somewhere out in the vast ocean, he'll want to go there.

And like they almost did with their foolish trek out into the Neverlands, they'll end up dead.

GRACE

"*I*t can't be true," Raze whispers in the twilight.

Grace snuggles closer to his warmth. "But what if it is? What if all the stories we've heard about Askala are lies?"

"Then our whole lives are lies." Raze lets out a long breath, shifting on the smooth piece of tin they'd found to sleep on.

They lapse into silence, the quiet surrounding them punctuated by Kallini's soft snores nearby. She'd insisted on sleeping away from them, saying she's not used to having anyone near her at night, but it was obvious she was trying to give them space. And neither Grace nor Raze had complained. Every second they spend together is precious. But every second they spend *alone* together is like a rare gem.

Hatch is also sleeping by himself not too far away, making them like the three points of the Summer Triangle twinkling above them in the sky.

It had been a busy day searching for lengths of curtains that don't exist. Brik and Mason never showed up. If Grace hadn't seen them running ahead to Fairbanks in the storm, she might have wondered if she'd dreamed they'd come along for the journey.

Brik had gotten along well with Barnacle. It's surprising he chose to disappear the moment he had the chance. Maybe he was worried Grace was going to ask him to carry Raze again? At least if he doesn't come back, she won't have to come good on her promise to make him second in charge. And she can't say she'd be sad to never see his tattooed face again.

"So, we're really going to Askala?" Raze brushes his cheek against hers.

"We need to know our enemy," she says, aware of the way the close contact has her stomach fluttering.

"I used to be your enemy," he reminds her. "Do you think you might fall in love with one of them?"

She pulls back in surprise. "Raze! Never. I'll never fall in love with anyone other than you. Not ever."

He seems to want to say something but holds back.

"You don't believe me?" she asks, fighting the insult she can't help but feel.

"I do believe you." He trails a fingertip down her cheek. "But I want you to promise me something."

She holds her breath as she waits for him to explain whatever it is that's troubling him so much.

"If we're ever separated, I want you to find someone strong to protect you." His words come out in a jumble. "You're a beautiful woman, Grace. Plenty of men will want to protect you. If you find one with a kind heart and strong body, you need to do whatever you have to do to secure his protection."

"I can look after myself," she says, horrified at the thought.

"I know you can." His hand slides to the back of her head. "But in the Outlands, it's always worth having someone else to watch your back."

"I have you," she breathes. "You watch my back. You told me you're coming with me wherever I go. As much as I'm not sure that's a good idea."

"I meant if…" He sighs, letting his hand fall. "If I can't come

133

with you. I want you to be safe. Always. Find someone to help keep you safe."

"Oh." He's talking about death. If he comes back with her to the Rust and they kill him, he wants to make sure she's protected. "I'm not promising you that, so you'd better make sure you don't die."

"I'll do my best." He leans in and his lips claim hers in a way that's fast becoming familiar.

She loses herself in him, pushing away all thoughts of having to seek protection from anyone else. If she learnt one thing in the Tournaments, it's that she knows how to look after herself.

Although, as Raze's hands roam her body sending delicious shivers down her spine, she decides she doesn't mind being protected by someone else. Just as long as it's him.

With darkness as walls to shield them, Grace tips back her head as Raze's kisses trail from her jaw to her neck. The warmth of his lips on her skin reminds her of the spoonfuls of honey they'd been given in the Never's infirmary.

It's sweet. It's unexpected. It's new. And she has no idea what's going to happen next.

She groans as Raze's mouth moves to her collar bone and he tugs at the hem of her shirt, pulling it up. He wants more of her. And she wants nothing more than to give all of herself to him.

A scream pierces the night air. Grace and Raze scramble to their feet as the terrified sound is cut short. And now Grace is panting for a whole new reason.

"Kallini," she says as Raze grabs her hand.

They climb over the rubble in Kallini's direction as deep regret thuds through Grace's chest. They should never have let her sleep away from them, no matter how much she'd insisted.

A few more careful steps and they reach the place they'd last seen her asleep on the pile of curtain scraps they'd taken from the ruins.

"Kallini," Grace says again. "What is it? Where are you?"

"She's dead," growls a familiar voice in her ear as a firm arm slips around her neck, holding Grace in a headlock. "And soon you will be, too."

"Brik!" she gasps, trying to loosen his grip.

There's a scuffle beside her as Raze fights off what Grace assumes is Brik's sidekick, Mason. She tries to see what's going on but they're more like shadows than solid forms.

Brik tightens his grip and Grace desperately attempts to drag in some air.

"I'm not going to be second in charge to a little girl like you," he hisses. "You insult me."

As Grace struggles to release herself from Brik's tight grip, Raze's earlier words come back to her. He wants her to make sure she always has someone to help protect her. And as much as she hadn't thought that was necessary, right now she knows it is. She'll never break out of this stranglehold on her own.

There's a loud *ooof* in Raze's direction that has ice running down Grace's spine. Even Brik freezes for a moment.

"Grace," grunts Raze. "Save...her...first."

"No," comes Hatch's agonized voice as the scuffle continues. "I'm saving you."

Trying to use the distraction to her advantage, Grace kicks backward at Brik, aiming for his shins as she claws at his thick arm to release her. But he has her held too tightly and her efforts are useless. She feels like one of the rats Trakk would catch in these very ruins—once they were in his grasp, their demise was inevitable.

As she weakens, the image of Trakk looms clearer in her mind. She's not ready to be reunited with him yet. Or Gray. She still has things to do. She's the Commander of the Outlands!

This thought gives her renewed strength, and she slams her heel into Brik's shin, dragging it down to the top of his foot. He groans in protest, but still, it's not enough for him to release her.

Not knowing if Raze is dead or alive, she continues to fight, not willing to accept her fate. Her chest screams at her for oxygen and just as the very last of her reserves are about to be used up, both Grace and Brik are slammed from the side and sent sprawling on the ground.

Broken glass and gravel scratch at her skin but the unexpected action has Brik momentarily loosening the headlock. Grace takes her chance, flipping her body around and kneeing Brik hard in the groin.

He howls and she leaps to her feet, stumbling toward a familiar shadow.

"Grace!" says Raze, putting his hands on her shoulders.

"I'm okay," she pants, heaving in deep breaths to fill her relieved lungs.

Raze drops his hold on her to surge at Brik. Dammit! Why does it have to be so dark?

Hatch's shadow sweeps past Grace to help Raze, while she continues to breathe in the night air, trying to refuel her body with oxygen as she fights her annoyance with how this is playing out.

She wants to be the one to help Raze! She wants to show him that she can fight, too.

Grace lunges towards the scuffle but is pulled back by an iron grip on her ankle that has her crashing to the ground.

"Not so fast," breathes a voice she recognizes as Mason's.

"Let me go!" she shouts, knowing what a foolish thing it is to say. This oaf isn't going to release her just because she told him to.

Mason drags her away from the direction she'd been so desperate to head, and she lashes at him with her free foot, landing a kick in what she hopes was his face.

He lets go of her ankle and she struggles to her knees.

Somehow, Raze is next to her again and he throws himself on Mason. More grunts and groans pierce the night air and then there's a frightening lull.

"Raze!" she cries. Please, he can't be injured. He only just got over what his father did to him.

There are breathless seconds of silence.

"He's dead," says Raze, hauling her to her feet.

She doesn't feel even one ounce of sadness. Just relief.

"We have to help Hatch." She breaks away and rushes toward the sounds of fighting. As tough as Mason was, Brik is tougher. He hadn't been the leader of Fairbanks for nothing. And he said he'd killed Kallini. If that's true then this piece of scum is even more evil than she'd realized.

Grace stoops and feels around on the ground for something she can use as a weapon, her hand landing on what feels like a sharp piece of concrete. Perfect.

She scrambles toward the shadows of the men on the ground, wincing at each grunt as punches are thrown, hoping that Hatch is getting the better of Brik. Hatch is a former Cy warrior but he's out of practice. She has to help tip the balance.

"I've got this," Raze hisses at her as he edges forward, waiting for an opening. "Stay back."

She doesn't answer him, deciding to take a leaf out of his own book and remain silent.

The men are so focused on each other, they don't notice her crawling toward them, shielded by the darkness.

A body slams to the ground just in front of her, the impact seeming to shake the entire world. That has to be Brik. He's at least twice the size of Hatch's lean frame. Only he could rattle the ruins in that monumental way.

She doesn't hesitate.

Grace raises the piece of concrete above her head, ready to bring it down.

But...she can't. Not if she doesn't know for certain that this is Brik lying here before her.

"Do it!" cries Hatch.

This is all the confirmation she needs. Grace brings her hand down fast, slamming the concrete into Brik's head, feeling the sharp tip pierce his skull and the warm splatter of blood showering her face.

He doesn't have time to scream. She doubts he even knew who or what just took his life. But there's no doubt in her mind that Brik's dead.

No longer the leader of Fairbanks. No longer her promised second in command.

She feels free.

Now she can only hope that Kallini is, too.

RAZE

*I*t's not until the first fingers of light touch the ruins of Fairbanks that they find Kallini.

They'd circled wider and wider throughout the night, Raze knowing it was near impossible to find her in the dark, but not caring. He refused to believe Kallini was dead until he saw it for himself.

As each hour passed, he wished he could've been the one to kill Brik himself. Kallini was collateral damage in this war between the factions. She never wanted the power others are thirsting for. She just wanted to help.

Raze is circling back to where Kallini was attacked, almost ready to give up, when he notices the scrape marks through the dust and gravel. His heart constricts when he sees the dark blood streaking through it.

"Here!" he calls hoarsely to Grace and Hatch.

He hears their light footsteps over the rubble, but Raze has already dropped to his knees. No wonder they couldn't find her in the dark. Kallini crawled into the space beneath a slab of concrete.

Either to nurse her wounds.

Or, to die.

"Kallini?" he asks softly. "It's me, Raze."

There's no answer from within the small, dark hollow.

Raze reaches in cautiously. "Can you hear me?"

He jolts when his hand connects with something soft. And warm!

"I found her!" he cries.

Grace joins him first, Hatch not far behind. "Is she…" Grace doesn't finish the sentence.

Raze swallows. "I think she's alive."

If Kallini's hand is still warm, then her heart is pumping blood through her body.

He flattens onto his stomach and shuffles forward. "Kallini. It's me, Raze," he repeats. "I'm going to get you out."

"Raze?" comes a faint voice.

"Yes," he whooshes in relief. "It's me. Are you hurt?"

"The men didn't get you," she says.

"They're both dead," he bites out, trying to keep his voice gentle. "They won't come near you again."

There's a soft sigh. "Or you."

"Hold onto my hand," he instructs. "I'm going to get you out."

He feels around until he finds her again, wrapping his fingers around her wrist. Then, he wriggles back, trying to be as gentle as possible as he pulls Kallini out of the hollow.

The small woman is light, which means he draws her out quickly. But when he sees what was blanketed by the dark, his stomach bottoms out.

Behind him, Grace gasps and Hatch takes a small step back.

"Kallini…" Raze whispers.

Her face is pale, damp tendrils of hair plastered to her forehead, and her lips are devoid of color. Because her entire torso is covered in blood. She releases Raze's hand and wraps her arms protectively around her, as if she can hide the destruction and crimson stains.

She closes her eyes, panting a little. Although she didn't cry out, being pulled from the hollow obviously took a toll. "I heard them…so I cried out." Her lashes flutter open. "And you're all still alive."

Grace moves closer to Kallini, her face tight. "You saved us."

"I like…to help."

Raze gently pushes the sweaty strands back from her face. "You've done nothing but that. We owe you our lives."

For some reason, a ghost of a smile plays over the woman's lips. "Good."

Hatch pushes to his feet. "I'll get some of the material to use as bandages. And I'll bring back some food and water."

Raze nods, not taking his eyes off Kallini. "Thank you."

"Tell him not to…worry," she says. "You have more important…things to…do."

Grace shakes her head. "Nothing is more important than making sure you get better."

"Just like you made me better," adds Raze. He flexes his shoulders. "See, it hardly hurts anymore."

Kallini tries to smile, only to grimace. She curls into herself further, her breathing shallow and sharp.

"What can I do, Kallini?" Raze asks desperately. This woman can't have touched their lives in such a sweet way only for her to bleed out onto the dirt.

"Leave me."

"No!" he says fiercely. "I'm not doing that."

"We're going to help you like you helped us," Grace adds, placing a comforting hand on Raze's lower back.

But Kallini is already shaking her head, even though the simple action seems to cause her pain. "There is a much more important way you can help me."

There's the sound of gravel crunching and Raze turns to see Hatch is back, holding shredded strips of material. He passes them to Raze, along with a small canteen of water.

Raze takes them and unscrews the canteen. "Here, drink first."

Kallini tries to shake her head again, but he's now cupping it, and she doesn't have the strength to fight his hold. "You... have it."

He smiles a little. "I'll have some after you do, not before."

She studies him for long seconds, but he maintains the determined expression on his face. "I'm a Cy. We don't negotiate," he jokes.

Kallini relaxes a little, her lips softening. Raze lifts the canteen to her mouth and she drinks a small amount before her head falls back again, exhausted.

Grace takes the canteen from Raze. "Well done," she praises.

"I didn't...have a choice," Kallini whispers, almost smiling.

Raze glances at Grace. "I learned from the best."

It was her insistence that he eat and drink back in the Tournaments that probably ensured he's alive today to tend to Kallini.

"It's amazing what a person will do when they care for someone," says Grace, her voice full of warmth.

That seems to comfort Kallini, because some of the pain washes away from her features as she closes her eyes.

"Now, what do we do?" he asks, eyes scanning her bloodied clothes. The wounds could be anywhere.

Her eyes flutter open. "Leave."

"No," Raze states flatly. "We're not doing that."

"You don't understand..." Kallini closes her eyes again, as if she's gathering her strength.

Raze and Grace glance at each other, a silent understanding passing between them. She picks up one of the strips of material while he takes Kallini's hand.

"Tell me. Help me understand."

Grace moves to the other side and kneels down. "Tell us, Kallini."

"Sit me up," she commands quietly.

With another glance at each other, Raze and Grace do as they're asked. With a hand under each arm, they carefully move Kallini into a seated position, propping her against a boulder beside them. She remains quiet the whole time, but Raze has spent his life learning that even the greatest pain can be contained within and kept silent.

Once they're done, Kallini's panting again, and a fresh stain of blood is spreading over her top. Grace moves in, a wad of cloth in her hand, ready to press it against the wound.

Not giving Kallini time to notice what Grace is doing, Raze leans into her line of vision. "Tell us," he implores.

Kallini's gaze flickers to Grace, her mouth opening.

"Because we're not leaving you," Raze adds.

That has her attention snapping to him. "You have to." Her face twists. "It's all I want."

Raze frowns. "I don't understand." Kallini insisted she come with them, but now she wants them to leave her?

Grace bites her lip as she presses the folded material to Kallini's wound. The woman draws in a sharp breath but doesn't break her focus on Raze.

"You have to kill Evrest. It's the only thing that will bring me peace."

His frown deepens. "When this is done, my father won't be alive," he promises.

"He will be if you're here. You must go to Askala. Learn what you need. Then come back here." Kallini draws in a sharp breath as Grace reaches around her to bandage the wad in place, but she doesn't stop her. It seems the words she wants to say are more important. "And kill him," she bites out, venom Raze didn't think was possible from this gentle woman dripping from her words.

Realization hits Raze. "You know him."

Kallini's eyes flicker. "Several Rust were out looking for

food. A long time ago. Evrest and his Cy warriors attacked." She looks away. "Evrest was unwell. I helped him, just like I helped you. But still, he took…everything."

They would've butchered any Rust who stood between them and food or water. Raze tightens his hold on Kallini's hand, Grace continuing her ministrations in the periphery. "That's why you hate him so much."

Maybe Corbin's father was killed. Her brother, her father. Possibly her whole family.

"I thought the Cy were all like that." She seems to shrink into herself. "It scared me."

Raze can barely remember the day he arrived at the Rust, it's so clouded by a haze of pain. And yet Kallini tended to him. Helped him heal faster than he ever has, just like she apparently did for his father.

"Why?" he asks, feeling like he's missing something. "Why did you help me?"

Kallini hisses as Grace wraps a length of material around her chest, but she doesn't even glance at her. Her eyes blaze with a strange mix of rational and irrational. "Because you are a son of Evrest."

"Yes, I am." No matter how much Raze wishes otherwise.

Kallini pulls him closer. "And so is Corbin."

Shock has Raze motionless. Unblinking. No longer breathing. Somewhere he hears Grace gasp. Maybe Hatch, too. But all he can see are Kallini's fervent eyes.

She's telling him the truth.

"Evrest hurt you…" Raze chokes through frozen lungs and a throat that's turned to stone.

"He raped me," Kallini spits. "He took my innocence. My peace. My sanity." She unwinds a little. "But he gave me Corbin."

Raze's half-brother.

"I was so scared my son would grow up defined by the Cy

144

venom in his blood. But you showed me he can be good. Gentle."

Raze draws back a little. He's not so sure he has a lot in common with Corbin.

With a quick glance in his direction, Grace returns to bandaging Kallini's wound. She even has to bring Kallini forward a little to slip the material behind her back, but Kallini acts as if it's not happening. She's totally focused on Raze. She wants him to understand.

"I've never hid Corbin's heritage from him," she continues. "He went to the Tournaments to win. To avenge me and kill his father."

Except Corbin was eliminated, along with all the Rust, in the first round. Which leaves Kallini with a thirst for vengeance and no way to quench it.

Grace shuffles back, her work complete. A gray bandage now circles Kallini's chest. It's not much, but it will stem the bleeding and protect it from the insects.

"The sooner you leave for Askala, the sooner you'll return." Her eyes blaze again. "And finish this."

Raze is about to object, when Hatch speaks up.

"It's fine weather. And we don't know how long that will last."

Raze grits his teeth, keeping his gaze on Kallini. "But you're injured."

"This is all I want," she whispers, the conversation having drained her. She closes her eyes and rests her head back. "It doesn't matter whether I live. Only that Evrest dies."

"It matters that you live," growls Raze.

Her shoulders drop as she lets out a rattly breath. "It matters that I have peace. The only way I'll have that is if you leave."

Grace's hand clenches the material of his shirt. "It's your call, Raze," she says, the weight of this decision heavy in her voice.

"And, she's dying," Hatch points out in a low voice.

Denial is Raze's first reaction, and it's swift and strong. They need to stay here! To do everything they can to help Kallini! And if she dies, to be there when she takes her last breath. No matter how long it takes.

Except that's not what she wants. If he stays, another Cy has taken her choice away from her.

Slowly, as if his body has multiplied in weight, Raze pushes to his feet. "Okay," he chokes. "I'll go. And when we return, I will end Evrest."

It's what needs to happen to unite every last faction.

Kallini's eyes remain closed, but peace fills her face with a softness he hasn't seen before. "Thank you," she mouths.

Grace stands, too, wrapping a tight arm around his waist. Hatch moves closer, placing the canteen and bag of food beside Kallini.

"For when you wake," he says, although it's obvious he doesn't believe that's going to happen.

Raze turns away, his heart heavy in his chest. He breaks into a run, Grace beside him and Hatch quickly catching up.

It's time to go to Askala and meet the enemy they've sworn to fight.

He's only run a few yards when Raze glances back. Kallini is where they left her, propped up against the boulder. Her eyes are closed, her head angled as if she's in a peaceful sleep. He silently says goodbye to the woman who, for a brief moment in time, was the mother he never had.

"You made the right choice," says Grace, her dark eyes full of compassion.

Raze nods, picking up his pace as they run toward the sun.

Kallini's rape. Her probable death.

Two more reasons to kill his father.

GRAY

*E*very moment spent in the Neverlands is a moment too long for Gray. Seeing Lexis for those brief few moments had been an agonizing mix of bliss and torture all at once.

He's not sure he can wait until the next rain to get out of this place. So, to keep distracted, he focuses intently on the things he needs to do.

Learn to walk without falling over.

Make sure his foot doesn't get infected.

Stay alive.

That should be simple enough. Except, Chicago keeps hauling him outside to do impossible chores like sweep out the tents or pluck insects from the air to add to the faction's watery stew they serve up each night.

But Gray would rather do either of those things for hours on end than the chore he's been instructed to do now.

He sets down the heavy bucket of human waste, aware if he spills even one stinking drop, Chicago will beat him. His instructions were clear. Carry the bucket past the edge of the Never camp to the lone straggly tree and tip it out over a sieve, which he is to then place in the sun so they can use the dried feces as fuel.

Nothing is wasted in the Never. Not even waste itself.

Drawing in a deep breath, he steadies his balance and grasps the handle of the bucket once more. He's getting better at walking, adopting the same uneven gate he witnessed when Shale had run ahead of him in the downpour. The problem is that whereas putting her foot down hadn't seemed to cause Shale pain, it sends hot bolts of lightning burning up Gray's leg. He just needs a little more time to heal, that's all. He'll get there.

He lifts the bucket and struggles forward, trying not to breathe in the putrid air. Winter once told him that when you smell something it's because tiny molecules are floating into your nose. *Poopicules,* she'd called them. He'd thought it was funny at the time, but now it only makes him gag.

Steeling himself against the stench, he works on making sure he doesn't vomit. He's been on limited rations of water despite the recent rain, which means he can't afford to lose a single drop of hydration.

Step by step, he gets closer to the tree, looking forward to standing underneath its patchy shade before he has to return to camp. Chicago isn't watching him. Nobody is. They know he's not going to run. Not without Lexis. And not without any water. Then there are his injuries, although without them, he'd still be on borrowed time.

He's trapped in a prison without walls, and even he's finding it hard to see the positives.

Somehow, he reaches the tree and carefully sets down the bucket, reaching for the sieve tied to his back. Better to get this over with. The sooner he tips over the bucket, the sooner at least some of the stench will seep into the cracks of the hungry soil.

"Ready for your breakfast?" he asks the tree, not entirely sure the contents of this bucket are going to fertilize it in the way the Never hope. "There's a good chance this is going to kill you, so I apologize for that."

He smiles, imagining Winter rolling her eyes at him talking to a tree.

"She wouldn't understand," he continues. "I know you can hear me. And I really am sorry about this…"

He squats down, relieved to take some of the pressure off his foot and lines up the sieve.

There's a small gust of welcome breeze and the tree's curled leaves whisper to him.

"Right, here it comes." He looks at the rough bark of the trunk. "Like I said, I'm really sorry."

Carefully, he tips the bucket, heaving as the smell rises up with force.

"Oh, fish shackles!" he cries out, hoping Rusty's favored words might take some of the discomfort out of the situation. But they don't. The task is just as revolting as it was a moment ago. Maybe even more now that he's getting a better look at what he'd been carrying.

Anything that's liquid rushes through the sieve, some trickling along the soil as more of it's absorbed.

He continues until the bucket is empty and the sieve sits on the damp ground, full to the brim. Somehow, he manages to keep the contents of his stomach in place.

Turning his head, he breathes in some fresh air while he waits for it to drain so the sieve will be easier to drag into the sun.

The tree groans and he looks up at the branches. "Don't you complain," he huffs. "You didn't have to carry it all the way here."

"You're funny," the tree says.

He jolts back and squints.

Shale appears amongst the leaves, grinning at him.

He presses a hand to his rapidly beating heart. "I thought I

149

really had lost my mind for a moment there. What are you doing up there?"

Shale doesn't answer, although that shouldn't surprise him. She may have entrusted him with a few of her precious words but that doesn't mean she's about to start cracking jokes, no matter how amusing she seems to find him.

"Where's Lexis?" he asks, seizing the opportunity for an update. "Is she okay?"

Shale points with a grubby finger and Gray turns his head and blinks into the sun.

It takes him a few moments to find her, but when he does, his heart both leaps and sinks.

Lexis is partially submerged in a shallow hole and banging at the hard earth with a stick. The sun is beating down on her and she's covered in dirt.

"What's she doing?" he asks.

Shale mimes drinking water, which confuses him at first as she's definitely not doing that. Then he realizes.

"She's digging a well?" he asks.

Shale nods, solemnly.

"But the water table could be miles down." He frowns, wanting to go to her to help but knowing that would only make things worse for both of them. "She could dig for months and not find it."

Shale lets out a long sigh as her response.

"Is that why your hands are so damaged?" he asks. "Is that what they make you do?"

Shale holds out her blistered hands. "Next rain. Next rain, we run."

Gray looks down at the sieve at his feet, needing to busy himself to stop the anger that's threading its way through his veins. How can a faction be so cruel? This poor girl is traumatized.

He picks the sieve up by one edge and drags it out of the shade and into the full sun.

Stepping back into the shade of the tree, his eyes return to Lexis.

"She told you to take a break, didn't she?" he asks.

Shale nods. "She said she'd cover for me. I'm not sure what that means."

Gray laughs gently. "It means she'll make up a story to explain why you're missing if anyone asks where you are."

A hint of a smile winds its way across Shale's lips. "I like Lexis."

"I like her, too," he says. "So much."

Shale climbs down a little lower and is about to put her foot on a thin dead branch still protruding from the tree.

"Careful," Gray warns. "That one won't hold you. It's about to snap off. Always check if something can take your weight before you step on it. My friend, Trakk, taught me that."

Shale nods, taking this in.

He watches Lexis for a moment, his legs itching to run to her. As if she senses his eyes upon her, she looks up. Her hand that's holding the stone in the air pauses and she raises her other to let him know she's seen him.

But he already knew. When their eyes connect, for a beat of time the world stops spinning on its axis. Or is that just his heart?

She waves and a small movement behind her hand catches his attention.

His spine stiffens and he rubs at his eyes, wondering if he imagined it.

Keeping his eyes on the expanse of dirt behind Lexis, he sees it again. It's like several small sections of oddly shaped dirt are shifting behind her, inching closer.

Then he makes out what they are, and he lets out a loud gasp.

"Shale," he says, trying to calm the rapid beating of his heart. "Climb down from there. I need you to get Lexis. Steal as many flasks of water as you can carry and bring her to me here. You're faster than me. Do it now!"

Shale slides down from the tree, clearly confused.

"It's raining," he says, not wanting to frighten her. "Tell Lexis it's raining."

Shale holds out a hand in the hot dry air, even more confused than she looked before.

"Just do it," he says, trying to keep the anxiety out of his voice and hoping Lexis understands his message. "Shale, it's time to run."

Shale takes off toward Lexis with her uneven gait and Gray snaps the dead branch off the tree. It has a forked end that can be used as a crutch. It's not perfect but it's going to have to do.

Because those patches of dirt coming toward Lexis, aren't patches of dirt at all.

They're Cy warriors.

He squints at their disguise. They have fabric caked in dirt draped over themselves as they crawl toward the Never camp. They're so well camouflaged that if Lexis hadn't waved at him and drawn his attention slightly to her left, he wouldn't have noticed them. They're clearly trying to take the Never by surprise. And he's willing to bet they're not here to ask for a cup of watery stew.

They're here to kill. Which means it's not only raining, they're about to get drenched.

What's about to take place here is going to be a better distraction than the biggest downpour. His foot's not ready for the journey, but his mind is. With the help of his crutch, he can make it.

He has to.

If they stay here, the Cy will kill them. They'll certainly kill Lexis. There's no way Evrest would allow her to live if he were to find out she's alive and turned her back on him. His pride wouldn't allow it.

Shale reaches Lexis and a hurried conversation takes place.

Gray knows Lexis trusts him completely. If he says it's time to run, those are the only instructions she needs.

She hauls herself out of the hole she'd been digging and dashes silently toward one of the tents. All the while, the Cy get closer.

Shale slides underneath the wall of the tent and moments later passes two large flasks out to Lexis, before scurrying out. Carrying one flask each, they run to Gray.

His eyes dart between the Cy and these two females he'd give his life to protect, knowing their timing has to be perfect. If they run before the Cy pounce, they'll never get away.

"Hey!" booms a deep voice and Gray's heart sinks. "What are you doing?"

Chicago.

The man who saved him yet wouldn't hesitate to kill them all. This is the worst case scenario.

Lexis and Shale don't pause. They push forward until they reach Gray. Lexis shoves her flask at Shale and immediately spins to face Chicago, leaping into her warrior's stance.

"The Cy are approaching," Gray whispers, so that Chicago doesn't hear.

Lexis doesn't acknowledge his words but the way her shoulders brace tells him she heard.

Gray tucks Shale behind him and leans heavily on his crutch, ready to back Lexis up if needed. Chicago is strong but he's a brute, his life experience not providing him with any finesse to the violence he's inflicted on Gray.

Lexis has totally got this!

Shale pushes on Gray's back and grunts.

"It's okay," he tells her, noting that the Cy are closing in on the tents. They have a few minutes now. Maybe less. "Watch this. Lexis is amazing."

"Get back to work," Chicago growls at Lexis. "Or I'll—"

"Who'll dig your well if you kill me?" snaps Lexis.

"The girl will." He glances at Shale. "She was doing just fine before you came along."

"She'd barely made a dent in the soil," says Lexis, holding her pose. "Unlike you're about to."

"Me?" Chicago's brows shoot up.

"Yeah." Lexis makes the tiniest of movements. "Wanna see?"

She pounces so fast it's hard to keep track, grabbing Chicago around the middle and slamming him to the ground.

"He made a dent!" Shale squeals pointing at the ground. "Look!"

This is without doubt the happiest Gray has seen this girl. It's like a drug. He just wants to see her face light up even more. Which it will when they get her out of here.

Chicago scrambles to his knees and raises two fingers to his lips, ready to call for backup.

"I wouldn't do that if I were you," Lexis warns.

Chicago hesitates, an overly confident look on his smug face. "And why not?"

Gray looks out at the Cy, seeing them reach the back of the line of tents. They slowly stand and drop their disguises, revealing that they're armed with spears, maces and murderous expressions on their faces. There are a dozen of them at least.

"It's raining, Lexis," says Gray, moving Shale behind the trunk of the tree and handing her his crutch and Lexis's water flask. "It's time."

Chicago draws in a sudden breath but before he can turn it into a whistle, there's an almighty battle cry from the Cy as they stampede into the village. "What the—"

Gray acts quickly, taking several uneven steps and picking

up the sieve filled with steaming feces. He returns and tips it directly over Chicago's head.

The man who'd held them captive roars in fury only to discover that opening his mouth so widely was an enormously bad idea as brown liquid streams down his face into every available crevice.

There's a squeal of delight from Shale, and Gray drops the empty sieve and takes Lexis's hand as they rush over to her.

Shale passes Gray his crutch and, together, the three of them run.

As fast as they can manage.

As far as they can manage.

They did it. No longer volunteers to one of the cruelest factions Gray's ever met. A faction that he's more than happy to leave to fend for themselves.

And it's all thanks to their biggest enemy—the Cy.

They're free. And boy the rain feels good.

LEXIS

It's hard for Lexis to leave the Never, knowing her people are closing in on them. Although she doubts her father is among them, there's still a simmering anger that demands to be released as the fireball it's destined to be.

And it's not because she feels the Never should be protected from the bloodbath that's descending on them.

The Cy need to be stopped.

It's the only way there's a chance the factions could be united.

But one glance at Gray and Shale, and Lexis knows she won't be turning around. It would be a death sentence for these two.

Which is why Lexis slips under Gray's free arm and takes Shale's hand, and runs as fast as she can. It's not nearly as swift as she'd like with Gray's hobbling steps and Shale's small legs, but it's momentum away. Momentum Lexis isn't willing to lose.

None of them look back as they half-run, half-stumble over the baked soil. Lexis has no sympathy for the Never, and she suspects the other two don't either. Especially Shale. Her childhood has forever been scarred by her time with them, both physically and emotionally.

Gray's panting far harder than he should be and Lexis knows he's in pain. She wishes they could slow down, give his injured foot a rest, but they can't. This is the first time she's run from a fight in her life, and she's going to make sure she does it right.

They have to ensure the Cy never find them.

The cries of the Never are faint when they reach them, the pain that caused them far removed. Gray winces while Shale looks as unaffected as Lexis feels. Her only wish is that the Never kill a few Cy before they're exterminated. Both factions haven't learned that cruelty isn't the ultimate power humans wield.

As they flee, Lexis wonders if the Cy have attacked other factions. It's probably a good thing Raze didn't live to see this bloodshed. He would've struggled to find hope in such a hopeless landscape. She wouldn't without Gray.

He stumbles, jerking down on Lexis's shoulder, and she hoists him back up. "You've got this."

"Do we have any idea where we're going?" he bites out through clenched teeth.

Lexis snaps her mouth shut just as Shale tugs on her hand. She glances down to see the little girl looking up at her, her gaze intense. Lexis imperceptibly shakes her head. She's not going to mention the nonexistent Treasure Island.

There will be no more chasing dreams.

"We'll think of somewhere," she says, trying to keep the grim edge out of her voice.

Gray grunts, his gaze focused on the ground, and she's not sure what that means. Shale tugs her hand again, but Lexis ignores it. They need to come up with a concrete plan. A realistic one.

Gray stumbles again and she slows her pace, deciding they're far enough away from the Never camp. They can no longer hear the cries, and it looks like the Cy didn't see them and haven't followed. They've escaped. They're free.

Lexis scans the horizon, noting that the sun is steadily climbing down toward the horizon behind them.

And with nowhere to go.

They trek in silence for long hours. Occasionally Shale tugs on Lexis's hand but she ignores it, focusing on keeping Gray upright. Even less frequently, they stop to ration out a few sips of water. Although Lexis holds the flask to her mouth as long as Gray and Shale do, she only allows enough to trickle in to moisten her tongue. They're playing the game of survival again, and it has the upper hand. The little water they have is the only advantage they possess. The one thing standing between them and losing. In other words, the only thing standing between them and death.

Suddenly, Gray's legs give out. Lexis tries to stop his fall but he twists and slips out of her hands, hitting the hard ground with a grunt.

"Gray," she cries out, kneeling beside him. His eyes are closed and she's worried he's lost consciousness. "Gray!"

His lashes flicker. "I'm thinking this is a good place to stop for a rest," he croaks.

Lexis glances around, but the landscape looks the same as every other mile they've traversed—barren, bleached. Patiently waiting for them to fall down and not get up again, just like last time.

"No," she cajoles. "Just a little bit further."

Gray opens his eyes. "What for, Lexis? We're using what little energy we have to go nowhere."

Lexis draws back, surprised at his words. He sounds almost…lost.

"We can't just stay here," she points out. With no food, no shelter, and dwindling water.

"Then where?" he asks again.

Shale squats next to Lexis, looking at her in silence, waiting for the answer, too. Lexis glares at her, warning her to stay silent.

"We could go to Fairbanks," she suggests.

"No, we can't, remember? Your father is going to be scouring that place." Gray looks away. "That is, if they haven't killed everyone already."

He's realized the Cy are on a deadly rampage, too.

Gray lets his head drop back onto the ground. "We can't go back to the Rust, and the Cragg are just as dangerous. I wouldn't even send Shale back to them." He sighs. "There's nowhere."

"Hey," Lexis says, shuffling a little closer. Gray doesn't sound lost, he sounds broken. Almost hopeless. "What happened to believing this will work out?"

"You mean being foolish?" he snaps, then seems to flinch at his own words. "I'm so sorry, Lexis. We should never have come out here."

"What?" she whispers. "You don't mean that."

Gray's eyes open again, and this time they're full of pain. Of desolation. "I'm injured. We have no food. Our water will be gone within a day or two. Then what?"

She thinks of their near brush with death after they left the Rust. They were in the middle of the Neverlands just like they are now. Except there's no spear to burn. And no Never to find them.

Lexis shakes her head, feeling something she hasn't in a long time. Fear. "But Shale..."

Gray was so determined to save this little girl. To show her how different the world can be.

"I have no doubt you didn't give her any empty promises." Gray swallows. "And that was the right thing to do."

Lexis can hardly breathe, not liking that Gray's talking the truth. A strange, stinging sensation peppers her eyes. She's seeing something she never thought would be possible. Gray's lost hope. His optimism has dimmed. Possibly been extinguished by harsh reality.

She falls back on her haunches, suddenly just as lost he looks. She realizes Gray's hope, his faith that they're moving toward a future worth living for, was the foundation for her own determination. After losing everything, especially Raze, Gray became her future. Her everything.

She'd follow him anywhere.

Except Gray doesn't seem to want to get back up. His eyes are closed, his breathing regular but shallow. Maybe it's the pain and exhaustion speaking.

But if it's not...

Lexis closes her eyes, surprised at the depth of pain that slices through her. She was part of what took Gray's hope. Even as she depended on it, she undermined it, telling herself she was being realistic. Sensible. That they needed to be to survive.

But hope is the foundation of survival. It's what the heart fights for. It's what powers the body to keep going.

As she sits there in stunned silence, a distant sound reaches her. A muted roar. But as Lexis focuses, she hears there's a rhythm to it. An ebb and flow.

Waves.

She turns startled eyes to Shale, finding her staring with her usual intensity. The girl has been steadily leading them toward the ocean.

Each and every tug on Lexis's hand was a pull toward hope.

Lexis swallows, knowing this new destination is likely to have the same outcome as their current aimless wandering.

"I know where we can go," Lexis whispers. She clears her throat, speaking louder. "Gray, I know where we can go."

He opens his eyes, something flickering in their dark depths. "The moon?"

No, but somewhere just as impossible.

Shale shuffles closer to Lexis. She knows the words are

coming. She knows they'll continue their journey to the rust-colored waves lapping at the edge of their hearing.

All because Lexis can't bear to see the light dimming in Gray's eyes. Because Gray *is* her hope.

And she will always follow that beacon, no matter where it takes her.

Gray sits up a little, his brows furrowing. "Lexis?"

She licks her dry lips. "We should find Treasure Island."

GRACE

*W*alking away from Kallini was one of the hardest things Grace has ever done.

But she was dying and they couldn't possibly deny her the last request she ever made. After what she'd suffered during her life, she deserved at least that respect.

She glances at Raze as they follow Hatch in the direction of the beach. It's difficult to believe Raze is Corbin's brother. *Half-brother*, she reminds herself, feeling a little better about that. Corbin's not someone she expects to ever warm to. Unlike Raze. He squeezes her hand as if he can read her thoughts. Not talking for so many years has meant he can read people better than most. Or maybe it's just her.

"It's just down here!" Hatch calls out, pointing ahead.

Grace notices the dirt below her feet is morphing into sand. They begin to descend a gentle hill and the ocean comes into view. The terrain is hilly but far flatter than that of where the Rust live.

"Where are we in relation to the Rust?" she asks Hatch as the gap between them closes.

He points. "They're a few miles that way. I didn't want them to see me building my raft. Not after what happened the first time."

"What happened?" asks Raze, before she gets the chance.

"It got stolen." Hatch shakes his head. "It was almost finished, too. So much work wasted."

"You think the Rust took it?" Grace lets go of Raze's hand so she can concentrate on not losing her footing as the thickness of the sand increases.

"Maybe." Hatch shrugs. "Could just as easily have been the Never. They're normally the ones who steal stuff."

"What would the Never want with a raft?" Raze asks. "Bit hard to carry around the desert."

"They don't always wander," says Hatch. "Sometimes they find a place to stay for a while. My raft would have kept their fires burning for some time."

"How do you know the second one you made is still there?" Raze asks.

Hatch shrugs. "I don't."

Raze shoots Grace a worried look.

"Now there's the serious boy I used to know," laughs Hatch, his eyes shining. "Don't worry. I buried it deep in the sand. I hid it so well I'm not even sure I'll be able to find it myself."

Raze's frown deepens and Hatch slaps him on the back.

"Just a little joke," he says. "I know exactly where it is."

"This is serious, Hatch." Grace narrows her eyes. "We need to get to Askala to see for ourselves the things you've told us about."

Hatch nods. "Wait until you see my son. Your nephew's a handsome kid."

Grace studies the proud look on his face. "Does he look like you? Or Grace?"

"A little of each." He walks ahead as he talks. "But luckily for him, mostly your sister. He has her dark eyes and hair. He has my nose, though. Maybe my chin, too."

Grace tries to picture this small boy. Her sister had been beautiful, and there's no denying Hatch is a good-looking guy. The kid must be cute. Hopefully, soon she can find out for herself.

Hatch counts his steps out loud as they hit the beach and Grace and Raze fall silent, not wanting him to lose track. When he reaches thirty, he stoops and starts digging.

"Feel free to help," he says, looking up.

Grace bends to her knees and scoops up some soft sand, Raze doing the same beside her. They hit dampness and keep digging.

"It's down here somewhere," Hatch says, beads of sweat forming on his forehead.

Grace doesn't question him but does wonder what they're going to do if it's not. They're expending a lot of energy right now. If he's got the wrong spot, they're not going to be able to dig up the whole beach.

Raze hits timber first, grunting as his fingertips scrape along the hard surface.

"Told you," says Hatch.

With renewed energy, they claw at the sand until the shape of a raft appears. It's smaller than Grace had imagined, although it was only built to carry one.

"Will we all fit on it?" she asks.

"A couple of skinny runts like you won't make much difference," Hatch replies as he lifts one edge out. Sand is caked to the timber, making it almost look like the whole thing is made from it, and it might crumble at any moment.

"Mangrove pine sap," says Hatch trying to brush some of it off. "Sticky stuff. But necessary so this thing doesn't break up in the water the moment we push it out."

Grace's eyes widen, not having considered this as a possibility before now. "Are you sure it's safe?"

Hatch looks at Raze and they seem to share some silent words.

"Nothing out here is safe," says Raze gently. "On land or at sea. Are you sure you still want to go?"

She pushes down her concerns. He's right. There are dangers everywhere they go. Just different kinds of dangers.

With the raft out of the sand, Hatch climbs into the hole and continues digging.

"What are you doing?" Raze scratches his chin.

"Supplies," says Hatch. "They're only basic and meant for one, but they'll be better than nothing."

Grace could just about leap into the hole and kiss this strange man who seems to have the solution to every obstacle standing in their way. It's like meeting him was meant to be.

He pulls a hessian sack out of the sand and passes it up to Raze.

"We should eat and drink everything now," says Hatch. "We can get more in Askala. I've been told they have gardens that grow as much food as you could ever want."

Grace shakes her head to think eating could be as easy as picking something off a tree. Surely, these people are as selfish as she's always believed. How could they have so much and not share it with the rest of the world? But Hatch had been so certain—

"Grace!" Raze holds out a flask, leaning forward to get her attention.

"Sorry." She shakes her head back to reality and takes a long sip of stale-tasting water.

Hatch hands her something that looks like a brown stick. "Eat this."

"What is it?" She turns it over in her palm.

"Dried, smoked rat." Hatch grins. "It's pretty much what I've survived on these past few years."

Grace takes a bite. She's eaten rat plenty of times, but never like this. It's chewy but her stomach doesn't complain about the sustenance.

"Thanks, Hatch," says Raze. "We appreciate it."

When all the supplies have gone, they push the raft into the water. The acid burns at Grace's ankles and she's relieved when Hatch gives them the signal to climb on.

"You okay?" asks Raze when she's safely on board. Trust him to notice her discomfort. She'd thought she hid it well.

"All good," she tells him.

Hatch pushes them over the breaking waves like the Cy warrior he is, then climbs on and unstraps an oar. They're pressed up against each other, but Hatch was right. It's big enough to hold them all. He drives the oar into the water, and they surge out to sea.

Grace holds on, understanding exactly why her sister had fallen so hard for Hatch. He's kind, strong, and resourceful. It's heartbreaking that their romance had been cut so short. If Askala had shared some of their riches maybe things would have been different. Maybe her sister would have been strong enough to survive bringing her child into the world. Hatch would have made for a wonderful big brother to grow up with.

The small raft begins the long journey, and soon they've traveled far enough that it would seem foolish to turn around. This is actually happening. They're going to Askala. It feels like the first real thing she's done as Commander. Her first step to uniting the factions and ensuring that *everyone* has the opportunity to sleep with a full belly at night.

Raze takes a shift with the oar, then reluctantly passes it to Grace who quickly develops a new respect for both males for making the task of rowing looks so easy. It feels like trying to breathe underwater.

Hatch takes the oar after several patient minutes of watching her struggle.

"It can get choppy out here," he explains. "Lots of currents in this section to watch out for."

At first, Grace thinks he's just using this as an excuse, but she soon sees he was deadly serious. The water is swirling in various patterns, creating white streaks on top of its rusty red surface. She can't help but think it looks a little like boiling blood but pushes away this thought as it does nothing to settle her nerves.

"Can we go around?" Raze asks, surveying the expanse of unsettled water.

Hatch shakes his head. "Quicker to go through. We'll be okay."

"He knows what he's doing," Grace reminds Raze. Her sister trusted him completely and therefore so does she. Everything is going to be just fine.

Raze squeezes her ankle as he nods. She gives him a small smile to show she's okay. His gaze goes back to the ocean, and he narrows his eyes in the distance.

"What's that?" he asks, pointing at a section of water that's swirling in a circular pattern, creating what looks like a hole in the ocean in the very center.

"A maelstrom." Hatch swallows. "We're well enough away, though."

Grace turns this word over in her mind, not having heard it before.

"What is that?" she asks Raze, although he seems just as perplexed.

"A whirlpool," Hatch answers for him. "The currents create them sometimes. They usually disappear as fast as they form. They're a little unpredictable."

Hatch steers them away from the worst of the swirling water as a grave sense of unease slides down Grace's spine. Unpredictability wasn't what she was hoping for out here. She had quite enough of that in Evrest's cruel Tournaments.

"Check that out!" Hatch says over his shoulder, motioning with his chin. "A trash island. Super rare! They form in the currents. I've never seen one before."

Grace turns her head and her jaw drops. Floating across the surface of the ocean in the distance is a large patch of brown sludge coated in colorful pieces of plastic trash. She can see narrow blue tubes that must've had some use in ancient times, white bags, clear bottles, and pieces of netting. And a million other things she can't even begin to recognize. She longs to inspect them one by one and imagine how it must have felt to live in a world where you could make things you needed from scratch instead of having to figure out how to reuse something that's already here.

"That's only a tiny island," says Hatch. "Rumor has it that there's one out there so big that people actually live on it."

"Who are you hearing rumors from?" Raze asks.

"You'd be surprised who passes through Fairbanks," says Hatch.

"I never saw anyone." Grace's brows pull together. "Although my friend, Trakk, claims to have seen others passing through."

Hatch nods as he turns the raft so they can get a better look at the trash island. "The Never pass through sometimes. They like to keep out of sight."

"Can we get a little closer?" Grace asks, fascinated by all the colorful treasures.

"Maybe just a little." Hatch moves them forward. "But not too close. This water is really unpredictable."

Grace smiles to have had her request granted, but this is quickly wiped from her face as she feels the gentle strength of a current beneath the raft. "Is it safe?"

"We should stay back," says Raze. "Let's not risk it."

"Hatch knows what he's doing," Grace reminds him. "I trust him."

"It's not about trust," says Raze as the current turns from gentle to slightly more forceful. "It's about risk."

"Yep." Hatch digs the oar into the water to haul them back. "I agree. Abort mission."

But the ocean seems to have other ideas and it pulls them forward, negating any strength Hatch puts behind the oar.

Raze leans over the edge of the raft, paddling with his hands. Grace follows his lead, doing the same despite the way it stings her skin. They need to get away from wherever this current is trying to take them.

The raft eventually pulls away, heading into calmer waters, only to be swept up by another current. This one is stronger, and it hurtles them directly into a small whirlpool that spins them around.

"It's going to suck us down!" Grace cries out, holding onto the edge of the raft as she fights the dizziness building in her head.

"The raft is too big for that," says Hatch, swapping his oar from side to side like he can't figure out what the next best move is.

Despite the reassurance of his words, Hatch is clearly worried. Sweat is dripping from his deeply furrowed brow. While the swirling force of the water isn't enough to swallow the raft, it's clearly stronger than Hatch.

They spin faster and Grace tries to hold onto her balance, reaching out for Raze.

He puts a steadying arm around her shoulders, her anchor in this tumbling world.

"I can do this!" shouts Hatch holding the oar in the water to try to stop the spinning. "It's okay!"

Grace can't help but think he's saying this more for himself than for them. She closes her eyes, waiting for this nightmare to be over. If only she hadn't asked for a closer look at the trash island. A simple request that could turn out to be a huge error.

There's a sudden jerk of the raft and Grace's eyes fly open to see Hatch has plunged his oar deep in the water. He gives it one giant pull and the raft is thrown out of the center of the whirlpool, spinning across the surface of the ocean toward safe waters.

Except Hatch has propelled them out at his own expense as he and the oar don't come with them. Hatch's legs kick up into the air as the oar is sucked into the maelstrom, taking him head-first with it. His back twists at an awkward angle and there's the sound of his skull cracking against the timber of the oar.

"Hatch!" Grace screams as Raze steadies the raft by digging his pink hands into the water.

Hatch completely disappears into the swirling red soup.

"Where is he?" she asks, scanning the water. "We have to look for him."

Raze points a shaking hand as the ocean spits out both Hatch and the oar.

Hatch is floating face down, his body turning in circles as he's slowly sucked into the whirlpool once more.

Tears slide down Grace's face as she watches him disappear. The situation is just so helpless. "Do you think he's…"

Raze puts a firm arm around her. "If he's not, he soon will be. I'm pretty sure his back broke when it twisted like that."

A few painful minutes pass before Hatch floats to the surface again. There's no sign of movement from him.

"We have to do something," Grace pleads, as the deadly cycle prepares to start again.

Raze shakes his head. "He's gone, Grace. If we try to help him, we will be, too."

She buries her face in his chest, seeking comfort that even he can't offer. He holds her tightly, knowing words are of no use to either of them right now.

Raze doesn't take his eyes off the horror scene and Grace

knows why. He's keeping her safe. Making sure they don't float back into treacherous waters.

"It's over," he eventually says.

She peels her head from his chest as he releases his hold on her to dip his hands back in the burning water, pulling the raft towards both Hatch and the oar.

Grace leans silently over the other side of the raft and helps. Together, they reach the oar, which Raze then uses to turn Hatch's body over so he's facing the sky, instead of the mysterious horrors of the ocean that just claimed his life.

"Thank you," Raze whispers to him, his head bowed in respect.

Grief grips Grace around the chest, as she wonders if Raze is thanking him for everything he did for him as a boy, or because of the way he just saved their lives. If they'd kept spinning on the whirlpool like that it was only a matter of time before she would have fallen off.

And all because Grace had asked to see the trash a little closer. This is all her fault.

She presses two fingertips to her lips then holds them out to Hatch. Instead of using the two simple words Raze had chosen, she chooses two of her own.

"I'm sorry."

Just as the words leave her lips, Hatch's eyes spring open and he looks directly at her.

He's alive.

RAZE

*a*s the sun sinks behind them, Raze almost doesn't recognize the strip of color on the horizon for what it is. He stares at it for long seconds, wondering if his exhausted arms need to start paddling the other way. It might be another trash island. It could be another danger they never imagined they'd face, just like the whirlpool. But as it steadily grows he realizes what the excess of green is.

Askala.

He nudges Grace where she's tending to Hatch. They had little to stem the bleeding from the wound on his head, but they used what they could. Strips from the hems of their shirts, shreds from the bottom of their pants. Eventually the blood had stopped, but it was clear Hatch was clinging to life. His breathing was raspy and irregular, his skin pale and dry.

Grace murmured encouragement as Raze continued to paddle. She reminded Hatch over and over that he'll soon be seeing his son. Although his eyes remained closed, at each mention of the boy his lips had fluttered up.

It's likely the only thing he was staying alive for.

Grace looks up at Raze's silent motion and he indicates with his chin at the mass they're approaching. Askala has gained enough form that it's undeniable they're looking at the island they've sworn to attack. To make their own.

"Oh," Grace breathes.

Raze admires that she got that one sound out. His own breath has disintegrated. His lungs have frozen. His throat is gripped with emotion.

As Askala rises from the sea, he tries to understand what he's seeing. For long seconds it feels like too much. Trees, and so many of them. He can't even count how many there are. Each one crowned with a riot of leaves, far more than he's ever seen before. And there's movement within them. Around them. Birds that have his mouth watering and his heart aching. He's so hungry he wants to devour every edible morsel. And yet he yearns to honor all the shades of life he never knew existed.

Grace grips his hand. "It's beautiful."

"It's...everything," he whispers.

Hatch moans, snapping them out of the spell Askala had cast over them. Raze spears the oar back into the rust-colored water with renewed vigor. The exhaustion that had dragged at his muscles is gone, burned away by a fresh burst of determination.

"We're almost there," Grace assures Hatch. "And it's just as we thought it would be."

Hatch's gaze flutters open, the same flash of excitement they're both feeling alive in his eyes. "My son..."

"Yes, you'll be seeing him soon."

Raze watches the mass of Askala grow, along with its verdant abundance and bold affluence. He wonders if Grace's words are true. Is this island going to be everything they expect it to be? A land of wealthy, greedy, selfish people?

Or have they been wrong all along...

Another draw of the oar through the water, and they're another foot closer. Another handful of seconds closer to having the answer.

Raze scans the pale beach that becomes apparent in the purple twilight. It's empty, but that doesn't mean it's free of threat or danger. An army could hide behind all those broad trunks and they'd never know.

Grace slips her knife from her belt, eyes scouring the approaching land just as intensely as he is. "Can you see anyone?"

Raze shakes his head, ready to drop the oar and pick up his own weapon. Something moves in the branches of a tree, and he does exactly that, ready to fight. But then there's more shaking of leaves and a bird far larger than he thought was possible flaps out, followed by a second. The first darts high, then low, then straight back into the foliage. The second bird is only a split second behind it.

Grace huffs out a laugh. "They're playing."

As they come closer, sounds fill the air. Insects buzzing, something that's making a strange croaking sound, the trill and song of birds. Raze's pulse increases, almost as if it's trying to keep up with the energy they're approaching.

He blinks, trying to assimilate this once more. All the noise and movement is fascinating and alarming at the same time. The Outlands are far more still. Silent. How will he hear someone approach? How will he know what's an attack and what's an animal with the time and energy to play?

The bottom of the ocean slowly appears as the water becomes shallow. Raze slips off the raft and the warm, acidic water wraps around him. He slowly drags the raft toward the beach, every nerve on high alert. Grace crouches low, staying close to Hatch, looking just as wired as Raze is feeling.

But as his shoulders appear above the water, then his torso, then it laps at his hips, no one appears. Angling to where the tree line is closest to the water, he scans the darkening beach.

Nothing.

There's movement and sound, but no people. What an alien world Askala is.

When the raft grates over sand, Grace hops off, too. Together, they drag it up, the barely conscious Hatch still on it. It's only a few feet before they're engulfed in more vegetation—grasses, shrubs, saplings, trees—than Raze ever dreamed could exist. Every shade of green fills his lungs, making his head swim. They release the raft, resting it on the layer of leaves that are beneath their feet.

"Raze," Grace breathes as she stares up.

He follows her line of sight, seeing a large, green fruit dangling just above. Grace reaches out and picks it, her eyes wide. She plucks it, teardrop-shaped and almost as large as her palm. With an excited glance in his direction, she bites into it.

Thick, leathery skin breaks under her teeth, revealing creamy flesh beneath that she quickly returns to her mouth. "Oh, Raze," Grace moans.

He wastes no time in finding his own bounty. He plucks another, even larger than Grace's, and uses his teeth to tear away the protective skin. And then, eyes closed, he takes his own bite.

The pale green flesh is hard and yet moist and creamy. Raze isn't sure whether he wants to freeze in shock or melt in delight. He eats it as quickly as he can, finding a large, smooth seed in the middle.

The food has barely settled in his stomach before he's picked another one and devoured it too. A look in Grace's direction reveals she's already done the same. She grins at him, her chin smeared with pale green. He smiles back.

They've found heaven.

Two more pieces of fruit have disappeared into Raze's eager stomach before he notices the tiny pools of water captured in some of the leaves. His eyes widen in wonder. The moisture has probably been sitting there all day, shaded and protected. It wasn't burned away before it even had a chance to settle. He dips his finger in it, almost as if to check it's real, before bringing it to his mouth.

It's the sweetest thing he's ever tasted.

Grace watches him do it, then quickly mirrors his action. The same bliss rolls over her face as the droplets of moisture touch her tongue.

The sight instantly becomes the most beautiful thing Raze has ever seen.

And this moment becomes the foundation of his vow. There's nothing he won't do to make sure Grace lives in this world. Like this.

Happy and healthy.

And for every other Outlander to have the same opportunity.

Grace picks another fruit, her beauty almost luminescent in this lush, dense haven. "One for Hatch."

She turns and gasps in the same moment Raze registers what she's seen.

Hatch is gone.

The raft is still behind them, obscured by foliage, but it's empty.

"He wants to find his son," says Grace, the same apprehension that's snaking through Raze apparent in her voice.

They move in unison, looking for Hatch's footprints. They find them easily in the leaf litter, then the sand. He's moved further down the beach. The prints are uneven and deep, showing he's staggering. It's a surprise he can walk at all after what happened.

It means it shouldn't take long to catch up to him. To protect him.

They hurry after the trail, and Raze is quickly surprised by how much distance Hatch has covered in the short amount of time they were eating the fruit and drinking the dew. The man is obviously desperate to see his son.

They round a curve in the beach and Raze throws his arm around Grace, hauling her behind a trunk far wider than any in the Outlands. Although Hatch is just ahead, weaving brokenly, two people just appeared from the tree line, a man and woman. If they see more than just an injured Outlander, they'll surely raise the alarm.

This way, Raze and Grace have the element of surprise.

There's a female gasp. "A Remnant!"

Raze peeks around the trunk, seeing the man step protectively in front of the woman. She looks a little older than him, her hair gray in a way many Outlanders never get to see.

"I...just want to..." Hatch lurches as he tries to keep himself upright, making the two people recoil. "Please, I've come for him."

The woman gasps again. "Stay back!"

Hatch staggers forward, his broken body unable to stay still. "I don't have time for this," he moans.

"Are you threatening us?" the woman gasps.

The man inflates his chest. Although Hatch is taller than him, he has the mass only a healthy, well-fed human can achieve. And if the Askalans know how to fight...

Grace grips his arm as if she sensed Raze's need to go to Hatch. She shakes her head imperceptibly. "If we go out there, they'll see us as even more of a threat," she whispers. "Surely they'll realize Hatch just wants to see his son."

Hatch lifts his hand as if he heard Grace, beseeching these people without words. The man leaps forward. "Stay away from my mother!"

He shoves Hatch back, making him stumble. Hatch tries to stay upright, but his legs give out. With a pained groan, he collapses onto the sand.

The man steps forward and cautiously nudges him with his

boot. "He's out cold. Should we help him?" he asks dubiously. "I'm sure Nova has something in the infirmary that could...save him." He says the second words almost distastefully.

"So he can take what we've worked so hard to build?" the woman almost spits. "I don't think so."

"But—"

"You've seen what they're like, Deniel. The Remnants are little more than leeches. They're causing trouble as it is."

The man, Deniel, grunts in agreement. "It's just that..."

"Have I taught you nothing?" the woman hisses. "All this talk of the Newlands shows us exactly what they want. More land. More power. What we have here isn't enough."

Deniel frowns. "Some new piece of land that's emerged several miles to the east won't be a threat, mother."

"It will be our biggest threat yet," she warns, her tone heavy with foreboding.

Deniel steps back, fear and distaste apparent on his features even in the half light. "Do we...kill him?"

This time, both Raze and Grace coil, ready to protect their friend. These two Askalans will be dead before they get a chance to hurt Hatch.

But the woman steps back, shaking her head. "I won't dirty my hands," she sneers. "Maybe a polar grizzly will take care of him for us, they need to eat just like we do."

With the callous words, the woman turns away, her son following her.

There's a child's cry, maybe a young boy, somewhere beyond the trees. "I'll save you, my lady!"

"So brave, Sir Luca," says a woman's delighted voice. "What would I do without you?"

"Nova, look, it's Zali and Deniel. Maybe they need saving, too?"

"We're fine, Luca," calls the older woman, Zali, hurrying

forward. "Nothing but a boring beach back there. And we all have an evening meal waiting for us."

"Yes, let's eat. I'm starving!" adds Deniel jovially.

Zali and Deniel disappear among the trees, off to see Nova and her son, Luca. And earth their meal.

Raze blinks as he watches them leave, trying to understand what they just saw. The Askalans are no different to the Outlanders. They're just as heartless.

They wait for breathless moments before racing out from behind the tree. Hatch hasn't moved from where he's collapsed, and they fall to their knees beside him.

"Hatch," Grace whispers. "Can you hear me?"

Raze rolls him over, gasping when two sightless eyes stare up at the indigo sky.

Hatch can't hear them. He's dead.

"No," Grace moans. "He didn't get to see his son."

Because the two people who found him weren't willing to help. How tragic that the people Hatch championed, the ones he believed didn't deserve a war, were the ones to stand back and watch him die.

Raze pushes to his feet. "We need to leave."

Grace nods, her shoulders low as if they're suddenly too heavy. "We should never have come here before we were ready to attack."

Hatch would still be alive.

Although, there would've been lingering doubt about what the Commander must do.

That's no longer the case.

Raze bends over and heaves Hatch's body over his shoulder. "They can't know we were here."

Grim faced, he trudges to the water and enters it. He doesn't stop until the water is at his waist. Then, he lowers Hatch into the acidic warmth, his chest tight as he pushes the body out into the ocean.

If Mother Nature is merciful, his flesh and bones will dissolve before a leatherskin finds him. But then again, she'll probably show as much mercy as the two people of Askala did.

Raze returns to Grace and they silently make their way back to the raft. They'll travel in darkness, but that's fine. They'll use the stars to navigate.

They've just reached it when Grace stops, frowning. "What about the boy?"

"I say we leave him here," Raze mutters.

If he's going to live with selfish people, he may as well live with wealthy ones. It's when they come back that they'll avenge his father.

Grace hesitates then nods. "You're right." Her face hardens. "We've seen enough."

They quickly fill their pockets with the fleshy green fruit. They'll need their energy, and not just for the return trip.

As Raze and Grace drag the raft back to the water, they glance at each other. The steely resolve he sees on her face matches the hard determination that wraps around his heart.

The people of Askala are everything they thought they'd be.

Selfish.

Greedy.

Willing to let Outlanders die so they can hoard their wealth.

Which means there's a war to wage.

GRAY

The sound of the ocean revives Gray just enough for him to stumble to its sandy shores. Lexis had said there's a place called Treasure Island. That there's another faction called the Origins who live there, hidden from the rest of the world.

And they were the most beautiful words he'd ever heard because Lexis's voice had been coated in her uniquely cautious brand of hope.

And cautious hope is so much better than no hope at all. He'll take it.

"You did it, Shale," he says, aware his voice is only a whisper. "You got us here."

The little girl shakes her head, stubbornly. "You got *me* here. I wouldn't have left the Never by myself."

The serendipity washes over him. They'd saved Shale from certain death, and in return it looks like she's saved them. Without her gently steering their path to the ocean, he'd be face down dead in the dirt right now.

"And we wouldn't have left without you." Lexis lifts a steadying hand from Gray's shoulder to touch Shale's cheek.

Gray plants his makeshift crutch in the sand and sinks down to stretch out. His foot is in agony and it's a relief to take the weight off it.

"Are they dead now?" asks Shale, her expression inscrutable.

Nobody needs to ask Shale who she's talking about. The difficult part is deciding how to answer.

"I don't know," says Lexis eventually. "But I know the people who attacked them, and they wouldn't have left anyone alive if they could help it."

Shale studies Lexis's face for a few beats. "Good."

Gray's heart shatters to hear a child speak like this. It's not right for anyone so young to have been so mistreated that they would think in such a callous way. He's about to find the energy to tell her that people being murdered is definitely not good when Lexis replies.

"It *is* good," she says. "I'm glad they're dead, too."

With these words, Gray lies down and protects his eyes from the sun with his arm. These reminders of how different he and Lexis are can sting. He wants them to be the same kind of person, headed on the same path, but how can they when their values are so far apart? Maybe the answer is that both of them need to shift a little. Perhaps, they already have? Because there's no doubt that Lexis is softer than when he first met her. Just as his own heart has hardened. The old Gray would have warned the Never of the Cy attack. All he'd done was run away, even if it had been to protect Lexis and Shale.

"How are we going to find Treasure Island?" Shale asks.

Lexis sits down beside Gray, looking out at the ocean. "I don't know."

Shale opens their remaining flask of water and takes a sip before passing it to Lexis. It's clear by the way they're handling it that it's almost empty.

"You finish it. I'm not thirsty." Lexis holds it out to Gray.

182

He shakes his head. There's no way she wouldn't be thirsty after that walk. "One sip each."

She nods, tipping the flask to her lips, then passing it to Gray.

He drains the last few precious drops of liquid, closing his eyes at the relief it gives him.

Shale giggles and he raises his brows as his eyes pop open. "What?"

"Lexis tricked you," she says. "She only pretended to drink."

Gray scowls at Lexis. "Is she right?"

"I told you I wasn't thirsty." Lexis pushes back up to her feet and takes a few steps to the ocean.

"It's not funny," he tells Shale, wishing he could take back the last minute and make sure Lexis had her share.

"Give me your stick and I'll find you more water." Shale puts out her hand, jiggling impatiently on her feet.

"It's not a stick," he says, holding it out to her and pulling a silly face. "It's a crutch."

"You broke it off a tree." She snatches it from him. "It's a stick."

"Then it's called a branch," he calls after her. "Do not belittle my branch. It has feelings, too."

Shale's turned her back and is firmly clutching the forked end of Gray's crutch with a section in each hand and the other end pointing outward. She heads away from the ocean back up the dunes.

"Don't go too far!" he calls out to her.

"What's she doing?" Lexis asks, returning with a puzzled look.

Gray shrugs and laughs. "She thinks she's going to find water. Let her go. It's a good distraction."

But Lexis doesn't join in the laughter. "She's a diviner? This makes sense, all of a sudden."

"What do you mean?" Gray rubs at his sore foot, wondering

if putting it in the ocean would make the wound better or worse. "What's a diviner?"

"You collect rainwater in the ruins in Fairbanks, but it's different in the Outlands." Lexis's eyes remain glued to Shale. "When it rains, it's great, but we can't count solely on that out there. There's water under the ground, but it's hard to find. Diviners know where to look. It's in their blood. The Cragg are known for it. That will be why the Never kidnapped Shale and had her digging wells. She knows where to find water!"

Gray turns around, studying Shale with more interest. She's walking slowly with the branch pointed out, pausing every now and then, moving steadily away from the ocean.

"Do you think—"

"Shh." Lexis holds up her hand and cuts him off. "I've never seen a diviner at work. It's fascinating."

Gray wonders if for the first time since he's known Lexis that she's being more optimistic about the outcome of this than he is. Perhaps they're not so different after all. Surely, Shale isn't going to be able to find water with a stick? *Branch*, he corrects himself.

Shale walks further away, turning in wide circles as the branch wriggles, and eventually Lexis wanders over to watch more closely. Gray notices her keeping a respectful distance so as not to interfere with Shale's work.

After what feels like hours, Gray hears a squeak of excitement and Shale's branch swings down to point at the ground.

"Here!" Shale calls out. "We need to dig here."

Lexis and Shale drop to the sand and start scooping. Gray gets to his knees and crawls to them, unable to bear the thought of putting weight on his foot again without his crutch. They could be expending a whole lot of energy for nothing out here. He has to do his share.

Shaking his head, he tries to inject some of his usual positivity into his thoughts. Shale had seemed so certain about her abilities. Maybe it *is* possible to divine water. It would certainly save their lives if it is. They're going to need time to figure out how to get themselves out into the ocean so they can search for this mysterious Treasure Island. Which means they're going to need a water source.

By the time he reaches them, the hole is already deep enough for Shale to be up to her waist. It seems digging in soft sand is a whole lot easier than the hard soil of the Neverlands. She continues at an impressive pace, leaving him feeling a little useless, hovering at the edges.

"We should hit water soon," says Shale, with a hint of uncertainty in her voice as she takes a breath.

"I believe in you," says Lexis with nothing but full confidence. "I saw the stick move, too. We didn't imagine it."

Shale nods, clearly pleased to have impressed Lexis.

"By the way, it's a branch." Gray reaches over to retrieve it. He'll need it back if they decide to start walking again.

Lexis rolls her eyes as she bends back into the hole to scoop more sand, and Gray smiles as he leans forward to watch.

There's a scraping noise and Shale and Lexis both sit up with straight spines.

"What was that?" asks Lexis. "Have we hit rock?"

Shale shrugs and Gray pushes down his disappointment. He'd almost begun to let himself believe they were actually going to find a water source.

The two females bend back down and dig some more, both of them gasping with what sounds like excitement.

"What is it?" Gray peers down, but it's impossible to see.

"There's something buried down here," says Lexis, not pausing to look up. "I think it's a..."

"A what?" Gray's voice is practically a shriek as he begs her to finish the sentence she started. "What is it?"

"I think it's a raft," says Lexis. "Start digging where you are, Gray. We need to widen this hole to get it out."

Pleased to be able to help, Gray starts scooping sand, as Lexis and Shale continue to widen their existing hole.

"It doesn't make sense," says Shale. "A raft isn't water. I'm sure there was water here."

"It's better than water." Lexis is huffing with exertion now. "This raft can take us to Treasure Island."

Gray makes quick work of the section he's digging and soon the sand dampens as he gets deeper down. But it's not timber that he hits. It's a hessian bag.

"I found something!" He pulls up the bag and heaves it out of the hole to investigate later. "It's heavy."

He continues working on digging out the sand, moving methodically toward Lexis and Shale to connect their tunnels.

"I think I can pull it out by this end," grunts Lexis.

Shale scurries beside her and they pull on the edge of the exposed timber. Lexis was right. Slowly, a raft emerges. Gray moves over to help and somehow, the three of them manage to work it out of its sandy tomb and set it on the flat sand above.

It's not a large raft, but big enough for the three of them. Shale only really counts as a half-sized person anyway. It will do just fine.

They climb out of the hole and sit panting on the sand as they smile at each other, hardly daring to believe their good fortune.

Gray reaches for the hessian bag and opens it up. He pulls out some brown sticks wrapped in cloth and sniffs at them.

"It's dried meat!" He passes them to Lexis who immediately holds them to her nose.

"I think it's rat," she says.

"What else is in there?" asks Shale, jiggling impatiently.

Gray pulls a large flask from the bag, shaking it to hear the miraculous sound of sloshing inside.

"You did it, Shale," he says. "You really did it."

Shale smiles so widely it looks like her face might break in half. "I knew there was water down there."

"I didn't doubt you for a moment." Lexis ruffles Shale's hair, proudly.

"I admit that I did," laughs Gray as he puts a hand to his heart. "But I do solemnly swear that I will *never* doubt you again."

"Even if I call your branch a stick?" She pokes out her tongue at him.

Gray waves his crutch at her. "What is this word *branch* that you speak of? I told you, this is a stick!"

"You did not!" Shale jumps on Gray and throws her arms around his neck squealing with laughter.

He's a little taken aback by the affection but only misses a beat before he wraps one arm around her and pulls Lexis to his side with his other. The three of them hold each other close in a way that Gray is certain Shale hasn't experienced since she was plucked from her home who knows how many years ago.

"You did good, Shale," says Lexis.

Shale shifts her arms from Gray's neck to Lexis's.

He sits back and watches the woman he loves holding this little girl, knowing that her tough exterior just crumbled that little bit more.

He'd grown up thinking Winter was the only person he had in this world. When he lost her, he consoled himself with the thought he had Lexis. But now he has Shale, too. It makes him wonder just how many more people he'll let into his heart if he lives long enough.

But just as quickly as Shale had thrown herself at him, she disentangles herself and runs back to the raft.

"When are we leaving, Lexis?" she asks. "When are we going to Treasure Island?"

Lexis looks at Gray and he smiles as he nods.

"Right now," Lexis says. "We have no time to waste."

LEXIS

They've just left the shore when a fission of worry trickles down Lexis's spine. The optimism that had powered her belief that Shale would find water, then the excitement at unearthing the raft and the supplies, the faith that had her announcing they should leave straight away, all discover how tiny they are compared to the expanse of red ocean they're now bobbing in.

Miles of rust water stretch in every direction, quiet and calm, as if Mother Nature doesn't have to boast of her power. It's apparent in the horizons that seem impossible to reach.

Treasure Island could be anywhere.

If it exists at all...

Lexis determinedly pushes that thought away as she spears the oar into the water. She can't think like that. She refuses to. Her world with Gray is founded on hope. There's no future without it.

And in that world, Treasure Island exists.

"So, which direction do we go in?" Shale asks, her young voice almost shivering with anticipation.

"Well, Askala is to the north, so we don't want to go that way," Lexis says thoughtfully. "So it's east or west."

And both directions look identical. A boundless expanse that dwarfs the small raft and the three souls sitting on it.

Shale looks left then right, then tucks in closer to Lexis. "We don't know what Treasure Island looks like, do we?"

There's a hesitation in her voice, and uncertainty creeping across her face. Just like Lexis, she's realizing what they're up against.

Gray turns to face the little girl, grinning. The hope that Lexis found in him is shining from his face like a second sun. It seems their time with the Never, his injured foot and missing toe, and the impossibility of what they're about to undertake, weren't able to undermine his optimism after all.

Her beautiful, idealistic, buoyant Gray is back.

Lexis finds herself smiling before she's even realized it's happened. If Shale wasn't here, she'd lean forward and kiss him.

In fact, that's exactly what she's going to do.

Lexis grips his shirt and pulls Gray in, planting her lips on his. She tastes the magic of this man. The desire that's never far away. And the power of their love.

And as always, she wants more.

Shale giggles. "You two are gross."

They pull apart, exchanging a heated glance. Gray winks at Lexis before turning back to Shale. "What I was about to say is that we should visualize Treasure Island."

"Visualize?" Shale asks, her face scrunched in confusion.

"Yeah. I used to do it as a kid. I'd close my eyes and imagine how I wanted a situation to turn out. I'd picture how I wanted my future to be."

Shale turns to Lexis. "Did you ever do that?"

Lexis's first response is, no, she's never done anything so ridiculous. Her childhood taught her over and over again that no amount of wishing for things to be different would matter.

But then she knows that response will do nothing but dim the light in the little girl's eyes. Possibly in Gray's, too. And she refuses to take that away from either of them, even if she doubts this will make any difference.

"I've never done it," she admits, glancing at Gray. "But what do we do?"

His smile broadens, either because he's looking forward to doing this, or because he knows Lexis is humoring him. "Well, we close our eyes and take a few deep breaths."

Shale looks around, no doubt a reflexive motion after being a slave for so long. With another doubtful glance at Gray, she complies. Lexis does the same, figuring this way she's less likely to roll her eyes.

"Now, I want you to imagine what Treasure Island looks like."

Lexis stares at the blackness at the back of her lids, wondering how they can picture something they've never seen? Something that possibly doesn't exist. Her eyes snap open as the insidious thought returns and she's about to suggest they just row, when she sees Gray and Shale's expressions.

Their eyes are still closed, their faces tilted up. Soft smiles grace both their faces.

"How big is it?" Gray asks almost reverently. "What will it feel like when we find it?"

"It's big," whispers Shale. "And green. With trees everywhere. Trees with fruit!"

Gray chuckles. "Oh yes, I see them. Who knew fruit could be so big! Wow, there's people, and they're waving to us. I think there's a welcoming committee."

Shale's smile grows wider as her eyes squeeze tighter, as if she's trying to hold onto the image in her mind. "There's other kids there. And they're jumping up and down."

Lexis closes her own eyes, not wanting to disrupt the

moment for these two, even if she thinks they're spinning dreams from nothing but wishes.

"And there are buildings," Gray says in wonder. "Like Fairbanks, but smaller and not crumbling."

Shale gasps. "And a waterfall! I've heard about them!"

Lexis remembers when Raze carved one of those. He'd found a round, flat stone, and used his knife to etch out the scene of a river tumbling over the edge of a cliff. They'd whispered about what it would be like to stand under so much water pouring down at once, filling their mouth, cleansing their bodies.

She can already see what it would look like. Such a peaceful, happy scene. It would be the four of them—

Her eyes fly open, no longer wanting to visualize this. Both Raze and Winter were there. Also smiling, well-fed, healthy. Alive. Laughing beneath the torrent of water.

She picks up the oar again, gripping it tightly. Even Treasure Island can't bring back their twins.

Gray opens his eyes and draws in a deep breath. "Okay, let's go find it."

Shale claps as she bounces on her backside, making the water slosh. "Yeah, let's go find it!"

Lexis digs the oar into the water, deciding to head east. "We'll try a different section of the ocean each day." Who knows how long this will take. Weeks. Years. "We'll need to be strategic."

Gray grins. "That's my warrior girl. Always thinking." He turns to face forward. "And we'll take turns rowing."

Lexis nods, happy to take the first shift. Her muscles were honed for hard work. She may not be able to buy into the picture that was just painted, but she can be the one to power them in the direction of whatever the future holds for them.

The Outlands quickly fade away behind them and Lexis makes a note of the direction they're heading in. They'll be returning at sundown so they can do this all again tomorrow. And when their supplies run out, they'll need to restock before they can do it again.

After an hour, they're nothing but a dot in a blood-red ocean.

After two, Lexis's arms begin to ache.

After three, Shale curls up in Lexis's shadow and falls asleep. There's nothing to see but ocean and more ocean.

Gray reaches a hand out. "Here, let me have a turn."

Lexis passes him the oar, acknowledging that she's best off having a break. They have to return to the Outlands, yet.

"We'll have to turn back, soon."

His lips thin as he nods. His optimistic soul probably expected them to find Treasure Island today.

Lexis sighs and scans the horizon. If she could conjure Treasure Island for him, she would. With everything just the way he and Shale imagined. She's about to look away, when something catches her gaze.

It's small, barely a smudge on the red ocean, but it's there.

"Gray," she says under her breath.

He follows her line of sight, and freezes, too. It's not Treasure Island, which makes it far more dangerous.

Lexis narrows her eyes. "It's another raft," she says disbelievingly, noting the way it's moving far quicker than she would've expected.

Which means it's Askalans. Or Outlanders.

And neither of those are friends.

Shale wakes as if she sensed the tension. "Have we found it?" She looks around, then ducks low when she sees the other raft on the horizon. "Have they seen us?" she whispers.

Gray shifts the few inches necessary so he can dip his oar in the water on the other side. "I'm thinking we head west."

Lexis nods, her muscles tightening. They came out here to escape the fighting, not find more. Gray begins paddling in the opposite direction. Watching over her shoulder, she notes the way the raft seems to be still moving quickly, but not going anywhere. Like the fools are going in circles.

"Lexis," Gray says quietly.

She turns around to see him pointing at something ahead. She climbs into a squat, her pulse tripping through her veins as she sees another blotch. Are they surrounded?

But this shape is smaller, lower. She wrinkles her nose as she recognizes what it is. "It's a pile of trash."

"It could have something cool on it!" Shale says excitedly.

Lexis and Gray glance at each other. There's no time to investigate it. They need to get out of view of the other raft.

He digs the oar into the water, hauling the raft forward. "We need to keep moving, Shale."

"We should head back," adds Lexis.

Gray nods, the edges of his lips turning down. "We'll try again tomorrow."

Shale glances over her shoulder where the raft is now just a dot. "Maybe next time."

"Yep, definitely next time," Gray says cheerfully.

Now that the raft is almost out of sight, Lexis allows herself to relax a little. "We just need to angle south a little more." The Outlands should only be a few hours away.

Nodding again, Gray pushes the oar a little deeper. The raft angles left a little before jolting straight back.

Lexis frowns. "You'll have to row harder to change the direction."

"I'm trying," he huffs. He jams the oar in deeper and pulls hard. This time the raft twitches, but continues moving forward.

Lexis takes the oar. "You're probably tired. I'll take over."

Gray looks like he's going to argue, but then releases it. Lexis adjusts her position so she can row, then pulls the wooden paddle through the water. She's surprised to find it's far harder than it was this morning.

And once again, the raft doesn't change direction.

"Good one, Lexis," gasps Shale. "We're going faster."

Realizing she's right, Lexis frowns. Their momentum is building in the wrong direction. She dips the oar in the water again. The water slices around it, as if the raft is powered by the wind.

"It's the current," says Gray. "It's pulling us along."

Except, it's pulling them west.

"We don't want to go this way," Lexis says through gritted teeth. Bunching the muscles in her shoulders, she tries again, this time harder. The raft shudders as if something's trying to pull it off its tracks and continues on. Another try and the edge dips below the surface, warm water rushing over the timber. Lexis quickly withdraws the oar, feeling like Mother Nature just gave her a warning—fight this and you will lose.

She looks at Gray, unsure and worried.

The current is drawing them away from the enemy, but further out to sea. They've avoided one danger, only to row straight into another.

"Let's all try to paddle," he says.

He and Shale scoop their hands through the water as Lexis rows with everything she has. With each burst of power, the raft picks up speed.

But stays on its course.

"We're just making it worse," Lexis pants. The hours of rowing from this morning have taken their toll. Although, even at full strength, she doubts it would be enough to overcome the current. She's familiar with fighting on land, not battling something as vast as the sea.

They all straighten, looking around as the lengths of timber they're on are pulled along. Further out to sea. Out into the expanse of nothingness.

Shale shuffles closer to Lexis. "What do we do now?"

Gray slips an arm around her bony shoulders. "We're better off saving our energy for the moment. Once the current has run out of steam, we'll take turns paddling back." He pats the bag of supplies with his other hand. "We'll be fine."

Shale glances at Lexis and she's about to nod encouragingly when the raft jolts forward. Shale grips Lexis's arm, her eyes wide with fright.

"The current's getting stronger," says Lexis, dread accumulating in her gut. "Stay close to the center of the raft."

Gray and Shale huddle in, closing the few inches between them. The raft powers on, gliding over the calm waters that disguised its existence. Lexis clings to the hope that Gray's right.

Surely the current has to slow soon, just enough for them to paddle in the direction of the Outlands.

The sun's trek toward the horizon counts out the minutes, then hours, that the current stays strong. They hold each other the whole time, only pulling apart to sip at their water or nibble at their rations. The knowledge that this is all they have weighs heavily in everyone's eyes. Throughout, the raft rides the surface of the heated ocean, dragged on an aimless journey following some unknown chart.

Although Lexis can already guess their destination.

Their slow, inevitable death.

A few times she tries again to change their direction, but the surface barely ripples as the sea ignores her attempts. Too soft and there's no acknowledgement that Lexis is even trying. Too hard, and the raft dips, threatening to tip.

Eventually, she curls into Gray, and Shale curls into her. The three of them hold each other as they watch. Wait.

And hope.

Although what for, she has no idea.

Lexis's eyelids are just beginning to droop when Shale gasps. Lexis pulls her in closer, instantly alert.

It's unlikely there are Outlanders or Askalans this far out, but the threat of leatherskins is very real. There's no way Lexis is going to have Mother Nature drag them miles out to sea just so they can be shark fodder.

"Look," Shale says, pointing straight ahead.

Another shape looms on the horizon, little more than a blot over the red sea.

Gray lets Lexis go as he leans forward. "It's probably another island of trash."

But they can't afford to be complacent. Lexis's fingers slip around the oar, the only weapon they have.

"Maybe this time we could check it out?" Shale asks. "There might be something on there we can use."

Lexis doesn't point out they don't have a choice. The current is pulling them straight toward whatever it is.

They slowly get to their feet, keeping their stance wide to stay balanced. The sun is setting behind the shape, making it hard to distinguish what they're approaching until they're far closer than Lexis would like. She holds the oar, wishing it was a spear.

The shape grows. Gains substance. And it soon becomes apparent what it is.

Lexis's breath evaporates but her lungs are too frozen to work. She stares, unblinking, as Gray's hand grips hers.

They've found Treasure Island.

And it's nothing like they imagined.

GRACE

Grace puts a hand to her belly and groans. That fleshy green fruit had been delicious but with every bump of the raft she fights having to keep what remains of it in her stomach.

Raze reaches for the oar to take a turn while she bends forward and drags oxygen into her lungs to steady herself.

"Maybe they were poisonous," she says. "I think I'm dying."

"You ate too much, that's all." Raze smiles. "I told you to slow down."

"Why didn't I listen to you?" She takes three quick breaths, hoping that might work better. "I will never not listen to you ever again."

"You didn't eat the seed, did you?" Raze frowns.

"Of course not!" Grace snaps. "It was like a rock."

"Sorry." He continues to row. "It was just a little hard to tell with the way you were shoving them all in your mouth."

"Says the guy who must've eaten about ten of them." She pokes out her tongue, enjoying the easy banter that flows between them. It's like she's known him for approximately forever.

"Lie down." Raze rests the oar to touch her gently on the shoulder. "Sleep for a bit. I don't like seeing you unwell."

She does as she's told. Well, not so much the sleeping bit, but the lying down bit. Resting her head on his thigh, she clutches her stomach while he continues to row.

"Where did that guy in Askala say the island was again?" she asks.

"Are you sleep talking?" Raze pauses again to smooth her hair off her forehead. "I told you to go to sleep."

She ignores him. There's no way she can sleep with her stomach about to split in two. "He said east, didn't he?"

He lets out a sigh at her stubbornness. "He did. If we row out far enough from this point, they can't see us easily from Askala's shores. Then if we bend around to the east, we should find these mysterious Newlands. If they actually exist."

"Why would they make that up?" she asks. "They didn't know we were listening."

"Who knows?" His voice turns serious. "But are you going to trust the word of someone who left an unarmed and injured man to die without even waiting to find out what he was doing there? And then go off to have their evening meal," he spits.

"Not when you put it like that." She lets go of her stomach that seems to agree with her change of position to lie on her back, being careful not to let her feet dangle over the edge of the small raft.

"At least the water is calm," Raze comments. "The rough water we saw earlier is well behind us now."

"You mean where we thought we saw that other raft?" she asks.

He nods as a frown crosses his face at the memory. The oceans are filled with just as many dangers out here as the land. Possibly even more. Thinking they might have spotted another raft hadn't been a good thing. This world is full of enemies right now.

"We can't be sure it was a raft," she reassures. "And it was going the opposite direction to us, so it doesn't really matter what it was."

He nods again but she knows that doesn't mean he won't keep a keen eye out just in case.

"Seriously, go to sleep for a bit," he says, changing the subject. "The water is calm here. You're safe."

She closes her eyes, feeling exactly that.

Safe.

Raze will always look after her. Just as she will always look after him. A nagging thought itches at the back of her mind, reminding her that she's anything but safe. She pushes it away. Right now, she's in no danger. If Gray were here, he'd tell her to enjoy that feeling.

She's unsure if she dozes off or just rests, but eventually she feels the turn of the raft as Raze heads east. Soon they'll know if the conversation they'd overheard was true. Could a slice of land covered in vegetation have really appeared in the water, ready to be inhabited? If so, they need to keep the greedy Askalans off it. Don't they have enough already?

Grace and Raze have to claim it first. It's only right.

It still amazes her how a race of people can be so selfish. Is it really accurate to claim to live in peace, if that peace is only extended to your own kind? Thoughts of the way they'd treated Hatch sting her eyes.

This is why she has to unite the factions and invade Askala. Nothing has ever been more important.

"You're talking in your sleep," Raze tells her.

"I'm not asleep," she says.

"Then you're talking to yourself." He grins affectionately. "Which is even worse."

"I was just thinking about the Newlands," says Grace.

He puts down the oar. "If you sit up, you can look at it instead."

"Where?" Grace sits up so fast she pulls a muscle in her neck.

It's impossible to miss. A long dark stripe in the ocean with tall trees stretching into the sky. Excitement floods her every cell, pushing away any thoughts of bringing up her food.

"It's actually there," she breathes. "Look, Raze. Isn't it beautiful?"

"A miniature version of Askala," says Raze, looping his arm around her. "No wonder they're so excited about it."

"They're not getting their hands on it." Grace rubs at her neck. "It's ours, Raze. That's our new home."

"You want to live there?" Raze drops his arm to resume his rowing.

"We *need* to live there," she says. "Look how many trees there are. Barnacle will be able to build his fleet so much faster with these resources."

"Pity we can't live there alone." Raze shoots her a cheeky grin. "I wouldn't mind living on a deserted island with you."

A rush of emotions swirl in her belly, upsetting the steadiness she'd only just found. She'd like nothing better than to spend the rest of her days living alone in the Newlands with Raze. But how does that help unite the factions? She's in a unique position here to make a genuine difference in the world and help the Askalans see just how selfish they are.

"Me too," she says. "But you know we can't. And it will be different with the Rust this time. They'll be on our turf. They won't lay a finger on you this time."

He nods sharply. "I'm not afraid of the Rust."

"I know." She touches his back lightly, needing the contact. "You're not afraid of anything."

"That's not true." He doesn't turn to look at her. "I'm afraid of losing you."

"You'll never lose me," she says. "I'll always be in your heart just as you'll always be in mine."

He doesn't respond, hearing her words for what they were—

the best promise she can give him. Because they both know that in the world they live in they could be separated at any time. Neither of them had expected a future without their twin, which has taught them that the only thing they can count on is a life that will continue to deviate off course.

Raze takes them the remainder of the journey in silence and when the raft touches the shoreline, Grace swallows down her nerves.

This moment feels...big. Like her life is about to change.

Raze leaps off and drags it up onto the sand so her feet won't have to touch the acid water. He holds out his hand to help her up. "How's your stomach?"

"I feel fine, thanks," she says, her legs aching as she stands. "Just a little guilty for letting you row practically the whole way here."

"I don't mind," he tells her. "It's what I do."

"I know." She tears her eyes from him to look back at the Newlands. "It's real, Raze. This place actually exists. And it's beautiful."

"So beautiful," he says, although his eyes haven't left her face.

"Let's look around." She swats at him, enjoying his compliment but far too curious to possibly stand still.

There are trees everywhere. All shades of green. Some with fruit. Some with bright flowers. Others with leaves that are gently waving in the breeze that's picked up since they left Askala. They're making a sound she's never heard before. She never realized when the wind moves something as delicate as a leaf, it actually makes a noise. But then again, there are thousands—perhaps millions—of leaves brushing up against each other, and all she ever saw in Fairbanks was one scraggly tree at a time.

"Can you hear that?" she asks. "The trees are whispering to us."

"What are they saying?" Raze drags the raft up onto the sand and they walk toward the trees.

"They're welcoming us," says Grace.

"Listen to the birds." Raze points to a flock of colorful parrots. "So many of them."

They step beneath that canopy. It's cool in the shade, reminding her a little of Fairbanks, except with trunks instead of concrete, and branches instead of fallen beams. It's like she's come home, except a much nicer version of it.

Raze's back stiffens the further they walk into the trees and his eyes dart around. This landscape may feel oddly familiar to her, but it's completely different to the barren landscape of the Outlands that Raze grew up with.

"It's okay," she tells him. "We're the only ones here."

"There are so many places to hide." He bends to look around a wide trunk. "How can anyone live in a place like this? It makes me nervous."

"You weren't like this in Fairbanks," she says, slipping her hand into his.

He shakes his head. "It was different there. Quieter."

"Except when a building falls on your head." She squeezes his hand, trying to let some of her calmness flow into him. "You'll get used to it here. We both will."

They break through into a clearing where there's soft grass clinging to the sandy soil.

Grace slips her arms around Raze's waist and leans her cheek against his chest. His heart is beating rapidly, and his breath is coming in short gasps. He's on high alert.

"Raze!" she says, standing on tip toes so she can press a kiss to his lips. "It's just us. It's okay."

"How can I keep you safe out here?" He returns her kiss before gently pushing away and turning in a circle as he scans the trees. "There could be an enemy right there and we wouldn't know it."

"Then we'll build ourselves a house," she says, deciding she's going to need to keep Raze busy if she wants him to stay here. "Somewhere we can protect ourselves. There's plenty of timber we can use. But first I need to write a note for Rust and see if I can attract a raven."

Raze nods his agreement. "I'll make a fire while you're doing that. It will be dark soon."

"Good thinking." She puts her arms around his waist. "We're going to be happy here, Raze. I can feel it."

"We are." He drops a kiss on the top of her head. "But then again, I'm happy anywhere you are."

Grace reluctantly moves away from him. There will be plenty of time to get lost in his embrace later under a blanket of stars. They have jobs to do now.

"Be careful!" Raze calls after her. "Stay where I can see you."

She smiles at his protectiveness as she walks to the papery tree and tears off a few pieces of bark until she has one that she thinks might be perfect. Just as she's about to walk away, she returns and tears off some more. The whole idea of ravens feels a little flaky. She's never even seen one before. But she's heard all about them. And it sounds like they could fly anywhere. She's going to have to send a few messages in the hope one might reach the Rust.

She tears off a long strand from a vine and strips it of leaves. If she's lucky enough to find a raven, she should be able to secure her note with this quite nicely.

Needing something to write with, she finds a tree full of what she's certain are poisonous red berries. She mushes them into a paste with a rock and finds a sturdy stick. She dips the tip into the paste and drags it across the bark to form the letters she needs. Reading and writing have never been her strong suit, but she's glad now that her sister insisted on teaching her when she was young.

. . .

New land. Sail north east. Come now. Commander.

She writes four copies of the same note, hoping these directions are enough for Barnacle to find them.

"I'm just going to the beach," she calls to Raze. "I'll be near the raft."

He looks up anxiously from the large pile of sticks and branches he's gathered. "I'll come with you."

She nods, deciding she'd better get used to this. With the unsettled way Raze is feeling, there's no way he's going to let her out of his sight. She could think of worse bodyguards...

Slipping her hand into his, they head in the direction of the beach to look for a raven. If they can find one heading for the Outlands, there's every chance it will reach the Rust first, given their proximity to the shore.

"Can I see the note?" Raze asks.

She hands one to him without hesitation, noticing the fascinated way he stares at the letters.

"You can't read," she says before she can stop herself, but he doesn't seem to mind.

"Lexis could understand the letters a little bit," he says. "Evrest didn't think I was worth teaching. There was no point."

"I'll teach you," she promises.

"I'm not as smart as you." Raze hands her back the note and stoops to collect a washed-up piece of shiny metal from the shoreline and angles it to the sky, trying to catch the last of the afternoon sun.

"You're smart," she says. "Much smarter than me. There are different kinds of smart, you know."

"Thanks," he says. "But I don't mind you being smarter."

Deciding to let it go, she scans the sky, seeing a dark shape move through a cloud.

"There!" she points.

Raze adjusts the angle of the metal, and a giant black bird swoops down.

It lands on the sand in front of them and she gasps at the majestic creature. Easily the largest bird Grace has ever seen, it has glossy black feathers, a shiny beak and beady eyes. It tilts its head to study them.

Raze reaches into his pocket to produce the same kind of red berry Grace had used to write her note. He squats down and holds his hand out to the bird.

"Would you like this?" he asks in a gentle voice. "I found it when I was looking for twigs."

"It could be poisonous!" gasps Grace.

"Oh." Raze grimaces. "I should have thought of that before I ate some myself. I told you that you're smarter than me."

"Do you feel okay?" she asks, her heart hammering at the idea of losing him. "Raze, are you okay?"

He nods, keeping his hand steady. "Definitely better than you felt on the raft."

She draws in a deep breath, telling herself that if it were poisonous, surely he'd have felt some of the effects by now.

"The bird wouldn't take it if it's not safe," she says as the bird ventures forward. "Ravens would know these things, wouldn't they?"

"Grace, I know as much as you do about this place." He sighs deeply. "Which is nothing. That's why it sets me on edge."

The raven comes closer again and takes the berry from Raze, eating it in one gulp then tilting its head as it looks for more.

Raze reaches slowly into his pocket as Grace cautiously ties one of her notes to the raven's leg.

Out of nowhere, two more ravens swoop down.

"These ones are hungry, too," says Raze, sharing his berries between the birds, while Grace ties notes to the other birds.

"Surely, one of these will find Rust," she says, when she's certain the notes are secure. "Maybe even the Cragg." The more people who can join them, the stronger they'll be.

Raze stands up and shoos the magnificent creatures back into the sky. The sound of their wings flapping makes Grace flinch as she steps back.

That was easier than she'd expected.

"We did the right thing, didn't we?" Doubt washes over her now that it's too late to take back her decision to alert the others.

Raze nods as he wraps an arm around her shoulders. "We did."

She's unsure if he's just saying that to make her feel better.

Because she didn't just choose her future. She chose one for Raze. And if things go well and she unites the factions, then she also chose one for every person left on this struggling planet.

Askala must be overthrown.

And now they have everything they need to win.

RAZE

*R*aze watches the ravens become little more than black dots in the bruised, twilight sky. If the birds reach the Outlands, others could be here in a couple of days.

And then it begins.

He's never been more excited and nervous in his life.

He turns and takes Grace's hand. There's planning to do. And a night alone to savor. "Let's get a fire started."

"Good idea," she says, smiling. "It'll keep the scary monsters away."

He scrunches his nose at her then tugs her hand. He'll always protect her. Do what's necessary for her to be safe. That was his role with Lexis. It's a privilege to do the same for Grace.

They return to the pile of sticks in the small clearing and Raze squats down, setting about starting a fire. Grace sits a few feet away, watching as he grips a small branch between his feet and rubs another between his hands, creating friction between the two.

"We'll be here a while," she muses. "Probably a few months."

Raze nods, keeping his gaze on the two points where the

wood meets. "Yes. It'll take time for everyone who can fight to get here. Then we need to build the boats."

"And the more we can build the better. Askala is strong."

Because they have all the food they need. Fresh water. Who knows how many people as they breed to their heart's content.

He squints, peering more closely at the wood. No sign of smoke yet. Gripping the stick tighter, he works faster. The wood is wetter here in the Newlands. Moisture actually has a chance to hang around in shaded patches and rich soil.

"They'll follow you now," he observes, not taking his eyes off the task. "You'll be presenting to them everything we need to win."

"*We* will be," she corrects softly.

Raze doesn't agree, but he doesn't say anything. The Outlanders will follow Grace. She's proven herself. But he's Cy. And a traitorous one at that. He suppresses a frown. He doesn't need them to like him. They just need to accept him.

Protecting Grace so she can fulfill her destiny is his only goal.

"We'll need huts," he says, changing the subject. "Houses for those who arrive."

As he says the words, a tiny tendril of smoke coils up from the sticks. He smiles in victory, rubbing his hands together even faster. The smoke thickens, becoming opaque and milky. He bends down, blowing gently, and is rewarded with a flicker of flame.

"Yes, Raze!" Grace hisses in excitement, as if she's never seen fire before.

His chest expands with pride. They've built something in the Newlands. He looks up and grins and she smiles back. It's small and fragile, but it's theirs.

Jerking his focus back, he sets about sprinkling finely shredded bark and tufts of dry grass on the fledgling fire. Within minutes, it grows, and they're adding leaves and twigs.

A gently crackling fire is throwing sparks into the sky and shadows on the trees around them when they both sit back, satisfaction soft on their faces. Raze lifts his arm and Grace moves to curl into his side, her arms wrapping around his waist. The warmth emitted by the fire is quickly dwarfed by the sweet heat kindling inside of him.

He draws in a deep breath. The leaves softly rustle and a strange hum fills the air, as if countless insects are hiding everywhere around them. Raze can feel them watching, but he ignores it. He's going to have to get used to it if this will be his home for the upcoming months.

"I think we build the first hut here. Around this fire," says Grace. "It can be the central meeting place for everyone."

"I like that." The heart of the Newlands will be founded by their own hearts.

"Me, too." Grace sighs. "There's a lot to prepare."

"So much." Finding a regular supply of water will be their first task. Learning what's edible and what's not. A loud *croak* somewhere to their left makes Raze tense. How big do the insects grow around here? He consciously unwinds, pulling Grace closer. Building shelter is also a priority.

"And I've been thinking," she says. "Maybe we should build the boats in the Outlands. The Askalans know the Newlands exist. They could turn up here at any time."

Raze frowns in thought. "That makes sense. We need to keep the element of surprise."

It would mean sending the wood to the Outlands. And keeping some men there so they can build the boats. This is definitely going to take several months.

Grace looks up at him, her dark eyes luminous in the firelight. "But all that can start tomorrow," she whispers.

His breath hitches somewhere deep in his lungs, but he's not sure he needs it. "I love you, Grace."

All this is possible because of her.

She moves up, her soft body grazing his. "I love you, too, Raze."

His lips crash down on hers, devouring her mouth. Since the moment they landed in the Newlands, the knowledge they're finally alone, that they have a reprieve, no matter how brief, has dominated his mind.

For now, Grace isn't the Commander. Death isn't hovering in the periphery. Their enemies are far away.

It's just the two of them.

And the love that's bloomed against impossible odds.

Grace pushes up, as if she needs more. And Raze is happy to oblige. His fingers spear into her hair as he cups her head, angling so he can explore deeper. Taste her. Make her his.

She moans, and the sound is like a spark to tinder, like he's spent all his life dry and desiccated. Waiting. Wanting.

Passion explodes as a wildfire is let loose. Raze's hands begin to move, sliding and caressing over clothes and skin. He wants to touch her everywhere. He wants to hear more of those moans.

He's rewarded with the sound of raw desire as he molds her against him, pressing her curves against his hard planes. Sculpting her to him. Making it so it's impossible to tell where the passion begins and whether it will ever end.

Grace's hands climb up his chest, scorching him as they wrap around his shoulders. She pushes and he tumbles, a willing surrender as his back lands on soft soil. And then she's kissing him, consuming him, touching him everywhere.

She's claiming him as absolutely as he's claiming her.

Their tattered, worn clothes disappear, an unwanted barrier between them. Raze can barely breathe, and yet his head swims with each gasping breath as skin touches skin. As mouth finds mouth. As body quivers against body.

Their movements become frantic, their need to consummate, to make this moment theirs, a primal drive. When they find the inevitable peak, their cries join the breeze tangling through the trees.

They collapse, Grace sprawled across him, their breaths coming in ragged gasps.

Raze wraps his arms around her, wishing he never had to let go. "Grace..." He stops, struck mute like he was for most of his life.

He feels her smile against his chest. "I know." She presses in closer. "We should've made time for that ages ago."

He chuckles, liking the way the vibrations in his chest ripple through both of them. "We really should've."

Reaching over, he throws another piece of wood on the fire. The warmth has him feeling languid and relaxed, both novel feelings, but he's not tired. He's not ready to let this night go yet. Time is inevitably drawing them toward war.

But for now, there's peace, and it's too beautiful to miss.

He rolls over so Grace is beneath him, tenderly brushing the hair from her face. His gaze roams over her cheeks, her lips, before returning to her smiling eyes. "We belong together," he says quietly. Fiercely.

She cups his face, tenderness softening her beautiful features. "I'll always be yours, Raze. No matter what."

Her words brand his heart and touch his soul. There's nothing he wouldn't do for this passionate, strong woman. She's given him everything.

A voice.

A heart.

A future.

Herself.

Grace wriggles a little, making him gasp. "I'm not ready for sleep," she murmurs as she reaches up to pepper kisses along the line of his jaw.

"I never realized how overrated it is," he groans. He angles his head and traps her lips. They kiss slowly, savoring the intensifying heat.

Tomorrow will bring responsibility and work. Tomorrow will bring them one day closer to war.

Tonight, they'll have nothing but each other.

Which is everything.

GRAY

*G*ray's jaw hangs open as he stares at the island they've washed up on.

"What is this place?" Lexis asks.

"It's Treasure Island!" squeals Shale. "Look at all the trees. It's exactly what you told me to imagine, Gray! There's even a waterfall. And the sand is so colorful. It's the prettiest thing I've ever seen in my life."

Gray glances at Lexis. That was a lot of words to tumble from the lips of this once-silent girl. Lexis's expression is a mixture of amusement and concern.

Because while Shale is right in what she's saying, these aren't any ordinary trees. And while Gray's never seen a waterfall before, he's certain this isn't an ordinary one of those either. Nor has he ever seen multi-colored sand.

"I told you it worked," says Gray, feeling a little smug. "We imagined it and here it is. Well, sort of."

"The trees are man-made." Lexis frowns. "Look at them. Those trunks are built out of metal. They look like old ship masts. And the leaves...are they strips of green plastic?"

"They sure smell like it," says Gray. He crinkles his nose at the artificial smell in the air, and scans the long line of trees on the edge of the island. The workmanship that's gone into these structures is impressive, even if bizarre. It's hard to tell from here how thick the line of trees is but it stretches far enough to shield their view of the rest of the island. These must have taken years to build. If not, decades.

"It's so cool," gushes Shale. "What's the waterfall made from? It's so shiny!"

"Broken glass," says Gray. "See the way it's catching the light at different angles. They're like tiny rainbows."

He shakes his head in amazement at the built up rock structure that's emerging from the trees a little way down the beach. The surface of the rocks at the front have been entirely coated with small shards of clear glass. A stream of water is cascading over it to a shimmering pool at the bottom where it gets scooped up by a giant wheel that's slowly turning, lifting it back up to the top of the waterfall to start the process again.

If only the water weren't full of acid, that pool would look good enough to swim in.

"I love it, I love it!" Shale scampers off the raft and onto the island. She immediately starts hopping from foot to foot. "Ouch! Ouch!"

Gray lurches himself off the raft toward her. He scoops her up, almost toppling them both over as he finds his balance.

"What's wrong?" Lexis asks from the raft.

"It's okay." Gray holds up a hand. "The ground is just..."

"Prickly," Shale finishes. "It's like a cactus."

"It's not that bad," says Gray. "Just a little rough on the skin if you were expecting soft sand."

Lexis joins them, dragging the raft out of the water and stepping cautiously. She doesn't seem too bothered by the coarse texture. Shoes are a luxury in the Outlands, worn only when completely necessary, which means the soles of their feet are tough. It's almost like they've grown an extra thick layer of skin to compensate.

Gray sets Shale carefully back on the ground and steadies himself. "It's okay. Just tread carefully."

Lexis stoops and picks up a handful of the colorful granules to study it. "It's ground-up refuse. This island has been covered in trash."

"What even is trash?" asks Shale, forever curious.

"It's things people used to throw away when they didn't want them anymore," says Lexis.

Shale looks at her like she's just sprouted an extra limb. Nothing is trash in the world they live in. "People did *not* do that."

"It's true," says Gray. "People had so many things that sometimes they would throw stuff away."

Shale's brows knit together as she tries to process this. "So, other people would find the trash and use it for themselves?"

"Sometimes," says Gray. "And sometimes they'd just put it into a giant dump for it to rot into the ground."

"I want to go to a dump," says Shale, impressed.

"What if it has ground-up trash on the ground?" Lexis teases.

"This isn't ground-up trash." Shale scoops up a handful of colored granules and lets them run through her fingers. "This is ground-up cactus."

"Hop on my back." Lexis's gaze darts around and she bends forward. Shale eagerly climbs on, trying to brush off her feet once she gets settled.

Gray hates that he can't take her, but he's only just figured out how to walk on his own without falling over.

"Hello!" Gray calls toward the line of trees as they move forward. "We come in peace!"

"Shh." Lexis scowls at him. "Let's just see what's here before we announce ourselves."

"Do you think the Origin people are nice?" Shale asks,

uncertainty creeping into her voice. "I mean, the Never used to be part of them, and they're not nice."

"I think they're nice," Gray says, trying to keep a confident tone to his voice. "Nobody nasty would build such a pretty pretend beach, would they? I think all the horrible people left because they didn't like the nice people they left behind."

Lexis shoots him a look. They both know that's not necessarily true. He shrugs. Maybe it is.

"I think so, too." Shale sits a little higher on Lexis's back to get a better view. "Nasty people don't normally like nice people."

"Hey, I'm not a horse." Lexis jiggles her into a more comfortable position.

"What's a horse?" asks Shale.

"An animal the ancient people used to ride," says Lexis.

Shale seems to like the sound of this. "What did they look like?"

"I've never seen one myself," says Lexis. "But I hear they looked like giant rats."

Gray smiles at the thought of riding a giant rat.

"I see one!" Shale squeals, pointing to the tree line made of rusted ship masts ahead. "I see a rat. Look! It heard you, Lexis. Or maybe it's a baby horse!"

Sure enough, a large rat darts out between two tree trunks and scampers away. Another one follows it. Then another climbs straight up the trunk and hides itself amongst the leaves. Now that they're closer, Gray can see the trees aren't in as good shape as he first thought. The ship masts are beginning to rust and many of the plastic leaves are in tatters. Some have writing on them from when they were used in their former life. Before they became trash, and then treasure once more.

Two more brown rats emerge from the trees, take one look at the three of them, then dash away out of sight. They're just like the rats in Fairbanks, only far fatter. It seems there's more food to be found out here than in the Outlands.

"They're definitely rats," says Gray, wishing Trakk were here to see such well rounded rodents.

Shale wriggles on Lexis's back. "We should catch them! I'm hungry! And thirsty."

"Not now," says Lexis, clamping her hands on Shale's ankles so she can't get free. "Let's see what else we can find."

A raven swoops down and lands on top of one of the trees. It tilts its head at them.

"And now a bird!" Shale jiggles even more excitedly. "So many creatures!"

This place certainly does seem to be teeming with life. Apart from human life, which is almost as strange as the rusted trees that are evidence of their existence. Gray's seen some clever creatures before, but none who could construct anything as elaborate as this man-made forest. There are definitely people around. But where?

"The bird has a note tied to its foot," Shale points out. "I've always wanted a letter from a raven. Do you think it will come to us?"

Gray squints, wondering if there's something wrong with his eyes. "How can you see that?"

"Look, silly!" laughs Shale, having the time of her life. "The bird is all black, but it has something brown attached to its leg."

The raven stretches its wide wings, and seeming to decide it's safe, the bird flies down, landing at their feet. Sure enough, there's a piece of papery bark tied to its leg by a vine.

"Let me!" Shale climbs down from Lexis's back, not seeming to be bothered by the cactus-sand and squats in front of the bird. Its eyes are black and beady, its beak long and sharp.

"Careful, Shale," Gray tells her. "Let it come to you, so it knows you're not a threat."

The bird inches its way forward, and taps its foot on the ground, waiting for Shale to untie the note. It looks to the sky as if this is all a huge inconvenience.

"Do you get the feeling if that bird could roll its eyes, then it would?" Gray whispers to Lexis.

"Move very slowly so you don't scare it," says Lexis. "We'll stay back so we don't crowd it."

Lexis slips her hand into Gray's and squeezes. The close contact is nice. Having Shale with them has been wonderful, but it's sure hampered the time they get to spend alone.

Shale unties the note, and the bird tilts its head at her expectantly.

"It wants payment," says Gray.

"But I don't have anything!" Shale's voice is high-pitched and worried.

"Shoo!" Lexis steps forward and sends the bird back into the sky.

It squawks loudly as its farewell.

"Sorry, raven!" shouts Shale. "Come and see me another time and I'll have something for you!"

Gray can only hope this is true.

"What does the note say?" Shale passes it to Lexis who studies it carefully.

"I don't know all these words." Lexis frowns. "I think it says something about directions. This word here is *north*."

She hands the note to Gray who curses himself for not paying more attention when his older sister had tried to teach him to read. Winter had been a far better student. If she were here, she'd be able to make sense of all these squiggly lines scratched out in red ink.

"I think this word says *land*." Gray squints like the other words are going to suddenly become clear.

"Oh!" says Shale. "Land in the north!"

"Pretty sure that's where Askala is," says Lexis. "And that's hardly news."

"We don't want to go there." Shale drops her voice to a whisper. "I've heard they eat their babies."

"Shale!" Lexis looks horrified.

"They don't do that," says Gray, wondering if the Cragg tell all their kids bedtime stories like this. It's no wonder they were such brutal competitors at the Tournaments if those are the kind of fairy-tales they grew up with.

"But you're right that we don't want to go there," says Lexis.

"What do you think the note's about?" Gray continues to study the strange combination of letters.

"My guess is…" Lexis lets out a sigh. "Evrest is preparing to invade Askala now that the Tournaments are over. Even more reason to stay well away."

"We don't need Askala." Shale sweeps out her hands. "We have Treasure Island! The most beautiful island in the world."

Gray laughs at her enthusiasm. Lexis remains serious, her eyes continually scanning for threat.

"Can I keep the note?" Shale puts out her hand and Gray passes it to her. She shoves it in her pocket. "Let's keep exploring. I want to see the waterfall."

"Let's find the people first." Lexis bends for Shale to climb up on her back once more. "We don't know if it's safe."

"I'm okay," Shale tells her, straightening her spine. "I'm used to the cactus-sand now."

"Let me know if you change your mind." Lexis ruffles her hair.

They walk into the trees and it's nothing like what Gray imagined standing in a forest would be like. The smell of decay winds its way up his nostrils as the shade envelopes them. There's no bird song or the sound of twigs breaking underneath their feet. Just the occasional rat scampering past and a raven cawing in the distance.

He turns to Lexis to see that his warrior-girl remains on high alert for danger.

"What's wrong?" he asks.

"Nothing." She shakes her head. "It's just there are so many places to hide. Let's move quickly. I don't like it in here."

Gray nods. Lexis grew up in a land of open spaces where an enemy could be spotted a mile away. Here, someone could be watching you from a yard away and you wouldn't have the faintest idea. It's no wonder it's making her nervous.

The band of man-made forest is only a few trees wide and soon they're exiting from the other side, their footsteps crunching on coarser ground. Gray blinks in the bright sunlight as the smell of decay intensifies.

Shale crinkles her nose. "What's that smell?"

Gray shrugs. "We're standing on ground-up trash, remember?"

"Ground-up cactus," she corrects. "And there's no such thing as trash. It's *treasure.*"

Lexis's hands shoot out, one to either side, as she stops Gray and Shale from walking forward. Her eyes are busy scanning, her breath held, every cell of her body ready to fight.

"It's a village," she says.

Gray's eyes adjust to the light and he takes in what Lexis has already seen. Stretching out before them is a wide path made from broken slabs of concrete with a long line of ramshackle huts dotted along each side. The path slopes down as it leads to a large colorful circular clearing in the distance. Branching off the clearing are about a dozen more paths at evenly spaced intervals.

The huts are made from a wide array of what Shale calls treasures. The Origins people seem to have cobbled together anything they could find for their homes. He can see roofs made of tin, others made from glass and some thatched from bracken. The crooked walls that are holding them up have been constructed from bricks, mud and tin sheets. They're a mish-mash of color, shapes and sizes, all lined up in perfectly spaced rows in an unlikely marriage of chaos and order.

Hundreds of people must live here. Thousands, perhaps. Yet there's not a single soul in sight.

Lexis lets her hands fall and she walks ahead, nodding at Gray to follow with Shale.

They move down the path and Gray is happy for the smoother concrete surface below his feet as he gets a closer look at the huts. They're only small, and most are falling down but they look well-loved. If people are living inside them, they're not giving themselves away just yet. Plants are growing in pots outside the doors, some bursting with fruit, and others struggling for life.

Lexis picks an apple from a small tree and passes it to Shale, picking two more and giving one to Gray. She then pulls a metal pipe from the roof of the house and tucks it in her waistband, no doubt to use as a weapon.

"Should we knock?" he asks in a whisper, feeling the eyes that are certain to be on them. "Maybe we should ask first?"

Lexis shakes her head. "Ask for forgiveness, not permission. We need to eat."

Shale is already chomping into her apple and Gray gives in and takes a bite. The fruity flesh instantly makes his mouth water and he immediately takes a second bite. Lexis is right. They need food and water, and these apples are providing them with both.

A rat darts out from one of the homes and scampers down the path. Just how many are there on this island? Trakk would absolutely love it here.

Continuing down the path behind Lexis with Shale's hand still gripping his own, Gray fights the uneasy feeling that's settling in his stomach. Something here isn't right. There's no way they aren't being watched.

"Do you feel that?" Lexis asks, pausing her steps as she chews her apple core right down to the stem it grew from.

Gray stills his movements and listens. "Feel what? People watching us?"

"No." She shakes her head. "The island is moving. Slowly. But it's moving."

Shale looks up at Gray with an amused expression. "Lexis notices everything," she whispers.

"She does." Gray nods as he finishes his apple, wishing he could eat several more. If these people don't appear soon, then maybe he will. His injured foot is already getting sore again. He really needs to sit down soon.

They make their way down the row of huts and step into the large circular clearing where all the roads intersect. It's completely deserted.

"Wow!" says Shale, her eyes wide as she takes in the mosaic pattern that's been paved into the ground. Broken tiles have been carefully sorted into bands of color. Red tiles line the outer ring of the clearing, bleeding seamlessly into orange, then yellow, then green then blue. A purple circle fills the center of the clearing with a ship's mast sprouting out of the middle. But instead of plastic leaves attached to the mast, this one has a long metal needle balancing on the top. Some kind of device to gauge the direction of the wind perhaps?

Having another idea, Gray turns around, counting the number of roads leading to this central area.

"Sixteen roads," he says, his eyes wide with realization. "I know what this is."

Lexis tilts her head in curiosity, waiting for him to continue.

He counts the roads again, wanting to be sure. "We're standing in the middle of a compass. This whole island is one giant compass."

"What's a compress?" Shale asks.

"Compass." Gray corrects, as he looks up to study the giant metal needle. "It tells you which direction is which."

"How does it work?" Lexis asks.

Gray points upward, his finger following the tip of the needle to the road it's pointing at. "A compass always points north."

"But this island is moving," Lexis reminds him.

"It's correcting its position," he says, certain he's right.

"Lexis." Shale's voice is shaking. "Gray. There are people..."

Gray gasps as he sees what Shale just noticed while he'd been distracted.

The Origins are emerging from their houses. A sea of people walk toward the center of the giant compass they call their home. They're blocking every possible road out, making him feel like one of the rats Trakk liked to corner in Fairbanks.

Lexis removes the metal bar from her waistband and assumes her warrior stance, even though she can't possibly fight all these people at once, and Gray tucks Shale behind his legs.

The center of this village no longer feels like an oversized navigational device.

They're standing right in the middle of a very elaborate trap.

LEXIS

Lexis tests the weight of the metal bar in her hand, jiggling it until she finds its center of balance. How many she can take out before she's incapacitated depends on the fighting ability of these Origins, but she's going to do everything she can to make sure it's a good proportion.

Even if the mass of people seems to be about ten bodies deep.

She feels the calm before a battle settle through her. Maybe she can create a path through them. If she's not surrounded, then she stands a chance.

The throng of people contract, as if they collectively just drew in a breath. They're all dressed in robes sewn from multi-colored scraps of...everything. Cloth. Plastic. Shiny pieces of metal. The flowing garments are reminiscent of the Never, just with more color. And less dirt.

Many of them squint at Lexis, Gray, and Shale, peering at them through narrowed eyes. It means they're surrounded by expressions full of threat. Lexis grips the bar. The first person to move is going to feel its wrath.

A woman steps forward, long dreadlocks hanging over her

shoulder, horns made of some sort of metal gracing her head and holding a short pole of her own. "Welcome to Treasure Island."

Lexis stills. No doubt it's a trap. Her muscles coil like springs, waiting for the demands. The bargaining. The threat that if they don't agree, they'll be killed.

The woman takes a step forward, cocking her head. "My name is Sage. I am the great-great-great granddaughter of the mighty Elijah," she announces. "And a child of Terra."

The crowd around her hums with excitement. Whispers move through the people.

"They came! Three of them!"

"Just like we prayed!"

"Terra has granted our wish!"

"We're saved!"

None of it makes sense, and that makes Lexis uncomfortable. She doesn't like being uncomfortable.

"What do you want from us?" she snaps.

Sage's eyes narrow even more and Lexis realizes it's not a threatening gesture. The woman has poor eyesight. She's trying to look at her more closely.

"Why, to share our riches. To care for you." Her nose twitches. "To bathe you."

Considering they're standing on an island of trash, the faint stench of rot hanging in the air, Lexis isn't sure that's a fair call. Although the Origins people seem to be the cleanest she's ever seen. But she's too confused by Sage's declaration to say anything.

Share? Care?

Gray steps next to her. "We're touched by your generosity," he says, giving Lexis a sidelong glance. He's asking her to stay quiet.

Sage flushes and the crowd collectively smiles. "No, we're grateful for your timely arrival."

Lexis opens her mouth to ask what the woman means by that, but Gray grips her arm, shaking his head imperceptibly. She snaps it closed, willing to admit Gray is the negotiator in their partnership. She's the protector who kills first and asks questions later.

"It's great to be here," Gray says loudly. "I'm Gray, this is Lexis and Shale."

The crowd's response is instantaneous. They throw their arms up in the air and cheer, rushing forward, shrinking the circle around them. Lexis's response is just as immediate. Snarling, she lifts her length of metal, holding it horizontally, ready to fight.

"Whoa," says Gray, extending his hands as the Origins people stop. "We just need a little space and time to get used to this."

"Of course," Sage says, blinking. She holds her arms out wide and the people move back, meaning Lexis can breathe again.

Sage turns to her people. "We'll prepare a feast!" she announces. "To welcome our gifts from Terra."

The crowd cheers, then disperses, streaming down the paths to huts and who-knows-where.

Lexis grudgingly lowers her metal bar but doesn't release it. Shale tries to shuffle around but she tucks her behind. She doesn't trust whatever's happening here. Friendliness is just as much a weapon as her pole.

A man remains behind, shoving a child forward as he whispers. "Go. Quickly."

The young boy, probably a little older than Shale, and far cleaner, sidles up next to Sage.

"Sage," he says hesitantly. "Maybe I could take them to the bathing pool while the feast is prepared?"

The woman reaches down, patting the boy's dark hair that's been twisted into countless short braids. "Ah, Atlas. Yes, that's a wonderful idea." She turns to look at Lexis and the others, squinting once again. "We'll prepare you a hut for when you return."

"Thank you," Gray says, sounding downright genuine.

Sage beams before turning and walking away, using her stick in a way Lexis has never seen before. She taps it from side to side on the path, as if she's finding her way.

"Is she worried about a rat running in front of her?" whispers Shale. "Or a baby horse?"

"I think maybe it's hard for her to see," Gray whispers back.

Lexis realizes he's noticed it, too. Sage is half-blind.

The boy shuffles closer, ducking his head. "I can show you the way, if you like."

Shale strides up to him, jamming her hands on her hips. "My name's Shale."

Atlas shrinks back. "I'm Atlas. Son of Kaj. Child of Terra."

"Your mom is the same mom as Sage's?" Shale asks, surprised.

"No," says Atlas, looking at her strangely. "We're all children of Terra."

Shale glances back at Lexis and Gray, but Gray just shakes his head again. Lexis bites her lip, unsure whether they should be waiting to get these answers.

"Food, a wash, and a good night's sleep first," he says under his breath as if he knows just what she's thinking.

She nods, seeing his logic. They need their strength before they find out the truth.

"Lead the way, Atlas," Gray says warmly. "The bathing pool sounds lovely."

Atlas flashes a brief smile before walking briskly down a path. South, judging from the angle of the tall compass not far away. At least they're not likely to get lost easily. Shale darts after him before Lexis can stop her, her hand catching nothing but air.

Gray takes it before she can decide whether she's going to

rush after the girl, weaving his fingers through hers with a grin. "This place is everything we've been looking for."

Falling into step, Lexis tries not to frown. It's true, the people are being openly friendly and generous. "There's got to be a catch."

"I think they're just excited to see new faces," says Gray. "Although maybe a few of them can't see so well."

Ahead, Shale is chattering away to Atlas, who's finally stopped flinching with every question thrown at him. The weird forest swallows them again, the leaves fluttering and making a strange hissing sound. Lexis glances over her shoulder, seeing several Origins people further up the paths. They're whispering excitedly among themselves. One or two wave, but Lexis doesn't wave back, instead almost glad for the protection of the fake forest.

If these people were hostile, she would've known what to expect. She could've followed the formula she has her whole life. But they're friendly. Excited to see them. Which leaves her without any idea of how to respond.

They round a bend and Lexis realizes they're making their way to the waterfall. The sound of crashing water greets them, the glittering pool beneath it. It's man-made, like the entire island, but the water cascading down is most definitely natural. And even Lexis can admit it's beautiful. She thinks of when she and Raze dreamed of standing beneath such a torrent of water. It hurts to think she's going to experience it and never be able to tell him.

"And they have freshwater, from the looks of things," Gray says in awe.

Atlas turns, standing at the edge of a clear blue pool. "This is where we bathe."

This is why the Origins people are so clean, despite living on a mound of trash. And they have so much water they can use some of it for bathing.

Shale peers over the edge. "The water's not red."

"That's because the bottom of the pool is blue glass," Atlas explains softly. "That's what colors the water."

"You're very smart," Shale says, looking a little wide-eyed.

Atlas flushes. "My dad said we should be friends."

Shale blinks. "Yeah, sure."

Atlas beams so hard, his smile swallows his face. He sits on the edge of the pool, dipping his feet into the water. "Terra has provided," he murmurs, almost to himself.

Shale glances at Lexis and Gray, her face clearly showing she's not sure what to do next. Gray moves to stand beside her, glancing down. "How about we go in together? Just at this shallow part? And we'll keep our clothes on. They need a wash, too."

The little girl nods eagerly, clasping Gray's hand tightly.

Lexis moves closer to them, eyes scanning the fake forest. Just as she suspected, several sets of eyes peer from behind the rusty trunks. They're still surrounded, still being watched.

Shale gingerly steps into the pool, the lapping water coming up to her calves. "Ooh, it's warm!"

Atlas grins with pleasure. "I love bathing here."

"Just take it easy," says Lexis. None of them know how to swim. Not to mention, this could be a trap.

Shale releases Gray's hand to bend over and splash the water on her face. She gasps, and it takes Lexis a moment to realize it wasn't in enjoyment. "What? What is it?"

"It's the water!" Gray hisses. "It's still acidic."

He scoops Shale up and tries to step up, only to wobble precariously because of his injured food. Lexis jumps in, helping them both out. She quickly wipes away the water from Shale's face, noticing the pinking of her skin.

"My raven note got ruined," says Shale, holding up a soggy piece of paper.

Lexis turns to Atlas, furious. "Why didn't you tell us?"

The boy shrinks back, cowering, and Gray jumps between them. "You're scaring him," he hisses to Lexis. He turns back to Atlas, crouching down. "The water's from the ocean, isn't it?"

Atlas nods, his chin tucked deep into his chest.

"But it doesn't bother you, does it?"

The boy shakes his head, peeking up from beneath his braided bangs.

Gray turns to Lexis. "They can swim in sea water," he says in wonder.

"We could swim in the ocean, but there are leatherskins there," Atlas offers timidly. "So we built this."

Gray straightens, eyebrows raised. Lexis glances at the pool, mulling this over. It seems the Origins people have evolved certain strengths.

Atlas darts around them, stopping in front of Shale as he wrings his hands. "I've displeased you? We're not friends anymore?" His voice rises in panic with each word.

Shale wipes at her face, the skin already returning to its normal, grime-streaked color. "I've never had a friend before, so I'm not really sure."

"You'll have many friends here," Atlas says solemnly.

"That sounds...weird."

"It'll be fine," he assures. "We're all children of Terra."

Shale nods, even though it's clear she has no idea what he's talking about. But it seems to be enough for Atlas because he turns and hurries down the path. "The feast is almost ready!"

At first, Lexis isn't sure how he knows, but she quickly smells what must've alerted him. Beneath the warm waft of trash is the smell of food. Meat.

The rumble of Gray's stomach tells her he's smelled it, too. He grins. "The feast is almost ready."

Shale jumps between them, clasping a hand each. "Well, what are we waiting for?"

Her own stomach cramping painfully, Lexis nods. She's not going to turn down any offer of food, especially protein. And the smell only becomes stronger as they make their way through the fake, hissing forest. By the time they exit the tree line, her mouth is watering and Shale's tugging on their arms with excitement. Gray's smile is almost as blinding as the sun they step into.

Except Lexis isn't ready to trust yet, no matter how good it smells. They were offered a bath, only to find Treasure Island isn't everything it seems. The feast could turn out the same.

Atlas runs ahead, disappearing among the people who have come out to see them. The crowd parts as Lexis, Gray and Shale make their way back to the center of the village, whispering again.

"They're beautiful."

"So healthy. And one is a child!"

"Terra has not forsaken us."

Lexis is about to ask some young woman exactly what's going on when she sees the large table set up at the base of the compass.

Roasted rats are stacked on platters, what looks like cockroaches on several others. A few apples sit on another, sliced, while a bowl of some sort of grain sits in the center.

Sage appears, waving her arm expansively over the table. "Our way to say thank you."

Before Lexis can ask for what, Shale darts forward, grabs a rat and bites into it. Her eyes roll with pleasure as she chews, her lips glistening. The crowd roars its approval.

Gray grins. "We don't want to let the people down." He takes a rat and passes it to Lexis, then picks one up for himself. Pure bliss blossoms over his face as he takes his own bite, the crowd once again cheering.

Lexis knows she should check if it's poisoned. Whether they should be accepting anything from these people. But the meat smells so good. And she can't remember the last time she had any...

The roasted rat crunches between her teeth. The flavors burst in her mouth as she chews. The sensation of something substantial in her stomach has her knees going weak. She opens her eyes to see Gray watching her, happy satisfaction lighting his beautiful features.

He's right. They have everything they need.

But can they trust the Origins? Or are they as fake as their trees and their sand?

GRACE

Grace is proud of what she and Raze have been able to achieve in such a short time.

Raze has managed to keep their campfire constantly burning. She likes the way the plume of gray smoke winds its way into the sky, marking their territory. And it's been a comfort at night when the stars haven't been enough to light their path.

It's also been handy for cooking the wild hares this island is inhabited by. They're fast and not easy to catch, but they're not quick enough for her warrior, Raze. The extra food in their bellies has given them the energy to begin work on planning out the village they intend to build while they wait for the others to arrive.

She surveys the foundations they've laid down for a large round hut they're constructing around the fire, affectionately calling it the Round House. This will make a good place to meet —somewhere they can discuss uniting the factions and sharing in the Earth's remaining spoils.

Not far away is the hut Raze built for them to sleep in. With so much timber at their disposal, it's a sturdy home with a solid roof that will be sure to keep out even the heaviest of rains. It still needs a little work, but Raze's skill with timber is impressive. Just another thing Hatch taught him that they have to be thankful for.

Grace had found a flowering bush growing in the forest and planted some offshoots near their hut's door. She looks at it now, certain they're growing already. It feels like home. Somewhere she and Raze can build a life together. Maybe they can return here after they invade Askala and live out their days. Perhaps even have a child.

"What are you thinking about?" Raze asks, catching her admiring their handiwork.

"Just how happy I am," she says. "Everything's falling into place."

He smiles, passing her a cup he made from a hollowed-out branch.

"Drink," he says. "It's rainwater."

"Did you have some?" she asks, knowing he has priors for letting her have his share.

He nods as he pats his stomach. "There are large leaves full to the brim on the beach not far from where we arrived. I'm going to make a barrel to collect it in."

She sips on the cool water, closing her eyes as she appreciates how precious this liquid is. When her eyelids flutter open, Raze is leaning in for a kiss. She presses her lips to his and lets out a small groan. Even an innocent kiss like this has the potential to become dynamite between them. Now that their passion has been unleashed, it's like she can't get enough of him. And judging by the way he's entwining his hands in her hair, it's clear he feels the same.

A branch snaps nearby, jolting them apart.

Raze leaps in front of Grace, taking the empty cup she'd only just drunk from, which is now a weapon, ready to strike.

"Who's there?" calls Raze. "Show yourself."

"It might be a hare," says Grace, her heart thumping wildly.

Raze holds up a hand to silence her. His head is tilted as he listens intently.

Holding her breath as well as her words, Grace listens, too.

Silence echoes back at them.

"Raze," Grace whispers. "It's nothing."

He shakes his head, his hand still raised.

"Well, wasn't that just the sweetest thing I ever saw," says Barnacle, stepping out from the trees. "So romantic out here. I might need to bring one of my wives over and do a bit of smooching myself."

Grace gasps, pleased that a kiss was all Barnacle witnessed. "You found us."

"Kind of a miracle, really." He runs his hand down his long beard.

"I gave you clear directions," says Grace, annoyed.

"*Sail north east.*" Barnacle rolls his eyes. "The ocean's a big place. Plenty of places north east."

Part of Grace wishes he didn't find them. She'd forgotten how irritating this guy is. But they need him. There's no way she can invade Askala and unite the factions alone.

"I've got to hand it to you though, Commander," Barnacle says, using her title. "This island is miraculous. I didn't think you had it in you but it seems I was wrong."

Grace tries to hide the smile that wants to spread across her face. Is this what it might feel like to have the respect of her people?

There's the sound of more twigs breaking, and Corbin appears beside Barnacle.

"Holy fish shackles!" He grins at Grace. "This island is awesome! How did you find this place?"

Grace pulls back her shoulders. "Hello, Corbin."

"Is it my imagination or do you look even more beautiful

when you're surrounded by trees?" His smarmy grin reaches his eyes in a way that's not at all appealing.

Raze bristles beside her, ready to defend her honor if needed.

"Leave him," she says firmly, wanting to handle this herself.

Corbin continues grinning at Grace. He hasn't even acknowledged Raze's presence yet. The guy he shares a father with. His own half-brother.

"How many of you came?" Grace asks, trying to keep this conversation on track.

"Not many," says Corbin. "We'll send for more now that we've seen this place. You've done well, Commander."

"She asked you how many." Raze drops his warrior pose but Grace knows he's still more than ready to fight.

Corbin shrugs as two more men appear beside Barnacle. "Let me see. There's the three of them. And me."

Scoria steps from the trees. "And me."

"Yeah, and her." Corbin points over his shoulder with his thumb. "She insisted on coming."

Scoria plants herself next to Corbin and tucks a possessive hand in the crook of his arm, which he immediately shakes off.

"Five was all we could fit in the boat," says Barnacle. "We're going to need to make them bigger for the invasion."

"Plenty of trees for that," one of his men mumbles, surveying the terrain.

"What's to eat?" Barnacle walks closer to their fire, where Raze has a hare cooking. "Smells like breakfast."

"They're not easy to catch," says Grace, following him. "But Raze is fast. He can trap as many as you can eat."

Barnacle looks at her and nods slowly. He knows exactly what she's doing—reminding him of why it's a good reason to keep Raze around. Even if he's a Cy.

Raze lifts the hare from the fire and lays it on a flat piece of bark. "Let it cool for a mo—"

Barnacle tears a leg from the hare and bites down. Jets of steam shoot from the corners of his mouth, but he doesn't seem to care in the slightest as he takes another bite.

His four companions crowd around for their share.

"Have you got any water?" Corbin asks between mouthfuls as he points to the empty flask hanging around his neck.

Raze shakes his head. "I can show you where to find some."

Scoria takes a bite of meat and blanches. Grace shakes her head at her ungratefulness. That was supposed to be Grace and Raze's breakfast. The least she could do is act like she's a little thankful.

"Nice hut." Barnacle tips his head toward their small home.

"Build your own," growls Raze.

"Relax," says Barnacle. "I'd never throw my Commander out of her own bed."

"We'll help you build one," adds Grace quickly. "We've been taking trees from around this clearing first. We can make a larger space for a proper camp. Once we've built your huts, we can continue work on the Round House. It will be like a meeting place for us all to use. You can see the foundations laid out here." She points, aware she's rambling to smooth things over.

"How long do you expect this all to take?" Corbin asks.

"We can't invade until we're completely ready," Grace says. "When we make our move, we have to succeed. No second chances."

"Shouldn't take more than a few moons." Barnacle licks some fat from his fingertips.

"We need to build the boats back at Rust," Grace says. "Askala knows this island exists. If we want to take them by surprise, we can't risk them finding our fleet."

Barnacle screws up his face. "Then moons will turn into orbits."

"He means years," Corbin explains. "This will take years."

"Yeah, we got that," says Raze.

"If it takes years, then it takes years." Grace nods. "What's important is that we do this right."

"How do you know so much about Askala?" Scoria asks with narrowed eyes, still not seeming to enjoy the taste of roasted hare. Maybe that's just her face. It's a little hard to tell.

"We went there," says Raze. "Not that they know it. We heard them talking about this island."

Corbin's brows shoot up. "What was Askala like?"

"Paradise," says Grace. "And if we work together, and we do this right, we can share in it, too."

The hare is merely bones now as their five new companions wipe greasy hands on tattered clothes and lick their lips. Corbin takes what's left of Scoria's share and finishes it off.

"So, where're you hiding everyone else?" asks Barnacle. "Where are Brik and Mason?"

"Yeah, where's my mom?" Corbin looks genuinely interested even though it took him this long to ask about Kallini's whereabouts.

"Brik and Mason tried to kill us," says Grace. "But they underestimated Raze. You'd be wise not to make the same mistake."

Barnacle studies Raze, his expression inscrutable. "We're all friends here."

"They killed Kallini," says Raze, looking toward Corbin.

Corbin flinches but holds steady.

"She loved you," Raze adds. "Her last words were about you. About your father…"

Grace is shocked to see Corbin smile to hear this.

"So, you know then?" Corbin asks.

Raze nods curtly. "Hello, brother."

"What in the fish shackles is going on?" Barnacle's cheeks are turning purple. "You're not saying that…Evrest…Corbin is a Cy?"

"I am *not* a Cy!" Corbin roars, seeming more upset by this than the news of his mother's death.

"Forget Cy!" Grace plants her hands on her hips. "Forget Never. Forget Fairbanks. We're Outlanders. And together we're going to put all the factions together so we can share in whatever bounty this planet has left to offer."

"The Commander has spoken," says Barnacle. "Now how about we build these huts? Not a fan of sleeping under the stars myself."

Raze nods his agreement. "If we get to work now, we should at least be able to get the frames up today."

"I need water first." Corbin pats his empty flask.

"I'll get it," says Grace, knowing she's useless next to Raze when it comes to working with wood. Besides, she needs to get away from Corbin just for a moment to clear her head. "That flask will be handy until we get a chance to build some barrels."

"I'll go with her." Scoria steps away from Corbin for the first time. "Need to talk to her about something."

Grace is surprised. So much for some time to clear her head! Scoria has made it clear in their short acquaintance that they'll never be best friends. Does she plan to threaten her to stay away from Corbin? If that's the case, she needn't waste her breath. Or is she approaching her as the Commander now that it appears her position is starting to be accepted?

Raze gives Grace some directions to where he found the rainwater this morning and tells her to be careful. She heads off, walking a little slower than she'd like with an exhausted Scoria trudging by her side.

Taking a leaf out of Raze's book, Grace lets silence hang in the air. Scoria will get to the point when she's ready.

"Listen, Grace," she eventually says. "I mean, Commander. I know we ain't always seen eye to eye, but we's the only two females around here. And I can't see that changin' for a while."

Grace nods, accepting the truth in this.

"I missed my monthly," says Scoria. "And I feel sick all the time. Tryin' hard right now not to throw up that meat."

"Oh." Now it makes sense why Scoria had reacted like that. She wasn't ungrateful for the meat. She's pregnant.

Scoria quickens her pace slightly. "Do you think I might be…"

"Yes, I think you are," says Grace, hoping this news might be enough for Corbin to finally leave her alone. "Congratulations."

"I think so, too." Scoria smiles proudly. "And I think it's a boy. He'll grow up to be just like his father."

"How…lovely." Grace pats Scoria on the back.

"I'm going to call him Raiden," says Scoria. "It means thunder, and our boy's going to enter the world just like a powerful storm."

"Girls can be powerful, too," Grace points out. "That name might work for a girl as well."

But Scoria shakes her head. "Corbin said he's always wanted a daughter called Charity. He said she'll be his gift to the world."

"So, he knows about this?" Grace is surprised. Scoria had only just seemed to have worked it out for herself.

"Not yet. But we've talked about having a family." Scoria bristles. "I know he jokes around but we're serious about each other. He loves me."

Grace isn't sure what to say to this new side of Scoria she's seeing.

"If you could keep away from him, that would be good." Scoria's voice hardens.

Grace opens her mouth to say that she'd be only too glad to oblige when the sounds of deep voices echo from the beach. She puts out a hand to stop Scoria.

"Quiet," she hisses. "Someone's here."

"That's not Corbin or Barnacle," Scoria whispers, fear creeping across her face. "Do you think it's Askala?"

"Wait here." Grace stalks forward, treading lightly so as not to make a sound.

She reaches the edge of the tree line and peers out, but the sun is in her eyes and she can't get a clear view of who's arrived.

Pulling back a little, she shields her face with her hand, and the figures on the beach come into focus.

Her jaw falls open in shock just as a blinding pain crashes over the back of her head and all her senses are swallowed up by a vortex of black.

RAZE

$\mathcal{R}$aze is on edge from the moment Grace leaves to collect water. It means the instant he hears Scoria's scream, he's running before it's a conscious choice. Branches whip his body and twigs crack loudly as he powers through the forest, cursing the obstacle course between him and Grace.

He sees the tree line ahead, his heart launching to his throat when he registers several men and women there, Scoria among them.

Grace isn't.

He snaps off a branch as he leaps over a log, knowing it's not much of a weapon, but a weapon, nonetheless. The warriors hear him coming, just like he knew they would—he's not trying to hide his approach. Raze quickly registers they're carrying clubs, along with their hardened features and clothes that far more resemble armor.

Cragg.

Scoria leaps in front of him, her hands outstretched. "There's been a mistake!"

Raze realizes the faction of the mountains have arrived just like the Rust did. He lowers the branch and slows. Then he sees Grace sprawled on the ground.

He roars, once more ready to attack. The Cragg haven't accepted Grace as their Commander. That will be their death sentence.

Scoria must see the intent on Raze's face because her features twist with panic. "No, they didn't mean it. Stop!" She turns to her people. "Step away, he just wants ta check on her."

The Cragg warriors, both men and women—although it's hard to tell the difference—do as Scoria says. Grace moans, rolling over and bringing her hand to the back of her head.

Raze falls to her side. "They hurt you," he growls. One word from her and they're all dead.

Grace looks around. "The Cragg came," she whispers.

"And we didn't mean no harm," says one of them. He takes a step forward only to quickly retreat as Raze glares at him. "We was all worked up with all these trees everywhere."

Raze blinks, not liking that he has something in common with the Cragg. The forest is definitely unsettling.

Grace tries to get to her feet and Raze helps her. "Why are you here?" she asks, a hard edge in her voice.

"We got ya note," the man says earnestly. "We came to git them people from Askala."

There are sounds through the trees and Barnacle, Corbin and the others appear, eyes narrowing as they see there are visitors. The Cragg warriors contract together, clearly going on the defensive.

Grace releases Raze's arm. "Welcome, fellow people of the Outlands," she says in a strong voice. "Thank you for answering my call."

The Cragg look at Grace, one scratching his stomach as they wait.

Grace straightens her spine. "Together, we are stronger. Together, we will be the might to defeat Askala."

Barnacle nods, Corbin following, as Scoria throws her fist in the air, her cry startling a bird or two. The Cragg glance at each other, their own nods slowly moving among them.

They came here to unite with the other factions. They came here to acknowledge their new Commander.

Grace glances at Raze, her face serious but he can see the glint of triumph deep in her dark eyes. "Now, all we're waiting for are the Never."

"The Never ain't comin," says one of the Cragg. "We passed one of their camps. Everyone had been killed. I don't think there's many of 'em left."

"There ain't *any* of 'em left," mutters another man beside him.

A chill slides down Raze's spine. The Cy must have attacked the Never, just like they did the Rust. His father's thirst for power and vengeance is still very much alive.

"Then it's good we found the Newlands," Grace says firmly. "This will be where we'll prepare, away from those who want to tear our unity apart."

The others glance at each other, looking thoughtful. Raze nods, showing his support, even as he considers Grace's words. They've decided they need to build the boats back in the Outlands. It means Evrest will have to be taken care of. Otherwise, he's a threat that will always hang over them.

"We're building huts," says Barnacle, straightening. "We will have a village."

"And there's hare to eat and water to drink," adds Corbin, patting his stomach.

"And more than enough wood to build a fleet to attack Askala," says Raze. He glances at Grace. "We should also train. Prepare to fight."

She mulls over his words. Hopefully she's considering that all these warriors have never fought on the same side. They all have strengths, but distrust and division will be their weaknesses.

Grace turns to the others. "We'll allocate two hours a day to training. Raze will coordinate and oversee the sessions."

There's a low grumble from the Cragg—no, the other Outlanders—as Barnacle and Corbin shift a little, their gazes flickering to Raze then quickly away. But no one objects, which is a testament to Grace's new status. They're willing to work with a Cy because the Commander has directed it.

It has hope fluttering in Raze's chest. A fragile butterfly, but a living, moving creature, nonetheless. They've found an island with all the resources they need. The Outlanders are willing to work together.

It's only a matter of time before Askala is theirs.

"Let's get back," says Grace. "There's work to be done."

People start making their way into the forest, and Raze waits beside her, deciding he's going to be her shadow for a little while longer. If anything happens to Grace, not only is his own life no longer worth living, but everything will be forfeit. Without a Commander, the Outlanders will fracture all over again.

He glances over his shoulder at the rusty sea, sending a promise to Askala. He will do whatever it takes to ensure Grace succeeds. And one day, he will stand on Askala's shores, with her beside him.

He's just about to look away when something catches his attention. A flicker of light, like the sun sparkling on the ocean. Most likely nothing. Light doesn't glance off rafts. But Raze double checks anyway.

And loses the ability to breathe.

The light didn't glance off a raft, although one appears several agonizing, airless seconds later. Then another. And another.

The statue of Cy stands proudly on the one in the center, the biggest one. It would have to be to support the weight of the silver-plated figure.

"Grace," Raze chokes through a tight throat.

She's by his side in an instant, no doubt having heard the alarm in his voice. "What? What is it?"

He knows when she sees it, too. She freezes. She gasps. She clutches his hand. "The Cy are here," she breathes.

Evrest has come to exact his revenge. To lay claim to everything they've built.

"Warriors of the Outlands!" she calls back into the forest. "We're under attack!"

Barnacle, Corbin, the Rust, and the Cragg come rushing back. They stand behind the tree line, staring as the figures on the sea steadily gain form.

The leaves above them flutter in the breeze, the agitated sound echoing that of the people below. Raze has no doubt Barnacle and the others know what they're up against.

They have no arrows. No spears. Nor was there any time to learn to fight as a united army.

The Cy have every one of those advantages.

Grace braces her hand against a tree trunk. "Hide yourselves. We'll use the element of surprise."

Everyone slips behind a tree, tension weaving through the forest. The rafts are now close enough to see the statue clearly, the six men on the rafts around it, and Evrest standing at the front.

A tremor shudders through Raze, but it's not fear. He stopped being scared of his father the moment he stabbed his own son. The moment he turned his back on his own daughter.

It's hatred.

Grace's hand settles on his arm and he covers it with his own, not taking his eyes off the approaching enemy. No matter what, they'll fight. This will be their baptism by blood.

And it will involve bloodshed, Raze has no doubt.

The rafts scrape over sand and the Cy warriors leap out to drag them further up, grunting at the weight of the statue. Evrest remains where he is, scanning the island with narrowed eyes. His gaze doesn't settle on any one point.

"He ain't seen us," whispers Barnacle.

Good. It's the one advantage they have. Although they outnumber them, every Cy warrior is worth at least two Rust or Cragg. The Tournaments proved it.

Once his raft has lodged on the beach, Evrest steps off. Sunlight strokes his scars, creating an ominous network of shadows over his face as he surveys the Newlands. He opens his arms wide as he breathes in deeply, as if he's the new lord and master. Raze's hands tighten into fists, his nails digging into his palm so hard it hurts.

Evrest's men spread out behind him, the rafts out of the water enough that they won't wash away. Everyone hiding amongst the trees holds still, waiting for the command. Once Evrest and the others are close enough, they'll attack.

Evrest stalks up the beach, his lip curling. His men's weapons are sheathed. Spears. Knives. One has a sword. And Evrest is empty-handed, but he likes it that way. It shows his confidence that he can kill with his own bare hands.

Good. That arrogance is what will have him killed.

Raze glances around. The Cragg have their clubs, the Rusts have knives, but he and Grace will have to use sticks or branches. He'll make sure no one gets close to her.

Evrest pauses halfway to the tree line. He glances down, his eyes trailing over where sand meets soil. He lifts his hand and his men stop as Raze realizes what his father is looking at.

Footprints coming down the beach and heading to the trees. Probably the Cragg's arrival. A sure sign someone has been here recently.

Evrest's lips twist into a smile, his gaze rising to the trees. He knows they're here. They've lost the element of surprise.

"Thank you for the invite, Outlanders," he calls out. "I received the note."

Someone stifles a gasp while Scoria whimpers.

"Come out and greet your Commander," he orders, a hard edge entering his voice. "We have work to do."

Raze's heart is thudding against his chest. They have very little chance of winning this. They'll be running into a blood-bath. Their own.

And Evrest will target Grace first.

Raze won't let that happen. Which means there's only one thing to do.

He steps around the tree trunk and strides toward the beach.

"Raze, no!" Grace hisses.

But it's too late. Evrest has seen him. His father's eyes blaze as he watches Raze walk toward him, stopping when there are several feet between them.

"You're not welcome here, Evrest," Raze calls out.

"Ah, he talks." His father studies him. "If I had known a blade to the back would get you speaking, I would've done it years ago."

Raze's scar flashes with heat but he ignores it. "Leave."

Evrest's nostrils flare. "I liked it better when you were silent." He looks up, facing the trees. "Join me, Outlanders. I will lead you to victory against Askala."

Which is exactly what Raze knew his father would do. Try to turn the Outlanders against Grace. Either before or after he kills her, Evrest won't care.

The only solution is for Evrest to die first.

"I challenge you, Evrest," Raze calls out, keeping his voice strong. "Winner elects the Commander."

There's a faint gasp from the trees behind Raze and it slices through him like lightning. He wishes he could have kissed Grace one more time. It's a given this will be a fight to the death. He just has to make sure it's his father's.

"With pleasure," Evrest growls, bloodlust flaring in his eyes.

Evrest rolls his shoulders as he walks forward. Raze steps to the side, and they begin a slow circle, sizing each other up. Father and son born of the same faction. Yet, two people far more fractured by hate than anyone in the Outlands.

That hatred pumps through Raze's veins like venom, demanding an outlet. Baying for blood. He steps slowly left, watching his father, waiting. Welcoming what's to come. This is the Tournament that will decide everything.

Evrest bares his teeth in a twisted parody of a smile as he reaches behind him and pulls out a knife. He twists it in his hand, letting the smooth metal catch the light. Raze doesn't bother to comment on it even as his pulse spikes. Fair is equated with weak in Evrest's mind.

"It's time to finish this," Evrest growls, leaping into action.

He runs at Raze, widening his eyes so the whites flash his thirst for violence. Raze vaults into motion, too, determined to meet him. Evrest slashes the knife the moment Raze is within reach, but Raze was expecting it. He twists, then maintaining momentum, spins past and shoves Evrest in the process.

His father stumbles, rights himself and turns back to Raze, snarling. He runs at him again, this time raising the knife high. Raze blocks it, his forearm crashing against his father's, then blocks the slash that aims for his abdomen. He powers a fist into his father's face, satisfaction bursting with the crunch of cartilage.

Evrest roars as he reels backward, spitting away the blood that trickles into his mouth. Raze narrows his eyes, communicating without words as he did most of his life.

You trained me to kill.

His father feints right but Raze moves left, predicting his father's angry slash of the knife.

And I know all your moves.

They circle again, and Raze sees that the Outlanders have

come out. Grace stands among them, her hand to her throat, her eyes pleading, no doubt for him to finish this.

He launches at Evrest, unleashing a volley of strikes, kicks, punches, using every memory of this man hurting him to power them. Evrest blocks most of them, but some get through his defenses. A fist powers into his father's solar plexus, an elbow to his jaw, a knee to his thigh.

But Evrest finds every opportunity to get his own blows in. Each one an explosive bruise or instant swelling. But even when the knife slashes Raze's arm, he hardly feels the pain. Within seconds, blood makes their strikes slick as it smears across their skin.

They separate again, panting. They're too evenly matched. It's obvious this will be a war of attrition, but Raze is determined he's the one who will walk away, bloodied but victorious.

The next clash is another barrage. Raze maiming his father. Evrest slashing with his knife, trying to slice his son. Raze gets in close, knowing he's nearer to the blade, but also giving Evrest less ability to make wide arcs with the deadly weapon. He twists and grabs, putting his father's arm in a lock as he kicks backward. His father yanks his hand back, trying to create distance between them, but the knife he's holding blocks his ability to withdraw, just as Raze expected. He kicks back again, putting all this strength into it as it connects with his chest.

But then his father releases the blade. His arm slips out, he drops to the ground and catches the knife before it hits the sand. A quick swipe of his leg across the back of Raze's knees and Raze is knocked to the ground.

He's just pressed his hands to the ground to push up when Evrest is above him, holding the knife high above his head. "You may know my moves, but a good fighter never gives away all his tricks," he snarls in triumph.

Raze powers his fist up into his father's jaw, hitting it so hard his teeth click. Evrest falls to the side, and Raze leaps on him, grabbing the knife from his limp hand. He presses it to his father's throat as his head lolls, barely conscious.

"A good fighter never assumes," Raze growls back.

Evrest assumed Raze would accept his fate. That he'd let Evrest kill him like he was trained to do with Lexis. But Raze has something to fight for now. A reason to live.

And a father he hates even more than that.

He raises the knife high, anticipating the flush of victory that will come with impaling it in his father's neck. The death will be fast, far more than Evrest deserves, but watching his blood gush onto the sand will be cleansing. It will purge his evil from his life.

Raze roars as he brings the knife down, seeing the knowledge of his impending death twist across his father's features. Death at the hand of his own son.

Grace's pleading eyes flash before Raze. Begging him.

And he realizes what she was trying to communicate.

He impales the knife to the hilt, victory exploding through his muscles. Nothing has ever felt so right. The crunch of metal through sand sends satisfaction shooting up his arm. Evrest turns to look at the knife skewered beside his head, then looks back at Raze, stunned.

Raze pushes to his feet, wiping away the blood trickling into his eyes. He's not his father.

He's not a killer by choice.

He turns to face the Outlanders. "Grace, our true Commander, rules with mercy and compassion. That is what the Outlands will stand for."

Except they're surrounded by Cy, each brandishing their deadly weapon. Before Raze can point out their leader has lost, pain punctures through his calf. He falls to his knees with a cry, hand reaching down and discovering the knife impaled in his muscles.

And then it's being yanked out, searing agony screaming up

his spine. Raze tries to stumble to his feet, but he's grabbed from behind, the knife now against his throat.

"You were always too weak," his father growls into his ear.

Raze freezes as the blade nicks his neck. His gaze latches onto Grace across the beach, her own agony reflecting his.

He's failed.

"Swear allegiance to your new Commander," Evrest half-snarls, half-shouts, making sure everyone can hear.

"Never," Raze spits.

He knows he's choosing death, but there's no other option. He will never align with his father again. Ever.

The blade pushes further into his skin and a warm bead of blood trickles down his throat. Raze closes his eyes, determined to do this with as much dignity as he can.

But then it's gone and he's pushed forward, face first into the sand.

"You will all swear your allegiance to me," Evrest shouts to the Outlanders. "Or every last one of you will die"

GRAY

"This place is amazing,' says Gray, stroking Lexis's forehead in the early morning light.

Shale is snoring softly beside them in the small hut the Origins allocated them. Lexis is awake but pretending not to be, so he continues talking, certain she can hear him.

"First, we have each other. Second, we have our very own home. Third, we have full stomachs. And fourth, we are completely safe." Excitement floods his soul as he feels the truth in these words. They actually did it! Not only did they find Treasure Island but it turned out to be everything they could have hoped for and more.

Lexis's eyes open. She seems to be trying to decide if she's going to argue with him or go with his outlook on the very fortunate situation they've found themselves in.

"Maybe it was our turn for some luck," she says.

He leans forward and kisses her, pleased she decided to focus on the positives.

Her lips respond under his and he deepens the kiss, wishing for one selfish moment that Shale wasn't here. He's going to combust if he doesn't feel Lexis's bare skin pressed against his soon.

There's a gentle tapping on the tin wall of their hut right beside where Shale's sleeping.

Lexis and Gray pull apart and sit up to listen. That sounded a little louder than the light footsteps of the rats that had scurried over their thin roof at night.

The noise comes again.

Lexis dives out the door before Gray can even react. She returns moments later, dragging a petrified Atlas by the plastic collar of his shirt.

"I just wanted to p-p-lay with Shale!" he stammers. "Let me go!"

Gray puts a steadying hand on Lexis's arm and she releases Atlas.

Shale is awake now, and she stands beside Atlas, tilting her head as she looks at him.

"Lexis means well," she explains. "She's not scary at all once you get to know her."

Atlas shoots Lexis an uncertain glance as he nods. "My dad thought it would be good to visit you now, but I can come back later."

"Now's good," says Gray quickly, memories of the feeling of Lexis's hands on him punching desire into his gut. "Why don't you see if you can find Shale something to eat for breakfast?"

Shale rubs her stomach and grins. "I've never had breakfast before."

"Let's go then!" Atlas is already at the door, just as keen to get away from Lexis as Gray is to get close to her.

"Yes, off you go." Gray makes a shooing motion. "Have fun!"

The door closes behind them and Gray practically melts into Lexis as he wraps his arms around her, wasting no time in trailing gentle kisses across her jawline.

"We found home," he murmurs. "We're safe."

In the Outlands they'd barely been able to sleep without watching out for an enemy. But here... here they finally have the chance to be themselves. Even if there's still a need to be fast, at least that's only due to the fear of being walked in on by a child, rather than being stabbed in the back.

Lexis pushes Gray back down to their sleeping mat. He thinks his foot might hurt a little as he sprawls onto his back and Lexis climbs on top of him, but it's hard to tell. There are too many delicious feelings surging through his body, overpowering every negative feeling or thought he's ever had.

Lexis kisses him.

Hard.

He strains his neck as he tries to drink in more of the sweet taste of her, his fingers entwining in her hair as he pulls her closer.

She resists and at first he thinks she's changed her mind, but when she undoes her bodice and throws it aside, revealing curves even lusher than he remembered, he realizes she's right here with him.

Every. Step. Of. The. Way.

Yanking his shirt over his head, then sliding down his trousers, it takes only moments for them to be completely bare, and his earlier wish of skin against skin is right here. And it's even softer and more incredible than he remembered.

"I'm addicted to you," he breathes, as she connects them in an even more intimate way.

Except, even as his addiction is being fed, he knows it will never be enough to sate his desire for this wild warrior girl.

They make love urgently, knowing their privacy could be ruptured at any minute. So, instead of stretching out the pleasure like Gray had the first time they were together, he concentrates on taking in every moment and locking the memory into the deepest parts of his mind. Forget food and water, this is what he needs to sustain him.

"Lexis!" he breathes when he feels her giving into the pleasure. He joins her and soon it's her calling out his name, and their world shatters and reforms to form something impossibly more beautiful than it was before.

Lexis lets out a long sigh then a soft giggle—a noise that's as unlike Lexis as being caught in a dense forest of trees. He enjoys this moment of bliss, thrilled that today is merely the start of many more days exactly like this. A simple life amongst these generous people who've welcomed them as their own. They can watch Shale grow, have children of their own, live to grow old...

He used to joke with Winter about the idea of living long enough for his hair to match his name. Maybe this is no longer a joke. Maybe he has decades left with Lexis, not years or months or days. Maybe in the future they might even get to take more time...

He can barely believe this good luck that Lexis had said it was their turn to have.

There's a noise outside the hut and Lexis scrambles off Gray and they dress almost as quickly as they'd removed their clothes. Their hut may have a door, but it most definitely doesn't have a lock.

Sure enough, the door creaks open and Shale returns, holding a bunch of small round purple fruits.

"They're called grapes," she tells them proudly. "Atlas's mom gave them to me."

"Where is Atlas?" asks Lexis, subtly retying her bodice. Her cheeks are flushed and Gray can only hope that Shale is too distracted by her grapes to notice.

"Atlas!" Shale calls. "I told you to get in here! Now!"

Gray's eyes widen. "Shale, speak nicely. It's not polite to be a boss."

Shale looks at Lexis, goes to say something, then changes her mind when Atlas appears at the door. He steps inside, choosing to stand on the side of the hut furthest away from Lexis.

Gray props open the door to let in some light and Shale offers him some grapes.

He puts one in his mouth and bites down. Intense sweetness floods his mouth and he immediately takes another one.

"This is the best thing I've eaten in my entire life," he declares.

Lexis rolls her eyes then takes one. A strange look of pleasure crosses her face, not all that dissimilar to the one he'd seen only minutes before.

"They're sooo good." Shale pops three in her mouth at once, making her cheeks bulge.

"Why are your people being so nice to us?" Lexis takes a step closer to Atlas. "What do you want from us?"

"Lexis," says Gray, shooting Atlas a reassuring smile. "People don't always want something in return for their kindness. Sometimes people are just nice."

"Not where I come from." Lexis sneers.

"You must come from somewhere awful," says Atlas, doing his best to stand tall. "Lucky you can't go back there."

"Can't? Why can't we?" Lexis takes another step. "We're not prisoners here. Are we?"

Atlas visibly swallows. "They broke up your raft. They needed it to cook the rats for the feast. We don't have a lot of spare wood around here."

Lexis's fists clench at her side and Gray puts a hand on her back, easing her away from the boy.

"That wasn't yours to destroy," she says through gritted teeth.

"The children of Terra don't have *yours* and *ours*," says Atlas. "We share. That's why you have this hut. And the grapes. We share what we have."

"We don't need the raft," Gray reminds her. "This is our home now. It's okay."

257

"Who's Terra anyway?" Shale asks, her cheeks still bulging with grapes. "She sure had a lot of kids."

"Terra is Mother Earth," says Atlas. "Everything we have is thanks to her. The sun to grow our fruits, the rain to feed our crops, the air to fill our lungs. It's all her taking care of her children."

Gray nods his head in understanding. "You worship Mother Earth."

"We need to show thanks," says Atlas. "At sunrise and sunset we meet at the Oasis, then we walk to the altar and give thanks to Terra for all her gifts."

"The Oasis?" asks Lexis. "What's that?"

"I know this one!" says Shale, jiggling. "That's what you call the circle place with all the rainbow tiles on the ground."

Atlas nods. "We're letting you rest today, but tomorrow my dad says you'll be expected to worship with us."

Lexis frowns. "We don't—"

"We'd love to," Gray finishes.

"Oasis is a funny name," says Shale.

Gray takes another grape, deciding he really needs to have a proper talk with Shale about manners.

"It was the name written on the side of the big ship," says Atlas. "It came to the Origins when Elijah took all the young people away. Those who remained decided to create an Oasis of our own. We can have nice things, too."

"Elijah was the name Sage used yesterday." Lexis narrows her eyes. "She said she was his granddaughter."

"Great-great-great granddaughter," corrects Atlas. "The Oasis came a long time ago."

"And where did Elijah take your young people?" Lexis asks.

Atlas shrugs. "To find a new world. One that doesn't float."

"And did they?" asks Shale. "The world we come from doesn't float."

"I don't know," Atlas whispers. "My dad says they're dead.

We're the lucky ones who stayed behind. We have our own Oasis now. And my mom thinks I might keep my eyes. Dad doesn't though…"

Gray glances at Lexis who seems just as perplexed by this last comment.

"Keep your eyes?" Shale is aghast as she holds out her foot. "The Never already took my toe. You're not taking my eyes."

Atlas reels back in horror at the sight of Shale's missing toe. Clearly he only just noticed it.

"He doesn't mean actually taking your eyes," soothes Gray, thinking he may have figured out what Atlas is trying to say. "He means his mom thinks he'll keep his eyesight when he gets older."

Atlas nods. "The Origins don't see so good. When the young people left, our skin grew tough but our eyes grew bad. That's why we need y—"

Lexis shoots Gray a glare. "I told you they wanted something. Nobody is this nice for nothing."

"What do they want?" Shale chews on her grapes with an open mouth. "Because they're not having my eyes."

Atlas takes a step toward the door. "I have to go."

"I don't think so." Lexis grabs him by the collar once more. It makes a crinkling sound under her grip.

"He's just a kid," Gray reminds her.

"Yeah, an honest one," says Lexis. "Which is more than we can say for anyone else around here. We need him to talk."

"I have to go!" Atlas wails, the braids of his hair seeming to tremble along with his legs.

"Why does your dad want you to be friends with Shale?" Lexis shakes him as if trying to dislodge the words from this throat.

Atlas winces. "He wants to mix the blood."

Shale takes two steps back, slamming into Gray's legs. He puts a protective arm around her.

"Shale is too young to mix blood." Lexis doesn't loosen her grip on the boy.

"Not now," squeaks Atlas. "When she's old enough. He wants us to mix blood so his grandchildren can be strong. I'm not sure what that means."

Lexis lets go of the frightened boy. "You keep away from Shale, you hear me?"

He nods, his feet seeming to want to run, but somehow staying planted on the floor. Tears stream down his face. "I'm scared of blood. I don't want to do any mixing."

"You're not having my blood," says Shale.

"It's okay," Gray squeezes her. "Nobody is going to take anyone's blood. That's not what his father means."

"Nobody is going to do any of what his father means." Lexis plants her hands on her hips. "Not now and not ever."

"But you have to," pleads Atlas. "Not Shale. Not yet. But you. And him." Atlas points a quivering hand at Gray. "My father says you're both old enough. They're talking about finding you mates."

A deep flush rises in Gray's cheeks as he realizes it wasn't their turn in life for some luck. How foolish he was to think that maybe they'd found somewhere safe to grow old.

The reason they'd been embraced so generously on this island wasn't out of any kind heartedness. These people want something from them.

Their bloodlines. Not together, but separately.

And that's the one thing they can't possibly give.

LEXIS

*L*exis storms out of the hut, fury flashing through her. She knew it! These Origins people were manipulating them!

She stops almost straight away as someone shuffles past, carrying a basket woven from wire and colorful strips of trash. The man smiles at Lexis and she snarls back. Their smiles are nothing but cunning ploys to get their defenses down.

So the Origins can share their blood.

Disgust shudders through her. They want to mate with them? The thought of doing that with anyone but Gray makes her stomach roll and bile sting her tongue.

And if they try to force her. Or Shale. Or even Gray...

"Lexis!" Gray calls, shooting out of the hut after her. He stops, surprised to see she's just outside. "Phew. I thought you might have..."

"Killed every one of them?" Lexis mutters, reflecting that she's gone soft. The old Lexis would've ended that man before he could smile at her, just so the Origins people realized what they'd trapped on their island.

Gray's face twists. "I'm sorry. I think I wanted this so much that I overlooked the warning signs."

Lexis's heart clenches. After losing so much, finding a home is all they've wanted. "It's okay. You were right, we needed to give them a chance."

And they've shown their true colors.

She picks up the pole she tucked in the garden beside their hut. It was actually easy to hide considering the flowers and shrubs were made of metal themselves. In fact, all she has to do is wrap some wire around it and tie a few strips of plastic and it will pass as a small tree.

Lexis looks around with new eyes. She's surrounded by weapons. She can keep Gray and Shale safe.

Now, she has to find a way off this trash island.

Shale comes out of the hut, Atlas right behind her. Lexis bristles at the way he's standing so close to her. No wonder his father was so keen for him to make friends with her.

"Atlas and I talked," Shale announces. "We'll swap blood when we're older."

Gray coughs out a choke. "Ah, Shale—"

"No," she says resolutely. "It's what children of Terra do."

Horror has Lexis freezing. They've been here a day and already these people are brainwashing the little girl.

The sound of tapping comes from Lexis's right and she spins to find Sage walking toward them, using her stick. The older woman smiles as she holds out her hand, revealing several pieces of flatbread, what looks like rat meat sandwiched in between. "Here. We break bread at the dawn worship, so I thought I'd bring you some."

Lexis almost knocks the food away. It suddenly feels like everything they take, they're promising another part of them away. Except, she doesn't move. Her stomach clenches, the energy flush of the sweet grapes already gone. They need their strength to escape.

She takes a piece, and her gaze follows Gray as he does the same. She likes watching him eat. There's something primal in seeing the bliss roll over his face. In knowing his body is receiving what it needs to continue surviving. Food means he, they, have a future.

Shale grins with her mouth full. "This is almost as good as the grapes."

Lexis acknowledges it's nice to see Shale eat, too. She's been through so much loss, so much has been taken from her, that the smiling, chewing face before her tugs at Lexis's chest. Her mouth twists. She really is going soft.

Sage smiles again. "I thought we might take a tour of the island," she says warmly. "So you can get to know your new home."

Gray subtly moves in front of Lexis, probably sensing the fury that just exploded inside her. "We know why you're being so nice."

Sage looks at him quizzically. "You understand we're all children of Terra? That what's ours is yours?"

"Yay!" calls Shale. "This is all ours, too!"

Lexis scowls at her. Her young mind doesn't understand what price this food and shelter involves.

She turns her glower to Sage. "No. You need fresh...genes."

The woman's face becomes subdued. "I see." She pulls up a smile as she glances at the two children. "Atlas, why don't you take Shale to the classroom? I believe they're learning letters this morning."

Lexis's hand shoots out to grab Shale's. "No."

The little girl stills, clearly torn. "But I might make more friends."

Which is exactly what Lexis is worried about. Friends. How many of them will be expected to be future mates?

"She'll be safe," Sage says, her voice low, as if it's weighed down by all the layers of meaning attached to it.

Gray glances at Lexis. "Let her go." He shifts a little closer. "Maybe the tour is a good idea."

Grudgingly, she releases Shale's hand. Gray's right. A tour will give them an idea of how to get off this awful island.

Shale skips away before Lexis changes her mind, Atlas scampering after her. It quickly morphs into a game of tag, their giggles lighting the air.

Lexis looks away. Shale is...happy.

"Come," says Sage. "Let me show you Treasure Island."

Gray takes Lexis's hand and squeezes. They fall behind Sage as she starts down the path, her stick tapping from one side to the other.

"How well can you see, Sage?" Gray asks quietly.

Sage glances over her shoulder. "Quite well considering my age. Many of us are blind by now, and although we care for them, their will to live tends to, ah, fade."

"They die," Lexis points out.

"Yes," says Sage, wincing. "They return to Terra."

They make their way to the forest of metal and trash, the plastic leaves rustling and hissing in the breeze. "So, can you see the trees?" Lexis asks.

"I can see outlines. Shapes. The rest I craft with my memory."

"And that's why you need us," Lexis says bitterly. Because the inbred people of this island are slowly going extinct.

"That's why we prayed for you." Sage smiles. "And you came."

Gray shakes his head. "We were brought here by currents. We didn't come here to save you."

By breeding with anyone who's willing.

"You were brought here by Terra," Sage says contentedly. "It was meant to be."

Lexis grits her teeth so she doesn't snap out that they have no intention of staying. All they need to do is build another raft. Somehow...

They pass the blue pool where several people are splashing and laughing. They wave animatedly at the three of them. Sage waves back but all Lexis wants to do is throw something at them.

Gray's hand tightens around hers and he tugs her along. "It's amazing they can be in there," Gray murmurs.

"Our skin has developed the ability to withstand the acidity. The ability to stay clean has helped prevent many illnesses," Sage says over her shoulder, putting Lexis's teeth once more on edge.

All the advantages of Treasure Island are being put on display.

They continue down the path. It curves, as if creating a large loop that will eventually bring them back to the village. More man-made trees line the sides, twisted in artful angles. Here, grass a foot or two high has been crafted from thousands of shards of plastic in every color imaginable. A rat scurries onto the path, sees it has company, and scoots back in. Several squeaks carry through the artificial grassland, indicating it's far from the only one in there.

"It creates a home for the rats," explains Sage. "They breed, becoming food for us."

No wonder the Origin people look so well fed. They've ensured an endless supply of protein for themselves.

Lexis turns her head away, not wanting to see it anymore. She always thought she'd do anything to have meat in her stomach. She never bothered to imagine what it's like to be clean. But giving up Gray so he can be with someone else isn't something she's willing to do.

Not ever.

Remembering why she's on this tour, Lexis takes another look around. But every tree and shrub is metal. Every piece of plastic was either already small and fractured, or the Origins people broke it up.

There's nothing here they could use to build a raft. There's no way to escape.

Sage continues, the curve continuing until they're heading back in the direction they came, but now on the other side of the village. Suddenly, she stops, spinning to face them. "We are good people," she says earnestly. "We will treat you well."

The anger is back in a hot flush but Gray quickly responds before Lexis can let Sage know exactly what she thinks of the bribe she's fashioned this entire island into.

He shakes his head. "We can see that. But what you ask of us…" He shifts closer to Lexis. "We can't agree to that."

Sage waves her arm out to the red sea in the distance. "Your children could swim in the ocean."

"No," snaps Lexis.

"You could pick who your mates would be," Sage offers gently.

"No."

Sage's hand tightens around her stick. "There's no rush. You're welcome to wait until you're ready."

"No."

"Shale won't have to consider this until she's of age."

Lexis takes a step toward the woman, expanding herself. "No. No. No." She bites off each word through gritted teeth, glaring at the woman as she hopes she's close enough for her to see the fierceness that's burning through her.

She and Gray have been through too much. Lost too much. Found love when Lexis wasn't sure it existed anymore.

The thought of breeding with others makes her physically ill.

Sadness drags at Sage's face as she takes a step back. She sighs. "Terra works in mysterious ways," she murmurs, almost as if she's reassuring herself. She glances at Lexis and Gray. "And you have time to think about it."

Because they're trapped here. Lexis suspects they burned the raft to ensure exactly that.

Sage turns and resumes walking. Lexis and Gray glance at each other, and she sees the same conviction in his eyes that's a hot, hard core in her gut.

The price is too high. They can't stay, no matter how much food and shelter are being promised them.

"Ahead is where we worship Terra every day at dawn and dusk," Sage explains, a warmth creeping into her voice along with her usual calmness. She sighs. "We have so much to be thankful for."

Gray winds his fingers through Lexis's and she sees he's staring straight ahead. She follows his line of sight.

And has to stop herself from gasping.

Ahead is the altar of the Origins people, and it seems Lexis and Gray also have much to be thankful for.

It's exactly what they need to get off this island.

GRACE

"*I*'ll say it one more time," Evrest sneers to the crowd. "Swear your allegiance to me. Or die. What's it going to be?"

Raze lifts his head from the sand and looks at Grace, pleading with her to stay alive, even though he knows as well as she does that they can't allow this pathetic excuse of a human to lead them as Commander. But right now, he's not giving them a lot of choice. This is a man who rules by fear. And if he's prepared to treat his own son in the way they just witnessed then nobody on this island has to question how he might treat them.

Barnacle steps forward, momentarily blocking Grace's view of Raze.

"Commander," he mutters to Evrest, bowing his head. It's clear he's not especially thrilled with this development, but he hasn't survived a life in the Outlands by being a fool. He knows when a choice is not really a choice.

His men follow, and Grace grits her teeth to see how flimsy their loyalty to her was. How dare Evrest respond to *her* note, come to the island that *she* found and take *her* men. Although, all of that is preferable to the thought of him killing Raze. At least their fight to the death hadn't resulted in any actual death. Not that she'd complain about Evrest ceasing to breathe right now...

She hates to admit it, but she now wishes Raze had killed his father while he'd had the chance. His death is the only possible way they can move forward. He's evil to the bone—a man who was born to divide, not unite. But Raze had shown him mercy because no matter how he was raised, the goodness in his heart is impossible to extinguish. In Evrest's case, Grace doubts there was ever any goodness there to begin with.

The Cy warriors fix their eyes on the Cragg next, waiting for them to make their choice. They, at least, seem more reluctant than the Rust, but eventually they move to stand behind Evrest. A woman with curly hair shoots Grace an apologetic look. It's clear who she'd rather call her Commander.

Grace gives her a curt nod. She understands. And she's witnessed enough death to not want to see Evrest snuff out this woman's life, too.

"Scoria," the woman pleads, extending her hand.

But Scoria stands steadfast beside the father of her unborn child, who in turn, remains beside Grace.

"Swear your allegiance," Evrest repeats, looking directly at Grace. "Although, the last person to bow down to me will have the pleasure of killing my son, so don't decide too quickly."

He kicks Raze hard in the ribs and Grace winces, feeling it in her own core, as she wishes once again that Raze had ended his fight differently.

"Come on." Scoria tugs on Corbin's hand. "I don't wanna kill no-one."

Evrest smiles. This is exactly what he wants. An excuse to try to force Grace to end Raze's life. He knows as well as everyone else here that she won't do it. Which means his sick game can continue until the shadows grow long and stars fill the sky. This is likely the most fun he's had since his violent Tournaments were brought to an abrupt end.

Corbin shoves Scoria forward.

"Go," he tells her.

"Scoria," the Cragg woman beckons. "Come on."

"Go!" Corbin practically spits at her.

Scoria obediently hurries over to take the Cragg woman's hand, turning immediately to face Corbin, willing him to follow her.

But his feet remain planted beside Grace. *Just what is this slimeball up to?*

"And then there were two," sneers Evrest, crossing his arms as he waits. "Which one of you will kill my son?"

"I'll make you a deal," Corbin whispers to Grace, his eyes fixed on Evrest.

"Go on," she says, knowing she has nothing to lose by hearing him out. No matter how she looks at this situation, both she and Raze are about to die. Possibly Corbin, too. They're outnumbered. Raze is injured and exhausted. Grace doesn't have the physical strength to take Evrest on. And Corbin couldn't win a fight to...well...to save his life.

"If I kill Evrest, you'll be my wife," hisses Corbin.

"Wife?" Grace blanches at the word. She's heard of out-fashioned terms like these but hadn't realized anyone still used them. And the idea of promising herself to anyone except Raze is completely abhorrent.

"My woman." Corbin keeps his voice low. "You'll pledge yourself to stay by my side forever."

"Never," she says through gritted teeth. "I'd rather die."

Then she looks at Raze sprawled on the sand, remembering the first time she'd seen him in Fairbanks.

Strong. Silent. Sleek.

A warrior for Cy who quickly became a warrior for her heart.

Their bond might not have been as instant as Gray and Lexis's, but it was just as all-consuming in the way it knocked her off her feet.

He's filled her with happiness she never knew was possible. And now she has to watch him die. Corbin can no more kill Evrest than he can fly to the moon. The deal he's trying to broker with her is as worthless as he is.

"Well?" Corbin nudges her in the ribs.

"Never," she repeats. "I will never be your woman. Or anything else. My heart belongs to—"

"A dead man," he finishes. "Why did you have to choose him over me, Winter?" She flinches at the use of her old name. "You chose the wrong brother."

Evrest lands another kick in Raze's ribs before walking over to Grace and Corbin.

"It's nice to see the womenfolk getting along," he says, mockingly. "But I need you to swear your allegiance, or I'll have my men kill the pair of you, along with that pathetic excuse for my son."

Corbin pulls back his shoulders. "I have something to tell you."

Evrest laughs. "Oh, it's story time, is it? How fun."

"You have another son," says Corbin. "A strong one. One who can help you lead. One who can provide you with grandchildren and continue your legacy long after you're gone."

Corbin gives his father a nervous smile, waiting for him to ask who this mysterious son might be.

"It's me," he squeaks when Evrest says nothing. "I'm your son."

Evrest tips back his head and laughs. "I have sons all over the Outlands. Daughters, too. What makes you think you're so special?"

"I'm the son of Kallini." His trembling lip gives his emotion away.

This seems to amuse Evrest even more. He looks at his men, not even giving Corbin the respect of his response directly. "He thinks I'm going to remember the actual names of all the wenches who throw themselves at me."

His men chuckle enthusiastically at this, patting each other on the back.

Raze gets to his knees, then his feet, approaching Evrest while his back is turned and his men are distracted. Grace tries not to look at him, not wanting to give his movements away. All he needs is a couple more seconds…

"Behind you!" shouts Corbin.

Before Evrest can turn around, his men have grabbed Raze and are dragging him roughly back. One of the men holds a blade at his throat.

Disappointment and fear floods Grace's gut. That could have been their chance. Their *only* chance. If those men are hurting him, she's going to…Tears sting the backs of her eyes. She's going to do what? There's literally nothing she can do.

Evrest fixes his gaze once more on Corbin. "See that piece of shit over there?" Evrest gestures with his head to Raze.

Corbin nods.

"He's my only son," he spits out. "Because he's the only one I raised. And look at what a disappointment he turned out to be. Which is why I'm going to enjoy watching him die. Sons are overrated. The last thing I need is another one to hold me back."

"I'm different," Corbin insists. "I'm better than he is."

"Pledge allegiance to me." Evrest keeps his voice level, but his anger is clear. "Or die."

"Do we have a deal?" Corbin asks.

It's only when he taps Grace on the arm that she realizes he's talking to her.

"Do we have a deal?" he repeats.

Grace swallows as she assesses her options. Corbin seems certain he can kill Evrest. A highly unlikely scenario. But one that would mean Raze would live. So would she. Which would be great if it weren't for the fact she'd be promised to the man who saved her.

Is living apart from the man she loves better than them dying together right now?

Raze's words that he spoke to her in Fairbanks come back to her.

If I can't come with you. I want you to be safe. Always. Find someone to help keep you safe.

She knows he meant these words if he were to die. But what if following his advice meant that he could live? What if somehow the *unlikely* actually happened? Because there's no way anyone would have bet on a skinny girl from Fairbanks winning the Tournaments. Why can't Corbin kill Evrest if he's so certain he knows how?

"You have a deal," she says, hating the taste of these words on her lips. "I give you my word."

"Oh, how sweet," Evrest laughs. "The womenfolk are talking again."

Corbin steps forward and shoves Evrest hard in the chest. It's a move that's so unexpected, it sends him stumbling two steps backward.

His men lurch forward and Evrest holds up a hand to stop them.

"I challenge you!" shouts Corbin, advancing on him again. "Just like your *real* son challenged you. A fight to the death. The last man standing chooses the Commander."

Evrest shakes his head. "This is getting sort of bor—"

Corbin shoves him in the chest again, robbing him of his words. "Are you scared?"

Evrest rights himself and glares at Corbin. Two men who are roughly even in height but not in muscle or skill. Corbin may have caught Evrest off guard twice by doing something totally unexpected, but that won't happen again. Evrest has the look of a warrior about him now. One that's ready to end this right now.

Grace takes a step back, trying to figure out her next move. When Corbin is dead, what then? Raze will be next. If she's lucky, Evrest will choose to end her life first so she doesn't have to watch. She catches Barnacle's gaze and he looks away, unwilling, or perhaps unable, to help.

If only there wasn't a blade to Raze's throat, they could run. Make it to a raft and get away before anyone could stop them. Because she'd rather die in a leatherskin's jaws than at the hands of the evil that's standing before her.

Evrest lands a punch squarely in Corbin's jaw. "I accept," he sneers. "But only because I'm going to enjoy it."

"You heard him!" shouts Corbin. "Whoever wins will choose their Comm—"

Evrest hits him again, this time in the stomach and it knocks all the wind from his lungs.

He doubles over and Evrest advances, pulling up his knee to smash Corbin's face. He collapses to the ground and howls.

"No!" screams Scoria from the sidelines, being held back by the Cragg woman. "Leave him alone! We have a baby coming! Your own grandchild."

Blood spurts in a shower from Corbin's nose as he pulls himself into a sitting position.

Evrest screws up his face at the sight of him. "Your mother must have been an ugly thing, going by the looks of you."

His men cackle loudly at the insult.

"Don't talk about my mother!" Corbin gets unsteadily to his feet only to be knocked back down again.

Grace is pleased to hear Corbin stick up for Kallini. Perhaps it's the last thing he'll ever do, which in one way is a nice thought given that his mother's last words had been of her son.

Enjoying himself immensely, Evrest gives his men a

dramatic shrug. "Even an ugly wench has her purposes. Must've been dark the night she came to my hut."

With all his theatrics, Grace sees something Evrest doesn't.

Corbin has reached into his pocket. She wants to shout out not to be foolish enough to bring a knife into this battle. Evrest will only use it to inflict even more pain. The best Corbin can hope for is a fast death. He's no match for this evil man who sired him.

But he doesn't produce a knife. Instead, he has something clutched in his fist. Whatever it is, it must be small. Too small to possibly be of any use in a fight with a ruthless man from the faction of Cy.

Corbin rises and stumbles toward Evrest. There's very little resemblance between these two men, but the distinctive profile of their noses gives them away. Grace isn't sure how she hadn't picked the link between them sooner.

"Impressive," says Evrest, turning to Corbin. "Ugly like your mother. But persistent like your father. Maybe there's a small part of me in that pathetic husk after all."

"My mother didn't go to your hut," says Corbin, wiping blood from his nose with his unencumbered hand. Evrest hasn't seemed to have noticed he's holding anything just yet.

Grace holds her breath, barely able to wait to see what has Corbin so confident he can win this fight.

"You went to her hut," Corbin continues. "You needed help. She saved your life and you repaid her by taking her innocence."

"No wench is innocent." Evrest advances on Corbin and now their faces are only inches apart as they sneer at each other. "Especially wenches who lure you to their huts with promises of help."

"You put your hands around her throat," says Corbin. "And you squeezed tight."

"Did I now?" Evrest smiles as he lifts his hands and wraps his filthy fingers around Corbin's neck and squeezes. "Like this?"

"No!" screams Scoria, who now has two Craggs holding her back. "Leave him!"

But Corbin isn't resisting. Evrest seems to be doing exactly as Corbin wants. Like he'd goaded him into doing this. But… why?

Grace holds her own breath. Whatever Corbin is up to, he has seconds to pull it off before his airways are cut off completely. And no matter the outcome, Grace's own future is about to change drastically. She'll either die herself, or be forever tied to a man who's as slippery as the blood that's still sliding from his broken nose down his face.

Corbin's fist flies up so quickly, Grace has to blink to make sure she's seeing right. With both of Evrest's hands busy, his face is exposed, and Corbin opens his palm and slips something into his father's surprised mouth.

"What the…" Evrest moves his head violently from side to side, and spits. But whatever Corbin had put in his mouth had been crushed into tiny pieces and he's having trouble getting it all out. His grip on Corbin loosens but he doesn't let go.

Corbin smiles, despite the hands clamped to his throat, almost as if he knows the vice is about to be released.

Grace's own hands fly to her mouth as she watches this unfold. Corbin had goaded Evrest into strangling him so he could put some kind of poison in his mouth. She's both impressed and horrified at how calculating he is.

"You…" Evrest chokes out. His face turns blue and a rattled wheeze emanates from his chest. "You!"

He lets go of Corbin, who draws in some much needed breath but doesn't back away.

"Do you remember why you went to my mother?" Corbin asks, as Evrest doubles over in an effort to drag air into his lungs. "Do you remember what you needed help for? Let me remind you. It was a severe walnut allergy. Unfortunately, you only had a very small bit that last time."

Evrest falls to his knees clutching at his throat seeming genuinely confused about the way this is playing out.

"I've carried a crushed walnut with me every day of my life since she told me," says Corbin. "Waiting for my chance to use it. Waiting...*to kill you.*"

A chill runs down Grace's spine as Evrest falls to the ground convulsing.

What kind of person carries a walnut in their pocket every day of their life in the hopes of killing their father?

The same kind of person who carries the exact evil in his heart as the very person he's trying to kill.

The kind of person she just agreed to pledge herself to if he succeeds, which is looking less and less *unlikely* with each of Evrest's gasping breaths.

What has she done?

Evrest falls still and Corbin plants his feet over his body to stake a claim on his kill, jeering at the shocked onlookers.

"He's dead!" he announces. "Which means I can choose the Commander."

"You must choose Grace!" Raze calls, only for Evrest's men to tighten their grip on him as they mutter threats of their own.

Grace straightens her spine, ready to take back the role that was once hers. And dreading telling Raze exactly what it's cost them.

"I choose myself," says Corbin. "I am your Commander."

A silence falls over the small crowd as they take this in. And then Barnacle begins to laugh.

"That's a wonderful joke, my friend, but I don't think so." He runs his hands down his beard as he steps forward. "I will never live in a world where you rule over me."

"Yet you were prepared to live under the rule of a woman." Corbin jerks his thumb over his shoulder in Grace's direction.

"She found this island," says Barnacle. "She gathered an army. She devised a plan for a fleet of boats like we've only ever been able to dream of before. Yeah, I'm prepared to live under her rule. Better her than you."

"Ai, ai," say his men. "And us."

"But that wasn't the deal," says Corbin, his jaw flapping. "Evrest agreed. Whoever won this fight would choose Commander."

"And who was Evrest to make that rule?" asks Grace, stepping forward and projecting her voice to sound far more confident than she feels. "I was the Commander when the Cy arrived, and I remain your Commander now. *I* never agreed to the rules of the fight."

"That's right," says Barnacle, clapping.

"Let go of him," Grace instructs Evrest's men who are holding Raze. "Let go of him, now!"

Slightly confused, perhaps still dazed by the death of their leader, they release Raze and he rushes to Grace's side.

She slips her hand into his, drawing in the comfort of him. He's alive. And the sound of his ragged breath is the most beautiful thing she's ever heard.

Corbin glares at Grace as he steps away from Evrest's body. "You may not have agreed to the rules of the fight, but you did agree to our deal. You gave me your word. And I kept my part of the deal."

"I can't," she says, unwilling to let go of the strong hand that's holding hers. Not now. Not ever.

"You must," Corbin counters. "What worth is a Commander who doesn't keep her word?"

"What's going on?" Scoria rushes to Corbin's side and clutches at his arm.

He shakes Scoria off. "The Commander has agreed to be my wife. We will rule side-by-side."

Raze stills by her side.

"Wife?" Scoria's voice is a shriek. "Wife?"

"You can still be my woman," he mumbles to Scoria. "This changes nothing between us."

Grace wants to vomit, both for this man's lack of morals and because she knows he's right.

What worth is a Commander who doesn't keep her word?

Nothing.

Nothing at all.

Which is why she knows she has to go through with what she agreed to.

She has no other choice but to become Corbin's wife.

RAZE

*G*race is alive.

They've won.

But it came at an unimaginable price.

As Raze watches his father's body sink into the rust-colored water, he ignores the sting of the sea around his waist. He ignores the irony that, ultimately, it was Evrest's own son who was the one to kill him. He ignores the cheers of the men and women back on the shore as the last of the puffy, scarred face that tortured him all his life disappears beneath the surface.

But he can't ignore the hollow agony that's replaced his heart in his chest.

He turns, finding Grace standing at the edge of the water. Her hands are gripped tightly at her waist. His pain is echoed in her eyes.

He walks back to shore, his feet feeling heavy. But he picks up his pace when he sees who's moving toward Grace.

Corbin.

Scoria notices too, and she quickly grabs his arm only for him to shake it off. Corbin comes to stand beside Grace and the cavern in Raze's chest expands. He stops, several feet between them, his feet sinking into the sand, sucking his ability to move.

"Tonight, we will celebrate!" Corbin announces. "We'll have a fire and food!"

A few Cragg cheer, but most of the Rust turn to look at Grace. The Cy glance around, eyes shrewd as they wait to see what's unfolding. She stills, realizing that right now she needs to be a Commander.

And that Commander is promised to Corbin.

She lifts her fist into the air. "Tonight we celebrate!"

This time, the cheers collectively punch the sky. "This way," Corbin calls. "We'll have a village with as many huts as we want!"

Another round of cheers and the Outlanders follow Corbin, Scoria hurrying to catch up. And yet, Raze and Grace don't move. The sound of the waves counts out the seconds as they stare at each other.

"I'm sorry," she whispers.

He shakes his head. "No. I am." He's the one who couldn't kill his father.

She takes a step forward. "The Raze I love was the one who chose mercy."

He mirrors her action, closing the distance between them. "The Grace who holds my heart is the one who saved me."

She saved all of them.

Two more steps and they're in each other's arms. The wound that is his heart heals a little as she curves into him. As he holds her with everything he has.

"I'll never be his," she whispers fiercely into his chest. "This is an agreement in name only. As the Commander I choose my mate."

But all those words do is burn at his soul. According to the very people she leads, she's with someone else.

Grace looks up at him. "We can make this work. This doesn't come between what we have."

She's right. Nothing can destroy the love they've found. Raze leans down and presses his lips to hers, showing her with aching tenderness exactly what's blossomed between them. Grace lets out a shuddering sigh, pressing closer as if she wants to crawl inside.

How he wishes she could do that. He'd keep her safe forever. But he can't.

He pulls back, glancing in the direction of the clearing everyone else would be at now. Grace needs to be there, too. She needs to show she's the leader, not Corbin.

She nods, the mouth that was so soft and sweet against his a moment ago now a tight, thin line. "I know. But we'll figure this out, okay?"

Raze nods, allowing himself a flicker of hope. Corbin may be her husband—the word makes Raze's stomach curdle—but he doesn't have Grace's heart. That's all that matters.

They've only just entered the tree line when voices ahead have them slowing. Especially when they realize one is Corbin's.

"Calm down, Scoria. You're overreacting."

"I'm carrying your child!" she hisses. "How could you do this?"

Corbin huffs. "I did this for us. To ensure our child grows healthy and strong." There's a pause then a rustling of leaves. "Besides, what we have doesn't need to come to an end," he cajoles.

"It don't?"

"We can still be together. I'm practically the Commander. I can do what I want."

Grace stiffens. This conversation is echoing their own only moments ago.

"I suppose that's okay…"

"Great." The grin in Corbin's voice is unmistakable. "Come on, let's get some food."

The sounds of their footsteps recede, leaving Raze and Grace in silence. And if she feels anything like him, with a bad taste in her mouth.

"The riches of Askala will be ours!" shouts a voice from not far away, several cheers following it. The excitement and elation in the voices is a stark contrast to the misery and mourning weighing Raze down.

And yet, this is what he fought for. This is what will ensure freedom from poverty for all Outlanders.

He takes Grace's hand and moves forward again. He also fought for a Commander who will be just. And that's exactly what they've been given.

They can't lose it all now.

They reach the clearing to find a fire has already been started. People are standing around, some squatting, their smiling lips stained with berries.

"Here's our Commander," Barnacle calls and another round of cheers rises through the forest.

Grace smiles. "Tonight, we eat and rest. Tomorrow, we build our village and our fleet."

More cheers and whoops grate along Raze's nerves.

Corbin strides over and stands on Grace's other side. He grabs her hand and lifts it into the air. "And we take what's ours!"

This time, the crowd's response is less enthusiastic. They glance from Corbin to Grace to Raze, realizing a strange dynamic is being born.

Their Commander is divided by heart and duty.

Grace stiffens, her hand held aloft by Corbin, her body moving subtly closer to Raze. But even as she does it, Raze knows she can't. He suspects she does, too.

So he does what needs to be done. He releases her other hand and takes a few steps back, welcoming the shadows.

At the same time, Grace raises her now freed hand. "We take what's ours!"

The roar that rises rivals all the others before it. Birds frighten into the sky. The ground thunders as the Outlanders stomp their feet. The forest fills with the promise of war.

The men slap each other's backs, grinning and shoving. "Let's go get us some dinner," Barnacle calls jovially.

Raze is as still as the trunks around him as the men disperse, talking among themselves as they plan their dinner. Grace flicks a glance over her shoulder before walking closer to the fire, her shoulders stiff and straight. Corbin joins her and when Scoria tries to do the same, he scowls at her. She immediately backs away, squatting down on the other side of the fire and staring into the flames sullenly.

This is the way it will be. Grace must stand by her word. She and Corbin will be husband and wife.

Scoria will be the mistress.

Raze will... He grips the trunk of a tree so hard the bark splinters off. Grace has made the decision she must. Now, he will have to do the same.

The afternoon comes, bringing with it the smell of roasting hare. The Outlanders start to plan their village, several staking a claim for their hut. As Raze watches, the legacy of the Commander unfolds, the lines between factions already blurring. Hope is kindling in their steps.

Grace finally comes to him when night falls and everyone else has curled up, their stomachs the fullest they've been, the promise of a home bright in their minds. Snores and grunts fill the air in an uneven rhythm.

Wordlessly, she takes his hand and draws him deeper among the trees. They walk far enough for privacy before stopping and crumpling to the forest floor. They hold each other tightly, arms and legs wrapping around the other, caressing and stroking.

Grace whispers his name over and over, as if she's binding him to her.

Raze is memorizing the feel of her.

Because they've won. And they've irrevocably lost.

He holds her as she cries. He holds her as she falls asleep. He holds her as his heart fractures all over again.

And then he stands up. Removing a small carved piece of wood, he presses it into her palm. Her hand curls around it despite the exhaustion making her face pale and drawn. Raze first started carving the small raven just after they sent the notes. It was intended to be a gift. A symbol of hope. A promise of tomorrow.

He just didn't realize it would also be a message of goodbye.

Walking away is the hardest thing Raze has ever done. One glance at Grace curled up on the forest floor and he almost changes his mind. But he clenches his hands and forces himself to keep walking. He can't stay.

He can't jeopardize Grace's role as Commander. Not after everything they've sacrificed and lost.

Their homes.

Lexis.

Gray.

He just didn't realize that they'd also have to lose each other.

Raze takes one of the Cy's rafts and pushes out to sea, the ocean water biting and lapping at his legs. He leaps on once he's far enough out and picks up the paddle.

Each stroke hurts.

Each stroke tears at the hole in his chest.

Each stroke takes him away from Grace.

But Raze doesn't stop. He'll return to Fairbanks and wait until Askala falls. It will probably take longer than his heart would like.

But he'll wait.

Then, one day, he'll return.

And their souls will be whole again.

GRAY

*G*ray walks beside Lexis, heading to the compass in the middle of the island. His foot still aches, and he has an obvious limp, but he's almost mastered keeping his balance now.

"I'm so excited! I'm so excited!" sings Shale as long shadows cast across the path in front of them.

Soon it will be dusk, and they'd promised Sage they'd join the Origins in worshiping Terra. She'd been so pleased, not realizing their real motivation was to get a closer look at the altar that holds so much promise for their escape. Gray hates being deceptive, having to remind himself of how these people had kept to themselves the reasons for their own excitement at their arrival.

Shale skips ahead when she sees Atlas and loops arms with him, practically dragging him along the uneven path. The way she's blossoming on this island both warms and breaks Gray's heart. She's unrecognizable from the scared, silent girl he'd met in the Neverlands. How can they think about tearing her away from this life? But then again, how can they possibly stay after what they've found out? Although, Sage had said Shale could wait until she was old enough to make her own choice…

Lexis yawns loudly.

"Are you okay?" Gray asks, detecting a slight shift in the way she normally moves. It's like her feet have suddenly become heavy.

She tilts her head. "I'm fine. Just a little tired."

If anyone else had said this to him, Gray wouldn't give it a second thought. Gray gets tired. Winter used to get tired. But Lexis?

No.

Warriors don't get *tired*.

"Should we turn around?" he suggests. "We can attend the dawn worship instead. One more night won't make any diff—"

"One night *will* make a difference," she insists. "It's an extra night here amongst these people."

He lets out a long breath. "Lexis, maybe they're not that bad. Maybe they're just—"

"Manipulative." She pulls back her shoulders. "They want us to breed with them. They want *Shale* to breed with them."

"Not right now, they don't," he says. "When she's older and if it's her choice. I don't thi—"

"Then I'll think for you."

"As well as finish all my sentences, apparently." He grins, trying to lift her mood.

"Sorry." She sighs. "I don't know what's wrong with me. It must be this place."

He loops an arm around her shoulders and pulls her closer. "There's nothing wrong with you. You're perfect."

"No wonder they want to breed with me then." A hint of a smile crosses her lips.

"Come on!" shouts Shale, spinning to face them.

"You two go on ahead," calls Gray. He can't possibly move any faster with his foot. And she's safe here. For now, anyway.

Shale needs no further encouragement and disappears into the crowd gathered on the rainbow of mosaic tiles surrounding the giant compass. Each and every person is facing west, watching the sun sink lower in the sky.

Sage had explained that their people gather here to form a procession down the road that leads to the altar to watch the sun either rise or set directly behind it.

"Do they have two altars?" Gray asks Lexis, a thought only just occurring to him.

Lexis shakes her head. "When Sage showed us the altar, she said it had just been used for dawn worship and was now waiting for dusk."

"But how's that possible?" Gray rubs at his temples. "The sun rises in the east. Sets in the west. How can they watch both of those from behind the same altar?"

Lexis frowns for a few long moments, then her brows shoot up. "Do you remember what I said when we first arrived here? This island is moving."

Gray gives a noncommittal shrug. "I still can't feel any movement, but I'll take your word for it."

"We're following the sun," she says, her eyes lighting up in fascination. "They're turning this island somehow."

He thinks about this for a moment. What Lexis is saying is the only possible explanation. And they already know this island made from trash is floating. But turning it with such precision would require a motor or technology he can't even begin to imagine. Is it possible these people are far more intelligent than they'd realized?

A hush ripples across the crowd as the people launch into motion, making their way down the road that leads west. And if Lexis is right, it's the very same road that had led east only this morning.

They follow, taking up the rear of the procession and holding their words for now. Somehow, it wouldn't feel right to talk while all those around them are in a revered silence. This is their sacred ritual and so few of those exist these days. Perhaps it's not as easy to believe in a higher power when everything around you is slowly dying?

The road eventually opens out onto the man-made beach, not far down from where they'd first arrived on their raft. The glistening glass of the waterfall can be seen far in the distance as the fading light glints off it.

People fan out on the beach in long lines, facing the water.

"There it is," Gray whispers, his eyes glued to the altar that sits several yards out into the ocean.

Lexis holds a finger to her lips as they take in the impressive sight of it. A holy relic to the Origins people. A means of escape for Gray and Lexis.

The centerpiece of the altar is a tall mast, much like the one that holds the compass. Except, perched on top of this one is an enormous six-pointed star made from broken yellow, orange and red glass. As the sun lowers in the sky, the star is catching its rays and fracturing them, sending thousands of smaller beams of light shining in all directions. With each subtle movement of the sun, the effect is becoming more and more spectacular. The people tip back their heads and bask in the dazzling energy. With their limited vision, Gray can see why this would be intoxicating.

But as captivating as the star is, it's not what has Lexis and Gray's interest.

It's the structure it's floating on.

A mast made from metal would never stand the test of time in the acidic ocean. But when attached to a platform made from treated timber, it would. A platform that looks like a larger and far sturdier version of the raft they'd arrived on. A raft they no longer have.

"It's bolted down," Gray whispers, trying to figure out how

they'll detach the mast. "And tied to the ocean floor somehow so it doesn't float away."

"Shh." Lexis warns. They'd agree to talk later when they'd return to their hut, but Gray can't help himself. With the sound of the crashing waves and the murmuring of the people praising Terra, he's pretty sure nobody else can hear him.

The sun drops just a little lower in the sky and light streams directly through the center of the star, shooting out thousands of golden fractured rays that reflect on the rust-colored ocean. It almost looks like it's ablaze.

"Praise Terra!" the people call out as their voices crack with emotion. "Blessed be, sweet Terra. Thank you for the life you give us."

Their enraptured faces tilt to the star, their precious altar showering them with warmth. Unable to resist the temptation to join them, Gray closes his eyes and watches the shades of light flicker across the back of his eyelids.

He gasps as something deep inside him shifts. It's like he's being flooded with love. For one brief moment, he's certain he can smell the scent of Winter's hair after standing in the summer rain. He feels the safety of his mother's arms cradling him as a child. Hears Trakk calling him to run through the ruins that were their playground. Tastes the joy of sweet grapes as a giggling Shale feeds them through his lips. Then Lexis fills all his senses and he's not just standing beside her, she invades his every cell, almost like she's become a part of his soul.

The light fades and his eyes flutter open to see the sun has dropped below the horizon, and he's left with tingles running down his spine.

"What happened?" he whispers, turning to see Lexis staring at him. "What was that? Did you feel it?"

Lexis tilts her head as she studies him. "I saw the sun pass through a man-made structure and send colored light onto the beach."

"No." Gray clasps her hands. "It was more than that. I saw...I felt... Lexis, it was incredible."

"Gray," she hisses, keeping her voice low. "Focus! The mast is supported by hooks. I'm certain I can prize them out with a metal bar. We get one or two out, then the star should fall into the ocean. Then we check what's under—"

"No," he says, deciding to finish one of her sentences for a change. "We can't. The acid will destroy the star. That altar is the only thing protecting it."

She narrows her eyes. "You can't be serious."

"Lexis." He glances around, unsure how to explain himself. "I saw something just now. I don't know how to explain it. We can't destroy the star. We can't. It wouldn't be right."

"Let's talk back in the hut." Lexis is on high alert. "We'll wait until dark and bring back what we need."

Gray sighs. She's not listening to him. It's like they're having two completely different conversations.

"Nobody can hear us," he says, sweeping a hand across the dispersing crowd. "We can talk here."

Shale races past them, skidding on what she once called cactus-sand but now seems completely at ease with. Atlas is behind her, catching up and tapping her on the back before turning and running the other way. Shale takes off after him, now her turn to chase.

Maybe that's exactly what's happening here.

"Don't you see it?" he asks Lexis. "Ever since we left the Tournaments, we've been the hunted. Then we decided to change our destiny and become the hunters. And we found this place. Do you really think we're going to find anywhere better? I don't want to go on the run again. Look at Shale. She's thriving. I'm thriving. And you've never looked better." His eyes rake her body, appreciating the soft curves and color in her cheeks after only just a couple of days of eating decent food. "They can't force us to do what they're asking. We'll just refuse. Or negotiate. These people will listen. I know they will."

"We won't bring Shale," says Lexis, still not prepared to let go of their plan. "You're right. She's thriving. It wouldn't be fair. We can't give her the kind of life she could have here. We'll leave, just the two of us. Find somewhere else to call home."

There's a tapping on Gray's back and he turns to find Shale standing behind them, her eyes spilling over with tears. He squats to her height, wondering how much of that she just heard.

She wraps her arms around Gray's neck, pressing her cheek to his as she looks up at Lexis.

"You're not leaving me," she says. "I'm coming with you. You can't leave me."

Gray lifts her and finds his balance, enjoying the comforting weight of this tough little girl in his arms. During the worship, he saw all the most important people in his life. Winter, his mother, Trakk, Lexis... and Shale. Everyone has been torn from his side, except Lexis. There's no way he's going to leave Shale behind, too.

He locks eyes with Lexis.

This is her call, and she knows it. Gray would follow her literally to the ends of the earth. And it seems Shale has decided that she would, too. Except, neither of them really wants to have to do that.

It's Lexis who wants to go. He has to make her realize that they can negotiate with these people. Nobody is going to force her to love anyone else in the way she loves him. The Origins are good people. He can see that. He needs her to see that, too.

Sage appears wordlessly beside them and bows her head. "Have you made your decision?"

"What decision?" Lexis crosses her arms.

"I may not see well, but I see well enough," says Sage. "And I noticed the way the two of you were looking at our altar earlier today. Have you decided yet if you're going to tear apart our most sacred relic and leave our shores, or if you're willing to forge a future and share your blood with us?"

Gray's eyes fly open as he decides these people are definitely smarter than he'd thought.

"We've already told you that's not happening," snaps Lexis. "Gray and I are already committed to each other, and Shale is far too young for any of this talk."

"That's right," says Gray. "We refuse to do that. We'd like to negotiate your terms."

Sage studies Lexis carefully, not saying a word. As she does, something seems to pass across her face. An understanding of some sorts. Gray looks at Lexis, trying to see what Sage has just noticed about her. But he sees the same beautiful, stubborn warrior girl he's always seen.

"I think Terra has sent us a gift." Sage beams at Lexis. "Not the gift we were expecting. But a precious gift all the same. One that changes everything."

Lexis looks at Gray with an expression of *has-this-woman-completely-lost-her-mind?*

"I've never had a present," says Shale, sliding down from Gray to stand on the ground and looking up at Sage expectantly.

"What are you talking about?" asks Gray.

"I'm talking about new life," says Sage, her grin practically incandescent. "Lexis, my dear, you weren't sent here to breed with us. I completely missed the signs."

"What signs?" Lexis narrows her eyes.

Sage pats her gently on the arm. "You can't breed with us. Terra works in mysterious ways, and this gift is one we'll have to be patient for."

Gray gasps as he thinks he works out what she's trying to tell them.

"That's right," says Sage. "Lexis, you've already been blessed. In case you hadn't realized it...you're pregnant."

LEXIS

*L*exis tries to process those two words.

You're pregnant.

She looks from Sage's serenely sure expression to Shale's surprised one to Gray, registering the biggest smile so far lighting his handsome features.

"Lexis," he breathes, joy infusing her name. "You're pregnant?"

Her hand lifts to her belly. She's been tired. Her breasts have been sore. She just hasn't felt herself.

As the truth filters through the shock, she blinks.

She's pregnant.

Not knowing what else to do, she spins on her heel and marches away. For the first time in her life, she runs from something. Her long strides carry her over the paths, past the compass, through the village, and into the forest. She doesn't stop until she gets to the pool, and only then because she doesn't have much choice. There's nowhere to go. They're trapped on this island…unless they escape with the raft.

She sinks to the ground, not even realizing she's cradling her flat stomach until she glances down.

Tears sting her eyes. *Why her? Why now?*

She never imagined she'd bring a child into this world. She swore she wouldn't.

And then she met Gray. And impossible things like hope and love and a future became possible.

And that sweet, soul-searing connection has created a child.

The knowledge simultaneously sits heavily in her gut and lightens her heart. Her decision now impacts not only Gray and Shale, but the life growing within her.

"Lexis?"

Gray's voice is soft, almost hesitant. She turns to find him several feet away, hovering as if he wants to go to her but knows she might need space.

"Gray," she says, her throat tight with emotion. "We're going to have a baby."

The smile that rivals the sun is back as he rushes to her. Sitting down, he puts his arms around her, pulling her close. But that's not enough. Lexis crawls onto his lap. She's never felt more vulnerable.

Gray tightens his hold. "My beautiful warrior woman is actually scared," he says gently. Almost fondly.

His words have her lips arching up at the edges. "Actually, I'm terrified."

"It's certainly the most wonderful and terrifying thing that could have happened to us." He chuckles. "And we've been in some scary situations."

Glad he understands, and not surprised that he does, Lexis leans back, gazing at him. "I don't know what to do," she confesses.

He cups her face tenderly. "Sage said we don't have to breed with anyone. She sees we belong together. I knew she'd be prepared to negotiate."

"But she'll want our child to breed with them. And Shale."

"They would've done that, anyway, once they grew up.

They'll find love, just like we did, and nature," his eyes glint, "Terra, will take care of the rest."

Lexis digests this, knowing he's right.

"And this is the best place for a child to grow up," Gray continues. "Food. Shelter. Water. A chance to play and learn and laugh." He sighs, his face tightening. "There's nothing for us in the Outlands."

Raze is gone.

So is Winter.

The world beyond is defined by death.

"So, you're mine?" she asks, not sure if she can believe the future that's being painted.

"Always. Just like you belong with me and no one else."

She chews her lip. "And we leave if anything changes?"

"I promise." He grins. "Maybe we'll take them all with us."

For the first time since she heard the news that just altered everything, Lexis smiles. "I think we should stay." Her smile grows. "For now."

To her surprise, Gray doesn't smile back. His other hand comes up to cup her face, his eyes becoming dark pools of truth. "I love you, Lexis. Thank you for giving me more than I could have ever dreamed of." His lips twitch. "And for a dreamer, that's saying something."

She kisses him hard, emotions flaring fiercely within her. "We're having a baby," she murmurs against his lips, awe finally infusing her.

Gray rests his forehead on hers, his eyes alive with love. "A warrior girl."

"A sweet boy who sees the beauty in everything."

His face lights up. "Maybe both."

Lexis's breath disintegrates. They're both twins—doesn't that make it more likely that they'll have the same? "Two babies?" she asks, dazed.

"To start with," teases Gray.

There's a rustle of plastic shrubs and Shale appears. "We're staying?" she asks, wringing her hands.

Gray glances at Lexis, and she knows he needs to hear it again. A part of her doesn't quite believe it herself.

"We're staying," says Lexis, opening her arms to the little girl.

Shale scrambles over, climbing into Lexis's lap even though she's still tucked on Gray's. "Yay," she says quietly. Excitedly. Gratefully.

Lexis and Gray wrap their arms around her, the same emotions creating a cocoon around them. Lexis rests her head on Gray's shoulder, staring at the blue pool. At the body of water in a color she didn't know was possible.

Shale is hope.

Their child will be hope.

They're the future generations who will mold all the tomorrows to come.

And Lexis is looking forward to seeing what that world will look like.

SIXTEEN YEARS LATER

GRACE

Grace has always liked the sound of her footsteps on the hard timber of the bridge that connects the Newlands to Askala. It's the sound of progress.

Healing.

And hope for the future.

It's a long walk between the two settlements, but thanks to falling ocean levels, the distance has been steadily closing. Both islands are far larger than they were when Grace first saw them. Which is just as well given that almost every Outlander lives here now.

Person, she corrects herself. There's no such thing as an Outlander anymore. Or factions. The world just has people who are doing their best to work together for a common goal—take care of the Earth, so in turn, it can take care of them. They've all seen what happens when you lose sight of this. Who knew that all this time it was the Askalans who had the right idea. It's just a shame it took so much bloodshed for the rest of the world to catch up.

Grace quickens her pace, keen to get back to Raze. It's only been two days, but after spending so many years apart, she doesn't want to waste a single moment. Her heart aches at the thought of him, leaving her unsure if it's from longing to be beside him, or the memory of the pain she felt when he left her all those years ago.

If she'd known exactly what it was going to cost her to keep her word to Corbin, she's not sure she'd make the same decision again. Her life had been miserable without Raze, even if she'd understood why he chose to wait for her in Fairbanks. Neither of them realized it was going to take over a decade to build a fleet of boats and mobilize an army. Perhaps that was just as well.

She could never have achieved what she had if any other path had been taken. This bridge she's walking on would never have been built. Newskala would never have been born. The world would still be divided.

"Commander." Two men walking in the opposite direction tilt their heads at Grace as they pass her.

She smiles brightly, appreciating the respect these former Cy warriors show her by continuing to use her former title. A title she's not entirely sure she deserves. Because while she may have led the invasion of Askala, it hadn't been a victory for the Outlands. Nor had it been a victory for Askala.

It had been a victory for them both.

They'd come to Askala's shores to seize power from a greedy, selfish race, only to find the people with their hands held in the air, refusing to fight. Grace had tried to take control peacefully, but Corbin had other ideas and almost killed her in his quest to claim the title of Commander for himself.

For a few horrible moments, Grace had thought all her hard work and sacrifice had been for nothing. And maybe it would have been if it weren't for two brave men.

Hawk had protected Grace from further harm, while Raze had permanently removed Corbin as a threat. And, somehow, all of this had become a catalyst for peace.

Because instead of fighting the Askalans, Grace's army chose to stand behind her. Perhaps they'd learned something during their years in the Newlands? Perhaps the Askalans known as Seekers, who'd tried to convince them that violence wasn't the answer, had made a difference after all? Or perhaps they were just hungry and tired, and wanted a better life?

Grace steps from the bridge onto solid ground and looks around, remembering when she'd first arrived in the Newlands with Raze. For a brief slice of time, they'd had this entire island to themselves. Yet as amazing as that had been, she far prefers the way it is now.

This island provides food, shelter and safety to hundreds of families. Children are being born into a life that holds hope.

Great pride swells in her chest when she thinks about the naïve determination that led her to enter the Tournaments back when she was no more than a skinny girl called Winter. If only Gray could have lived to see what she did with her title after she won. He'd be proud. He'd probably also tell her he wasn't surprised. Her twin always thought more highly of her than she thought of herself.

"Grace."

She spins around to see Hawk standing close by. His small daughter, Cormorant, is perched on his shoulders, tugging at the thick orange tufts of her father's hair.

Grace smiles up at her. "Hi, Cormie."

"Hi, Auntie Grace," she says, insisting on calling her the same name her cousins do, even though they're not related. Not having had children of her own, Grace is more than happy to be Cormie's honorary aunt.

"You need to get some rest," says Hawk, touching Grace gently on the arm.

"And you need to stop being so protective of me," she laughs.

"There's Mommy!" Cormie wriggles to get down from Hawk's shoulders and runs to Sam who scoops up her daughter.

Grace can't help but admire the way Sam's improved her prosthetic hand over the years to enhance its function. One of these days she might even convince Hawk's uncle Dex to allow her to make one for him, too. He says the bridge is proof he doesn't need it, given he practically drove its construction *single-handedly*. They all know that's not true, though. His partner Wren was right by his side every step of the way, tapping her foot impatiently and pointing out that his jokes are getting even worse over the years.

"How were things in Askala?" Sam asks, glancing at the bridge. "Is Luca far behind you?"

Grace shakes her head. "Not far. Mercy insisted on coming with him which meant they needed to bring all the kids. Your parents decided to come, too. You know what a nightmare it is getting everyone across the bridge with Tarquin daring them to jump off every second step. They should be here soon."

Sam looks at Hawk affectionately. "Are you glad now we stopped at one child? With such limited resources in the world, it doesn't make good biological sense for the longevity of the planet to reproduce more than once."

Hawk ruffles Cormie's hair as Sam moves in closer to him. "We only needed one. We hit perfection on the first try."

"I'm going to find Raze," says Grace. She's not jealous of the close family unit Hawk and Sam have together, but seeing them like this has her yearning for the only man who's ever made her heart skip a beat.

She says her goodbyes, leaving Sam and Hawk to wait for their family to arrive, and makes her way toward the children's center.

It was Raze's idea to set up a place where the orphans of the Outlands could be cared for. Grace had readily agreed, and it wasn't long until they decided to add a room for themselves at the center and make it their home.

Living amongst the children has been the greatest joy of

Grace's life, the feeling surpassed only when they manage to successfully place a child with a family of Newskala. This work feels just as important as anything she did as Commander. The next generation are the ones who will inherit the future. They need to be raised with love.

"Hey, Kimber," says Grace, pushing open the gate and seeing her dear friend supervising the children in the yard.

"Look who's here!" Kimber gives her a warm smile and the children rush at Grace, hugging her around the legs.

She pats as many of them as she can on the head and groans theatrically as she tries to walk forward with the weight of so many children clinging to her.

"Everything okay?" Grace asks Kimber as she wanders over.

"Never better." Kimber smiles. "Kids, show Grace what you've been doing."

The children let go of her to run to a small rock-climbing frame Kimber's set up. Using rocks as footholds, they climb up and over to the other side, squealing in excitement before running back to start again.

"'Bout time these little-uns learned how to climb rocks," says Kimber.

"Look how strong you all are," Grace gushes with pride as the children check to see she's watching them.

Kimber goes to the frame to help a small girl, and Grace watches her with the same kind of pride in her strength. When Kimber first came to live here, she was a mere shell of herself. Originally from Cragg, she'd had her daughter stolen from her by the Never. She hadn't been able to get over it. Not until she'd come to the children's center to help out and something inside of her had lit up. None of these children could ever replace her daughter, but they went a long way to ease a little of her pain. Each time a new child is brought to the center, Kimber's eyes light up and she whispers her daughter's name.

Shale.

Despite her daughter not having shown up yet, Kimber lives in hope. Which is a gift in itself.

"Keep going," Grace calls to the children. "I'll be back."

She heads inside and sees Raze at a table showing a small group how to carve from wood. He's so good with the children, especially the quiet ones. He understands them in a way nobody else can.

He looks up the moment Grace enters the room, almost as if he felt her presence.

She holds up a hand, telling him there's no rush. It's enough for her just to watch him for a while. To drink in the sight of the man she loves.

But it's not enough for Raze, and he goes to her, wrapping her up in his arms and pressing his cheek to the top of her head while the children giggle as they watch.

They stand there for long moments, not moving apart from the rise and fall of their chests. He doesn't say anything, and she knows it's because he's speaking to her with the beat of his heart as it falls into sync with hers.

They have everything they need right here.

They have peace.

They have a future.

They have each other.

And for that, Grace is thankful. It's more than she could have ever hoped for.

"I love you," she whispers into his chest.

He tips up her face and kisses her forehead, giving her a look that she knows is a promise.

For tonight.

For tomorrow.

For every day of the rest of their lives.

Together.

RAZE

*R*aze pulls back, but not before quickly dropping another kiss on Grace's temple. The luxury to be able to do that has never worn off. Actually, the years of separation, everything that they had to endure to stand here, in this moment, makes each touch precious.

"I have something to show you," he murmurs huskily, the children's laughter and shouts a whirlwind around them.

She looks up, eyes alight. "You've made another one?"

He nods, his heart warming at her excitement. "The idea came to me last night."

Today is the day they send their annual message. He always likes to create something to honor the day.

Grace slips away, lithe and youthful in a way only joy can make you, and skips toward their room. "I have something for you, too."

Surprised and curious, he watches as she returns clutching something wrapped in cloth. It's square and flat and not very big, and Raze can't think of what it might be.

Grace slips a hand into his. "I'll give it to you on the beach."

Raze nods and they weave their way out of the children's

center, leaving Kimber in charge. Patience is something he learned in his long years in Fairbanks. For the first few he had Kallini as company after she determinedly healed from her injuries. But when she passed away peacefully in her sleep, a smile on her face because she lived long enough to learn Evrest had been avenged, he was alone.

Waiting.

Watching for a sign.

Wishing this was all over so hard some days it was a soul-deep ache.

And it had paid off. As they walk through the gardens and huts of Newskala, hand in hand, a future that in his darkest moments didn't seem possible stretches like a breathless dawn before them.

Grace wraps herself around his arm, the hard edge of his gift pressing into his bicep. "We did it, Raze."

One or both of them still breathe those words each and every day. A little disbelieving. Deeply grateful that they are part of what stretches before them.

Unity.

Peace.

Prosperity for all.

Well, for all who are willing to share in the vision of what they fought so hard for. A few Outlanders still roam the waste-lands beyond the red-tinted sea. They'd be people like his father, those who believe violence is power. Those unwilling to give that up.

The trees disperse as they reach the beach. Although they're a little away from the bridge that stretches to Askala, the sound of squeals and giggles still reach them. They both smile as they watch Mercy chase Luca as if they're still teens, Mercy light footed despite the rounded belly clearly carrying their next child. Tarquin, Hope, and their toddler twins quickly overpower him as he's more than happy to be caught. He collapses under the weight of their love and laughter and they tumble around on the sand while Kian and Nova watch on, laughing.

Raze and Grace wrap their arms around each other, holding tightly. They've heard the stories that brought everyone here. Nova and Kian, the childhood sweethearts whose love transcended Bound and Unbound. Wren and Dex, an Outlander spy and an Askalan who were the first to forge love between enemy factions. Sam and Hawk, Seekers who showed what courage and faith can achieve. Luca and Mercy, living proof of the power of love and passion and dogged determination.

And this is where Raze and Grace stand each year to celebrate their own story.

Grace gasps. "Oh Raze, it's beautiful."

She says that every year, and yet the wonder never fades from her face. She steps closer and crouches down, her finger hovering over the drawing.

The scenes he etches so carefully into the sand have always paid tribute to their past. They capture the moments of victory that were scattered among the hardships.

Grace winning the Tournaments.

Arriving in the Newlands.

Reuniting in Askala.

But today, the scene pays tribute to what may have been.

There are four people scratched into the sand, all with their backs to them as they face the ocean. In pairs, they have their arms around each other's waists just as Raze and Grace do.

But Raze and Grace aren't together in the image.

They're each clasping their twin.

Grace and Gray cling tightly, their heads pressed close. Raze and Lexis are more upright, more alert, yet just as inseparable.

"This is what it would have looked like," Grace whispers.

The four of them, gazing out, wordless and proud. Conscious of the gift that they found each other. Deeply thankful they still have one another.

Grace pushes to her feet. "Gray used to talk about imagining your future. It's how you make it come true."

Bittersweet grief slices through Raze. "Lexis would have scoffed at the idea." His practical sister believed you forged your future, not dreamed it.

Grace rests her head on his shoulder. "Gray would've said he knew this is how it would have turned out all along."

They stand just as silently and wordlessly as the image, two instead of four. Raze tries to focus on everything they now have. They're so blessed. So undeniably lucky. But there are moments where the wounds of their battles gape and bleed. Some losses never heal.

With a shuddering breath, Grace lifts the wrapped gift she brought him. "Here. I'm glad I made this."

Curious, Raze quickly unwraps it, his heart lighting up when he sees what it is.

A book.

He saw them in Askala and was instantly fascinated. Holders of knowledge, places of silence, and the truly beautiful ones are enriched with art. He opens it, surprised to find the pages blank.

"I made it from pulped bark. Sam helped me. She's excited to expand her journals and records." Grace smiles, her dark eyes luminous. She pulls out a whittled piece of coal from her pocket. "So we can keep all your beautiful art. Will you draw more like this?" She waves an arm to the scene in the sand.

"Of course," he says quietly. Humbly. Achingly.

"This way we can always have them with us."

Raze nods, his throat tight. "In more than just memory."

"Yes," Grace chokes. She pulls something else out of her pocket and Raze already knows what it is.

The reason they're here. Just like they have all the other times since they reunited, they'll send a message out to the horizon.

She holds up the tightly folded piece of paper and a small

piece of shiny metal. "I try to tell them as much as I can. About Newskala. The bridge. That we're happy." She squints into the sky. "Now, we just need a raven."

"I can hear Lexis rolling her eyes," Raze says affectionately.

A sad peace settles over Grace's beautiful features. "Gray's smiling." She lifts the metal to catch the sun, turning to look back at the trees. "I have an extra-large cricket," she calls out.

Something out on the water catches Raze's attention. He stills. "Grace," he says tightly.

There won't be time to send the raven this year.

She turns, seeing it, too.

A shape on the horizon. Far bigger than anything they've seen before. As they stand there, frozen, it grows. Dark and shapeless, it moves inexorably closer.

The only thing it can be is an attack. A fleet of ships even bigger than they had built over a decade ago.

But the people here aren't prepared for war. They have no weapons, no training.

If the Outlanders have been secretly amassing an army far bigger than any of them could have imagined, they don't stand a chance.

Everything they sacrificed, all the loss and the pain, has been for nothing.

Raze puts an arm around Grace. Whatever happens next, they're never going to be separated again.

GRAY

"*L*ook!" Gray points in the distance as Lexis slips her hand into his.

"I see it," she breathes.

The wind catches Lexis's hair as Treasure Island inches toward Newskala using the motor that once turned the island. All these years later, she's still the most beautiful woman he's ever seen.

He digs his feet into the artificial sand that's now so familiar he's forgotten what real sand feels like and fixes his gaze back on the horizon.

This day has been a year in the making and Gray can barely contain the gratitude he has to sweet Terra for making it possible. It was the storm she sent that caused the raven to fly off course and end up on Treasure Island with the note attached to its foot.

A note just like the one they'd found when they first arrived on the island.

A note that he now knows was unmistakably written by Winter.

If that wasn't a gift from Mother Nature, then he's not sure what is.

Shale had found this latest note and brought it straight to them, her hands shaking, aware of the impact of the news it contained. Gray and Lexis had never learned to read beyond the basics, but Shale had and she'd read the words aloud that changed the entire course of their lives.

Winter and Raze are alive. Not only that, they'd managed to unite the factions. *All* the factions, including Askala. He always knew his sister was capable of such a monumental act. That part of the note was the only thing that hadn't been a surprise.

To think that for all these years Lexis and Gray had thought their twins were dead, only to learn that Winter and Raze believed the same of them.

Another part of Terra's plan, no doubt. There's no way they'd have given up looking for each other if they'd believed anything else. And if they hadn't gone their separate ways Winter and Raze would never have been able to unite the Outlands, and Lexis and Gray wouldn't be standing here now bringing the Origins to the Newlands.

"Are we doing the right thing?" Lexis asks, scanning the long line of people fringing the shoreline. "Should we have gone ahead on our own first to make sure it's safe?"

"It's safe," Gray reassures. "We've been through this a hundred times."

Lexis nods, knowing this is far from an exaggeration. They've had countless conversations with each other and the rest of the Origins since receiving the note. In the end, it was impossible to argue for any other course of action than the one they're taking now. The Origins had known for years they needed to add to their gene pool for the optimal health of their people. And while Gray, Lexis and Shale's arrival had been a good start, they were never going to be enough. And now the world beyond the island is safe. The real purpose Terra had sent a current to drag their raft directly to Treasure Island was so they could one day take the Origins to the people, and not the other way around.

Like Sage used to always say, *Terra works in mysterious ways.*

The sound of a baby squawking steals Gray's attention and he turns around, smiling to see Shale holding her newborn daughter.

"Hey," says Shale holding little Kimber out to him. "Can you take her for a bit please? Atlas and I just can't get her to go to sleep. You have the magic touch."

Gray reaches out for his beloved granddaughter and snuggles her to his chest as he rocks from side to side. Kimber's squawks quickly turn to gurgles as she closes her eyes and settles immediately to sleep. He leans down and kisses her soft head, breathing in her precious warmth.

Shale shakes her head. "We've been trying to get her to nod off all day. How do you do that? I swear I held her in exactly the same way."

Lexis rolls her eyes. "He was like that with Aurora and Orion, too. Super annoying."

"Not annoying." Shale yawns. "At this stage I'll take any break I can get."

"It's his special connection to Terra," laughs Lexis. She hasn't embraced the Origins' belief in the powers of Mother Nature in quite the same way Gray has, but he doesn't mind. One of the things that drew him to her so strongly in the first place was how stubborn and individual she was in her views of the world. She was like nobody he'd ever met back then and remains so now.

"We're nearly there," says Gray, indicating the ocean with his chin as anticipation builds in his gut. This past year of planning is about to come to fruition. Both he and Lexis are about to see their twins. Something neither of them had thought was possible ever again.

Shale turns and her eyes open wide with both fascination and fear. Lexis slips a comforting arm around her. They know she's afraid for Kimber, not wanting her daughter to experience any of the pain she went through herself as a child. Shale loves her life on Treasure Island. She was one of the most difficult of everyone to convince that it was time for things to change. In the end it was Atlas who talked her into it.

There's a murmur around the crowd as they draw close enough to the Newlands for the Origins people to see with their limited vision. It had taken Gray years to figure out that the will to live that these people seemed to lose in their twilight years wasn't due to them not being able to see the faces around them. It was due to them not being able to see any hope.

And it feels good that's what he and Lexis have been able to give them.

Gray smiles to see their twins, Aurora and Orion, join them on the beach. Orion leans in to give Kimber a gentle kiss on her forehead, forever the soft-hearted, doting uncle. Aurora stands on Shale's other side, offering her comfort, even though Gray knows his fiercely independent daughter would rather stand alone.

"What are you thinking?" Orion asks.

"That this is the happiest moment of my life," Gray says, looking at the five people he loves the most and knowing when he sees Winter, this number will expand to six. Joy sings through his veins at the thought. It's hard to fathom that soon he'll be able to hug his beloved sister as they try to catch up on all the years they lost. "I mean it. I've never been happier than I am right now."

"Oh, Dad." Aurora shakes her head, laughing affectionately at him. "You're so mushy."

"Leave him." Orion puts a hand on Gray's back. "This is a big day. Imagine how you'd feel if you hadn't seen me for nearly two decades."

Aurora grins. "Actually, that wouldn't—"

"Stop it," admonishes Shale. "You'd miss him like crazy. Families aren't meant to be separated."

Aurora falls silent. Shale's made her point. They all know how much she misses her mother, especially since becoming a mother herself. Over the years as Shale had grown, so had her hope that her mother might still be alive. After all, the Never weren't exactly known for their honesty. But even Gray wonders if this might be a stretch.

"Yeah, alright. I'd miss you, Orion," Aurora says reluctantly.

"Tell us again what they're like," says Shale, leaning her head on Lexis's shoulder. "I want to hear about Winter and Raze."

"We've told you a million times," says Lexis.

"Tell us again," says Orion.

Lexis stands a little taller. "Raze is like me, only far braver. Blond and fair, he was born a protector. Strong and fearless, yet sensitive all the same. Remember that he doesn't talk so don't be upset if he doesn't say anything to you. But I promise he'll speak to you with his eyes."

"And Winter?" prompts Aurora, looking at Gray.

He lets out a soft sigh. "Like me, only far more sensible. She's a fighter. A leader. Ambitious. Sometimes a little reckless, but she believes in what's right and wrong. I always knew she was destined for greatness. She looks like you, Aurora, except with darker features like mine."

"I can't wait to meet her," says Aurora.

"Won't be long now." Shale points ahead. "I can see the bridge Winter mentioned in her letter."

"There are people standing on it," says Lexis. "They've seen us arriving."

"We're a little hard to miss," laughs Gray. Kimber lets out a groan of complaint and Gray obediently falls silent and jiggles her back to sleep.

"Let me take her," says Shale, knowing he's going to need free hands to greet his twin.

Gray gently transfers Kimber to Shale, relieved to see her settle back to sleep in her mother's arms.

"Maybe we should have sent a raven," says Lexis, returning to Gray's side. "So that they know we're not here to fight."

"They don't want to fight us," says Gray, taking her hand and noticing she's trembling. "They live in peace. This is all part of Terra's plan."

"What if the note was a trick?" asks Lexis.

He's never known her to be so unsure about any of her decisions, although maybe that's because none of them have been as important as this one.

"It's not a trick." He kisses the top of her head. "We're putting the last piece in the puzzle, that's all. We're making the world a better place."

Lexis nods, trusting him like she has no other, apart from the brother she's about to be reunited with. She tucks herself into Gray's chest, keeping her eyes on the Newlands.

He wraps her up in his arms and decides they, too, are like a puzzle. Different shades and different shapes but somehow, they just seem to fit.

LEXIS

*T*he low grinding noise as the bottom of their island hits the rising ocean floor tells them they've come as close as they can.

"We'll need the rafts," someone calls out, except Lexis doesn't turn around to see who it was.

She can't take her gaze off the shores of Newskala. More people than she expected are standing along the sand, all watching the large island that just docked a hundred yards away.

But there's only one person Lexis is looking for.

One person her heart hasn't quite been whole without.

She sees the blond hair. The strong shoulders. The outline she never thought she'd set eyes on again.

Raze.

Her shadow. Her protector. Her reason for living for the first half of her life.

Her twin.

Beside her, Gray gasps, and she suspects he just saw Winter beside Raze. The same disbelief and wonder must be coursing through him. Neither of them expected this day would ever exist.

People start pushing the rafts sitting on the multicolored sand down to the water. Shale, Aurora and Orion begin to head down, glancing over their shoulders when their parents don't join them.

"Mom?" Shale asks.

"Dad?" Aurora and Orion say simultaneously.

Except they're both frozen. Lexis is too scared to move. Too terrified she'll shatter this moment.

She can see Raze. Feel the intensity of his gaze even over the distance. How many times did she wish to see him just one more time? How many times has Gray called out Winter's name in his sleep, even after all these years?

And they've been given that gift. That precious, impossible gift.

"Winter," Gray chokes out.

The one word snaps Lexis out of her daze. Suddenly, seeing Raze across the distance isn't enough. She needs to touch him. To confirm he's real.

And there's no way she's sitting on a raft and waiting long minutes as they row over.

Lexis breaks into a run, feet digging into the pebbly sand, then splashing through the water. A few more strides, and she dives into the ocean. Warm water encases her, instantly prickling her skin, but she doesn't care.

Raze is on the other side of this divide.

Lexis swims with powerful strokes, pulling through the water with everything she has. The sea stings her eyes, tries to get into her mouth, but even a school of leatherskins wouldn't stop her. She'll reach Raze no matter what.

Her foot kicks sand when she sees that the water ahead of her is splashing and churning, too. Lexis stands, wondering if

320

her frantic swim did, indeed, attract a leatherskin. Always prepared, she pulls her knife out of the halter on her belt.

When she sees who was coming toward her, she drops the knife. It sinks to the bottom of the ocean, forgotten.

Like it no longer exists, along with the rest of the world.

Raze is staring at her, water streaming into his rapidly blinking eyes. His mouth works, but no sound comes. Lexis's heart stutters. Shudders. And soars.

"Raze," she breathes.

They're holding each other without even realizing they've moved. She grasps him so tight her arms ache. "Raze," she says again, wanting to say it a million times more. He's a little taller, thicker and impossibly stronger, and very much alive.

In that moment, her life is complete. Her heart is whole. And her future a blazing, beautiful prospect.

She has Gray.

Their children.

And now Raze.

He pulls back, still blinking in amazement. "Lexis. You're alive."

Her eyes snap wide. "You're talking."

He laughs, and the sound is so beautiful it dances through her soul. "We have much to share."

There's more splashing, then the sound of delighted laughter as Winter and Gray also meet in the ocean, unwilling to wait for the rafts. They collide and Gray lifts Winter and spins her around, creating a whirlpool of happiness in the rose-tinted ocean.

"I knew you'd succeed," Gray cries.

"I can't believe you've been alive all this time," Winter says, sobbing and laughing simultaneously.

Lexis and Raze squeeze each other again, the joy of their partners only multiplying their own. She decides she never wants this moment to end.

Until she registers the water lapping at her waist.

She looks up at Raze, devouring his features. Older and sun-weathered, but her beautiful brother, nonetheless. "Shall we go in? The water stings. I'm not like the Origins." Their skin has all but made them immune to the acid, a quality that Shale's daughter will likely inherit.

"The Origins?" Raze asks, Winter also looking curious.

"Our people," Gray says proudly.

Winter presses a hand to his chest. "They can meet our people."

The four of them make their way out of the ocean. Lexis and Raze startle simultaneously, their bodies jolting from relaxed to alert when a roaring rises from the shore. Clapping. Shouts. Words of congratulations.

The people of Newskala are celebrating with them.

Lexis and Raze smile at each other sheepishly. Their vigilance was too deeply ingrained during their childhood. It's nice to have someone who understands.

Winter lifts her and Gray's clutched hands. "Our twins have come to join us!"

"And we bring friends," calls Gray.

Exiting the water, they turn as the people rush down to stand around them, cheering even louder.

Lexis and Raze, Winter and Gray stand on the beach, each twin with their arm around the other, watching as the rafts steadily approach the shore.

Lexis's heart clenches when Orion waves enthusiastically and Gray waves back. Aurora is watching everything with eagle eyes. Shale is clutching baby Kimber, scanning the shores with an edge of desperation. Lexis almost presses her hand to her mouth, wanting to tell her not to get her hopes up. Death is far more common than long life in the Outlands.

But her hand remains by her side. Because her other hand is holding onto her twin.

If she can find Raze, Shale could find her mother. What a reunion that would be, with Shale's daughter evidence of their resilience. That despite it all, they've not only survived, but thrived.

The rafts scrape over sand, the people on board squinting nervously.

The Origins are about to meet the people of Newskala.

Shale hands Kimber to Atlas and runs toward a woman in the crowd and they embrace, sobbing in a way that tells Lexis that Shale was right to hold onto her hope. Perhaps they all should have.

"This is amazing, Winter," Gray breathes.

She smiles, resting her head on his chest. "My name's Grace, now. I'm living the life our sister couldn't."

Gray blinks in surprise, but doesn't say anything, just nods his understanding.

The rest of the Origins people clamber off the rafts as the people of Newskala move to greet them. At first there's hesitation. Uncertainty. But it all dissolves with the first smile. The first gasp of wonder.

And then there's greetings and laughter and questions.

"An island that moves? How long have you been out there?"

"Are the wars truly over? Is it really safe?"

"You must see our trees. We made them ourselves."

"You must see our forest. It stretches for miles."

Her heart bursting inside a too-tight chest, Lexis lifts her free arm, looking over at Gray. The two sets of twins gravitate toward each other until she's pressed against him. Lexis's eyes sting with rare tears. Even rarer than the few that have fallen before.

Because these are tears of joy.

She has her brother on her right. The love of her life on her left. Raze and Winter—Grace—smile at each other over the heads of their twins.

Like Raze said, there is much to tell. A past to understand.

But also a future to forge.

One that will be beyond anything they could have imagined.

One that defines faith. Hope. Unity.

The undeniable power of love.

And sweet Terra, Lexis can't wait.

THE END

Want more of The Thaw Chronicles?

Check out Book 11, The Oasis Trials, now!

http://mybook.to/OasisTrials

THE OASIS TRIALS

BOOK 11, THE THAW CHRONICLES

Five trials to prove your worth. Two teens with everything to lose. One chance to escape.

In a world ravaged by global warming, an unconventional leader plans to sail away and start again in a mythical place known as Tomorrow Land. He's decided to take one hundred young lives with him...if they pass a series of tests.

Fyve's grown up in the poverty and violence molded by environmental and economic collapse. Passing is his only ticket to escape a life of starvation and struggle. But it also means leaving his family, the ones he's spent his life protecting.

Halo is the daughter of the leader, and she's determined to compete in the Trials just like everyone else. As the tests become more deadly with each one that passes, she questions if the future she yearns for is worth it. Especially if Fyve is adamant he won't set foot on the ship her father has promised will arrive.

As the fight to leave becomes the fight to survive, as passing the tests means leaving behind everything and everyone they love, Fyve and Halo are about to discover that being chosen comes at a price.

You will be blown away by this epic dystopian adventure brought to you by Tamar Sloan and Heidi Catherine, authors of the smash hit series, The Thaw Chronicles.

Grab your copy now
http://mybook.to/OasisTrials

WANT TO STAY IN TOUCH?

If you'd like to be the first for to hear all the news from Tamar and Heidi, be sure to sign up to our newsletter. Subscribers receive bonus content, early cover reveals and sneaky snippets of upcoming books. We'd love you to join us!

SIGN UP HERE:

https://sendfox.com/tamarandheidi

ABOUT THE AUTHORS

Tamar Sloan hasn't decided whether she's a psychologist who loves writing, or a writer with a lifelong fascination with psychology. She must have been someone pretty awesome in a previous life (past life regression indicated a Care Bear), because she gets to do both. When not reading, writing or working with teens, Tamar can be found with her husband and two children enjoying country life in their small slice of the Australian bush.

Heidi Catherine loves the way her books give her the opportunity to escape into worlds vastly different to her own life in the burbs. While she quite enjoys killing her characters (especially the awful ones), she promises she's far better behaved in real life. Other than writing and reading, Heidi's current obsessions include watching far too much reality TV with the excuse that it's research for her books.

MORE SERIES TO FALL IN LOVE WITH...

ALSO BY TAMAR SLOAN AND HEIDI CATHERINE

The Sovereign Code

Elemental Games

ALSO BY TAMAR SLOAN

Keepers of the Grail

Keepers of the Light

Keepers of the Chalice

Keepers of Excalibur

Zodiac Guardians

Descendants of the Gods

Prime Prophecy

ALSO BY HEIDI CATHERINE

The Kingdoms of Evernow

The Soulweaver

www.ingramcontent.com/pod-product-compliance
Lightning Source LLC
Chambersburg PA
CBHW021447240626
47153CB00001B/330